TARBIN'S TRUE HEIR

TARBIN'S TRUE HEIR

THE RECHARGING

KELLY LYNN COLBY

Cursed Dragon Ship
PUBLISHING

To those who think they can't fulfill their dreams:
This book in your hand is proof that you can.
Do the thing.

CHAPTER ONE

THE WOODEN BOW curved in Talia's hand as she pulled back the string. The tension of the cord mirrored that in her muscles. Her head tilted and aimed down the shaft of the arrow toward the tawny buck. The tip pointed behind his front leg, at his heart. Talia's arm clenched. She had to make a clean shot. Despite her father's expectations, Princess Talia Winterlaus must not return to the castle empty-handed.

The animal's head shot up. He pawed the ground and grunted. Talia gripped her bow tighter. She didn't know what had startled him. Regardless, she couldn't let him escape. Talia focused on her prey. Time to prove her worth.

Shouts erupted from deeper in the forest. Talia grimaced as she recognized her brother's chortle. Tanin always ruined everything. Talia's fingers flexed in anger and slipped from the bowstring.

The release flew over the buck's head and embedded in a tree. The deer sprang toward the bushes. He reached the edge of the brush as a snap sprang from beside Talia. Her husbandry companion Ial's quick shot lodged into a leaping haunch. The deer bleated a high-pitched squeal as it disappeared into the underbrush.

No need for stealth now. The chase was on. Talia threw the camouflaged cover off her head. Her strawberry-blonde hair jumped from its confinement. She rushed across the clearing. Her petite frame pushed through vegetation as high as her waist.

Since his hunting experience outweighed the rest of the companions', Talia nodded at Ial to take the lead. "That shot should give us a blood trail to follow. We must get my sacrifice back before Cook's deadline."

Ial's thin waist and wide shoulders gave him a top-heavy look, belied by the grace with which he wove through the underbrush. He crouched by a darkening stain on a bush and trotted ahead.

"I feel sorry for the fluffy thing." Medicinal guardian Nyna pushed back her deep brown hair as she bent to pick a curly-leafed herb from the edge of the clearing. Educated in the culinary arts as well as the ways of healing, she recognized the greenery. "Parsley will bring out the savory goodness of the venison. Cook will be thrilled."

"How did you go from 'poor deer' to 'can't wait to eat him' in less than an eye blink?" Dew pushed Nyna forward.

Nyna's svelte build and slouching shoulders contrasted with Dew's curvy figure and bouncy curls. Coupled with her never-met-a-stranger attitude, Dew made the perfect cultural guardian.

Nyna raised her eyebrows as she took her time adjusting her bag. "Princess Talia must provide dinner for her guests at tonight's Graduation Ceremony. With the buck already injured, the Light tells us to end his misery and fulfill the royal duty."

"It was a rhetorical question, Nyna. I have long stopped trying to define your thought process." Dew's dancer grace made it easy for her to dodge the forest debris.

Talia glared at her companions, hoping to hurry them. She wished they felt the same drive she did. At the princess's look, Nyna quickened her pace to catch up with Ial.

A loud crack startled Talia. Ial was by her side in a moment, with Nyna and Dew flanking her in front.

Naul, the defense guardian, shrugged his shoulders in apology. "I stepped on a rotten log. It didn't like that." Naul shook broken bits of wood from his shoe and rubbed his shaved head. His wide girth could have swallowed the entire party and still had room for a small child or two. It made him an imposing and fierce competitor, which contrasted with his jovial and gentle personality.

The tension drained from her companions.

Talia sighed with envy. Her stress increased with the delay. "Let's go!"

Ial ran in front, directing Talia along the deer's flight path.

Though the princess remained in charge, she easily relegated responsibility to her companions. Upon her tenth birthday, Talia had been presented a selection of students of her age from each school of discipline to bond with her for life. The princess resisted many traditions of her heritage, but not this one. So far, she had no cause to doubt those she had chosen. The guardians had grown from servants to friends, the only people Talia could be herself around.

Talia's mood darkened with the forest as the party traversed its depths. Her brother, Prince Tanin Winterlaus, irked her. She trampled through the underbrush hunting for a dignified offering in order to compete with him. Her father told Talia she could set rabbit traps by the garden wall and entertain guests, while her brother brought in the main course. Talia refused to take the easy way out.

Talia and Tanin had been rivals since birth. She'd left the womb first. Talia felt that made her the heir apparent. All of Tarbin disagreed with her. A woman had not sat upon the throne in all its known history.

The princess covered ground quicker as the foliage thinned. The dense canopy allowed meager light to penetrate, controlling the wild growth seen on the edges of the clearing. Ial knelt at a large wet spot on the forest floor.

"That's a lot of blood. You must have hit an artery." Talia studied the stained leaves, crushed in an elongated fashion. The deer had obviously collapsed on this spot.

"Such blood loss will bring him down soon," said Nyna.

"Let's find him and get out of here. By the ever-present Darkness," Naul cursed, as he shook his foot, trying to free it from a twisted vine, "I think the Royal Forest is out to get me."

Ial traced the divots in the soil, indicating the direction the deer had staggered as it had struggled to stand in its weakened state. Talia nocked an arrow to her bow and crouched to remain unseen for as long as possible. The buck might still have enough adrenaline left for one more sprint. The husbandry guardian prepared his bow as well.

"No, Ial," whispered Talia. "I have to make the kill."

He nodded and hung his bow over his shoulder, his expression unchanged. The princess appreciated his stoic acceptance of his role.

Dew whispered over her shoulder, "The law dictates you need to provide a feast for your Graduation Ceremony. You don't have to hunt anything. Organizing your servants and guests proves your capacity for leadership of the kingdom."

"I understand the law, Dew. But Tanin is bringing in a large boar, if the shouting means what I think it does. I can't let him outshine me." Talia squeezed her bow too tightly. Ial's quiet hand on her fist made her loosen her grip.

"King Roland won't allow you on the throne, regardless of who brings the best... " Dew's voice trailed off.

Talia's jaw tightened. "I know." Talia continued forward. She had to do this to prove her worthiness to herself.

Ial waved a hand for the group to quiet. Talia spotted the fallen buck at the base of the naddle tree. His chest heaved as he gulped breath. His tongue protruded from his mouth, a leaf stuck to its pink surface. The stem flipped back and forth with the animal's breathing.

The deer lifted his head to look at the humans. With his back end seemingly paralyzed, he kicked his front legs wildly as he struggled to stand. Talia lifted her bow, aimed, and released. The arrow sunk deep into the animal's chest, piercing his heart. He collapsed. Wet with his spittle, the dried leaves made little noise.

Talia crouched before her kill, removed the leaf from his tongue, and closed his eyelids. Ial tilted his head, holding up his hunting knife. Talia accepted the offered shaft. The light filtering through the canopy glinted off the long blade.

She had cleaned fish and rabbits, but never anything as large as a buck. Talia placed the tip of the blade below the rib cage. She closed her eyes and prayed to the Light to guide her hand. The sharp blade cut through the layer of skin and fat. Steam rose from the gash as the innards fell to the ground. Talia crinkled her nose at the sickening smell of salty metal. She refused to show weakness and finished the job with quick efficiency.

Once done, she stuck the knife into the ground. She removed her bloody gloves, leaving them inside out to keep the muck from soiling her bag. Talia looked up at Ial, who put his hand on her shoulder. His single nod was all the approval she needed.

Talia pulled the knife from the ground, grasping the blade to offer it handle first to her husbandry guardian. As she stood, a bout of dizziness overtook her. To steady herself, she searched for a solid handhold and gripped the knife blade too aggressively.

"By the Dark!" cursed Talia, releasing the knife to Ial. A small but deep cut graced her palm.

"Let me see." Nyna grabbed Talia's hand. "Deer blood and dirt. A challenge. Let me get the cloth and ointment from my bag."

"It's fine. We can clean it when we get back to the castle." Talia resisted the urge to put the dirty cut in her mouth to stop the bleeding.

"Nonsense. I have everything I need here." Nyna rifled through her shoulder bag, pulling out a small clay jar and a rag.

"We'll get dinner ready for transport." Naul pulled the carry pole from its strap on his back. "Ial?"

The husbandry guardian grabbed the rope. As the two manipulated the carcass, the smell intensified, turning Talia's stomach. She focused on the bright green leaves of the naddle tree overhead.

"Ouch!" Talia snatched her injured hand from Nyna.

"I have to clean the wound." The medicinal guardian hummed, taking Talia's hand once more.

"Do you have to take such pleasure in my pain?"

"Ending your suffering brings me pleasure." Nyna tapped the bottle on the cloth, but nothing came out. "I need some water to loosen up the ointment. We don't get injured enough. It's gone dry."

Dew waved her water bladder at Nyna. "Oh, you poor dear, we'll have to go back to our weekly stabbings to keep your supplies circulating."

While her companions bantered, Talia leaned against the naddle tree. She had always loved this tree. The only one of its kind in the entire Royal Forest. Sometimes, in the middle of the night, she would feel it calling her. As a little girl, she would sneak out and hide in its roots. When the guardians joined her life, all five would frolic in the clearing under its towering branches. Talia thought it fitting the key for her Graduation Ceremony ended at her favorite childhood playground.

A tingle coursed through her body. Talia took a deep breath and let it out slowly. She normally wasn't bothered by blood. She didn't know why she felt so out of sorts.

By her feet, she noticed a flash among a pile of leaves. She pushed the clutter away with a booted toe, revealing a ring mounted with a small green gemstone. It looked like an emerald. The tingling she'd felt intensified. Her limbs hummed. Forgetting about the cut on her palm, she picked up the stone and turned it between her hands, trying to determine its origin. The green stone had to be cut glass. No one would misplace such a valuable piece of jewelry and not report its loss.

Talia frowned as her blood smeared across the faceted piece. Holding the ring pinched between her fingers, she reached into her satchel for a cloth, then froze as an eerie feeling swept through her. Afraid the weirdness came from the ring, Talia held the mysterious emerald at arm's length. From deep inside the gem, a light emanated and intensified as her blood soaked into what should have been a solid surface. Talia jumped back and dropped the ring into the forest debris. The glowing faded as it fell.

"Did you see that?" Talia backed up until she collided with Nyna.

"See what?" Nyna grabbed Talia's hand and smeared cool ointment on it without looking up.

A glowing ball of light flew into the branches over Talia's head. She pointed, her mouth agape. Had the ring flown from the ground to the branches? She'd never seen a flying ring before.

"We're ready if you are." Naul lifted his end of the litter to his waist while the other end lay on Ial's shoulder.

The buck hung upside down from the sagging pole perfectly horizontal. The entire image was disorienting. Talia's mind wanted to slant the pole at an angle since it was in one companion's hand and on the other's shoulder. Yet, the difference in height between Naul and Ial was so drastic, the pole remained level with the ground. Dew and Nyna burst into laughter.

"What's so funny?" Naul asked.

Ial cocked his head at the hysterical women.

"I think Naul might be part giant." Dew managed to squeeze out between laughs.

"Or Ial part dwarf." Nyna covered her giggles with her hand.

"Can you laugh at us later?" Naul kept walking past the women. "This deer is heavy."

Ial stuck his tongue out at Nyna, who fell to the forest floor, clutching her bag to her chest.

Talia couldn't find the same glee Nyna and Dew had. The whole ring incident still boggled her. "Did anyone else see that light?" Talia stared up into the thick branches. Beams bounced among the boughs. Maybe the shine she had seen had simply been filtered from the Light's Daughter.

She bent down and tossed aside half-composed leaves, releasing a wet mold smell into the air. The emerald was gone. Talia held her bandaged hand against her chest, puzzled. Her companions stopped laughing.

"Are you all right, Princess?" Dew bent down beside Talia, searching her eyes.

Talia stood and looked away. Her guardians couldn't fathom the stress she was under. At the Graduation Ceremony, Talia would receive more attention, but not the kind she hoped for. She'd earned higher marks than her brother in every area of study, including hand-to-hand combat. Her success should thrill her. If only it meant something more than a story to tell her children someday. As Tanin liked to point out, her in-depth schooling prepared her to be the perfect wife for a noble husband. That's all. Her only purpose.

Talia's soul screamed she was meant for so much more. Instead, she answered Dew the only way she knew how, "I will be."

Talia leaned against the familiar bark of the naddle. A warmth enveloped her chilled muscles. Her anxiety faded, as it always did when she touched the beloved tree. A gentle breeze brushed her hair from her face. The taste of ripe blackberries flooded her mouth. She opened her eyes and focused across the clearing.

"Blackberries." Talia spoke out loud before she knew her intention.

Heavily leafed vines engulfed a fallen tree. Deep blue clusters hung on the surface. While Ial and Naul headed back to the castle with their load, Talia waved Nyna and Dew to follow her. She bent before the prickly growth, intent on leaving with every one of the ripe berries. She unfolded her neckerchief as a makeshift container.

Nyna joined Talia, piling fruit into Dew's tunic. "Blackberries pair well with venison."

Talia heard the castle bell, muted by the trees. "A guest has arrived. It's still early, isn't it?"

Talia popped a berry in her mouth and moved into the clearing to locate the Light's Daughter in the sky.

Nyna nudged Dew. "Maybe it's Lordling Gregor Rivenwood of Kenia. He spoke excitedly about this ceremony last time we saw him."

"What are you hinting at? You know guardians can have no priorities outside of their charge." Dew raised her eyebrows, indicating the princess. "Besides, he's shown more interest in Talia than me."

"He has?" Talia sat on the ground by the bushes, eating another berry. "Lordling Gregor spends all his time womanizing with Tanin."

"As an excuse to see you." Dew held her shirt with both hands, keeping the pile of berries in the center.

"By the Light, Dew, stop it." Talia threw a berry at her cultural guardian. "The last man I will have feelings for is Lordling Gregor Rivenwood."

Dew ducked and tossed a berry back. "Don't let his strong nose and deep brown eyes shake your determination."

Talia popped up onto her knees and threw another berry.

"Or his crooked smile and smooth dance moves." Nyna added more berries to the melee.

Talia aimed her next shot at Nyna. "Aren't you two supposed to be defending me, not ganging up on me?"

"The rules on blackberry fights are unclear." Dew held her tunic to her chest, trying to prevent the loss of all the fruit as she pelted Talia with her other hand.

Talia exchanged berry artillery with her companions until there were as many squashed ones at her feet as whole ones in her neckerchief. She felt free. A temporary feeling, but a welcome one, before she had to fulfill her princess duties for the dignitaries attending the duel ceremonies.

"I surrender." Talia collapsed on her back. "He is kind of handsome."

Nyna and Dew fell giggling beside Talia.

The castle bell announced more arrivals. The girls rolled off the ground, clutching their berry hoard.

Talia sighed. "Off to princess."

She walked backward a few steps. The naddle tree's smaller branches swayed in the breeze. Talia felt like there was something she was forgetting. Not until she reached the garden wall did she realize there was no wind.

CHAPTER TWO

Talia burst through the kitchen doors with Dew and Nyna beside her. The succulent scent of roasting meat and yeasty bread filled her senses. She closed her eyes to enjoy the aroma. Her stomach growled, followed by Dew's and then Nyna's. The three burst out laughing. Talia held her neckerchief of blackberries close as a servant hurried by. The kitchen was bustling with activity as the cook and her assistants prepared for the night's feast.

"Must be nice to be so carefree." The flickering light from the oven fire illuminated the smirking face of Prince Tanin Winterlaus. "I wish my only responsibility was to marry well and have fat babies."

Talia's icy blue eyes reflected back at her from his face, the only feature that marked them as related. Tanin stood tall, like their father, with round cheekbones and thin lips. Talia's face tightened as she resisted the impulse to tackle her twin. Instead, she said, "We can switch, my dear brother. You have the hips for childbirth."

Nyna dumped Talia's blackberries into a basket before the princess squeezed them into juice. Dew added hers to the pile and moved close to her charge. Two of Tanin's guardians stood in the same position next to the prince.

"I know father said you could snare bunnies, but all you could find were berries?" Tanin held his hand out to his defense guardian, Rory, who smacked it with his palm, and again in reverse.

Rory's dark, hairless skin made his expression difficult to interpret in the dim light. His deep laugh blended with the prince's lighter one, though the man's eyes did not lighten with joy.

"I shot a buck as my sacrifice. The berries are an added bonus. I'm perfectly capable of providing for my people." Talia thought about spinning for a dramatic exit, but Tanin blocked the door to the wing she needed.

"Not bad, my dear sister. What say you, Kettlor? Will a buck feed more than, for example, a wild boar?" Tanin cocked his head at his husbandry guardian.

"I believe the boar my Prince wrangled to be about... " Kettlor's shoulder-length curly hair bounced as he rocked back on his heels, doing his calculations in his head. "Five times the weight of the average buck, so it should feed a few hundred people more."

"We could smoke the deer meat and take it on our *long* journey, I suppose." Tanin turned his back to his sister.

"Let's go, Princess. We have a ceremony to prepare for," Dew whispered in Talia's ear.

Talia shrugged her off and stepped toward her brother. "At least I chased down my sacrifice, instead of having servants dig and bait a hole the previous night."

Tanin swiveled on his heel and stared at his sister with a raised eyebrow. "Are you accusing me of being wise? I'm having trouble interpreting that as an insult."

"I'm accusing you of sleeping in this morning and collecting your sacrifice as if you went to market and bought it with Father's gold." Talia's words spit from her mouth with seething anger. She could not tolerate another minute of her brother relegating her to an inferior position.

Tanin's faced darkened to almost purple. "How dare you question my contribution! If you were not my sister... "

The twins stood a few inches apart, noses almost touching, both with hands on the grips of their belt knives. Their guardians tried to squeeze in between them to prevent an all-out brawl. The rushing kitchen servants froze in place, waiting for the resolution.

"Well, well, well." A male voice emanated from the root cellar. "I see the Winterlaus twins are at it again. Maybe you should take up a hobby that does not include screaming at each other."

Talia squinted into the shadow. An athletic man wiped his hands together as he walked into the fire-lit kitchen.

"Lordling Gregor." Talia took a step back from her brother. Her face flushed in embarrassment for the childish way she was acting in front of their noble guest.

The flickering flame reflected off Lordling Gregor Rivenwood's shiny black hair. His dark eyes danced with joy above his toothy smile. Talia's breath quickened. Her heart beat so loud, she placed her hand over it to quiet the rhythm.

"I had to make sure the servants stored the grain properly. Father would have a fit if Cook was unhappy with his donation." The presence of the jovial man lightened the room's atmosphere.

The servants returned to their pot stirring and vegetable chopping. Dew and Nyna backed away from Rory and Kettlor.

Talia took a deep breath and asked the Light for strength. "Did you get the flooding under control in Kenia? I heard two villages were completely washed away."

"Father has it under control. He insisted I represent our province at the Graduation and Forging Ceremonies." Gregor clapped his hand on Tanin's shoulder. "Judging by the prince's luck with the ladies, this could be the last such ceremony in my lifetime."

Tanin brushed his sleeves and straightened in front of his classmate. "I have much better luck when you're not around." The prince headed farther into the castle, the smirk on his face showing his amusement. "Don't make me send you on a diplomatic mission to the north. I hear the Ngaroans have special assignments for pretty boys."

Gregor threw his hands up in surrender. "Forgive me, my Prince. I will let you have first pick from now on."

"Let me? Prince wins over Lordling. Just in case you're forgetting how to play the game."

Gregor winked at Talia from the doorway as he followed her brother. She blushed and lowered her eyes. Scolding herself for letting him have any effect on her, she looked up in time to watch the backs of Tanin's guardians exit the kitchen. Talia leaned against the wooden prep table, tired, as if she'd run from the back of the forest to the castle.

"He's delicious," Dew muttered.

Naul came in from the butcher building behind the kitchen. "Can I have some? I'm starving."

A servant scowled at the guardian as he grabbed an apple and took a big bite.

Ial shook his head.

"I'm not sure you're his type," Dew quipped. "I was talking about Lordling Gregor."

"I'm glad I missed him. He makes me lose my appetite." Naul tossed the core into the fire. The kitchen servants jumped as it sizzled. "He moves from one conquest to the next faster than a—"

"Bee pollinating flowers," Ial's soft voice added.

"He does, doesn't he?" Talia brushed Gregor from her mind. She didn't have time for such nonsense. "We should probably check our equipment and verify everything is ready for the Forging Quest. We leave in two mornings."

"Cook said she almost has the food packed. She'll finish tomorrow when the chaos of tonight's feast is over." Naul grabbed a warm roll on the way out of the kitchen, ignoring the annoyed look on a servant's face.

As the companions turned down a corridor in the castle, a page skidded to a halt in his slippers.

"Princess, I have been searching for you." He leaned on his knees, his breath ragged. He coughed and clutched his chest.

Nyna pulled something from her bag. "Here. Breathe this in slowly. Calm. Calm." The medicinal guardian's soothing voice quieted the servant's breathing.

"Thank you, Guardian Nyna." The page bowed his head and then turned to Talia. "Princess, your father, the king, has requested your presence in the Royal Meeting Hall."

"I guess we'll collect the supplies later." The princess bit her lower lip, pondering why she had been summoned. Looking down at her soiled and bloodstained clothing, Talia wondered if she had time to run to her chamber. As long as her mother, the queen, was not present, her father wouldn't notice her unladylike attire.

The royal family and their elite servants were the only ones allowed in the Royal Meeting Hall. The room was her sanctuary from the expectations of the world.

Naul and Dew pushed open the double doors without knocking. The room was quiet compared to the rest of the castle, flooded as it was with bustling servants and boisterous guests. A solid wood table with cushioned chairs around it took up the center. Sconces along the walls held torches instead of candles to brighten the stone-lined room. Within the folds of cloth that burned upon each torch, the steward had wrapped dried lavender, adding a soothing fragrance to the air. When the Winterlaus family gathered for a meal, anything to maintain serenity was appreciated.

Raucous laughter she did not recognize stopped Talia in her tracks. King Roland Winterlaus sat at the head of the table in a high-backed chair. Tall, with dark hair and a frame thickened by age, the king held up his large silver mug to toast with another man. The guest seemed familiar, but Talia could not place him. The stranger's chair was engulfed by his large frame and fur coat. His gravel-filled laugh held no merriment as he clunked the king's mug with his own.

"My darling princess! Come give your proud father a hug." King Roland pushed his chair back with the help of one of his guardians.

He swayed a bit on his feet before stabilizing. Talia frowned. He'd started drinking far in advance of the feast. Mother would not be pleased. The king wrapped the princess in his arms, lifting her off the ground in a tight squeeze. Talia's face cracked into a smile. She couldn't stay mad at this man who loved her so dearly.

"How did the hunt go, Talia? Did you trap a family of rabbits?" Roland tumbled back into his seat, his arms still around Talia's waist.

"I brought in a buck, Father." Talia's back straightened with pride.

Roland looked around her at Ial. "Well done, guardian."

Ial blanched.

Talia pushed her father's arm from her waist. Lines formed on her forehead. "No, Father, I shot the buck and cleaned it myself."

The stranger huffed. Talia glared at him, her arms crossed. How dare this man disrespect her in her family's private hall.

"Good for you, my darling." Roland sloshed some yellowish liquid into a mug and set it in front of Talia. "You have to try this Darvis mead. I'd forgotten how much I enjoy it. I don't know what they feed the bees in Darvis, but it's blessed by the Light."

"Centuries of crafting, Your Majesty."

Talia stared at the man, more annoyed than ever by his presence. Something was going on and she was not privy to the details. He held her unwavering gaze, his dark coal eyes shadowed by eyebrows so bushy, they tangled in his bangs, erasing his forehead. His dark wiry hair blended with the collar of his fur coat, transforming him into a beast.

"Darvis mead? Where did this come from? We haven't had the pleasure since King Vanderlae closed the borders." Even as she asked, she realized who the stranger was. *Darvis. Of course.* "Lord Bello Hilderamn."

"At your service." Bello bowed his head without taking his eyes off the princess.

"Did King Vanderlae open trade relations with Tarbin and send you to broker the details?" From what Talia understood, Bello had become a trusted adviser to the Darvisian king. His reputation painted him as a cutthroat merchant whose temper turned violent when deals did not go his way. He looked quite different from the last time she saw him when she was a little girl. His menacing visage, nevertheless, had left an impression.

"My, my, the princess is very concerned with the running of the kingdom, isn't she?" Bello kept his focus on Talia while addressing King Roland.

"She's always been daddy's little girl. Strong-willed and eager to fight." Roland swayed a bit as he took another large swallow of mead. "But don't let that fool you. She's all girl and will make a stunning wife."

Talia's hands fidgeted. She didn't like the direction the conversation was taking. "Did you call for me, Father?"

"Yes, my sweet girl, but you have spoiled the surprise." Roland put a hand on Bello's shoulder. "Lord Hilderamn and I have been working for months on a bargain to get the trade routes flowing again."

"That's why the Giant Eagle flights to and from the west have been so frequent." Talia sat down next to her father and sipped some mead. The initial spice of cinnamon cooled as the fermented honey filled her mouth. "By the Light."

Bello leaned back in his chair, his fingers steepled over the large bulge of his gut. "There's much more where that came from."

Talia cocked her head, contemplating. She was missing something.

"Indeed. It was the most efficient way to get messengers across the continent. Too bad they can't carry more than a couple light-weight people. I could get used to regular shipments of this elixir," Roland continued, unaware of the staring contest between his daughter and his guest. "I wanted you here to meet Lord Bello Hilderamn as the young woman you have become. It has been so many years since he saw you last."

"I am honored to remake your acquaintance, Lord Hilderamn." Talia bowed her head at the Darvisian.

"It is *my* pleasure, Princess Talia." The way he said her name sent a shiver down her spine.

Talia sat up straight. "By the Stars in the night sky, is this my mission for the Forging? Am I to travel with Lord Hilderamn to Darvis to negotiate the trade agreement?"

"You know I'm not supposed to tell you of your quest before tomorrow night." Her father winked at Bello.

The men chuckled. Talia didn't understand the joke, but the excitement of her important mission overwhelmed her doubts. She was going to complete a mission worthy of an heir. Even if she couldn't serve her people by ruling. Talia felt confident she could prove that a princess had more to offer than fancy dresses and lavish balls.

"I must go prepare for tonight's ceremony. May I be dismissed, Father?"

"Of course, sweetheart." The king stood on shaky feet and kissed his daughter's hand. "I have an important announcement tonight. It's vital that you look your most beautiful."

Bello rose from his seat and took Talia's hand as Roland dropped it. He kissed her fingertips, his wet lips lingering. She yanked her hand away and wiped them on her tunic. The hunger in his stare heightened her awareness of his possessive body language.

Talia marched toward the door before she could rebuke her father's guest for his inappropriate behavior. She had to control herself. If she was to be tasked with making nice with Darvis, she would have to start with this vile man.

CHAPTER THREE

————————

A FLICKERING BALL of light flew through the hallways of the castle. The route to the princess's chambers was quiet. Nevertheless, she flew cautiously to remain unseen.

As soon as she landed on one of the two crossbeams of the princess's door, the light transformed into a humanoid figure, no bigger than a finch. Her wings quietly vibrated. Her unclothed body represented the perfect female form, except for the dragonfly wings sticking out of her back.

The fairy removed a sealed note from her satchel. The paper easily fit through a crack in the wooden door from which it drifted to the floor on the other side. Pressing both hands to the wood, she closed her eyes and whispered. The letter grew to human-size. Across the top, bold handwriting spelled, "For the eyes of Princess Talia Winterlaus only."

With her message delivered, the fairy dropped backward from the wooden ledge. She transformed into a ball of light once more, as her wings regained their flight rhythm. She hovered at the top of the door, waiting. She had to make sure her note reached its target.

INSIDE THE CHAMBER, Talia sat clenching the arms of her chair as her mother fixed her hair in the latest upturned style. Piling the tresses of red-streaked gold proved to be quite a battle for Queen Shantia. Yet, her huge smile, as she cursed another stray strand, showed she loved every second of it. Talia, however, would rather be anywhere else. Dressing up was not her favorite duty.

Nyna sat beside Talia, getting her dark hair styled in intricate braids by Chary. The queen's servant, had no children. Any time she spent with Talia and her guardians was precious to the older woman.

As only Talia's female guardians were allowed in her inner bedchamber, Dew acted as the required second. The cultural guardian stood her duty by the modest fire that worked to keep the early spring chill out of the room. Dew's hair required no taming. She always managed to have every curl in place without neglecting her role as companion to the princess.

As a child, Talia had asked her mother why she only had Chary as a servant when father had four guardians. Shantia explained the guardians protected the Tarbin Light-blessed bloodline, which the queen did not share.

"Ow!" Talia complained, as her mother pulled at a particularly challenging knot.

"What? A show of discomfort from the girl who recently ran around the forest hunting?" Shantia tightened her lips disapprovingly as she pulled on another lock of hair.

Talia crossed her arms over her chest. "I have every right to hunt in *my forest*."

Talia's muscles tingled as an odd sensation flowed through her limbs. It felt like it came from outside the door.

"Dew, is there someone in the hall?" she asked, looking over her shoulder at the carved wood as if it held answers.

Dew opened the door. "I didn't hear anything."

The only light from the antechamber came from the modest fire and the candelabra on the table where Naul and Ial played cards. The large wooden entrance to the princess's suite of rooms remained closed.

"Boys, did you hear anyone at the hall door?" Dew called to her fellow guardians.

Naul looked at Ial, who shook his head.

"We didn't hear anything." Naul put his hand down and crossed to the door.

The candlelight reflected off the defense guardian's shaved head as he opened the door. Torchlight flickered in the hallway as a cool breeze brushed past the large man all the way into the inner chamber.

Naul shrugged his shoulders, making his formal jacket groan as his flexing muscles strained against it. "I don't see anyone." He closed the door and rejoined Ial at the table.

Chary put Nyna's hand on an incomplete braid. "Hold this for a second, would you, dear?"

The servant moved to the outer room and bent down by the door.

"Never mind." The queen's companion messed with her skirt as she returned to her hairstyling. "I thought I saw shadows of feet. My big imagination. Did I ever tell you the story of the dolphin and the mermaid?"

"That's one of my favorite legends, Chary. Let's hear it again," Queen Shantia urged.

Talia chewed on her cheek. Her mother was acting odd. She wouldn't have enlisted Chary to tell her story unless she was trying to distract them. Shantia didn't believe in the mythology of the old gods.

Dew shivered as she closed the door to the bedchamber. "It's cold out there."

Goosebumps popped up on Talia's skin. That eerie sensation, as though someone were watching her, invaded her nerves. There had to be someone at the door. What else could she be sensing?

"I'm going to check further down the hallway. I can't shake this feeling. It's making me nervous."

"Oh, no, you're not." Shantia firmly pushed her daughter back onto the padded stool. "Your hair is not done yet. You will not embarrass me at the Graduation Ceremony with a disheveled appearance."

"Dew?" Talia pleaded.

"I'm on it." Dew swung the inner door open.

Reading his fellow guardian's face, Ial put his hand of cards on the table. The husbandry guardian stood as tall as Naul sitting. He opened the outer door and stepped into the hallway.

"I don't see anyone." Ial's voice echoed down the stone walls, as if proving his point.

As he closed the door, Naul picked up an envelope from the floor. "What's this?"

"I didn't see anyone, but someone must have shoved it under the door." Ial seemed perplexed by the delivery. He took the note from Naul and flipped it over. "It's addressed to the princess."

Chary jumped, bumping the table with the flowers for Talia's hair, sending them to the floor. Shantia exchanged a concerned look with her friend.

"Bah. Anyone who leaves notes under my door... " The princess scoffed. "Read it for me."

Ial opened the envelope with the thin dagger from his belt.

"Um, it's blank." Ial handed the parchment to Talia.

"Ha, ha, very funny. I know they taught you to read," she joked.

Talia took the missive and held it up for the room to see. Words in solid writing filled the page in poetic structure. Ial stared at the creased paper, eyes blinking.

Nyna giggled. "Looks like a love note to me."

For a moment, Talia feared the note had come from Lordling Gregor. Or worse, Lord Bello. Sniffing the letter, she detected no cologne. Instead, the paper smelled of the outdoors, woodsy and fresh. She read out loud:

"It is time for you to seek your destiny.

The truth of your birth cannot forever be hidden.

Search the Succession by Forging Clause in the Articles of Royal Deference.

You have been preparing for that which you do not know.
It is time to know."

Queen Shantia stumbled, dropping the strand of hair she held. Chary rushed to her mistress's side.

"Mother, are you okay?" Talia jumped up to help Chary get the queen on the bed. The layers of Talia's pristine white skirt hindered her movement.

"I'm fine, Talia. The preparations for two once-in-a-lifetime ceremonies in two days has me exhausted." Shantia accepted the glass of water offered by Chary, holding the servant's hand and gaze for a fraction too long.

"You can rest here for a little while. The Graduation Ceremony isn't for a couple hours." Talia brushed back blonde curls from her mother's chilled face.

"Truth of your birth?" queried Nyna, bringing Talia's focus back to the mysterious message.

Talia read the letter again to make sure she hadn't missed something. "Royal Deference? Since when does royalty defer to anything?"

Shantia spoke up, "We don't know who wrote this letter or what their motives are. It sounds like a setup or a cruel joke."

"I'll ask the rest of the staff if they know anything about the deliverer," Chary offered. "The servants usually know what's going on, and they're more likely to speak with me." She held out her hand to take the note.

"Of course. You're right." Talia tucked the note into her bodice, pretending not to notice Chary's outstretched hand. Something about the letter had sunk in deeper than she wanted it to. When she tried to formulate an explanation, she couldn't find a reason for anyone to send a message of this nature. Yet, could there be any truth to a destiny beyond marriage? What were the motives of the note writer?

"Let me know what you find, Chary." Talia ended the debate in her head. It was a dilemma for another time. Now, they had to finish preparations for the feast.

As the women left the princess's quarters, the fairy slipped out through the top of the door. She flew back to report the delivery of the note to her master. He would be pleased with her persistence, even if she had been forced to use more magic than expected. She must tell him of the princess's ability to sense the usage. Since the brother did not have the blood, they were lucky the sister's link was so strong. The fairy's hopes were renewed that her world, along with that of her master, would return as prophesied.

CHAPTER FOUR

TALIA APPROACHED THE GREAT HALL, walking awkwardly in her dainty slippers. The layers of her dress scratched her thighs. She wished she had left her leggings on underneath. She preferred more practical attire. She hated dressing for formal ceremonies.

Beside her, Naul pulled on his collar ferociously, trying to make room for his massive neck. Ial held his shoes in his hand, waiting until the last minute to force his flipper-like feet into them. Nyna kept reaching to adjust the strap of her absent bag. Talia wasn't the only one uncomfortable in these garments. Her scowl softened as she watched her guardians fuss with their clothes.

Dew, however, appeared perfectly at ease. Her dress, the same style as Nyna's, looked like a completely different outfit. The fabric cinched at her modest waist and blossomed at her chest, showcasing her impressive cleavage. Talia made a mental note to never wear the same dress as Dew. Ever. She'd lose that battle.

Arriving at the double doors leading to the Great Hall, the trepidation over the mysterious note weighed heavily on Talia's mind. She shook her head, dislodging a flower. Watching the white petals float to the ground without a choice in their destination, Talia felt trapped by the same invisible force. The note spoke of her destiny. Something deep inside whispered to the part of Talia that she kept suppressed. There was something she was supposed to do, something she was supposed to accomplish. Talia brushed a light strand of hair off her nose. Her thoughts turned to her father's big announcement. If it wasn't her Forging Quest, what did he have in mind?

Talia's guardians took up their positions around her. Though these young people spent the majority of their time together and were irrevocably bonded, Princess Talia Winterlaus had to remain detached, due to her rank and responsibility. As the kingdom's only princess, Talia had to present herself as regal, well-bred, and educated.

Talia peeked through the crack in the solid oak double doors of the Great Hall. Soft blue fabric hung at the back of the hall and darkened as it progressed along the ceiling, tucked along the rafters in flowing arches. By the time the silk reached the front, the blue turned to black, cascading as the backdrop to the main table on the stage. Stars, meticulously sewn in preserved patterns, represented the night sky at the moment of the twins' birth.

Long, rectangular tables were covered in deep blue silk cloths. Unique candelabras, each designed in the shape of a constellation, decorated the centers.

The Weeping Child shone on the table closest to her. The story of this constellation had intrigued her growing up, because it changed depending on who was telling it. Her father told a story of a disobedient child completely despondent over disappointing her king. Chary told her a grand story of ancient gods and how the child wept at their departure. One night, when she was about six, her mother had focused on the constellation and explained the child had been ripped away from her homeland and forced to live in exile in a strange kingdom.

None of these interpretations rang true for Talia. During her Giant Eagle flight training at the Husbandry School, Talia saw a side of the world that was new to her: natural beauty. As Talia soared over the land and sea on her first night flight, she understood the constellation. The child of light experienced an overwhelmingly beautiful view from such a great height, leaving her with no choice but to weep at its power. Tears welled from Talia's eyes as the emotional memory compounded upon the other struggles inside her head.

"My darling sister, congratulations," spoke Tanin, startling Talia out of her inner turmoil.

Talia turned from the door to see her brother approaching with open arms. He gave her a big hug, which only served to further confuse her.

"Good news travels quickly. I hear Father has finally chosen your future husband." Tanin mocked. "I have to admit I'm a bit jealous."

Talia pushed her brother away. "What are you talking about?"

"You do have it easy, sis," continued Tanin, ignoring his sister's retort. "While I must negotiate with kings and trade with dwarves to serve my country, all you have to do is lie on your back!"

Some of Tanin's guardians made lewd gestures with their hips to drive the point home. Talia's group tensed, ready to defend the honor of their beloved princess.

Before the fists could fly, the hall's large oak doors opened, forcing the participants to smooth their expressions. Princess Talia Winterlaus took a calming breath. Her training took over as a smile plastered across her face. She focused straight ahead, afraid to meet the gaze of the onlookers in case someone saw through her façade.

At the herald's introduction, Talia glided in to the sound of the royal players stationed near the back. The new composition had a strong drumline led by a bright and cheerful shawm. As Talia entered, the guests rose to their feet as one. Her guardians marched behind in two lines, scanning the crowd out of habit more than need.

Tanin and his guardians were announced and followed close behind. Talia heard the ladies in the crowd sigh in admiration of her brother's looks. Talia swallowed her disgust. If they knew him as she did, would they still be impressed?

The order of those standing at the head table on the dais caused

Talia's perfect smile to falter. High Priestess Nomyra loomed with crossed hands inside her robe at the end of the table. Next to her, Queen Shantia stood behind her tall chair. The unoccupied spot to her left—to the right hand of King Roland—belonged to the prince, as the unofficial heir to the throne. Nothing odd there.

It was the person standing on the other side of the king that confused Talia. Lord Bello Hilderamn took Talia's traditional spot on King Roland's left. The seat meant for the princess seemed to be to Bello's left. Talia hid her shock with a slight cough to regain her composure. Impossible. She replayed the meeting between her, King Roland, and Lord Bello. She had known she was missing something but hadn't been able to imagine what it was. Tanin's words came back to haunt her.

"Father has finally chosen your future husband."

It couldn't be. Lord Bello Hilderamn was to be her husband? This vile man from an estranged kingdom was her father's choice?

Talia slowed her pace. Her blue eyes darkened. As she met Lord Bello's gaze, his facial expression morphed into that of a predator. His bear paws gripped his coat with such intensity, Talia's instincts told her to run.

Her guardians stood by their table before the stage as Talia climbed the five steps, approaching the king from his left. She couldn't allow her father to make this horrible mistake. She was first-born. The Light gave her privileges. How could her father treat her with such disdain? She thought he loved her.

Her face flushed red as she made her decision. Talia passed King Roland to take the place at his right hand.

King Roland laughed and kissed his daughter on her forehead. The king broke protocol and addressed the crowd, "Our beloved princess is not ready to leave her father's side."

The audience awed appreciatively. Her father still smelled of mead, but his steady stance and quick wit showed he had sobered up —at least partially.

High Priestess Nomyra twisted the ruby ring around her finger in agitation. Talia smile meekly, acutely aware of the astropriestess's proclivity for complete order.

Tanin climbed the stage, his rage barely contained. Lord Bello discretely moved one seat over, allowing the prince to claim the spot on his father's left.

Roland ignored his son's outrage. The king reclaimed his seat, one hand holding his daughter's. Tanin fell heavily into his chair. Talia thought steam came off her brother, his face was so swollen with fury. The rest of the table and the guests took their seats as the orchestra moved on to a familiar piece of music: The Creation of the Universe.

High Priestess Nomyra alone remained standing. "All we are is determined by the Dark." Her voice engulfed the audience in the reverence she preached.

Queen Shantia rubbed her daughter on the shoulder. Talia watched the performers enter the hall.

A male dancer dressed entirely in black sauntered down the aisle. He brought with him a long skein of flowing gold silk. An identically dressed second male dancer held the other end. Together, they produced undulations in the fabric using graceful arm movements. The gold represented the primordial energy distributed throughout the universe.

"Long ago, the Light divided the Dark, allowing life to enter the universe."

A flicker caught the corner of Talia's vision. Nomyra lit a single candle, which she held high in front of her face.

On the floor, two female dancers, dressed in costumes cut from the same golden skein, rose from the center of the fabric. Back to back, they mirrored each other's arms and legs. Their seamless movements created the impression of one point of light.

"The First Dark and the Last Dark grew jealous of the attention the beautiful Light gave to nascent life."

The music changed to a minor key as the high-pitched gemshorn took over the melody. The dark-clad men fought over the cloth, ripping it into two pieces.

"The Light protected its creation by dividing itself and distracting the First Dark and the Last Dark."

The women separated and beckoned to the men. The Dark danced with the Light, switching partners as the music changed to a gay tune of celebration.

"The peace proved temporary as the First Dark grew jealous of the Last Dark, feeling he was spending more than his share with the Lights of the universe."

The men quarreled, their dancing turning erratic.

"The Light could not allow the two Darks to tear apart existence. Light decided to split into billions of pieces, spreading its energy throughout the night sky."

Gentle flutes flitted above the fray as the female dancers shredded the fabric wrap. They sprinkled the golden bits around the tables, on the guests, over the sparring men. The male dancers traveled through the aisles on different paths, sometimes admiring the shiny fabric, other times covetously hiding a piece in their pocket.

"Overly fond of human kind, the Light watches the mischievous Dark and warns us of his intentions. As long as we bear witness to the Light's messages and obey its commands, life will prosper."

Silence fell as the music concluded. The dancers returned to the wide center aisle to bow before King Roland. The king stood and bowed in return. The audience erupted in applause and cries of approval. The performers blushed with pleasure and relief. Dancing for the king had risks and rewards. It looked like this time, they earned a reward from the king.

"A beautiful telling of the Beginning. A performance worthy of a royal graduation." King Roland remained standing, straightening his cloak as he waited for the crowd to settle down. A subtle clearing of his throat was enough to promote a quick end to the cheering.

"Eighteen years ago as of tomorrow, the Light blessed Tarbin with a long-awaited heir." Roland held his left hand out to his son, who rose and accepted it. "Prince Tanin Winterlaus."

The prince bowed to the cheering audience. With his head down, he spared his seated sister a smug look.

"Because we waited so long for an heir, the Light decided to bless us with an extra special gift." Roland held out his right hand for Talia. She smiled sweetly at her brother before turning her attention to the audience. "Your beloved Princess Talia Winterlaus."

The crowd erupted into cheers. Talia bowed deeply, wishing her hair was down so she could hide her blushing cheeks. For a moment, she forgot about antagonizing her brother. Her people believed in her. She wished she could serve them as she felt called to.

"These two young people represent the best of the new generation. Today, we celebrate the completion of their formal education." The king threw his arm over Tanin's shoulder.

"Each institution prepared Prince Tanin in different ways to reign when my time ends. Sadly, your prince will have to wait many years for his chance." King Roland gave his son a solid punch to the arm.

Tanin winced. Talia swallowed a giggle.

"The same schools taught Princess Talia skills that will aide her husband with his responsibilities."

"Here, here!" Lord Bello smacked the table hard enough to make his place setting bounce.

Color drained from Talia's face, taking her good humor with it. The audience hushed. The princess could not discern if their silence bespoke their understanding of her future binding or shock at the foreigner's outburst.

King Roland's hearty laugh joined Lord Bello's chortling. Talia watched the tension leave the guests on cue from their king. She, however, felt no relief.

"I was going to wait until tomorrow's event to make the big reveal. But apparently, the secret has not been sealed as tightly as I had wished." Roland held his daughter, using his other arm to beckon Bello to his feet.

Tanin moved out of the way to allow the large man room. Talia had never seen her brother so accommodating. His enthusiasm for this union made her despise the prospect even more. Anything her brother wanted for her couldn't be good.

Talia stared straight ahead at her guardians, refusing to meet the eyes of the beast. They crouched on the edge of their seats, ready to mount the stage as a group if Talia called to them. The loyalty of her companions bolstered Talia's courage. She met Lord Bello's gaze with a look of disdain. She might not have a choice in whom she would wed, but nothing would stop her from expressing her disapproval.

"Tarbin's beautiful princess will join Darvis's most powerful nobleman, Lord Bello Hilderamn, once again building a bridge between our two kingdoms." King Roland put Talia's left hand in Bello's right.

The middle-aged man's fleshy hand possessively gripped Talia's. He held her hand up as if displaying a trophy. Talia allowed the crowd to clap for a few seconds before snatching her hand out of his grasp. She regained her seat before the urge to run overtook her sense of duty.

"Now, let's eat." King Roland sat, followed by Tanin and Bello.

Troupes of servants entered the hall, carrying trays of the most decadent food. Six servants carried in Tanin's wild boar on a large flat board. Two servants followed with Talia's buck. The king handed each of his children a large carving knife to make the first ceremonial cut of their sacrificial offering. All sustenance hailed from the king. At the Graduation Ceremony, the royal children had to prove they could support their people as well as their father. As kitchen staff carved the rest of the meat and distributed the succulent-smelling main courses, King Roland drank and laughed with Tanin and Bello.

Talia found she had little appetite. She nibbled sparingly at her food to keep up appearances. At one of the guest tables below, Lordling Gregor sat between two ladies, who flirted with him nonstop. Gregor winked at Talia. She scoffed at his unsolicited attention. If it wasn't one entitled nobleman seeking her attention, it was another.

Talia took attendance of the rest of the guests. She saw lords and ladies from all over Tarbin. The only foreigner she could pick out was Lord Bello. When her father had hinted that her Forging Quest would be to reestablish a trading relationship between Tarbin and Darvis, did he mean by marrying the foul foreigner? The whole time she thought her father was finally seeing her worth, he was actually planning on pawning her off for his own political gain.

"Where's King Vanderlae?" Princess Talia realized the oddity of a powerful nobleman of Darvis attending a royal Tarbin ceremony without the presence of his king.

"Odd, isn't it?" Queen Shantia leaned toward her daughter. "Lord Bello claims his king sanctions your union."

"So, they suddenly don't hate us? What changed?" Talia snuck a look at the beast down the table.

"I'm not sure, but your father is convinced." The queen put a spoonful of potatoes on Talia's plate.

High Priestess Nomyra spoke from around the queen, "The Hilderamn Trading Company's net worth is rumored to be more substantial than King Vanderlae's holdings. The balance of power seems to be shifting in Darvis."

Realization flooded Talia. "Lord Bello cannot be king unless he is connected to royalty."

"And his immense wealth will sustain you in the manner you are accustomed to." Queen Shantia leaned in front of Talia, blocking Nomyra. "Your father does love you."

Roland laughed heartily with food in his mouth, as he shared an amusing tale with Tanin and Bello.

"In his own way." Talia stared at her plate. Her father might love her. Yet his actions showed no consideration for her as a person.

The meal seemed interminable as course after course was placed in front of Talia and then cleared untouched. Her mother tried to make small talk. The princess couldn't put on her fake smile and play along anymore. Her mind churned with nightmare visions of her future.

Her mind returned again and again to the note. It suggested an alternative. She dismissed the silly dream as an alternative for a regular girl, not a princess. She had a responsibility to her father and to her kingdom. The note was nothing more than a distraction.

King Roland raised his hands, instantly ending the feast. "Let's dance in celebration of the royal graduates." He cued the musicians to strike up a lively tune.

Roland grabbed Shantia, leading her to the center of the Great Hall. Couples quickly followed their sovereign's lead.

Bello offered his hand to Talia. She couldn't think of a way out of the duty. She placed her small hand in his monstrous one and followed him to the dance floor. Naul and Nyna dropped their utensils onto their plates, joining the princess on the floor.

Bello held Talia too close for polite society. His unnatural grace left her feet surprisingly untrampled. Her breasts, however, were pressed uncomfortably against his chest. He was being too familiar with her body. She didn't belong to him yet. Talia tried to step back, but Bello forced her against him.

Bello leaned down to whisper, "You have been promised to me, my dear. You might as well grow accustomed to my will. I will give you a purpose in life as you bear me fat sons of royal blood."

Talia clenched her jaw, fighting the urge to verbally retaliate. She wanted to kick him and run away. Deep inside, she feared the monster was right.

"And that little stunt you pulled today with the seating at the grand table will not be tolerated." To prove his point, Bello squeezed her hands painfully.

When the song ended, he released her to bow. Lordling Gregor stepped in front of her, hand extended. She offered a strained smile to Bello, allowing him to kiss her hand. Gregor lead Talia to another part of the floor before Bello could refuse. As her partner spun her around, Talia saw the sneering confidence on Bello's face. He didn't look intimidated by the attention of the young whelp on his intended. The beast's complete assurance in her future terrified Talia.

"Did you know this was going to happen?" Gregor asked. "I would have brought a wedding gift."

Was the concern Talia heard in his voice. Before she pondered the emotion's meaning, Gregor winked at a young noblewoman they waltzed past. She sighed at her naivety.

"No," Talia confessed, wondering why she was confiding in the Lordling. "And I desire no gifts from you."

"If you need anything I can provide... " Gregor left the sentence open, his look seeming to confess his willingness to move mountains if required.

Talia didn't know how to respond. No wonder so many women fell for his charm. He certainly felt authentic. Though grateful the lordling had saved her from another dance with the beast, she couldn't figure out what he was looking for from her.

Dew waved at Talia from the guardian table to get her attention.

Thankful for the out, Talia freed herself from Gregor's warm embrace. "I have to go."

With Nyna and Naul close behind, Talia made her way to the table as another girl took her place in the lordling's arms. Talia swallowed the flutter in her throat.

"Lord Hilderamn has left," Dew said as soon as Talia was within earshot. "Now what?"

"I think we should escape while no one is looking." Nyna whispered, one hand grasping for her missing bag strap. "I don't like the way Lord Bello manhandled Talia."

"Let's get out of here." Talia moved to an outside wall to avoid the mass of dancers in the center of the room. She had to get away from the stifling castle.

CHAPTER FIVE

Princess Talia Winterlaus dashed through the Royal Forest. Whenever her life felt out of control, she ran until she couldn't breathe. On this night, her fancy dress and ill-fitting shoes kept her pace too slow to meet her needs.

Usually her first choice, the thought of sitting under the branches of her naddle tree offered no comfort today. Instead, her flight ended in front of a fearsome dragon carved from the blackest basalt. The dragon sat on extraordinary haunches with its wings thrust open. Its arm-like claws splayed, looking for flesh to sink into. The strong neck held the head to the top of the tree line, where piercing red ruby eyes were inlaid. The tail of the beast trailed behind, equal in length to the body. Talia was sure if dragons were real, they would leave onlookers with the same quiet awe that washed over her now.

Her companions breathed heavily by her side, their formal clothing spattered with dirt and stained with sweat. Her own white dress had been torn by grasping vegetation.

"At least now we know what King Roland was hinting at this afternoon." Nyna put a hand on the dragon's tail for balance as she flung her shoes off.

"We knew we were going west based on our preparation for the Forging Quest." Talia thought about the hours with High Priestess Nomyra. "I thought it was for an important diplomatic mission. Not a one-way trip to matrimony. I thought I would have some time."

"It does explain why the high priestess was always annoyed with us. The Forging Quest is meant to prove the worth of the heir. She probably thought she was wasting her time teaching us about the mountain terrain and the dwarven language." Dew walked in small circles, trying to catch her breath.

Naul pointed up. "Maybe we can bribe Lord Hilderamn with the dragon eye rubies."

The moon straight overhead reflected in the red gemstones.

Talia folded her arms over her chest. "A bribe won't help. He wants my name."

Talia appreciated her companions' support but knew she would have to face her betrothal alone.

Ial's quiet voice offered a distraction. "We couldn't trade the rubies anyway. The dragon won't allow it."

"The legend." Talia passed into the darkness. She remembered playing hide and seek under those wings, running in and out of the red lava stones with her brother, as Chary told the twins the legends of their kingdom. "Two thieves climbed to the top of the statue and pried out the jewels. When they tried to escape with the rubies, the thieves grew lost, unable to find their way out of the forest. Desperation drove them, tired and hungry, back to the dragon. They climbed to the top and put back the dragon's eyes. The path reappeared before the failed thieves, and they ran without looking back."

Dew interrupted Talia's moment of self-pity. "I think we need to visit the library. The old librarian is a bit coarse, but her knowledge of Tarbin history is unparalleled."

"Dew, I know you find comfort in old books, but I need to *do* something." Talia bit her lower lip.

"The note, Talia. We have to know what it means." The cultural guardian grabbed Talia's shoulders to look her straight in the eye.

"We don't know who the note is from or what their motives are. We need to find the Articles of Royal Deference. The librarian will know where to find them."

Princess Talia pulled the note, which she'd felt compelled to keep with her, from her bodice. "'The truth of your birth.' What could that possibly mean?"

Naul crossed his arms. "Let's go find out." His stern expression made Talia feel protected.

Would Talia be able to keep them safe if she was thrust into an unknown household in a foreign land? She had to use every resource available to her.

"It speaks of your destiny," Nyna said. "No one can avoid their destiny. Best to learn what you can."

"Ial?" Talia turned to her quietest companion.

He scratched the back of his head. Then he placed his hand palm down in the middle of the companions. Talia added hers on top of his, followed by the rest of the guardians.

The group chanted as one. "For the Light despite the Dark, we will shine in knowledge to fight the shadow of doubt."

Their hands raised as their volume climaxed. The mantra that had aided the companions throughout the years echoed eerily in the nighttime forest.

"First thing in the morning, we'll go to the library." Talia headed toward the castle. Slowly this time, assured of the path ahead.

CHAPTER SIX

High Priestess Nomyra Highwind watched the sunlight change colors as it poured into her chamber window. She pulled the knot loose from her hair, shaking out the waist-long locks. Despite being in her mid-fifties, her hair remained youthfully thick, though most of the color had bleached out decades ago.

The sun was not responsible for the loss of color. Her soft white, wrinkle-free skin attested to that. Though the Light's beloved daughter, the sun was little more than interference to the high priestess. Its bright light forced the eyes to focus on the ground, when the sky held the answers. The Stars led the educated observer to true power. Her family's legacy was close at hand. The mishap of one rogue priest had broken the cycle, leaving the Highwind family, as well as the world, struggling to gather what remained. A thousand years later, Nomyra poised on the edge of the Recharging.

Her full-length black robe slid across the floor as she made her way to her bed. After her minor role in the Graduation Ceremony hours ago, Nomyra spent the night atop her tower. While the rest of the castle filled their sheets, the High Priestess studied the Stars, scouring the night sky for any signs she might have missed. The Light shared nothing new. The learned woman interpreted their silence as acknowledgment of her careful preparations.

She was ready.

As the sun rose, Nomyra claimed her pillow. She kissed the Krag ring, ever present on her right middle finger. The steel band, mounted with a ruby the size of a human eye, represented the power of the astropriests. One ring mounted with a precious gem was granted to each high priestess and high priest at their anointing. Few understood the true strength of the rings. Nomyra's family was not one to share powerful secrets.

Closing her eyes in her darkened room, Nomyra drifted to sleep, confident in her preparations for her performance at the Forging Ceremony that night.

CHAPTER SEVEN

EARLY THE NEXT MORNING, Talia and her companions stood at the small wooden door to the castle library. The simple entryway gave no hint of the contents it hid. This was Talia's first visit, but Dew had spent many hours here. She motioned for her cultural guardian to take the lead.

Before Dew knocked, the librarian, Ms. Giddeona Feltwith, opened the door. The middle-aged woman's completely gray hair was piled carelessly on her head. Her overused gray eyes and oversized gray tunic made her appear a ghost on the threshold. Grasping onto the edge of the door, her fingers, longer than her palm, added to the supernatural image. Her second hand held a magnifying glass to aid her abused eyes. Appearing more curious than surprised, the librarian stared at the young people before her.

Talia stared back, lost for words. Giddeona slammed the door shut. The young people covered their faces as dust flew up off the floor.

Talia coughed to clear her throat of inhaled dust. "What just happened?"

Dew shook her head. "Well, Ms. Feltwith's always been peculiar, but I have no idea what that was."

Naul reached over Talia and Dew and banged on the door. "Peculiar or no, that was no way to greet the princess."

The wood swung open immediately, as if the librarian had been waiting in the same spot for the guests to make the next move. Again, the older woman said nothing. She held the door open but blocked the way in. She stood there with eyebrows raised, waiting.

Talia opened and closed her mouth twice, trying to put her thoughts into words. What was it about this woman that intimidated her? Giddeona shrugged and started to swing the door closed again.

"Wait!" pleaded Talia, as she placed her hand flatly on the door to keep it open. "How did you know we were here?"

"The way you young people clomp up and down the hallways, how could I not hear you coming?" Giddeona responded in a raspy voice. "Is that why you came all the way down here at this ridiculously early hour? To check my hearing and my patience?"

"No, ma'am." Dew but a hand on Talia's shoulder. "We were hoping to do some research."

"Before anyone else knows what you're up to?"

The companions exchanged looks of awe at the woman's keen perception.

"Knowledge is power, and it is about time you started to seek yours." Giddeona stepped aside and ushered them in.

That phrasing was so similar to the mysterious message that sent Talia to the library, she had to wonder. "Did you send me the note?"

"Note? What note? I don't have time to send little missives to royal children too busy with their own personal bickering to stop for a moment and notice who is doing all the real manipulating and what her plotting adds up to." Giddeona continued to mumble to herself as she moved further into the library.

As she passed the entrance, Talia's focus drifted upward. The unremarkable door hid a wondrous room nearly as big as the Great Hall.

Shelves reached to the ceiling in even columns throughout the space. Talia made out rope tying the tops of the shelves to the rafters. Volumes filled every level of every bookcase. The lack of furniture along some walls didn't stop the books from piling up vertically. Talia felt contrite for never having visited the library. Apparently, few people did. The dust of age covered every surface from the floor to the highest shelf.

As she followed Giddeona deeper into the chamber, Talia found it difficult to make out the details of her surroundings. The dim light masked the true depth of the massive space. Talia wondered where the light, however modest, came from. No windows could be discerned through the stacked shelves. Torches were unlit along the walls. It was probably safer that way, considering she had used many of the materials in this room to start fires.

Talia froze at the sound of a pile of books thumping to the ground.

"Sorry." Naul's shoulders hunched as he bent to try to pick the books up. Nyna beat him to it. She piled the books neater than they had been in their clumsily stacked column.

Giddeona waved her hand without stopping or turning around. Talia shrugged, meeting her defense guardian's gaze. If the librarian didn't care, why should she admonish him?

The companions passively followed the old woman through the maze, along a path relatively clear of dirt. Giddeona walked confidently along the makeshift passageway. She halted suddenly in front of a large collection of books with deep burgundy covers.

"Dragonhide. Sturdy, noncorrosive, colorful. The Articles of Royal Deference. Your forebears wanted to ensure the stability of their institution by creating a nearly indestructible index of the laws the royal class must not only enforce but obey themselves. The dragon skin was donated, of course, by Aninion the Great Unifier, if I remember correctly."

Ial rolled his eyes at Dew. "Dragon?"

Giddeona bored into Mal. "Only believe what you see, do you, young man? It is true dragons have not been seen for centuries, but I assure you they do exist. They were here before the mountains formed, when the sea was still raging with fire, before humans could write or govern, before the beginning of history."

The old woman turned her gaze to Talia. "Where they have gone is the real mystery."

The cryptic talk was starting to piss Talia off. "If you didn't write the note, how did you know what we wanted to research?"

"The Forging Ceremony is tonight. The rules governing the event are in this volume." Without deliberation, Giddeona removed a dusty tome from the shelf and placed it in Talia's hands.

The old woman gripped the younger woman as their joined hands held the book. Pulling Talia close, Giddeona leaned in, her breath smelling of ink and mildew. Talia refused to be intimidated.

In a whisper, Giddeona advised, "Consider carefully what lies before you. Despite what others might label your destiny, you have a choice. What is written can be rewritten."

The librarian held the princess's attention. The next moment, she released Talia and backtracked through the way they had come. Talia followed behind, walking by instinct, lost in her own thoughts and confusion. Arriving at the door, Giddeona ushered her visitors into the hallway. Without a word, she closed the door with finality.

Talia grew cognizant of her position outside the library with a grimy book in her hand. The bewildered princess had never been so lost in her life. She'd had perfect focus through her schooling, organizing her responsibilities and reaching her academic achievements. When did her life become so cryptic and aimless? Irrational angry that everything in her life was occurring outside of her control, she twisted around to the wooden door. She raised her arm to bang on the wood and demand an explanation, a reason, a direction to aim.

Before her knuckles hit, Dew stepped in front of her.

"Should we make sure the volume is what we came for before we disturb Ms. Feltwith again?"

Ial nodded in agreement.

Talia had her doubts. "How are we supposed to know what we're looking for? Did you hear the way she spoke, almost trance-like at times? She had to have written the note. I want to know why she's denying it and what her game is."

"Talia, let's take the book back to your chambers," pleaded Nyna.

"We're never going to get through this book in one day, especially when we don't know what we're looking for." Talia held the note in one hand, the book in the other.

"Here." Talia handed the note to Dew. "If you're going to help me look, you should read the message yourself."

Dew looked at the parchment for only a moment. "Wrong sheet. This one's blank."

"It's the only one I have." Talia stopped under a lit torch.

Bewildered, Talia gave the book to Naul so she could use both hands to search her pockets. Empty. Out of options, she took the slip of paper from Dew. As soon as her fingers touched the paper, the familiar handwriting reappeared, as if freshly written. Eyes wide, Talia touched the ink, expecting it to smear, but it was dry.

"That's what it did when I picked it up from the floor." Ial held his hands behind his back. "I knew I wasn't crazy."

"I thought you were joking." Talia tapped Ial's shoulder in apology. "I wonder if the words have changed."

Talia read the directive again:

"It is time for you to seek your destiny.

The truth of your birth cannot forever be hidden.

Search the Succession by Forging Clause in..."

As soon as she began the third line, the index in Naul's hand began to rustle. The defense guardian held it out at arm's length, flat on his open palms, as it opened. Its pages flipped rapidly. The companion curved his back, putting the book as far from his body as possible. As soon as the pages stopped moving, Naul closed the book and tossed it to Nyna.

She instinctively caught it. "It's warm."

Dew set the book on the ground and motioned to Talia. "Read the note again."

As Talia reached the words "Succession by Forging," the book spontaneously flipped open, appearing to stop at the same page as before. Talia finished reading the note to see if the pages had more moving to do. They remained open to that particular part.

Talia handed the note to Dew and picked up the book from the ground. "I believe this is Elvish." She showed the flowery writing to Dew.

"Definitely Elvish," agreed the cultural guardian.

"Why would a law book meant to instruct a human royal line be written in Elvish?" asked Nyna.

"I have an Elvish dictionary in my chamber," Dew offered, obviously anxious to get to translating.

"I think we're missing the bigger picture here." Ial pointed to the book as if it were a naughty child.

Talia raised an eyebrow. "And that would be?"

"Are we just going to ignore the disappearing and reappearing ink and the spontaneously opening book?" asked Naul. "It's like—"

"Magic." Talia looked down at the inanimate object in her hand.

"I don't know what to make of the enchantment. But I do know how to make sense of the written words." Dew used the note, blank at her touch, as a bookmark in the leather-bound tome.

Magic. Talia couldn't believe she used that word without sarcasm. No one would have characterized the princess's life as ordinary, but the last two days had transformed her existence into another state of being altogether. Oddly, she was not afraid. Maybe fear would come later.

CHAPTER EIGHT

NOMYRA'S EYES FLASHED OPEN, fire burning around the deep blue irises. A knock on her outer door disturbed her rest. She dismissed the uninvited visitor as a new servant. No one familiar with the castle and its habits would dare make noise in the Astropriest Tower at this early hour. Nomyra's girl would shoo away the intruder. Tucking her pillow below her neck and closing her eyes, the high priestess forced her heart to slow and her breathing to calm.

The knock rang through her chambers again. This time, it was accompanied by a muffled voice. "High Priestess, are you awake? I have important information for you."

"Seamus." Nomyra threw her sheets aside with a growl. "That nephew of mine must be taught some manners."

The middle-aged woman ignored her aching shoulders as she threw her robe on. She flung the door open as Seamus raised his hand to pound on it again.

"The Stars themselves better be falling from the sky for you to disturb my sleep on this pivotal day. You know what is at stake." Nomyra left the door for Seamus to close.

"Precisely because the Forging Ceremony is today, I had to

awaken you. I apologize for the ill timing." Seamus's mouth pinched on one side.

Nomyra could feel his eagerness to tell her the bad news. Still seeing him as the petulant youth who had come to the castle seeking his future, Nomyra had to remind herself that the now-forty-year-old man had ambitions of his own. She needed to keep an eye on him. Her nephew had played his part eighteen years ago, which he never failed to remind her. His past pivotal role wouldn't protect him from Nomyra's wrath if he disturbed her careful planning. Every piece had to fit precisely where the Light directed.

The high priestess poured herself a cup of water and leaned against the table. She stared at her nephew. His frame was so thin, it barely cast a shadow in the filtered light.

Seamus rocked on the balls of his feet, unable to stand still. "Princess Talia visited the library this morning."

Nomyra dropped her cup onto the table, spilling water across the surface. She twirled Krag around her finger. "Did she speak to Giddeona?"

"I don't know for sure. I couldn't get down the hallway without being seen." The younger priest pulled on his right ear. "She left with a burgundy leather-bound book. That could only be from the—"

"Articles of Royal Deference. What could she possibly be researching? Only the heir is part of the prophecy. His sister is irrelevant." Nomyra sat in her armchair by the fireplace, folding her legs beneath her. She stared at the curved walls of her tower chamber, lost in her thoughts. Her mind raced through the possibilities. "What have I missed?"

The clap of Seamus's heels on the stone floor invaded her thoughts. She needed him to go so she could think.

"Thank you for the information. You can leave now."

"But I can help you solve this problem. We can make a contingency plan." Seamus bent his back like a groveling dog. "Tell me what you planned, and I can help ensure its success."

"You have already served the prophecy in the only way required of you." Nomyra slowly unfolded her legs and rose to her full height, forcing Seamus to look up at her. "Thank you for the information. You can leave now."

"Please, Auntie. I want to make up for my mother's treachery. I can be of much more service to the family name. Let me help."

Nomyra moved to the door. Her nephew's begging turned her stomach. His shuffling steps followed her.

"I know secrets the king would be most interested to learn." The threat dripped from his mouth.

The high priestess pivoted so quickly her hair rose in the air. Her flat hand landed fiercely on her nephew's cheek. The sound of skin on skin echoed from the stone walls. Krag scraped his face. Seamus's hand flew to his reddening cheek, eyes wide in shock.

"If you dare threaten me again, your place will be outside the Highwinds for eternity."

As the dull glow from the soaked blood into the ring faded, Nomyra glared at her nephew. A knock broke through her angry tirade.

"Did someone post a celebration in my chambers and forget to tell me?" she yelled as she flung the door open.

Prince Tanin cocked one hip, his hand on his sword hilt. He raised his eyebrows at the high priestess's exclamation. The youth tilted his head, his eyes focused on the woman's slightly open robe. "If you need me to come back another time... "

"Priest Seamus was just leaving, my Prince." Nomyra tucked her robe closed, hiding any peeking skin, and bowed. She was grateful her long hair hid her face enough for her to compose her expression.

Seamus bowed as the prince and two of his guardians entered the tower chambers. The priest left without another word, though Nomyra could feel his repressed anger. She'd have to deal with him sooner rather than later.

The high priestess closed the door, checked her robe, and took a deep breath, before turning around. "How can I be of assistance, my Prince?"

"High Priestess Nomyra, I wanted to verify there were no changes in the evening's plans. My sister has been acting erratically. Wedding jitters, I'm sure." Tanin winked at Rory, his defense guardian, and Tyler, his cultural guardian who happened to be Nomyra's cousin. While Rory snickered with Tanin, Tyler refused to meet Nomyra's eyes.

Nomyra's voice lowered soothingly. "There have been no changes, my Prince."

The Stars had chosen Tanin to return the Highwinds and Tarbin to its golden age of power. His insecurity and constant posturing made the high priestess question the Light's choice. As long as he followed Tyler's guidance and her own, he could not fail. His destiny was clear. Plus, he wouldn't be around after the Recharging to cause much of a problem anyway.

"The kitchen staff and livery have assured me that all the preparations have been made for my year-long quest, as well as my sister's. Do you know what they are talking about?" The prince stood entirely too close to the older woman. Rory and Tyler sat on the sofa, ignoring their charge's inappropriate behavior.

Nomyra laughed to weaken the prince's tension. "Perhaps she is planning on running away." She moved to her work table and pulled out a bottle of wine. She needed something stronger than water if she was to deal with the boy.

"Of course, what else would that silly girl do?" Tanin's shoulders relaxed. He held up his hand for her glass of wine.

Nomyra stared at him for a moment. His audacity ate at her temper. The sweet-sour nose of the expensive red wine filled the woman's senses as she handed the boy the glass she had poured for herself.

Tanin gulped the wine. "Have you heard from the dwarves?"

Nomyra scowled at his lack of appreciation for the complex flavors, wishing she pulled out the cheaper bottle. "Yes. Tyler should have informed you." One look at her cousin told her he had. "The diamond has safely left the Eckerd Mountains and will be delivered to the port before you leave for the Kiwi Islands."

"Excellent. I'm going to sneak in a nap before this evening's main event. I want to look my best as I leave Talia far behind and rise to the position my father has prepared me for." The prince grabbed the bottle of wine from Nomyra's desk.

The high priestess's mind whirled as she calculated the punishment for throttling the spoiled prince. It might be worth it.

At his charge's cue, Rory opened the door and inspected the hallway. With an apologetic smile, Tyler took up position behind the prince. One of Nomyra's eyebrows rose ever so subtly. What dangers did the paranoid guardians imagine would jump out at Prince Tanin in his own castle?

"You should get some rest too, High Priestess. The Forging Ceremony will be the pinnacle of your career. Topped only by my return when you officially crown me the True Heir," Tanin spoke over his shoulder. "You don't want the kingdom to see those dark circles under your eyes."

"Yes, my Prince." Nomyra bowed her head, hiding the smirk on her face. *My eyes will be the last thing the crowd notices.*

She closed the door behind the prince. The high priestess couldn't shake the doubt that had seeded in her mind. Why would the princess take a volume of the Articles of Royal Deference? Nomyra knew Giddeona would never allow her into the library to discover which volume the princess possessed. The library was Giddeona's realm, the one place in the castle Nomyra had no power. Something in there must offer Talia a way out of her engagement. Nomyra couldn't fathom any other purpose for her research.

The woman closed her eyes and leaned her head against the back of her chair. She'd deal with the princess later, if necessary. Right now, she had to concentrate on the Forging Ceremony and keeping Tanin on track.

She hoped meek Tyler had enough presence to guide Tanin through the yearlong trial. Tanin had been expected to sit through all the tutoring sessions to prepare him for the journey. He'd only spent half the time Nomyra recommended. Studious Tyler understood the importance of the heir's mission. That should keep him motivated to stand up to the prince's laziness.

With the Recharging only two years away, everything was falling into place as planned.

Soon.

Soon Nomyra would be free of the eternal royal bickering and ridiculous request. The Highwinds would return to their ancient status as rulers of the Renquist continent from the ancient desert city of Raqmu, with Nomyra leading the way. Generations of her family had sacrificed to get Nomyra to the position she now held so she could fix the last broken element.

She would not fail them.

CHAPTER NINE

Talia sat in the same Great Hall that had held her Graduation Ceremony the night before. The same Stars adorned the stage, the only aspect to hint it was the same room, since rows of benches replaced the banquet tables.

Nyna placed a comforting hand on the princess's twitching legs. Talia knew what to do. The translation of the note-chosen section of the *Articles of Royal Deference* had been more than enlightening. The follow-through, however, was putting her on edge. Standing up to her brother was something she'd done her whole life. She looked forward to one more stab in that direction. Yet, the high priestess terrified her. Talia hoped the Stars were on her side this night.

Talia's companions flanked her on both sides of the bench, wearing their formal guardian garb of dark blue leggings, bright-white tunics, and gold sashes, which denoted their schools and ranks. Talia had chosen to wear leggings as well as a conservative tunic. If she was going to play with the boys, she wanted to avoid looking like a delicate flower.

Dew and Nyna had worked all day translating the passage indicated by the note. With Elvish a dead language, Dew had learned it in school as a tradition, not as a tool useful to her duties. Therefore, she had relied heavily on her Elvish dictionary. Luckily, Nyna knew a bit of the extinct language from translating old medicinal scrolls. While the two had worked, Ial and Naul had packed their supplies for a cross-country trip. Talia had paced most of the morning, completely useless.

As Tanin and his four companions entered the hall, Talia forced her mind to focus. Her brother's party claimed their seats to the right of Talia's group. The prince's guardians were dressed identically to Talia's. Tanin wore an outrageous, bright-silver shirt with black leggings.

Nyna elbowed Talia. "Who dressed the prince for the ceremony?"

Talia chewed on her lower lip. "You know my brother chose that particular outfit to glow like a Star in the night sky. He already thinks himself a god. What happens when he finally wears the crown?"

"Light help us all," Dew answered.

A few rows back, Talia spotted Gregor talking with a noble daughter adorned in a flattering gown with every hair in place. Gregor flashed his characteristic smile at Talia. The noble daughter followed his gaze and frowned slightly. She motioned to her entourage, who turned and giggled. Talia suspected they laughed at her untraditional outfit. The princess smiled to herself. If the girls were scandalized by her attire, wait until she interrupted the ceremony.

Talia's mood faded as quickly as it had risen with the entrance of Lord Bello.

Talia recognized certainty in his expression, not much different than the one her brother held. Lord Bello was convinced he would leave this chamber with the princess on his arm, one step closer to his ultimate goal. Proving Talia's interpretation, Lord Bello patted the empty seat next to him, inviting her to take her rightful place. Talia's companions scowled at his audacity. The intense emotion emanating from the group caused the room to grow quiet, anticipating the next move.

Before anything could occur, High Priestess Nomyra took the stage, refocusing all attention to the front. The flamboyant speaker held up her arms, causing the sleeves of her brilliant-white robes to slide to her elbows. Nomyra spoke words unrecognizable to the crowd. She brought down her arms with a flourish, emitting flames from her fingertips. The fire caught the gossamer fabric encircling a raised object on the stage.

The heat washed over Talia, who gripped her seat, resisting her instinct to flee.

The fire consumed the fabric in a matter of seconds, revealing a large dais in the shape of a five-pointed star. Nomyra stepped upon the head point, facing the crowd. Atop the dais on the left branch stood an empty pedestal. On the right branch sat an ornate, high-backed chair embroidered with the Seafarer constellation, King Roland's birth sign.

"A ruler is forged, not born. The fire cleansed the dais as it heats the forge." Nomyra's voice boomed through the hall, taking complete command of the audience.

It took Talia a moment to shake her spell and notice King Roland walking down the aisle to the stage. His guardians wore the same uniform as the younger group, though their gold sashes contained more awards and higher rankings. Talia recalled that three of her father's current guardians had accompanied the once-prince on his Forging Quest almost thirty years ago. The king climbed the stairs and stood before his throne.

"I am the blacksmith who has tempered the raw metal," King Roland proclaimed, proudly looking down at his son.

"Are you prepared to have the strength, endurance, and will of your creation tested for the good of Tarbin?" Nomyra asked.

"I am," replied the king, bowing his head to the high priestess.

Nomyra removed the Tarbin crown from Roland's head. Holding it high with the tips of her fingers, Nomyra gracefully crossed the dais to the pedestal. She lowered the crown to the silk top as the king took his seat, both coming to rest at the same moment.

The heirloom represented all the power of the kingdom, the symbol of Tarbin's rule for hundreds of years. No one remembered when the crown was forged. Its makeup baffled the best alchemists. Tradition said gold, which the weight of the crown supported. The firm nature of the molding, however, bespoke of some harder agent solidifying the malleable metal. Mounted on the crown were five precious gems, each the size of a goose's egg. A ruby, an emerald, a diamond, a sapphire, and a black opal each adorned one of five rectangle projections evenly spaced around the crown. Fox fur lined the bottom, providing a comfortable fit for the wearer.

The high priestess reclaimed her spot at the head of the star. She extended her arms to the audience. Tanin straightened his tunic and brushed back his hair, preparing for his cue.

"The forge has been heated, the metal tempered. Now the would-be ruler must be put to the anvil." Nomyra's focus fell on Prince Tanin, who rose at her last word.

"I am ready to walk through the fire and succumb to the hammer to become the strong, flexible, and well-balanced weapon my people deserve."

The last few syllables fell from Tanin's mouth without emphasis, as his words echoed beside him. Talia stood tall beside her brother, repeating the same script. Tanin pivoted, throwing an accusatory look at the high priestess. Nomyra's face flushed at the interruption of her carefully planned ceremony.

Talia witnessed a moment of panic break through the carefully crafted façade of High Priestess Nomyra. Maybe she was human after all.

The king waved his hand at his daughter. "Sit down, child. Only the heir participates in the Forging Ceremony. Yours will follow."

Talia swallowed. She either stood up for herself now or accepted whatever future was laid out for her. "The heir is undetermined until the conclusion of the Forging Quest per the *Articles of Royal Deference*," Talia proclaimed with more confidence than she felt.

The king didn't seem to hear her. "Now, my darling, your time will come."

Ignoring the murmuring of the assembled guests, Nomyra focused on Talia. "The law you speak of can only be used by illegitimate children of the current ruler when the child comes of age or is of age when the legitimate heir comes of age." Exasperated, the high priestess attempted to reclaim control. "Now please step forward, Prince Tanin Winterlaus, and hear your quest."

Tanin sneered at Talia over his shoulder as he approached the stage. The audience whispered behind her back. Talia saw her chance to prove herself slipping away. She looked down at her companions. All four motioned her forward toward the stage.

Talia shouted over the commotion using volume to show her determination to proceed. "The Forging Clause specifies all of-age children of royal blood!"

Nomyra threw her closed fists down at her sides. "It does *not!*"

Cowed by High Priestess Nomyra's will, Talia froze.

The audience quieted.

"Actually, High Priestess, it does."

Talia, along with the entire audience, pivoted to see who was supporting her cause. In the back of the room, holding up the leather-bound book from the princess's bedchamber, stood Giddeona Feltwith. Nomyra's face fell. A flash of fear flickered in the powerful woman's eyes.

Clearly tired of the evening's interruptions, King Roland said, "How can a librarian question the high priestess on matters of religious rights?"

"When the librarian was high priestess first." Giddeona walked up the aisle to the foot of the stage, offering the book.

Nomyra grabbed the older woman's hand, pulling their faces close. If Talia hadn't been so close, she wouldn't have heard a thing.

"Why are you doing this? You walked away from your responsibility, leaving me to fulfill our family's duties." Nomyra shook with anger.

"Because our family was wrong," replied Giddeona, slipping her hand out of her sister's grasp. Addressing the audience loudly, the librarian continued, "The *Articles of Royal Deference* clearly outlines the ascension of power. Each royal child of age, regardless of prior quest status, is called to go on a Forging Quest. The contender who succeeds becomes the rightful heir, regardless of birth order or gender."

Nomyra slammed the book shut and tossed it back to the older woman. "She's right."

Giddeona caught the book and shooed Tanin up to the dais. The librarian offered Talia a hand up as the princess followed her brother.

"Thank you," Talia implied gratitude for more than the assistance to the stage.

"Do not thank me, young one. The path you have chosen is painful and treacherous. One day, you might wish I had stayed in my dusty library." With her last words spoken, Giddeona walked up the aisle and out of the hall as unobtrusively as she had entered.

Talia watched her leave, wondering what the reclusive librarian meant by being the high priestess first. What was the family wrong about? Before Talia could work out an answer, her father demanded her attention.

"Let the princess participate. She might be able to help her brother." The king glanced dotingly at his daughter.

Talia held her breath as she watched the high priestess react. The woman's fists balled up so tightly the princess expected to see blood drip onto the stage.

"I read the Stars and know what they foretell. I follow their orders above all others. The quest the Light laid out calls for the True

Heir to participate, *not* his sister." Nomyra's voice sounded calm and steady, though her jaw tightened as fiercely as her fists.

Talia impressed herself with her ability to talk even as her entire body shook. "According to Tarbin's law, we don't know who the True Heir is until the quest is complete."

Tanin twisted to face his father, mirroring Nomyra's clenched fists. The king held up a quieting hand to his son.

King Roland faced the fuming high priestess. "I allow your presence as a matter of tradition and reverence. But make no mistake, your roll is advisory only."

"Father," Tanin protested in the same hushed voice.

King Roland quieted the prince's argument. "Tanin, remain quiet and accept your quest. You will triumph and fulfill your destiny to rule after me. A man will always sit on the Tarbin throne. Let your sister have one last adventure before fulfilling her duty as wife and mother."

Talia opened her mouth to voice her own complaint.

"You be quiet, my daughter. I am indulging your last childish whim. Be grateful I do not call your betrothed to fetch you from the stage."

The king sat and planted his elbows on his armrests, a sign the conversation was over.

High Priestess Nomyra unfolded her fingers and loosened her jaw. She focused on the twins, ignoring the king and the audience.

"Kneel," she ordered, indicating the last two unoccupied points of the star. Nomyra closed her eyes and inhaled deeply, her white hair surrounding her head like a mane.

Nomyra regained her theatrical voice as she slipped back into her prepared script. "Tarbin's crown is a symbol of unity established millennia ago. Though the crown appears whole, it has been fractured over time."

The crown was in perfect condition as far as Talia could tell: no staining, no cracks, no fingerprints.

"The five Holy Gemstones mounted on the Golden Crown

represent the six kingdoms of Tarbin. The original size of this grand country has left the common knowledge, leaving us to believe our current borders envelope the entirety of Tarbin. This is false."

Nomyra verified she had the complete attention of her audience. "Tarbin once spanned the whole of the Renquist continent, from the Southern Sea to the Ngaro Ocean, across the Great Desert to the forest of Althuin. Each mountain peak, every island. All inhabitants called themselves Tarbinians. We were the greatest kingdom in the known world. The Stars blessed us, and the Planets turned for us."

She paused, gripping the crown close to her chest. "The crown truly represents our kingdom's downfall. As we have shrunk in size and favor, so has it shrunk in value."

Nomyra ripped the diamond from its mounting, holding it up to gasps from the audience. The king popped up from his throne, ready to throttle the high priestess for her impudence. Before he could reach her, Nomyra pitched the diamond at the center of the dais with all her might.

The gem shattered, flinging pieces in every direction. Tanin and Talia covered their faces. The audience stood in shock. The guardians of the royal twins rushed the stage.

"That's not possible. Diamonds don't shatter," the king bellowed. "Reight, Allius, search her!"

The high priestess removed her robe and tossed it at the lunging men. Nomyra stood with arms outstretched, completely naked. The audience fell back in their seats at the sight of the head of their religious order's statuesque presence. Her defiant eyes challenged the guardians to lay hands on her. For the first time, Talia truly understood the power of the high priestess.

"I have nothing to hide," Nomyra proclaimed, handing the damaged crown to the guardians, who delivered it straight to the king without touching her.

"All the gems on the crown are forgeries." The high priestess focused on the young royals kneeling before her.

Talia watched Tanin struggle to keep his gaze on the woman's eyes. Talia knew Nomyra and Tanin had spent hours preparing for this ceremony and researching for the journey ahead. It was part of what made her so nervous to join so late in the process. Obviously, the high priestess hadn't prepared Tanin for this particular portion.

Talia concentrated on Nomyra's words, trying to glean all meaning from their content. She didn't have the advantage of private tutoring with the high priestess.

"Your Forging Quest will lead you outside our current borders. You must find the original stones and return them to their rightful place upon the crown. Uniting the jewels with their original mounting will be the beginning of uniting the lost lands to the current. You have one year to complete your Forging. One year from today, we will meet again, at this place, with the recovered gems ready to be mounted. So say the Stars."

The crowd chimed in together, "So say the Stars."

"Above all else, the blood of the True Heir will determine the champion of the quest." High Priestess Nomyra held the twins' eyes for an intense moment. Abruptly turning, she strode off the stage.

The audience erupted in chaos. Voices shouted questions at their ruler. King Roland whispered to his guardians, who tried to encourage the attendants to retire to the banquet hall where the bull was prepared for the slaughter and the formal dinner would begin. Tanin jumped off the stage and exited with his guardians, without a word to his father or sister. Talia rejoined her companions, relief flooding her brain, causing her to sway. Naul held her steady.

Nyna adjusted her sash. "You were so brave, Talia. I don't know if I could have stood up to High Priestess Nomyra."

"And now?" Ial asked, surveying the agitated crowd.

"I guess we're going on an adventure." Delighted her voice still worked, Talia sat on the edge of the stage, finding some problems with her feet.

"Can we talk after we get out of here?" Naul pointed at a figure pushing his way through the crowd.

A furious Lord Bello shoved people out of his way as he stormed toward the stage.

Talia's body vibrated with renewed urgency. "Good call. Let's go."

CHAPTER TEN

IN THE RELATIVE quiet of the hallway, Gregor paced. Talia smiled, despite the stress of the evening.

Lordling Gregor sighed in obvious relief. "Oh, good, you escaped the crowd. More importantly, Lord Bello."

Talia strode down the hall toward her chambers. "I don't have time for your harassment right now. I need to figure out what I'm supposed to do next."

"How did you know about the *Articles of Royal Deference?*" Gregor trotted to catch up. "I've never seen Tanin so angry."

"I don't see how any of this is your business."

"Do you know where the gems are?" Gregor continued to push.

"No, not a clue. Look, we have to figure out where we're supposed to start." Talia's heart raced at the magnitude of the quest before her.

"That's why I was looking for you," explained Gregor. "I think I know where one is."

The train of youths stopped as one, causing Gregor to bump into Ial.

"How do you do that?" questioned Gregor, impressed with the group's synchronicity.

"Did you know the gems were fake?" asked Dew, unable to keep herself out of the conversation.

"No," Gregor claimed, throwing his hands in the air. "Well, I wasn't sure."

Talia continued leading her group back to her chambers. "We don't have time for this. We need to leave before someone changes their mind and locks me up."

She studied Gregor's face as the group moved down the hallway. Was he working for her brother? Why would he wait outside the hall and offer advice?

Talia stopped, unable to continue without discerning the lordling's motives. "Okay, fess up. What do you know?"

"At the Defense School, I bonded with Head Master Lutch Overstone. He was more of a father to me than my real father."

Naul smacked Gregor on the shoulder. "I remember that old dwarf. Always going on about conspiracies and ancient secrets."

"Master Overstone was obsessed with Tarbin history." Gregor rubbed his shoulder. "After class, he would study ancient manuscripts and sketches from before the Great Sundering. During breaks, he would lead expeditions to long-lost ruins to gather more information. The old dwarf started to believe the true Holy Diamond rested on the scepter used in the annual Dwarf Peace Ceremony, commemorating the end of the Dwarven Civil War."

"Does he have a theory on where the other gems lie?" asked Dew.

"I don't know. I graduated before Overstone took his theory to the Dwarven King. Last I heard, he was forced into retirement by the Defense School administration."

"Look. That's a nice story, but I'm not sure what I'm supposed to do about it? Go to the Dwarven King and ask him nicely to let me have the diamond?" Talia looked up at him expectantly.

"The thing is... " Gregor hesitated. "In the end, Master Overstone started to rant about a conspiracy orchestrated by the astropriests and that the cause of the Great Sundering had nothing to do with the wars, but with a natural phenomenon. He claimed the diamond on the scepter was a copy. The old dwarf claimed to know where the real Holy Diamond was. It was probably why they forced him to retire and leave the mountain."

The group arrived at Talia's chamber. The princess ushered her companions in but blocked Gregor from entering.

"Thank you for the information, but we'll hit the library and see if Ms. Feltwith has more information for us." Talia dismissed him.

Gregor stuck his foot in the closing door. "Please, I know I can help."

Talia stared at Gregor. Tanin was ahead of the game. Her brother might have to share the Forging Quest, but she knew he wouldn't allow her to tag along, regardless of what their father suggested. She'd have to discover her own path. What she couldn't figure out was what Gregor expected to get from helping her.

"Princess Talia," Nyna called from inside the chamber.

Talia left the door ajar, allowing Lordling Gregor to enter behind her.

A dusty tome lay on the round table by the fireplace. The book was thick enough to be three volumes. It was bound in dark-colored leather, the exact shade difficult to discern in the dimly lit chamber. On the front, Elvish lettering proclaimed its title.

"*Secrets of the Key*," Dew translated. She opened the book and flipped through the pages.

Talia noticed a note beside the book. Opening it, she read its contents aloud:

"Princess, I am sorry I cannot journey with you. I'm afraid I've made myself more unwanted than usual. This book will give you the background information you need to find the Holy Gemstones. I wish I could tell you everything, but alas, it seems the Light wants you to discover everything yourself. I hope you succeed in your quest. The world needs to be rebalanced, and I doubt the prince is up to the task. May the Stars guide your journey. Giddeona Feltwith, Librarian."

Talia shook her head. "Is this supposed to make me feel better? Why can't she give me a guide if she knows more? Is she too busy letting dust gather in the library?"

Dew petted the book like it was a precious treasure. "This could be just what we need Talia." She flipped open the pages reverently. "It contains the history of the Golden Crown and the Holy Gemstones."

It didn't make Talia feel any better, but at least it was something to start with.

Nyna moved her finger as she read the text. "The table of contents lists the crown with the humans, the ruby with the dragons, the sapphire with the elves, the emerald with something called the nadph, the black opal with the mermaids, and the diamond with the dwarves."

"There are a lot of make-believe creatures on that list," Ial remarked.

"The diamond with the dwarves supports Master Overstone's story," reiterated Gregor.

Talia sized the lordling up. She didn't know if she could trust him. She chose the side of caution. "I believe you, but you still can't come with us."

Naul simplified the decision. "So, we need to visit the dwarves and find the diamond. Maybe Dew and Nyna can get more of the book translated along the way, giving us a clue on where to go after that."

"What if the diamond is a fake like Master Overstone claimed?" asked Dew. "How do we even know which one is the original?"

"Maybe the book will tell us?" Talia speculated.

Gregor crossed his arms. "Or maybe you can talk to Master Overstone."

Talia studied him again. His boyish charm swayed her heart, but she was determined to use her brain.

"We can ask the master dwarf when we get to his kingdom." Talia tried to dismiss the lordling.

"But he was exiled," Gregor reminded her.

"So how were you going to question him?"

"I might know where the old dwarf went into hiding." Gregor studied his fingernails. "I possibly could have exchanged correspondence with him over the last couple of years, in secret."

"Great! Tell us where he is." Talia used her most authoritative voice.

"I promised him I wouldn't tell a soul."

"Why bring it up, then, if you weren't going to tell us?" demanded Talia, annoyed with the wordplay. She was ready for some action.

"If you were to follow me as I made a visit to my dear old master, I couldn't be blamed for that, right?" Gregor grinned with a half-raised eyebrow.

Talia finally understood.

"So you are refusing to tell me where Master Overstone is in order to sneak your way into my party. Is that it? Who do you think you are? I am Tarbin's Princess Talia Winterlaus, heading out on a vital quest. And you're playing games?"

"I have no choice, Princess. My word is all I have. If I break it every time royalty asks me to, I would have nothing." The young nobleman held up his hands in surrender. Talia's anger seemed to only amuse him.

"Fine." Talia started toward the door. Her guardians exchanged looks as Nyna stuffed the large volume into her bag. "Let's go."

"Does that mean I'm in?" asked Gregor, balancing on the balls of his feet.

"No, it means we will travel together to Master Overstone, who had better answer questions about the Holy Diamond." The princess threatened Gregor. "Then you can stay and visit with your old friend while the rest of us continue our quest."

"Great! Let me pack a few items and—"

"We're out of time. If you're coming with me, you're leaving now. We're heading to the stables and leaving before the moon rises."

Talia waited for Gregor to argue. She had to make sure he didn't have an opportunity to relay their whereabouts to Tanin. Talia was surprised at her paranoia. This quest was her one opportunity to determine her own destiny. She wouldn't let the smile and easy charm of a boy sway her.

"All right. Let's go." Gregor exited in front of Talia, heading toward the stables.

Talia paused with the door in her hand. Closing this door would shut out her childhood. She was progressing into adulthood at an alarming pace. Talia sincerely hoped she was up for the challenge.

CHAPTER ELEVEN

TANIN STORMED into High Priestess Nomyra's chambers, unable to contain his anger at the surprises of the evening. Nomyra sat calmly, wrapped in a thin robe with one leg flung over the arm of the lavishly upholstered chair. Her control infuriated the prince.

"What happened tonight?" Tanin demanded. "You told me everything was under control. What game are you playing?"

With his hand on the hilt of his ceremonial blade, Tanin glared down at the unperturbed high priestess. On high alert, Rory and Orui, his husbandry guardian, flanked the prince. Tanin watched the woman languidly rise and walk over to a sideboard to pour two drinks. She stepped up to Tanin, offering him one of the glasses as she sipped from the other. He took his hand off the hilt and accepted it.

Feeling petulant, Tanin downed the spirit in one swallow and then threw the glass against the far wall.

Nomyra didn't flinch.

Tanin grew angrier at her lack of reaction. He was the prince. She should fear him.

He grabbed Nomyra's shoulders to shake some sense into her. The high priestess stiffened, her piercing blue eyes boring into Tanin.

He released her and backed up a step. For a moment, Tanin had forgotten the raw power wrapped up in the slender female form. The high priestess took another sip of her drink and sat down.

"Talia's odds of success are so insignificant, her interruption of the ceremony only added to the drama for the audience. She can offer no competition for you in your quest." Nomyra watched her protégé. "The little princess is playing a game without knowing the rules. You will follow the map I gave you, along with the specific instructions for your interaction with each people you encounter. Tyler is well-versed in proper etiquette and multiple languages. You will return triumphant with the proper Holy Gemstones to be mounted on the proper crown with the proper heir ready to don it."

Tanin's breathing slowed as Nomyra spoke. Of course, everything would be fine. Until tonight, Talia couldn't have known the jewels were fake. How could she possibly know where to search for the real ones? He'd be halfway around the world before Talia finished looking under her bed. Reassured of his inevitable success, Tanin crossed to the sideboard to pour another drink.

"To a successful journey," toasted Tanin.

Nomyra rose from her chair, her robe accentuating her curvy figure, and raised her glass. "To the return of the True Heir."

Both parties emptied their glasses.

"I must make an appearance at the feast." Tanin exited with his guardians close behind.

The high priestess's research had better be accurate. If Tanin ran into more surprises like his sister's inclusion in the quest, the prince would make sure Nomyra remembered who really ruled Tarbin. Maybe it was time to appoint a male high priest. Tanin had grown tired of a woman being privy to more knowledge than he. That would be his first act when he took the crown: no more priestesses in Tarbin.

"Come, men," Tanin addressed his guardians outside Nomyra's chambers, as he led them down the hall toward the feast. "Let's find us some busty women to wish us a fond farewell before duty calls us away."

CHAPTER TWELVE

A‌fter a week of travel, Talia's hind end molded to Ruix, her chestnut horse, even if she had trouble walking when she dismounted. Her muscles ached but the end of this part of the journey was within view literally. From her vantage point on a hill, Talia gazed down at the gates of the largest city they'd seen since leaving Tarbinulus.

"Babla Village. The center of trade between the dwarves and the Tarbinians." Gregor dismounted his gray steed and flexed his shoulders.

The mixed dwarf and human town snuggled against the bottom of a tall hill. The location provided the town with easy access to the coveted clay that made the region famous. The mound appeared no more than a hillock compared to the Eckerd Mountain range behind it. The home of the dwarves and the Defense School stood starkly gray against the striated greens, reds, and oranges of the lower hills.

"Babla Village? I think it's outgrown that name." Naul nudged Nyna sitting beside him in the wagon. "It's time to call it Babla Metropolis."

Talia estimated the size of the town as half the size of Tarbinulus. Considering the capital was the largest city in the kingdom, Talia agreed with Naul. It might be time to rename Babla. An entire forest of trees must have been cut to build the spiked fence surrounding the town. The population spilled outside the gates into stables and inns and smaller trading markets. Most of the buildings along the west up to the gate were constructed using what looked like the same logs. Stucco dyed to match the clay hillside covered the timber of the fancier residents. A few buildings on the east side were stone constructions.

"Babla was founded by human clay artists centuries ago,' Gregor continued his description. "As their artistry grew popular and people from all over the world wanted to own a piece, roads were built to make isolated Babla more accessible."

Clay, mined from the hill, acted as the base for the most beautiful beads and pottery renowned throughout the continent and highly sought after. Talia fingered her beaded bracelet, remembering how proud her mother had looked when she gave her daughter the colorful jewelry on her tenth birthday.

"Once the roads were built, Babla became a bustling trade center," Dew added.

"You're from this area, aren't you, Dew?" Talia remembered.

"West of here. A tiny hamlet called Mahanagara. A former bustling city that turned into a ghost town when the roads to Babla were completed. It happened generations ago, but Mahanagara is still bitter. The current residents' grandparents weren't alive when the city faded from prominence. Yet everything that's wrong with their lives is because of Babla's existence." Dew looked off to the west.

"Shall we?" Ial started down the hill, leading his solid black horse. "After days of camping, I'm ready for a forgiving mattress and a soft pillow."

"And some fresh ingredients. I'm out of ideas for sprucing up corn meal," Nyna added.

Talia nodded her agreement. Though experienced travelers, the royal party usually had days to plan and pack for their journey with other castle servants helping load the cart. Ial and Naul had packed extra provisions for the longer trip while Dew and Nyna had worked on translating the library book. In their rush, the men had forgotten to include flour and potatoes.

"Where to, Gregor?" asked Talia as the rest of her guardians dismounted and stretched their legs to walk the last two hundred yards to the outskirts. The princess still doubted the lordling's motives, but she needed him. For now.

"The dwarf side of town." Gregor lead the way.

"I'm guessing that's the predominately stone buildings?" Naul rubbed his head. "Not up to their normal standards, are they?"

"No. The dwarves who settled here were metalworkers, not stonemasons. When these dwarves wanted something more permanent to commence the trading of their skills in Babla, there were some disputes over who was allowed to build and who wasn't. The war between humans and dwarves was still fresh in everyone's mind. Distrust ruled any decisions. But the dwarves wanted access to the traders and the humans wanted access to the superior dwarven metalwork. In the end, they reached a compromise. The humans gave the dwarves a section on the east side of town to do with as they wished. The dwarves provided all the weapons necessary to defend the town from invasion but were forbidden from carrying arms themselves."

"Hard to believe a dwarf would ever agree to a demand from a human?" Naul pulled back on the pack mules, keeping the cart's speed controlled as the group descended the grassy hill on the well-worn road.

"Well, the dwarves who wanted to live in Babla didn't support the war between the two factions during the Dwarven Civil War. Both the Eckerd and the Krimmel tried to persuade the skilled weapons masters to supply their army. Refusing to choose a side, they were banished from both kingdoms and sent to wander the mountains. When the skilled dwarves grew tired of eternal roaming, they were eager to accept any deal that offered the possibility of stability."

"How do you know so much about the history of Babla, Gregor?" asked Dew. "Kenia is far to the north."

"My father has had me exchange our wheat in Babla each season. I think this is where my love of architecture developed. That's why I took so many stonemason classes at the Defense School."

Naul and Gregor lifted their right fists over their heads and chanted the school motto in deep-throated Dwarven:

"Shape it boldly,

Wield it wisely,

Stone and Metal will not fail."

"But bone and muscle will," Dew answered in Common. She pointed to a sign with a painted mug and cot. "Can we stop at that inn outside the gate to rest our tortured feet and bottoms?"

"The horses could use a thorough grooming and a quiet night." Ial patted his mare on her forehead. She nudged him with her muzzle, searching for a treat hidden in his jacket.

Talia tried not to growl out loud. She was frustrated with the slow progress of their party thus far. They had yet to spot her brother or his guardians on their journey. She hoped they had chosen well and were heading toward the proper destination. While Tanin had the benefit of High Priestess Nomyra's tutelage, Talia was making it up as she went along. She glanced sideways at Gregor. If he had been sent to throw her off track, she would end his noble blood before another generation.

She took a deep breath and refocused on the task at hand. Her companions were right. She was exhausted too. Maybe a night's sleep in a real bed would do them all some good. Who knew how often that would happen as they completed the world's largest scavenger hunt?

"Nyna and Ial can secure us rooms and facilities for the animals. Naul and Dew, you're with me and Gregor. I want to see if we can track down Master Overstone." Talia flashed her eyes at Gregor, trying to communicate that if the dwarf was nowhere to be found, he'd regret it.

The companions heading to the inn took the animals from the four heading to the dwarf side of town. Dew grabbed the book from Nyna's bag before relinquishing her mount.

GREGOR FOLLOWED a branch off the main road, heading around the wooden fence to the east side of Babla.

"We're not going inside the gates?" asked Talia.

"Master Overstone has spent his entire life underground. He's not about to start breathing clean air and basking in the sun's glow now," Gregor half-joked. "I'm sure he's locked himself in a stuffy chamber surrounded by dusty books."

Talia glowered at him. "So, what you're saying is you have no idea where he lives."

A group of giggling dwarven children ran around the companions. Talia noted that the sound was so similar to the urchin children running around Tarbinulus, always in a hurry to go nowhere. The stone houses she passed had doors no more than four feet tall, with wood-framed windows two feet above the ground. A few houses were grander with a second story. The roofs were timber and straw. A merchant flag hung above the average-sized door of another building. That particular structure had tall ceilings to accommodate customers of all sizes.

The companions followed a busy street to an intersection that opened up into a town common. Sheep with different-colored wool tied around their necks feasted in part of the grassy field. On the other side, a well-used stage, decorated with a set of fake stones and trees, slanted up away from the audience.

To the right of the stage, sliced logs, thick enough for dwarf children to sit on, were arranged in three concentric circles around a small platform with another larger log. Every seat was taken by an engaged young one, mostly dwarven, but there were some humans as well. They were all focused on an elderly dwarf standing on the central platform.

Naul smirked and nudged Gregor. "Or Master Overstone could be entertaining children in the middle of the town square."

"He *hates...* " Gregor's jaw dropped.

Master Overstone looked centuries older than Talia remembered. His face had so many wrinkles, the excess skin could create a new one. Colored like marble—mostly white with streaks of black and gray throughout—his hair reached his shoulders. His simple tunic and worn trousers bespoke of poverty, though Talia knew the master professors at the Defense School made a good living. She wondered how much the master had been able to take with him when he fled the accusations.

The old dwarf reached the climax of his tale. He jumped off the platform with his calloused hands above his head, shaped like claws. He roared like a vicious beast. The children straightened their backs in shock. Some shrieked in fear and delight. He pulled a wooden dagger from his belt and pounced back onto the platform like he was tackling a monster. He rose slowly, a pretend animal trophy held high in one hand, the wooden dagger in the other. The children clapped and cheered.

"You got 'em, Old Stoney!"

"I knew you could do it."

"Old Stoney is the best hunter ever!"

Gregor waded through the children with the rest of the party behind him. The dwarf spotted his former protégé.

"Old Stoney?" queried Gregor, one eyebrow raised.

"The children named me." Overstone's face cracked into a huge smile that accentuated the wrinkles but brightened his gray eyes. The old bard turned his attention to his audience. "That will be the last story for today, you rowdy cubs. Go home and do your chores so your mothers allow you to return tomorrow."

His announcement was greeted by groans, but no arguments.

The children left the area in groups, some in a bigger hurry than others.

Gregor, Talia, and Naul placed their right fists over their hearts and bowed to Master Overstone. The dwarf's face turned serious as he returned the gesture.

Gregor made the introductions. "You know, Princess Talia and her defense guardians, Naul. This is Dew, graduate of the Cultural School."

Dew bowed with her fist over her heart, imitating her princess. The old dwarf repeated the greeting.

"From feared master stonemason to children entertainer? I thought you hated children." Gregor threw aside formality to hug his mentor.

Overstone returned the hug on tiptoe as the human bent in half. "The children expect nothing more than a good tale. Their parents, on the other hand... " Overstone sighed. "I'm too old for politics. Never had the heart for it anyway." The old dwarf led the group down smaller streets toward the clay mountain.

"What story were you telling, Master?" asked Talia.

"Call me Old Stoney, Princess. This is who I am now," Overstone claimed, though Talia thought she heard regret in his tone. "I was telling the tale of The Lions Three."

Talia understood why she didn't recognize the story. "The Lions Three ends with the third lion eating the hunter. I've not seen an ending with the hunter triumphant."

A sneaky smile broke Old Stoney's melancholy. "Ah, but the hunter in my story is a dwarf warrior. And a dwarf warrior would never lose to a mangy lion."

Gregor laughed. "Always spinning a tale. Though I'm not sure I remember you so animated while sober."

"The worst part about living with these dwarves is no liquor. They don't believe in consuming spirits of any kind." Old Stoney shook his head, lamenting. "It's like they've forgotten what it means to be a dwarf. Luckily, the humans inside the fence don't share the same detestation."

Old Stoney stopped at a wooden door set into the clay mountain. He knocked on three specific spots on the solid wood. Each knock popped open a hole, wherein Old Stoney placed a wooden peg to hold it ajar. He pulled the latch, revealing a small stone chamber, large enough for ten average-sized people to fit.

He ushered the humans in, closing the door behind the group. Old Stoney carefully pulled out each peg with a click. The sealed door left the group in complete darkness. Talia fought claustrophobia. A chill ran down her spine as the temperature dropped. She jumped as the old dwarf brushed by her to the stone wall opposite the wooden door. A metallic tapping on one of the stone walls, followed by a loud scratching noise, pierced the quiet. Talia felt Dew and Naul on either side of her.

A bright light filled the chamber, blinding the group. Talia covered her eyes with her left arm while reaching for her sword with her right. She thought she heard Naul draw his weapon.

"Calm down," Old Stoney reassured. "Never seen young people so anxious about an old dwarf opening a door."

Talia blinked her eyes to see him standing in a cluttered chamber of awkwardly stacked books and a few worn-through upholstered chairs. Torches were lit on the wall, as was a large fireplace. Gregor nudged Talia and raised his eyebrows in an I-told-you-so expression.

"I hope you're not here to ask me to return to the school." Old Stoney's mood changed to the grouchy old dwarf Talia associated with his reputation. "I will never go back and nothing you say would convince me to change my mind."

Talia could hear the longing in his response. Despite his protests, Talia believed the old dwarf would jump at the chance to return to his home.

Dew seemed anxious to get to the point. "No, sir. We have some questions about your theories regarding the Holy Diamond."

"Always looking for answers, are we? I would be careful what questions you ask, young lady. Some questions are threatening to people of power. They'll take everything away from you to keep you from asking them. Even your identity." Old Stoney sat heavily in an armchair by the fire.

Gregor sat in a chair across from his mentor and leaned forward pleadingly. "We believe you."

"All of it?" Old Stoney leaned forward as well.

"Yes."

Talia sat beside Gregor. "I've been sent on a mission to recover the original gems from the Tarbin royal crown. We know the ones on it are fake."

Dew pointed to the burgundy book she carried. "Our research suggests the Holy Diamond was sent to the dwarves for safekeeping."

"Yes, it was." Old Stoney grew excited despite his attempts at staying aloof.

He plundered the stack of books by his chair and retrieved a black unnamed tome with a cracked binding. He offered the book to Dew, who promptly sat on the floor cross-legged. She perused the volume while the old dwarf continued.

"According to this post-Civil War account, the Eckerd dwarves possessed the Holy Diamond. It was kept on the king's scepter brought out for special ceremonies and celebrations. One of the concessions of the Peace Treaty ceded the Holy Diamond to the Krimmel dwarves."

"So the Krimmel dwarves have it now." Dew repeated. Her finger followed a passage in the history book.

"Maybe that's why we haven't seen Tanin. He might have headed directly to the Krimmel Mountain range," Talia speculated, standing up to pace. She glanced at Gregor to see if his expression gave anything away. Nothing.

"No one's seen the Krimmel for well over a century. How are we supposed to find them?" asked Gregor.

"And if we find them, will we be able to convince them of the importance of our quest? Why would isolated dwarves care about the succession of rulers in Tarbin?" Talia felt her chances dwindling.

"I know why the dwarves were given the Holy Diamond." The sparkle in Old Stoney's eyes bespoke his excitement at having an audience for his research. "The astropriests spread the Holy Gemstones among the intelligent races to guard them until the next Recharging."

Dew looked up from the book. "The next what?"

"Recharging," the dwarf repeated, leaning toward his audience. "I have no idea what it is. But it has something to do with an alignment of celestial bodies. The Holy Gemstones must be united with the crown within the next two years."

"What happens if I fail?" asked Talia, afraid of the answer.

"I don't know." Old Stoney sat back in his chair, tapping his hand on the arm. "I was looking for more details when the Eckerd Council shut me down. Out here in the middle of nowhere, I have no access to the research materials beyond what I smuggled out with me." He absently kicked at the pile of books.

"We'll figure out how to make contact with the Krimmel and worry about everything else later," Talia decided. She turned to Old Stoney, who was staring into the fire. "Do you know how to get to their kingdom? I heard they sealed themselves in. Is there an entrance anywhere?"

"Of course there is, Princess." Old Stoney gestured toward Dew on the floor. "There's a map in the back of the book your guardian holds."

Dew flipped to the back. "By the Light, I'm not sure we'll be able to get there."

Talia took the book from her to get a closer look. The ink was a bit faded but still easily discernible. The mountains in the west had a dotted line enclosing the Krimmel kingdom. Three entrances were marked on the east side of the outline. Gregor and Naul looked over Talia's shoulder.

"It's bigger than I pictured, but we should be able to get there easily enough," Naul commented. "It looks like this path hits the middle entrance. The terrain appears to be a steady incline from where we are."

"I agree." Gregor traced a path with his finger on the map. "We can cross the Overpass River at the bridge and head south until we hit whatever this mountain is called and then head west."

"That's Randoian Mountain. The weather there is unpredictable, especially with the recent spring melt. Who knows what challenges it will offer?" Dew outlined a route to the northern entrance. "This one might be a bit steeper, but it should be clear."

"Randoian has behaved himself the past three springs. By the time you get there from here, the warmer summer sun will have dried any remaining mud slicks." Old Stoney traced the middle path. "This is the best choice."

"You should come with us," Talia offered, seeing sadness engulf Old Stoney.

The dwarf stood, hips popping, and ushered his guests into the entryway of his home. "My old legs wouldn't carry me halfway. I'm afraid to say my adventuring days are over. Plus," he winked at Lordling Gregor, "it is not my destiny to fulfill."

Old Stoney pulled a lever that slid a stone into place behind them, plunging them into darkness once more. Talia heard tapping on the wooden door leading to the outside. She was amazed the dwarf could perform the complex maneuvers in the dark. As the sunlight blinded her, Talia held up the book to give it back to the dwarf.

"Keep it." Old Stoney held up his hand, refusing to accept it. "It's doing little good piled in my hermit cave."

He smiled as he shook the hand of each adventurer. "Good luck."

The wooden door closed, leaving the four companions outside looking at each other.

Naul rubbed his rumbling stomach. "Food and rest?"

"Yes." Talia lead the group back to the inn at the gate. She needed to fill in the rest of the party on what they'd learned.

Talia wondered how much High Priestess Nomyra knew about

this Recharging. Maybe that's why she had chosen this particular quest.

One thing at a time. Talia still didn't know where the rest of the Holy Gemstones were, only which race was rumored to guard them. Since some of the creatures were mythical, Talia was at a loss on where to start. The princess put it out of her mind. She knew what they had to do tomorrow. For now, that would have to suffice.

CHAPTER THIRTEEN

AFTER A MONTH of travel by land then sea, Tanin felt relief as the ship approached its first official stop. The crew in front of him tied up the main sail, using the foresail to control the vessel's approach. Tanin was shocked by the meager port. Never having journeyed to Kiwa, Tanin only had its reputation to go on. With its predominately ocean-going community, Tanin expected a large port with many slots for trading vessels. Instead, no human structures beyond the modest wooden dock marred the pristine beauty of the cold water island.

"My Prince, the temperature has dropped." Rory offered a wool cloak identical to the one he already wore. Rory's dark complexion glimmered in the low sun as he draped the cloak around Tanin's shoulders. Tanin thought his companion could have been very successful at the Cultural School learning the martial arts. Rory's lithe form melded with his weapons as he danced with his opponent. That's probably why Rory preferred two swords. It made his arms equal length.

"Thank you, Rory." Tanin gripped the cloak tightly around him as the salty air bit into his flesh. The cold seemed to have come from nowhere. Tanin's thoughts had remained focused on his mission, his body disconnected. Now he felt the wind chafe his cheeks. His hands tingled. Ahead, the fog lifted, revealing snow-topped mountain peaks.

"We will drop anchor in a few minutes, Your Highness." Captain Leslie Sonacevontes reminded Tanin of a homeless man from the streets of Tarbinulus with his scraggly beard, sun-wrinkled skin, and unwashed clothing. His unruly appearance tended to put off most trading partners, which was why the experienced captain employed a young, handsome first mate to do the talking for him. If he had not been reputed to be the best captain in the shipping fleet, Tanin would never have chosen Sonacevontes to lead the ocean-going section of his mission.

"I will prepare the men." Rory bowed his head to his prince as he headed below decks to rouse the rest of the party.

"Do you need my first mate to come ashore?" asked Captain Sonacevontes after a nudge from his second-in-command.

"It would be my pleasure," Martin Maritoss offered. "We have traded extensively with Kiwa, bringing back exotic seafood, much-sought-after furs, precious pearls. The deals I receive are incomparable to any other crew in the Southern Sea. I would gladly introduce you to my contacts for a modest convenience fee."

Tanin watched the ship approach the shore, resisting the urge to toss the first mate into the freezing waters. Maritoss couldn't have been more than a couple years older than Tanin, but he presented himself as a superior with vast pools of knowledge inaccessible to the prince. The officer's soft white skin and unblemished hands showed his hatred of physical labor, choosing to use his good looks and fast tongue instead. Tanin had taken an instant dislike to the man as soon as he boarded the ship. Fourteen days at sea watching Maritoss shirk all responsibility had done nothing to change Tanin's mind.

"My men and I have it under control," Tanin replied succinctly.

The last thing he wanted was the nosy Maritoss discovering hints of the true mission. Tanin suspected the opportunist would ingratiate himself into the quest to run off with the gems to sell to the top bidder. With that thought, Tanin checked the pouch string on his neck. He felt the large diamond against his chest. The dwarf representative had delivered it to the prince as promised. Hopefully, the rest of the expedition would run as smoothly.

"Wait for us here ready to go at a moment's notice."

The captain and first mate nodded in acknowledgement. The captain yelled at his crew to drop the longboats. Rory reappeared beside the prince. The guardian buckled on Tanin's sword belt for him. Then he handed the prince his weapon. Tanin accepted his sword, adjusting his belt until the weight balanced.

"Good luck, Your Highness." Maritoss bowed.

The captain offered a slight nod and then distractedly went about ordering his crew. Tanin felt Maritoss studying him.

"I don't trust him," Rory grumbled, looking at the first mate over his shoulder.

"Neither do I." Tanin agreed.

After Kettlor and Orui climbed down to the first longboat, Tanin swung his leg over the railing and descended the rope ladder onto the second one.

"I can't believe Kiwa's dock is too small for the ship. The rumors of this vast trading city have been greatly exaggerated." Orui complained in his deep northern accent.

After eight years of service to his prince, Orui should have shed himself of his traditional speak, but it stubbornly stuck around, as did his bright red hair and dull green eyes. The days at sea had multiplied Orui's freckles, adding one for each mischievous trick he had played on the crew during their voyage. Sometimes, Tanin wished Orui would use his Medicinal School training to treat the ill more than make healthy people sick. Though his skill with herbs would come in handy when Tanin was king and needed Orui to quietly take care of an enemy for him.

Tanin steadied the ladder for Rory. The chief translator on this trip, Tyler was the last companion down. Tyler excelled in languages at the Cultural School and was anxious to try speaking the Kiwa tongue with natives. He had stuck to his bunk most of the voyage, brushing up on verb conjugations and proper pronouns. No wonder he looked paler than the other companions.

Tyler sat down and carefully tucked his satchel with his Kiwa dictionary under his seat to grab an oar. The small, frail-appearing linguist was eager to help. Tanin had learned it was best to leave Tyler to his books. The cultural guardian exhausted quickly from any physical exertion, which was almost as frustrating as his inane clumsiness.

"I'll take the oar. I don't feel like going for a swim today." Tanin insisted.

"Of course, my Prince. Whatever you require." Tyler looked slightly disappointed but obliged Tanin's request, moving to the bow of the boat.

"Are we ready?" Tanin surveyed the longboats, fully packed with trading goods. His men held up their oars.

"I wish we could travel by Manta." Kettlor used his oar to push his longboat from the ship. He tossed his head to get his curls out of his eyes. The husbandry guardian tightened the straps of his cloak before joining the paddling.

"We'd probably freeze to death." Rory's head followed a piece of ice the size of the longboat that floated by.

"There is that," Kettlor admitted.

The longboats made their way to the floating dock. Tanin watched the snow-peaked mountains approach, lost in the rhythm of the strokes. The deep green covering every surface of the mountain range surprised him. Kiwa was covered in snow most of the year, with the ground showing itself for a couple months in the late spring and summer. Tanin expected a frozen wasteland, full of abused gravel and craggy cliffs. The dense bushes highlighted with gorgeous red and purple flowers looked more like a jungle paradise. If not for the chill biting through his cloak as the arctic air blew around the long-boats, he'd think he was about to embark on a tropical adventure.

When the docks were only a few strokes away, native Kiwas poured onto the beach from the dense forested landscape. The natives wore thin leather shirts with matching short pants. Tanin wondered how they avoided frostbite as he observed their shoeless feet. Of course, the weather was summer for them and the Kiwas were enjoying the warmth.

The natives balanced on the floating dock, guiding the longboat into a slip. The companions tossed ropes to the natives to secure the vessel.

Tanin held a bag of trade goods. He inspected the Kiwas who stood in rows looking at the prince without offering greeting or assistance. Tanin rolled his eyes at their silence. And so began the first test of the many ridiculous traditions he would have to follow on his quest.

A visitor could tell one position from another based on the insignia each member of the tribe wore on their sleeve. The king possessed a complicated patch of many smaller people sewn into the figure of one larger Kiwa. Tanin searched for that patch. He spotted it on an unassuming middle-aged man in the second row of the staring Kiwas.

"King," Tanin addressed the stocky man, looking directly into his weathered eyes surrounded by skin already tanned like the hide of his clothing. "I offer your tribe fresh oranges and a cast-iron pot."

Tanin did not break his stare while Tyler translated in the Kiwa tongue. Tanin judged the king's reaction, hoping Tyler's translation was flawless.

"What do you ask in return?" the king's lips barely moved. He maintained Tanin's eye while Tyler translated.

"Only your friendship," the prince replied.

Tyler almost repeated the sentence at the same time. The cultural guardian had studied the ritual more precisely than Tanin had. The only reason Tanin had to make sure he said the right words in Common was just in case someone understood what he was saying without Tyler's filtering.

The king stepped in front of the gathered Kiwas. He raised both his hands, palms up. The crowd nodded as one in what Tanin assumed was acquiescence. Two Kiwas, both wearing the cook patch of a metal pot hung over a fire, accepted Tanin's gifts and left the beach. They chatted together excitedly. Tanin thought they probably hadn't seen an orange in months and were excited about dinner that evening.

Such a simple life, to be thrilled by fruit. Tanin pitied them.

"How can I make your stay a pleasant experience?" asked the king through Tyler. The rest of the guardians stood around their prince, eyes darting around the beach.

"I wish for a viewing of the Great Spirit Clam," Tanin proclaimed, trying not to sneer. Nomyra claimed the Black Opal lay hidden inside the giant clam.

As Tyler finished the request, Tanin watched shock wash across the king's face before the older man hid the emotion under a stern expression. "No outsider may approach the Great Spirit Clam. Most do not know of its existence. How did you come by such knowledge?"

"I have been instructed by the High Priestess Nomyra of the astropriests to commune with the Great Spirit Clam to seek its guidance on my quest to assure ascension to the throne." Tanin left out the part about having to tear the clam open to get its hidden treasure.

The Kiwa observers remaining on the beach murmured. Tanin hoped they weren't preparing to send the group away. He didn't want to use force on the primitive tribe, but nothing would stop him from getting what he came for.

The king watched Tanin and his companions for a full minute. Tanin fought the urge to start shivering as the cold sank in. The king turned, heading to a path through the trees. Tanin looked questioningly at Tyler.

"Did I miss something?"

"I don't think so, my Prince." Tyler fingered the book in his bag.

He spoke a few questioning words to the lingering crowd on the beach. A young woman answered as she motioned for the foreigners to follow the path.

Tyler translated. "It seems we are to follow the king to the village, where he must discuss your request with the village elders."

"It would've been nice if he'd told us," Orui complained, rubbing his hands together and blowing on them.

"Orui and Kettlor, stay and guard the longboats. Make sure they are prepared for a hasty departure in case the negotiations don't go as planned," Tanin ordered.

The medicinal guardian groaned but neither offered further complaint.

Tanin motioned to Rory and Tyler as he followed the king's path into the woods. Entering the relative protection of the forest broke the cold wind, raising the ambient temperature.

The troop followed the path lined with gravel identical to the white stones on the beach. Tanin wondered if the stones lay beneath the underbrush naturally or were placed there by the Kiwas. The path led the group through the evergreen forest, dumping them into a clearing.

"Is it me, or is the village laid out like one half of a clam shell?" asked Tanin.

The scalloped treelike was trimmed in an almost semi-circle around the village. Where a clam shell would have multiple ridges running from the scalloped end to the joined piece, the Kiwa village had rows of leather-covered structures stretched over wooden frames. The lines of huts ended in a flat rectangular area similar to the valve part of a clam. This section hosted one large building with its canvas flap wide open at the end of the path.

"It's exactly like in the book." Tyler held up the Kiwa dictionary. A sketch of the village in the shape of a clam shell mirrored what the companions observed. "It says the large hut at the intersection is the center of the village where the elders meet, meals are cooked and served, special ceremonies are performed."

"So, are we supposed to enter the building or wait for an invite?" Tanin already grew tired of the formal rules and it was only the beginning of his quest.

"Everyone allowed on the island is welcome inside the lodge of any village. But don't go into any of the family huts. It's the only bit of individuality allowed within the Kiwa culture," Tyler cautioned. He retrieved a pencil from his satchel and started taking notes in the margins of his book.

Rory walked through the open flap of the large tent with one hand on a sword hilt. Apparently the interior was innocuous, because Rory nodded for Tanin to enter.

Tanin ducked as he entered the warmth of the lodge. He was surprised by the temperature conditions inside, resisting the urge to take off his cloak to soak in the glowing warmth more thoroughly. In a far corner of the one-room structure, a group of older men huddled together, arguing. Tanin motioned Tyler to head in that direction so he could eavesdrop on the conversation. The cultural guardian continued to sketch the lodge in his book as he slowly made his way to the corner.

Two children greeted Tanin, offering small wooden bowls full of a steaming thick soup or stew. Tanin noted both wore the child patch with a cook symbol inside. Tanin accepted a bowl.

Tanin and Rory took the seats open to them on the floor around a lively fire. Without any utensils, Tanin tipped the bowl cautiously into his mouth. The mystery meat was a bit chewy and full of briny flavor. As Tanin started on his second bowl, Tyler returned. He took the space left empty for him beside the prince.

Tyler loudly sipped the steaming soup handed to him. The children servers giggled at his noisy eating. "This is very tasty. What's in it? We need to take this recipe to Orui. It will be a hit at the prince's coronation."

"Which will never happen if you don't get to the point." Tanin growled, annoyed with Tyler's lack of focus. "Is the debate leaning in our favor?"

"Oh, no," Tyler responded, chastised into cooperating. "The king doesn't trust us. The elders are divided. Some think good favor with the astropriests will add luck to their hunt. Others fear risking the ire of the Great Spirit Clam so close to some kind of conjunction."

Tyler took another long drink of soup, dribbling some of the broth on his cloak. The children laughed again, one offering a cloth to clean the mess.

"Oh, and they talked about a prophecy." Tyler remembered, as he spilled soup on his knee while wiping his chest. "One of the elders, the really elder elder in the back, the one sitting against the corner piling, mentioned our arrival as a fulfillment of the prophecy. Whatever that means."

Tanin observed the continuing argument of the tribe's council. Some of the elders glared at the rest. The elder Tyler referred to sat with legs crossed, staying out of the heated argument. The old man stared fixedly at Tanin as if anticipating his next move.

"What are the odds of us finding the giant clam without their help?"

"We'd have to search the whole island and the surrounding sea." Tyler's eyes looked up, his mouth scrunched. His fingers moved, though they were holding a bowl of soup and a cloth.

Tanin blinked at his guardian. Was he actually trying to calculate the odds?

"So, impossible." Rory took the soup bowl from Tyler before the rest of the contents ended up on his tunic.

Tanin took the second bag of trade goods. He marched to the corner as his guardians jumped up to stay with their prince.

"I am prepared to prove my worth to be in the presence of the Great Spirit Clam," Tanin said in his most authoritative voice. He reached into the bag and pulled out an exquisite knife. The eight-inch blade was sharply curved on one side with a jagged end on the opposite. He set the tool on the ground in front of the Kiwa king. "I gift a perfect hunting knife made of the strongest metal my people have mastered."

Metal objects were coveted by the islanders, where no mining or metalwork of any kind was practiced. Tanin dumped the rest of the contents before the stunned men. "I present eight metal spearheads strong enough to pierce the hide of any sea creature. We wish only to worship before the Great Spirit Clam to gain its blessing for my quest."

"The Great Spirit Clam does not crown you as worthy simply because you claim to be." The elder Tyler had described spoke in perfect Common. "You must successfully return from a poulpe hunt with the eye of the slain as evidence of your worthiness."

Some of the council protested vehemently. The seated elder silenced the dissent with one authoritative sentence in Kiwa. The group grew silent. Each elder bowed his head once and then turned to the king.

Tyler skidded to a halt beside his prince, ready to translate.

"If you wish to appear before the Great Spirit Clam, you will accompany my men on a *poulpe* hunt." Tyler struggled over the foreign word.

"If you refuse, you will never view what you seek. Cowards may not sully the Great Spirit Clam with their fear." The king drew a deep breath. "Failure may not sully the Great Spirit Clam either. We must succeed in slaughtering the beast, or the Great Spirit Clam will refuse to welcome us."

"Can we leave immediately?" Tanin was tired of waiting. He was ready for some action.

"Hunting the poulpe in the dark is suicide. We leave at sunrise."

Tanin had missed the sunset. With the Light's Daughter so low on the horizon, it must pass below the sea quickly this far south.

"I suggest you make peace with the Stars this night. You might be joining them tomorrow."

A Kiwa woman guided Tanin and his companions to their tent. As he followed Rory under the flap, Tanin slammed into his guardian's arm.

"There's someone in here." The defense guardian's deep voice contrasted with the scratching of his sword against its scabbard.

"It's just us, Mr. Paranoid." Orui's brogue accent greeted his companions. "Some villagers practically carried us and dumped us in here."

"Short of slaughtering them, I don't know how we could have resisted." Kettlor supported Orui's story.

Rory stood by the door. "Looks like we get to slaughter something tomorrow in some sort of formal hunt."

"A hunt?" asked Kettlor, his voice rising in excitement. The husbandry guardian came from a long line of avid hunters.

"We have to participate to win a viewing of the giant clam." Tanin chose a spot for himself.

"Do we know what we're hunting?" There can't be much large game on this small island." Kettlor's eyes shone with more enthusiasm than he had showed for the whole expedition.

"It's called a poulpe." Tyler found a pile of furs to curl up in. "I haven't seen that word mentioned anywhere in my research."

"We should try to get some sleep before daybreak." Prince Tanin faced the tent wall, ending all conversation. He didn't care what they had to kill as long as they could do it quickly and move on. He wanted a real bed on solid ground.

His guardians settled down around him, except for Rory, who would stand first watch at the door.

"Tyler," Tanin whispered, unable to quiet his mind. His body rocked slightly as if still on board the ship. "What did the old man in the corner say to quiet the others?"

"Oh, something about outsiders fulfilling the prophecy to rebalance the world and awaken the ancients." Tyler yawned.

"Prophecy?"

"I don't remember seeing a prophecy connected to the Giant Spirit Clam in my studies, but those books are a couple centuries old. Maybe it's a new prophecy." Tyler's voice faded into a mumble as fatigue claimed his consciousness.

Or maybe the books aren't old enough, thought Tanin. Nomyra spoke of a thousand-year cycle. Maybe the prophecy was connected to that event. Good. Then he was on the right track. He would have to thank Nomyra when he returned home and claimed his crown.

Maybe he wouldn't have her killed when he replaced all the priestesses with priests in Tarbinulus. Tanin fell asleep with the image of the high priestess stretched across his royal bed, beckoning.

CHAPTER FOURTEEN

When the king said sunrise, Tanin had forgotten the southern sun hid beyond the horizon for only a few hours this time of year. His eyes had barely closed when the king's hunters woke Tanin and his companions.

Now, Tanin still struggled to shake the groggy feeling as he sat in a canoe on the quiet water. The touch of sleep made him more tired than if he had waited a few hours to set out. His breath formed a mist around his head in the cold early morning air. He rubbed his hands together, trying to keep them agile for the battle with the unknown beast. The two canoes held five warriors each: Tanin's men in one boat, the king's men in the second.

"How exactly are we supposed to use this?" asked Orui. He held up a serrated blade the length of a broadsword with a large hook on the end. Two such weapons were attached to each boat.

"That is the hook blade." The king, with Tyler translating, motioned for one of his hunters to demonstrate. "You hook a tentacle with the end and drag it on board. The second hook blade is used to secure the pouple's jaw away from the hunters. Then you saw back and forth with the blade to remove the tentacle from the beast."

"Sounds simple," Tanin said, thinking that wasn't simple at all.

Kettlor searched the water's surface. "At least we know whatever we're hunting has tentacles. That narrows it down a bit."

The king and his men placed their oars under the seats of the canoe. Tanin and his men mirrored their actions. The Kiwas bent their heads, closed their eyes, and started a deep-throated chant. Tanin looked to Tyler. The linguist shrugged his shoulders.

The waves picked up as a breeze blew back Tanin's hood. After a couple weeks aboard ship, he'd thought he'd found his sea legs. The rolling of the relatively small canoe, compared to the larger vessel, left Tanin's stomach twitching with the old pangs felt at the beginning of the voyage. He couldn't wait to leave this part of his journey and return to horseback.

Quiet fell on the hunting party as the Kiwas stopped singing. The king pulled the lid off a wicker basket at the back of his canoe. He dumped a spoonful of the contents into the water. Tanin gagged as the wind carried a whiff of rotten fish to his canoe. Tyler leaned over the boat and vomited, adding to the assault on Tanin's senses. He became hypersensitive to the salt in the air and the odd musty smell from the wooden vessel.

"Make yourself known, ancient poulpe! We would prove our worth!" the old man shouted across the water, standing with ease in the rocking canoe.

The king's voice sounded robust and formal as it called forth the beast. Tyler's gargled voice was not as demanding.

"I don't think I'll ever eat fish again." He moaned, rolling up in a ball on the bottom of the canoe.

Rory kicked his fellow guardian. "Keep your place, boy. A battle is to ensue. We must protect the prince and bring victory to his name."

"Boy?" questioned Tanin, amused with the title, considering the two were the same age.

"He acts like a child, he will be treated as a child," Rory

defended. He forcibly yanked the cloak Tyler was rolled in, nudging him back into place on the seat.

"Uh, my Prince?" Orui pointed to a disturbance on the water a hundred yards out. A deep orange shape peeked through the greenish-blue of the glacial meltwater.

"Could it be... ?" Kettlor gasped, standing up to get a better view. "I never thought I would see one in my lifetime."

The orange hue faded into the deep, only to reappear halfway to the waiting vessels. Tanin could make out a bulbous, almost red body with long tentacles. The undulating suckers explored the water filled with bait.

"What is it?" asked Tyler, turning greener as the poulpe approached.

"A giant squid." Kettlor pulled out his bow and arrows. "They're the major predator of our Mantas but have never been spotted alive. Sucker scars on the mounts who survived an attack are the only evidence of their existence."

"Until now." Tanin pulled out his sword, unsure how it would help with the water beast but unwilling to be unarmed.

The king emptied the remaining contents of the bucket over the side. One of his men handed him an oar, which he used to stir the water. The giant squid grabbed a fish head and shrunk under the surface again. One Kiwa hunter held a hook blade ready. The king took hold of the second weapon, then looked at Tanin expectantly.

Tanin sheathed his sword and picked up a hook blade. He weighted it in his hand, trying to establish its balance. Tanin wanted to use two hands to heft the weapon after feeling its mass but couldn't figure out where to grasp it. A sticky substance coated the handle. He hoped that would help him hold on as seawater weakened his grip.

Something rammed the canoe. Tanin stumbled, glad to have a free hand to grab the side. As the vessel tipped steeply, Tanin faced an eye the size of his head. The cold pupil constricted.

"My Prince!" Kettlor yelled in warning.

Tanin tore himself away from the beast's gaze. Kettlor nocked an arrow to his bow, legs wide for balance. A suckered tentacle reached for Tanin's leg from the other side of the canoe. He tried to dance out of the way as he brought the hook blade around. Rory ducked to avoid being swept overboard as the weapon swung past. Kettlor's arrow penetrated one of the suckers, pinning the tentacle to the wood. Deep red blood gushed across the bottom of the boat. The metallic smell overshadowed the fish odor.

Tanin thrust the Kiwa weapon into the water, trying to snare the large creature. The beast churned the ocean to a foam. More tentacles burst from the surface, forcing Tanin to the center of the wobbly vessel.

Tyler screamed, a distinct tone of pain in it. One of the beast's appendages had wrapped itself around the guardian's leg. The squid yanked Tyler toward the edge. Rory grabbed his dagger from his belt. He stabbed the tentacle, pinning it to the wood. The beast released Tyler, though its limbs thrashed about the crowded boat. Tanin flattened against the side, intent on escaping the suction cups.

The giant squid tried to swim away. His power towed the vessel across the icy water. Tanin held on with the awkward movement of the injured animal. The blood made the boat's bottom slick, causing Tanin to lose his balance and skid on the surface. He held the hook blade up to prevent it from catapulting into the sea. The serrated edge cut through one of the attached tentacles. The canoe spun in a circle, pressing Tanin into the port side.

"Sever the other one," the prince shouted to Rory.

The defense guardian pulled his sword and sliced through the huge tentacle in one stroke. Tanin found his feet as the movement of the boat slowed to a crawl. He wouldn't let that cursed thing escape.

Tanin thrust the hook blade into the water again. The weapon snared the beast deep into the flesh near the eye. The ocean darkened to purple as the giant squid's life bled out.

The king's voice carried across the water. Tyler rocked back and forth, unresponsive.

"Tyler! Translate!" Tanin kicked his foot to the second hook blade. Rory grabbed it.

"Do not damage the eye!" Tyler's voice managed to squeak out the words. "The Great Spirit Clam demands the eye as witness."

Orui griped as he bandaged Tyler's leg. "Really? Why can't he just ask for a tentacle? There's a bunch of those?"

Rory snagged the base of a tentacle near the body. Kettlor helped the prince haul the struggling creature on board.

A tentacle flailed, searching for purchase. The suckers attached to Orui's arm. The medicinal guardian growled in anger. He pulled Tyler's sword from its scabbard and sliced through the orange flesh. Tanin fell backward as the load lightened. He looked up in time to see the dead weight of the sucker-attached tentacle plunge Orui into the icy waters.

Tyler dove for Orui's feet before they fell below the surface. The much smaller guardian couldn't haul him back aboard. Sensing a vulnerable target, the squid swung toward the overboard man. Orui pushed away from the creature. Kettlor released the prince and grabbed Orui's other leg. The two guardians hauled the sputtering, shivering medicinal guardian out of the sea. Kettlor ripped off the tentacle. Orui screamed as some of his flesh was wrenched off along with the suckers.

Tanin pushed his injured guardians from his focus. He had to succeed. "Rory, on three. One... two... three!"

They pulled with all their strength. Tanin's arms shook with the strain. His feet fought for traction on the blood-slicked decking. With a suckering pop, the giant squid's body flopped into the canoe between Tanin and Rory. The wing-like protrusions on either side of the head flapped aggressively.

"Watch the beak!" Kettlor warned.

"The what?" Tanin fought to hold on to the hook blade.

Kettlor pushed past the prince with an oar in his hand. With a burst of unexpected energy, the squid swung around. The hook blade tore free, knocking Tanin off his feet. For a moment, the prince thought the beast had swallowed a bird. A black-tipped beak, twice as big as any Giant Eagle's, snapped at him. Tanin tried to scoot back but rammed into a canoe seat. Kettlor pounced on the beak, straining to keep the oar steady over the struggling animal.

Orui bounded around the prone prince, retrieving the hook blade with his one good arm. He plunged the serrated edge into the squid's mouth. The screech of the beak on metal split the air like a scream. The orange blob of flesh took up half the boat. The prince saw Rory's arms shaking with the effort of holding the squid on board.

Tanin climbed onto the slippery body. He dug a knife into the flesh beside the eye and cut all the way around the socket. The eye dilated to a black emptiness. The canoe rocked with a shift in weight as the remaining tentacles flopped into the water, twitching. The organ slipped from Tanin's mucus-covered hands.

The orb, the size of a large, round watermelon, slid toward the bow of the canoe. Tyler swept the large eye into his lap.

The squid's movements faded to death spasms. Tanin heard an odd rushing sound. Unready for the next surprise, he stood unsteadily on his feet.

The men on the king's boat held their oars over their heads, cheering. The voices across the surface sounded like a waterfall. The king nodded once at the prince.

Rory removed the hook blade from the head of the beast and collapsed. His arms and legs shook from muscle fatigue. Kettlor and Orui, favoring his injured arm, used paddles to leverage the giant squid's convulsing body over the side of the canoe. Tyler held the eye against his chest.

Tanin let out a hearty laugh, releasing the stress of the last few minutes; for it was only a few minutes, even though it had felt like hours. He roared with laughter, with his hands on his hips and his mouth wide open. His guardians stared at their hysterical charge. Squid blood fell from his hair into his open maw. The thick, metallic gel stinking of salt and fish overwhelmed Tanin. He fell to his knees, grabbed the side of the canoe, and vomited into the sea.

From that vantage point, Tanin watched the darkness of the icy ocean swallow the remains of the giant squid. He took stock of his guardians. Orui's arm looked like it had gone through a meat grinder. Tyler's leg wasn't much better. Kettlor and Rory looked exhausted but were otherwise unharmed.

The group had been highly trained but never fully tested. Now Tanin knew his men wouldn't fail him. By this time next year, he would be the sworn heir of Tarbin with his loyal guardians protecting his birthright.

CHAPTER FIFTEEN

"I still don't think we should go this way," Dew complained for the fifth time that morning. "The northern entrance looks the most promising. I've been to the eastern door hundreds of times and never seen any sign of life."

Talia sighed. Since she was born in the area, the group had allowed Dew to lead them as they left Babla. The companion claimed to know the route like the back of her hand. Four hours later, Nyna realized Dew was leading the group to the northernmost door. That way meant they would have to climb through two canyons. The people and horses might survive the steep slopes, but the wagon wouldn't.

Talia didn't know what to do with Dew. She claimed she had gotten turned around. It had been many years since she'd been home. Nyna returned the group to the path heading to the more approachable eastern entrance. Dew had kept up a tirade ever since the recalculation.

"The people of Mahanagara speak of vicious wolf packs that attack all who approach," Dew warned.

"I thought you said you'd been there often as a child and there was nothing there?" Naul rolled his eyes at the change in tactic.

"No, she said there were no guards at the grand doors. She thinks they're only a façade," Nyna defended.

"I'm pretty sure Dew described the path as full of dangerous sinkholes able to swallow any pack animal that sets a hoof on it," Ial added.

"Maybe there are griffins that will swoop down and impale intruders with their vicious talons," Gregor teased.

Dew tried to defend herself. "I said nothing of griffins."

"I know." Gregor held his hands up, his horse continuing to trudge along. "I wanted to make up a fun story too."

Dew huffed at the lordling.

Nyna giggled at the banter. "Why do you really not want to take us to the eastern entrance?"

Talia listened without turning around. She didn't want her annoyance to force Dew to create another lie.

"Please don't make me go home," Dew whispered her plea in a childlike voice.

"It's time for lunch." Talia stopped at the front of the group and dismounted.

"But it's only a few more miles to… " Before Gregor could finish his protest, Talia's glare silenced him. He dismounted, taking Talia's reins. "Picnic on the side of the road it is."

Talia clasped her hands behind her back, like the queen often did whenever she was preparing for a pep talk with her daughter. "Dew, will you come walk with me for a minute? I need to stretch my legs before eating."

Ial helped Dew down and took her horse for water. Dew looked pleadingly to Nyna, who handed the map to Ial. The princess had to be guarded by two, which meant any conversation with her was never completely private.

The evergreen forest exuded a sap smell into the relatively warm air. A rabbit scampered through the pine needles heading for a cluster of yew bushes. Talia wondered how many rabbit eyes were on the companions as they passed the patch of green. A woodpecker's drilling for bugs echoed through the trees, but there was no other movement. This path wasn't often traveled. People walking around might be odd enough to keep the forest animals quiet and hidden.

"Reminds me of home." Dew inhaled the pine. She kicked a pile of needles out of her way. "I hate it."

Talia found a log to sit on and waited for Dew to open up. Watching her pacing guardian, Talia noted once more her stunning beauty. The filtered sunlight played on her bouncy golden hair. Her bodice moved gently as her round hips swayed under her riding pants. The guardian could have had any man she wanted if her station in life had allowed it. Dew stopped pacing and sat at Talia's feet. She crossed her legs and looked down, letting her hair fall over her face.

"My mother was born in Mahanagara. But the small village provided little opportunity for a woman like her. She learned to read and write on her own from the few books she was able to scavenge from neighbors and traveling salesman. My grandparents recognized potential in their little girl. They sold everything they owned to pay tuition for the Cultural School. A gift that might have freed her from an unfulfilling life."

"Your mother was a cultural graduate?" Talia was surprised two women from the same obscure village were able to gain admittance to the prestigious school.

"No. She never graduated." Dew pushed a curl behind her ear. "Mom used to regale us with tales of her school years. She described it in loving detail. When I arrived on campus all those years later, it felt like coming home."

Dew grew quiet.

Talia prompted her. "What stopped your mother from graduating?"

"During her fourth year, a horrific accident rocked the campus. Remember the scorch marks in the north tower? They trail up the stone bordering the windows on the top floor."

Talia nodded. She'd always wondered what had happened. With only two years at the school to cram in as much knowledge as she could, the princess hadn't had time to explore the history.

"My mother never mentioned it. She refused to tell us any details. All I knew was the incident left my mother's left arm and hand terribly burned and shriveled. She wore a shawl draped low over her left shoulder to keep it hidden. Scars on her face were harder to hide. Years later, my curiosity led me to find out what I could."

Nyna put a comforting hand on Dew's shoulder.

"I discovered three students died and six others were brutally disfigured. As many times as I tried, I couldn't get into that room. The door was sealed by means I couldn't detect or defeat. And the professors refused to talk about it. All I know is my mother left the school after the accident. Whether she was expelled or quit... " Dew shrugged.

She reached down to pick up a black spider with brown stripes before it ran under the log. Distracted by the creature in her hand, Dew continued, "She spent five years on her own as a street urchin in Babla, as close to home as she dared. When she ran into her old friend, she barely recognized him. He traveled down the mountain to sell his freshly picked flowers at market. I don't know that it was love at first sight for my mother, but my father said he had been in love with her since they were toddlers. Her withered arm and scarred face added character to her inherent beauty. My father proclaimed his love as he convinced her to elope with him. I think my mother was so tortured by the street life she was looking for any escape she could find." Dew paused in reflection. "Actually, I think my mother was always trying to escape but never found the way out.

"My grandparents adjusted to the idea of their children's union after the grandchildren were born. My sister, my brother, and then me. Our family thrived in the small town, cultivating flowers and bulbs to sell every spring and chopping wood to sell through the winter. My mother returned to her childhood habit of finding books whenever she could, putting in special requests for father to bring back anything he found at market. She taught us how to read and write, which set us apart from the rest of the villagers. But overall, we got along fine."

Dew braided and unbraided a chunk of her hair while staring straight up at the sky. "Until we didn't."

Her foot tapped the ground as if she needed the rhythm to continue her tale. "My brother dared me to climb the tallest ruin on the cliff behind our village. We were forbidden from going back there at all, let alone to climb anything. But I had been challenged and I wouldn't show weakness. I felt the dry stone sapping the moisture from my hands, which oddly made the limestone more slippery. The ancient walls were weather-beaten enough to leave the porous stone full of holes. I used these as footholds to scale the vertical face. I probably could have made it to the top, but it started raining. My brother got scared and ran away, leaving me there. The rain intensified into a full-blown storm. I froze, plastering my body against the stone, trying not to get swept off the side. The cold mountain rain seeped into my bones, making my hands grow numb. I was going to lose my grip.

"I didn't know it at the time—I couldn't see or hear much below me—but my sister saw my brother run from the ruins. She's the one who found me hanging from the cliff and ran to the center of town screaming for help. Half the town, including my mother and father, braved the storm with ropes and ladders to try and get me down." Dew shivered. "By the time they arrived, water rushed out of the hole I had my right foot planted in. My foot slipped, and I teetered on the edge. With no control of my numb hands, I couldn't balance any longer. Someone below me screamed. Before my mind could grasp what was happening, I was falling.

"It felt like everything was in slow motion"—Dew looked straight in Talia's eyes for the first time since starting the tale—"until my descent really was in slow motion. Somehow, my body hit a warm blanket that wrapped me in its folds. I could feel the fabric protecting me from the rain. It gently carried me to the ground. I didn't notice the blue glow until I sat up and looked at my legs.

"Next thing I knew, my father picked me up and ran to my mother. She was slumped on the ground, shaking. My sister helped her up. I thought she was traumatized by my near-death experience. That's when I noticed no one was cheering. An invisible ring had formed around my family as the villagers backed away from us. Through the rain, I heard whispers of 'witch.'"

Dew sunk her head into her hands, sobbing. Talia had never seen Dew shed a single tear. Her hysterics unnerved Talia as much as the tale that inspired them. Nyna joined Dew on the ground, offering her shoulder as a pillow. Talia knelt on the dead pine needles and placed a hand on Dew's knee.

Dew took a steadying breath, then continued, "That night, the townsfolk broke into our home. My twelve-year-old brother felt guilty for abandoning me. He fought the angry men as equals. They tossed him aside aggressively. He hit his head on the hearth and didn't get up. Father did everything he could to defend Mother, but the townsmen subdued him and dragged her away." Dew stared off into nowhere. "By the time my sister and I freed Father, the townspeople already had Mother tied to a stake over a large pile of wood."

"She looked pale and thin. Her damaged left arm, usually kept carefully hidden, lay out in the open for everyone to see," Dew squeaked out between sobs. "She screamed for my dad to go away. She begged him to take us and run."

Dew rose to her feet. Dead leaves crunched as she paced in front of Talia.

"My father ignored her pleas, intent on saving her." Dew swallowed, Nyna by her side. "The wood was still wet from the storm. Men were dousing the wood with oil so it would light. While their hands were full, father jumped onto the crudely constructed platform. The oil covered everything. He had trouble getting his fingers through the knots on the rope. Without warning, the villagers lit the bonfire."

Nyna gasped. Talia's fingers twitched, anxious to help, yet powerless to change the atrocity committed a decade ago.

Dew pushed away from Nyna, wiping her nose with her sleeve. "My sister journeyed with me to the Cultural School and demanded they take me in for what they did to our mother. I don't know where she went after." She marched toward the road.

Talia struggled to catch up, with Nyna on her heels. "Wait! Dew, where are you going?"

The petite guardian moved quickly through the undergrowth, hitting the lunching party before Talia could stop her. Dew untied her mount, releasing the four other horses tied to the same tree.

Gregor jumped up, dropping his bread, to grab the reins of the spooked horses. Ial jogged calmly down the path a couple yards to retrieve his nervous mare.

Distracted by the chaos, no one stopped Dew as she mounted her horse. The cultural guardian took off at a gallop, heading toward Mahanagara.

"Ial." Talia saw him with his horse. "Please follow her."

The husbandry guardian cantered after Dew before his feet were fully in the stirrups.

"What happened?" asked Gregor.

The guardians gathered the vestiges of lunch and tossed it in the wagon, prepared to join the flight.

"Childhood trauma," said Talia, without explaining further. "Is everything secure?"

"Safe and sound, if a bit topsy-turvy." Naul tightened the last strap over the covered wagon.

"To Mahanagara?" asked Gregor, handing Talia the reins to her chestnut.

She climbed onto her horse with her eyes on the road ahead. Dew had taken off determinedly. She hoped Ial would stop her from diving off a cliff in grief. Talia was surprised Dew had traveled toward her hometown, instead of away from it. Then again, Talia had never seen the cultural guardian out of control. She wasn't sure how to react to Dew's current state of mind.

"To Mahanagara." Talia kicked her horse into a gallop.

CHAPTER SIXTEEN

TALIA and her companions slowed their horses as they entered the clearing. She estimated Mahanagara at three dozen homes, with a few larger buildings interspersed throughout. Most of them had colored flags defining their role in their community. Talia smelled the bakery before she saw the loaf of bread inscribed on a weather-beaten orange pennant. All the larger buildings and some of the smaller dwellings were raised on wooden stilts. Observing the trenches in the hardened mud road, Talia imagined the runoff from melting snow would cause flooding most years.

She spotted Ial and Dew in front of a sprawling wooden building uplifted on thick beams, leaving an opening half the size of a man below it. A stable sat off to the side on the ground proper. Talia assumed the building was the inn, based on the image of a bed and foamy mug on a faded blue flag. The cloth dipped low in the dry mountain air.

Ial blocked the steps leading up to the inn. Dew screamed at him with a flaming torch in her hands. Talia threw a look at Nyna as the women dismounted.

"Dew!" Talia shouted. "I know it seems like justice to burn down the town that took so much from you, but—"

"It is justice!" Dew pivoted on her heels, the flames of her torch getting dangerously close to her hair. Townspeople came out of their homes and businesses, lining the one main road through Mahanagara. "How dare they continue their lives as if my parents never existed! How dare they destroy my family and move on unharmed! I have never known peace. Now it's their turn to burn."

Dew turned gracefully backward. She delivered a swift side kick to Ial's abdomen. The young man collapsed. Dew leaped over him with the torch held high.

"Dew?" A woman appeared at the top of the steps.

The guardian froze. She pulled her hair out of her eyes with her free hand. Dropping the torch, Dew flew up the last few steps. She threw herself into the arms of the woman. Gregor rushed forward and stomped on the torch before the fire could take root.

Nyna helped Ial up, checking him for injury. Talia patted her husbandry guardian on the shoulder in thanks as she approached the inn. The whispering of the gossiping townspeople followed Talia up the steps. This might be the most excitement the small town had seen in years.

Talia climbed the steps. She grasped when she got a closer look at the middle-aged woman holding Dew. It was like seeing twenty years into the future. The woman had the young guardian's curly hair, though it was a shade darker. Her green eyes radiated the same emotional intelligence, while her curvaceous form spoke of a silent grace. Only the freckles spread generously over the older woman's face and arms separated the two women.

"Rebekka, my sister," Dew uttered, her voice muffled by the older woman's shoulder.

Talia shared a shocked look with Nyna. The guardian's surprise verified Talia's suspicion. Dew's sister was only six years older than her. The woman holding the cultural guardian looked at least a couple decades older. If Talia hadn't known better, she would have pegged Rebekka as Dew's mother.

"I knew you were coming. The tree never lies." Rebekka held Dew's tear-streaked face in her hands, covering her with kisses.

"Rex! Horil!" Rebekka shouted over the railing of the inn's porch.

Two boys—Talia guessed they were closer to ten than fifteen—jumped off the roof of the stables. "All right, you nosy, lazy louts, do your job and care for this party's animals!"

Talia nodded her approval at Gregor's questioning look. He helped the stable hands lead the horses into the barn. The wagon wouldn't fit, so Naul unhitched the animals outside the enclosure.

Rebekka addressed the gathered townspeople. "The rest of you can go back to your routines. I told you she was coming, and she is here. The tree never lies!"

Talia could hear the disdain dripping from Rebekka's voice as she pointed an accusing finger at the crowd below her. Talia expected the people to defend themselves. Instead, the villagers obeyed. They turned around, almost as a group, heading back to their homes and businesses.

"And we're closed for the night."

Ial held the door open for the women. Talia followed them inside, half-expecting Dew's sister to shoo the companions off as she had the villagers. She would find the princess not so easily dismissed.

Warmth seeped into Talia's body as she passed the threshold. She realized how deeply the mountain chill had sunk into her bones as they started to defrost. A welcoming fire in the middle of the room fed its smoke into a low funnel leading to the roof. Hung from the rafters above the long tables were varieties of herbs and hops. The smell of meat stew, bubbling in a large kettle suspended over the fire pit, partially masked the stench of stale beer. Unlabeled bottles with amber liquor stocked the shelves behind the long bar. Kegs lay under the stairway.

"Atika!" shouted Rebekka.

Talia was beginning to think the woman's voice had two volumes:

whispering and shouting. A girl popped her head through a door behind the bar.

"You have the night off. I'll take care of these guests. Be back early to gather eggs."

"Yes, ma'am," the girl replied.

Talia caught a hint of disappointment in the barmaid's voice. Unlikely to be sad about having a night off, Talia guessed Atika's friends expected a full report on the new arrivals and she'd have nothing to offer.

"Here." Rebekka filled mugs and flung them on the bar. "Grab one and have a seat."

Naul and Gregor arrived in time to grab a mug for themselves. Ial, favoring his midsection, sat beside Dew, who never took her eyes off her sister. Rebekka sat on the other side of Dew, across from Talia.

"Who are your friends, my sister?" Rebekka focused on the group for the first time.

Dew introduced her companions, leaving Talia for last.

"A real princess? In Mahanagara?" Rebekka's eyebrows furrowed and lips pursed. "You're not here to take the trees, are you? Because you can't have them." Dew's sister slammed her fists on the table, bouncing the closest mugs.

Naul stood up with his hand on his hilt.

Talia motioned the companions to be at ease. "We're only passing through. We seek passage into the Krimmel Kingdom."

"Ridiculous," Rebekka scoffed, dismissing Talia with a wave of her hand. "No one enters the realm of the dwarves. The only guests we've had since I've been running the inn, and for decades before if you believe the prior owner, have been pilgrims trying to gain passage into the Krimmel Kingdom. Dwarves and humans alike spend a night or two with us, excited about the prospect of penetrating the mountain. A couple weeks later, every one of them returns defeated. Only a fool would waste his time on such a silly venture."

Talia raised her eyebrows at Rebekka's disrespect. The princess had tolerated abuse, but never complete dismissal. She wasn't sure how to react. Rebekka moved along with the conversation as if the rest of the party had left the room.

"I have thought of you every day since I left you at that school." Rebekka stroked her sister's hair, brushing it out of the younger girl's eyes. "I hoped you would find happiness, but I could live with peace."

"I've never stopped thinking of you." Dew echoed her sister's sentiments. "I imagined you off exploring the kingdom. How could you come back here and live with these people?"

"We left so abruptly, I had to return and make sure they had a proper burial. When I made it back weeks later"—Rebekka took a deep swallow of beer—"brother lay putrefied on the hearth of our family home. I burned it to the ground, hoping his angry spirit would whip the flames into a fever to consume the town, but it didn't."

The innkeeper tapped her fingers on her mug as if the sound would keep her in the present as her memories tried to drag her into the past. "After seeing Brother, I knew the town had left our parents where they had died. The platform stood, cracked and blackened by the fire. The middle post where mother had been bound was replaced by two aspens wrapped around each other like they had grown that way for decades."

Nyna perked up. "Aspens are found in this part of the mountains?"

Rebekka shook her head. "We have no such trees in the valley. It's a mystery where they came from. The villagers I bullied into talking to me said the trees popped up overnight."

Rebekka's eyes shown with the light of discovery. She touched her forehead to her sister's, as if they were children again sharing a secret. "When I touch the trees, they speak to me," she whispered.

Talia's eyebrows shot up. Gregor nudged her under the table with equal concern. The princess catalogued the innkeeper's actions more carefully in search of further signs of madness.

"Can we see the trees?" Gregor asked, sipping his beer casually.

"I knew you were after the trees!" Rebekka shot up from her seat knocking into the table. Mugs of beer tipped, sloshing some of their liquid onto the stained wood.

"No, Bekka." Dew took her sister's hands and gazed up at her, eyes wide. Talia watched the older woman's anger cool as she stared into the depths of those eyes. "Princess Talia has been assigned a sacred mission she must complete. The trees are not part of that mission. But before I journey on, I would see the resting place of our mother and father."

"Of course, Dew. But only you. They may not come." Rebekka glared at the group, daring one of them to argue.

Before Talia could accept her dare, Dew stepped in.

"Bekka." The younger sister stood. "When I swore an oath to dedicate my life to protect the royal bloodline, I also promised to hold my fellow guardians as my new siblings. They are my family."

Dew left out the part of the oath when the guardians had bled into a fire symbolizing the severance from their old family blood. Legally, Rebekka was less a sibling to Dew than the other three guardians.

"Fine." Rebekka's shoulders slumped in submission. "If the trees don't want you there, they'll tell me."

She took Dew's hand and started for the door behind the bar. The companions abandoned their mugs and quickly followed. The door led to a storeroom with a brick oven for baking bread. The shelves were sparsely stacked, mostly with flour, salt, and a few root vegetables. Talia recognized the sour smell of a starter batch of dough coming from a covered wooden bowl on an island table.

The companions exited the kitchen through a back door after Rebekka and Dew, who walked onto an animal trail through the overgrown yews and evergreens.

Talia felt like an intruder in the quiet of the afternoon. Naul's scabbard tapped against his thigh. Nyna's medicinal bag slapped on her hip. The princess had a feeling they were entering sacred ground and wished her guardians would approach more respectfully. She made a mental note to practice stealthy movement with the group.

The trail emptied into a large clearing devoid of plant life. The grayish soil was packed down as hard as rock. Talia doubted the ground became muddy in the rain, because it was so solid. She resisted the urge to bend down and pick at it to verify that it was dirt, not rock. Odd, oval-like shapes indented the clearing in concentric circles, drawing Talia's eyes to the center.

Talia gasped as her vision filled with the grotesquely beautiful living monument. Two ninety-foot aspen trees were intertwined, as if hugging each other. Their white bark sparkled next to the burned cinder remains of an old platform. The dark green of summer colored the heart-shaped leaves clustered on the branches. They rustled softly. The princess understood why Rebekka thought the trees talked to her. Their majesty and strength spoke to Talia as well.

One hand grasping her sister, the other holding Ial, Dew collapsed in tears near the base of the tree. Her lower legs fit in the grooves on the ground. Talia nodded in understanding. The ovals must be from the townspeople giving homage to the trees by kneeling before them. Judging by the number and seeming permanence of the marks, Talia assumed it was a regular occurrence.

"Where did they come from?" Nyna walked around the trees, studying the ground and the surrounding clearing. Her perplexed expression intrigued Talia.

"Don't trees grow from ashes all the time?" Talia asked, keeping her voice low.

"Not aspen," Nyna clarified. Something high in the branches caught her attention. "Princess, do you see that?"

Talia followed Nyna's eyes to a flock of white cotton-like fibers attached to a smaller branch near the top of the tree. "The fluffy white stuff?"

"What's so unusual about a seeding plant?" asked Gregor. "Without the seeds, there would be no baby plants, and my father would be the duke of sand fields instead of wheat."

"Female aspen trees are *covered* with white, fluffy seeds when they decide to reproduce that way. I've never seen just one pod on a tree, not even in a cultivated garden." Nyna pulled on her bag strap, obviously agitated.

"Talia." Dew, still on her knees but no longer crying, waved the princess over. "Rebekka asks that we pray before the trees to ask for a safe passage through the dwarf kingdom."

Talia didn't know how the Light would feel about her worshipping a couple of twisted aspens. Then again, if she were to be anointed the True Heir, she would need to participate in many customs outside her heritage. Finding a couple grooves of her own, Talia looked expectantly at the rest of her companions. They followed her lead, creating a circle surrounding the trees. Well past midday, the sun seemed to sit on the peak of a mountain in the west.

Rebekka's singular voice, crisp and clear, sang in a language Talia couldn't identify. Dew joined her sister in her deeper alto. The haunting lyrics carried through the glen. Movement arose from the perimeter bushes. Naul and Nyna reached for weapons.

Before the companions could jump into full defensive mode, soft music radiated from the shaded area. The townspeople parted the underbrush as they entered the clearing, adding their voices to Dew's and Rebekka's. As if carefully choreographed, the flood of people flowed around the trees, kneeling in concentric circles. A forest of joyful faces looked up at the trees with religious zeal.

Talia smiled to herself. She was right about the indentations. Though she wondered how long the villagers must stay in this position for the marks to be so permanent.

The trees moved. Talia knew that was impossible. She saw it out of the corner of her eye. The day's events had her exhausted and imagining things. She squinted at the perfectly still trunks, daring them to move again, but nothing happened.

Talia looked at her companions on the other side of Dew. They were trying to sing the song with the rest of the worshipers. The simple melody got stuck in her head with the lyrics on a loop. She wondered what they meant.

The trees moved again. A wind must have caused them to stir.

She studied the tops of the large pines outside the clearing. The needles remained completely still with no detectable swinging branches. It was not the wind.

The worshipers put their hands in the air and swayed back and forth. The companions, a bit out of sync, caught up quickly and added their hands to the crowd. Talia lifted her arms as well, mimicking the rhythm of the villagers. The intertwined trees picked up the pace of their movement, swaying with the crowd. Talia's jaw dropped. The inanimate aspen danced with the music.

Drawn to the unplant-like movement, Talia stood. In a trance, she ambled toward the steps rising to the rotting platform. She saw her companions look at each other, but all she could think about was approaching the twisted trunks. She had to talk to the dancing trees.

Naul stepped to the side of the platform. Talia felt his presence, but didn't respond to his pleas for her to come back down. His voice seemed so far away, the trees so near. The rest of the guardians gained their feet.

Nyna and Dew were closest to the steps. The companions headed toward the rotting wood. Rebekka blocked their path. "The trees call her forward. She must obey."

Talia saw everything from the corner of her eye. But nothing distracted her from the calling of the aspen.

The townspeople rushed the companions, tackling them to the ground before they could draw a weapon. Talia barely noticed the commotion. She reached forward, putting one hand on each white trunk. A burning sensation flowed from the trees, enveloping her body in warmth. Her muscles relaxed as tension left her body.

Rebekka's voice drifted from behind Talia. "That is what love feels like."

"Love," Talia repeated in a whisper of escaped breath. The burden of royal duty seemed so far away. She wanted to stay here forever, curled up under the shady branches.

"The trees knew you were coming. They have worked hard to be ready." Dew's sister stood so close to Talia she could feel the warmth of her breath.

"Ready."

Rebekka reached around Talia's back, holding one of her forearms in each hand. "You will rebalance the world. It is your destiny."

"Destiny." Talia blinked.

The innkeeper gently pulled Talia's hands from the tree bark and held them up in the air. The trees shook violently, eliciting gasps from the crowd.

"Look out!" Gregor shouted.

Talia looked up in time to see a seed-laden branch falling toward her head. She and Rebekka caught it. The extra weight proved too much for the rotting platform. The structure collapsed, sending splinters and old char into the air. As she fell, Talia gripped the branch as if it were still attached and could stop her descent.

Talia hit the ground with a crunch. She recognized the sound of breaking bone but felt no pain. Pushing herself up, Talia found Rebekka underneath her. The older woman lay unconscious with a bleeding wound on her skull.

"Talia?" Gregor threw large planks off the pile with Naul beside him.

"It's fine." Talia found she still held the branch full of fluffy white seeds. The young heart-shaped leaves reminded her of the love the trees had poured into her.

"Rebekka?" Dew's voice squeaked as she squeezed through the debris to get to her sister.

The memory of the injured innkeeper brought Talia back to reality. "She broke my fall, Dew. It's like she knew what was going to happen," Talia explained, trying to comfort her guardian. "She saved me."

"Rebekka?" Dew dropped beside her sister, brushing the blood out of the fallen woman's eyes. "Speak to me. I just found you; I don't want to lose you again."

Nyna's gentle voice broke through Dew's grief. "Let me look at her, Dew."

The cultural guardian gave the medicinal guardian room, but refused to release her sister's hand.

"I have to stop the bleeding." Nyna tore a strip from the cleanest part of her shirt. She motioned Gregor to hold the scrap on the wound.

"I don't like the look of this leg. It could be broken. Naul, can you find two sticks about as long as Rebekka's leg?"

Naul surveyed the pile of debris surrounding them. "I think I can manage."

"The villagers left," Ial reported, entering the debris field.

Talia focused on the scene before her, trying to clear her head. The surrounding area was deathly quiet except for Naul breaking wood over his knee. Covered in dust and Rebekka's blood, Talia stood in a pile of splintered wood. Behind her, the aspens stood unharmed except for a mar across the bottom where some of the platform must have scraped the trunk on its way down.

With Ial's assistance, Talia climbed out of the pile, favoring her right ankle but otherwise uninjured. The crack she heard must have been Rebekka's leg.

"What did she say to you up there?" Ial asked, while examining her twisted ankle.

"I don't remember." She tried to recall Rebekka's words, but failed. "I'll ask her when she regains consciousness."

"We need to get her back to the inn." Nyna instructed Naul and Gregor on how to carry the prone woman without aggravating her injuries.

Nyna held Dew close as she guided her back to the village behind her sister.

Ial waited for Talia to move forward, but she couldn't quite remember how to put one foot in front of the other.

He nodded at the heavy branch in her hand. "Do you need me to carry that for you?"

Talia flushed with jealous anger and turned away from his outstretched hands. She held the gift of the aspens against her chest, cradled like an infant.

Ial remained still, his only reaction a slight raising of his eyebrows.

Talia felt silly and had no idea why she overreacted to his offer of help. "Thank you, Ial. It is quite a burden."

She handed the seed-laden branch to her husbandry guardian and marched after the rest of the party before she changed her mind.

CHAPTER SEVENTEEN

Tanin experienced déjà vu as he and his men paddled the longboat toward the Kiwa Island. The group had successfully brought back the giant squid eye to the villagers. The population had celebrated their victory. Tanin's skin still tingled from the ceremonial scrubbing he had received to cleanse the squid goo from his limbs. He hoped the smell of mint from the bathwater wouldn't alert the islanders to their sneaky approach.

After the feast yesterday, the hunters had led the foreigners through the island forest. The hike had ended on the side opposite from Tanin's moored ship. This side ended in a steep cliff with a fifty-foot plunge to the waves below. Tanin frowned, remembering his frustration at not being able to lay his hands on the Holy Black Opal.

The king had placed the giant squid eye on a flat dish at the top of a large, elaborately carved pillar. As soon as he released the organ, Tanin heard the screech of stone on stone. The pedestal slid into the ground.

"The Great Spirit Clam accepts the testimony of the poulpe." The king spread his arm toward the cliff edge. "You may commune until the eye returns to the circle of life."

Tanin didn't see a clam anywhere.

"My Prince." Rory peered over the cliff, directing his charge's gaze down.

The water at the base of the cliff bubbled oddly as a shadow rose from the depths. The shape emerged at the same speed the obelisk sank. From the distant cliff, it seemed a monster broke the waves, leading with giant, blue-tinged teeth. Kettlor crawled on his belly to the edge, allowing him to stick his head as far out as possible.

Kettlor whistled his appreciation. "This cold water does breed monsters, doesn't it?"

"That clam could feed the village for a week," Orui commented, bent over beside the husbandry guardian.

"There must be a mechanism that lifts the shellfish above the water with the proper counterweight." Rory nodded toward the squid eye on the disk of the pedestal.

Tanin raised his eyebrows. Of course, the Great Spirit Clam couldn't move on its own. He marveled at the ingenuity of the rulers who had hidden the gem so safely. They had created a religious mystique so powerful, it led an entire society to dedicate its practices to protecting the Holy Black Opal, and they didn't even know they were doing it.

After an annoying amount of kneeling and chanting, Tanin and his men were finally led back to the village. Tanin thanked them for their hospitality and promised to sign a trade deal giving the Kiwas a monopoly on all seal fur trade with Tarbin. He refused the offer of another night's rest on land. The prince insisted the group had to continue their mission of exploration in order to make it back to Tarbin by the end of one year.

The villagers waved them off, sitting on the docks until the ship sailed away due west.

Once they had crossed the horizon, Captain Sonacevontes ordered the crew to tack the vessel to the south. The sailors expertly maneuvered the trading ship to the cliff side of the island, where the clam sat above the surface. The captain ordered the longboat down.

Tanin and his men again took up oars and headed toward the Great Spirit Clam. The companions were armed with crowbars, metal rods, and chisels. Kettlor wasn't sure what they'd need to get the clam open. The group came with everything they thought might come in handy. Tanin was certain they wouldn't get a second chance.

"What if the clam gets away? How do we follow it to the depths?" asked Orui.

"Tell me that is not a serious question," Kettlor scoffed. "Clams don't move."

"It looks like this particular specimen is attached to whatever platform lifted it into place," Rory added. "Though it does look a little higher above the water than it appeared from above."

"Look at the birds." Tyler pointed to the top of the cliff, where the companions had stood during the raising ceremony. Dozens of seagulls with bright white bodies and completely black heads swarmed the sacrificial disk containing the rotting eye. Something spooked the birds, sending them into the air all at once. The giant clam sank slightly lower in the water.

"Did you see that?" Orui shifted his oar, favoring his injured arm.

"Interesting," Rory squinted at the cliff.

"Of course." Tyler put the full picture together. "As the birds eat the squid eye and the weight on the obelisk lessens, it rises, causing the clam's platform to sink under the water."

"What happens if the birds knock the eye off altogether?" Tanin wondered, fearing the answer. "Row faster!"

Urgency over losing the clam to the depths drove the companions to paddle swiftly, regardless of the noise they made.

The sun approached the horizon more quickly than Tanin had hoped. The Light bounced along the water's surface like a smooth rock on a pond. The prince prayed for a speedy recovery of the Holy Black Opal.

As the longboat drew up beside the giant clam, its true colors became clear. The mountain-sky blue of the tissue lining the inside of the zigzag mouth looked dyed, the color shone so vividly. Fuzzy green algae covered the outside of the undulating shell. The tiny filaments flowed back and forth as water washed up onto the platform with the rise and fall of the waves.

Orui and Tyler kept the longboat close. From this distance, Tanin saw the stone holding the mass of the clam mostly above the water. He tentatively stepped onto the smooth surface, followed by Rory and Kettlor. Tanin almost slipped into the freezing water as the platform sank five inches. The sudden movement of the mechanism spooked the birds again, causing the clam to sink farther.

"We better hurry," cautioned Rory, reaching for the clam.

The blue-and-green sea creature was closed with just enough space available to fit human fingers between the wavy halves. With one on each side, the men pulled, trying to separate the shells with the least amount of effort. The slippery footing combined with the strength of the clam provided no progress.

Tanin grabbed a crowbar. He levered the iron bar against one shell, prying the opposite side open. Despite the cold, sweat popped out on his forehead at the exertion.

"Interesting," commented Rory. Instead of a big open space with meat and slimy bits like most clams, the giant one had a blue membrane stretched across the opening with one large hole off to the side.

"I suppose I have to stick my hand in there and dig around?" Tanin scrunched his lip in disgust. The color would be gorgeous on a cape for a formal ball. The stench that emanated from the sea beast negated any visual comfort the earth colors provided.

"It is your quest, my Prince." Kettlor took the leveraged crowbar from Tanin, keeping it open.

Tanin pulled up his sleeve and shoved his arm roughly into the opening of the tissue. He imagined the clam protesting, but it didn't move. The prince rummaged through slimy bits. He tried to ignore the unpleasant sensation as he searched for the hard texture of a gemstone. Rory slipped, knocking Tanin into the side of the shell.

The prince's hand rammed into a firm object packed against the side of the shell.

"I think I've found it. Help me get it out, Rory."

Unable to maneuver in the same hole, Rory pulled out his belt knife and sliced through the connective tissue. With the curtain pulled back, Tanin could see the hard object. It didn't look like a black opal at all. In fact, it was a dull gray color, nowhere near deep enough to be black.

"Wait. That can't be it." Tanin pulled out his own knife.

The two men started cutting pieces out and tossing them into the water. Kettlor threw the crowbar into the longboat since the clam no longer tried to close on them. The chunks of meat sank into the water around the raised platform, lightening the load. Orui pushed the longboat back as the platform rose further.

"I don't see anything else. Do you?" Tanin asked Rory. The companion shook his head.

In a rage, Tanin kicked the giant shell. The violent action threw him off balance as his cold-numbed hands and feet refused to obey. Rory caught his charge and shoved him to safety, sacrificing his own balance. Tanin watched Rory plunge into the frigid waters. Orui reached out and hauled Rory onto the side of the vessel. His injured state prevented him from pulling Rory fully aboard. Tyler helped the defense guardian over the edge.

Tanin. spit in the water trying to get the briny taste out of his mouth. "That's it. We're leaving. I'm not wasting another second on this leg of the voyage. High Priestess Nomyra will have to do better research to find the Holy Black Opal." He climbed into the longboat. Rory shivered so violently, the vessel vibrated.

"Not a swim I'd recommend." Orui put his oar in the water with his good hand.

"Let's go!" Tanin grabbed an oar. He shot an impatient look at Kettlor, who was still on the platform. The husbandry guardian was cutting the bulbous pearl, easily the size of a fat house cat, out of the clam carcass. "Come on! Leave the garbage behind."

"I'm sorry, my Prince. I've never seen anything like this before. Master Gravis would appreciate such a specimen." Kettlor removed his soaked cloak and wrapped it carefully around the gnarly object. He flung his hair out of his eyes and climbed into the longboat behind Tanin.

With everyone off, the platform jolted up a few feet. The sudden movement forced the obelisk down with enough force to knock the squid eye from the counterbalance high up on the cliff. The eye wobbled to the edge, then rolled over it, splashing to the water below. It landed a foot away from Tanin's paddle, sending a torrent of cold water over the companions. The loss of the bird mass and the eye caused the pedestal to rise fast enough to slam to a stop. The flat offering disk broke and tumbled from the stone column.

The mutilated giant clam fell rapidly into the depths, the freezing saltwater bubbling angrily. A deep groan, like that of a dying giant, roared from inside the cliff face.

"Paddle!" shouted Tanin.

They put all their force into moving as far away from the cliff as they could. The rumbling grew as rocks poured off the steep incline. One boulder hit the submerged clam platform with enough force to knock it onto its side. The moaning grew into a roar. Tanin realized the cliff was manmade wall as the façade broke apart in large pieces. The waves from their impact on the water rushed into the boat. The companions rowed more urgently, while Tanin worried the water would swamp the vessel.

As the wall peeled away, a complicated mechanism of gears and chains revealed itself.

"Incredible. I've never seen anything like it." Tyler clutched his oar, motionless.

"You can gawk later. Keep rowing," Tanin ordered.

"Duck!" yelled Rory.

A gear the size of one of the boats headed for the fleeing men. Everyone tucked their heads into the boat. The metal projectile brushed over them close enough to feel the wind.

A chain large enough to restrain a dragon fell loose.

"Hurry!" Tanin heard one of his guardians yell.

The chain fell a couple feet behind the fleeing longboat. The vessel rushed forward on a wave. Tanin heard a sickening crack. Hoping the sound didn't indicate a structural collapse, he kept paddling.

His muscles ached from the strain. The temperature dropped as the boat picked up speed. The dying machine continued to spew parts of itself. Every article of Tanin's clothing was soaked from the turmoil of the disintegration.

"We're taking on water," Orui cautioned.

"Almost there," Tanin said through clenched teeth.

The men arrived at the ship, bumping into the side in their haste. The violence of the collapsing mechanism produced enough energy to send the larger vessel swaying. Captain Sonacevontes barked orders from the deck. A rope with a loop tied on the end was thrown down to Tanin. Freezing water filled half the boat. It wouldn't stay above water much longer. Tanin grabbed the offered salvation. The crew pulled him aboard. More ropes were tossed for the rest of the companions.

"Bring these men dry clothes and warm tea." First Officer Maritoss commanded while the captain organized the recovery of the longboat. "Prince Tanin, you have made a miraculous escape. I have never seen anything like that great machine."

Tanin allowed the first officer to help him remove his wet clothing. His muscles were frozen beyond resistance.

"What is Tyler doing?" Rory asked as the cultural guardian limped to a trunk on the deck.

"Who knows with that one?" Orui muttered. He clenched his injured arm to his chest. "I'm going to need help rebandaging this."

"I've got you." Rory grabbed the aid kit from one of the sailors.

Tyler hopped to the railing, dragging his injured leg behind. He held a book, a feather, and ink.

Kettlor dropped the blanket he was wrapped in to help his fellow guardian. "Hand me the book."

"I have to draw everything I can before there's nothing left." Despite his protests, Tyler obeyed Kettlor.

"I know." The calm companion gave the book and writing tools to Maritoss. He helped Tyler into dry clothes, then gave him back his instruments.

Tyler hugged Kettlor in gratitude. The cultural guardian stood at the railing and sketched the great mechanism in the cliff face as Kettlor wrapped his injured leg. Rory joined Tyler, helping him fill in the empty spots.

Tanin looked at the ugly pearl hanging from Kettlor's belt. "I can't believe I've wasted so much time on this part of the journey with nothing to show for it."

"We will set sail for Naddle Swamp immediately, my Prince." Orui bowed and left to talk with the captain.

Tanin tried to take comfort. If he couldn't find the Holy Black Opal, neither could his sister. He only had to obtain more gems than she. High Priestess Nomyra was focused on the young ruler bringing back all the gems. He didn't know why the woman was so concerned about the legitimacy of the stones. He'd deal with that problem later. Surely the rich Darvisian market would have a black opal comparable to the missing stone.

Tanin parted his blue lips in a smile. The ship moved west toward Naddle Swamp. The Holy Emerald better be where Nomyra said it was. If she had made him memorize the script required to obtain the gem from its guardians for nothing, heads would roll.

"We will reach our destination in three weeks, my Prince," Orui reported.

"Make it two and a half."

CHAPTER EIGHTEEN

DRAGICK WATCHED the intruders through the holes in the stone wall. The young dwarf, taller than most of his peers, pulled on his beard with one hand. His other held his assigned guard spear, which stood twice his height. Not that the weapon would do him any good in the close quarters of the tight cave behind the granite wall. But tradition was tradition.

He tucked the spear in the crook of his shoulder to free both hands to rub his strained eyes. He had a headache from staring into the sunlit mountainside from inside the candlelit cave. He smoothed out his clay-red uniform jacket and chose a viewpoint a bit higher up to give his back a break from bending awkwardly.

The dwarf guard had studied the human troupe for days as they pushed and prodded the door, searching for a way in. Dragick had lost three silvers in the guard pool, betting on how long the humans would try to breach the entrance before giving up and going home. Occasionally, humans found the entrance to the Krimmel Kingdom, by purpose or happenstance. In Dragick's memory, no group had stayed so long, fiddling with the immovable object.

Of course, the humans didn't know it was immovable.

The arched door, carved out of the gray mountain granite, stood four dwarves tall. Adorned with ancient writings from legends long forgotten and symbols with obscure cultural meanings, the facing was only a façade. When the dwarves fled their homeland, the stone masons had devised the massive door as a diversion from the actual entrance located underground, around the south side of the granite wall. An impressive stone structure, with oblique clues on how to gain entrance, attracted enough attention to keep the befuddled humans from realizing the door was a fake.

The second duty guard, Gallick, filled the boring hours on duty differently than the studious Dragick. His partner set down his spear, dropped his pants, and mooned the humans.

"You know they can't see you," said Dragick, shaking his head.

"Maybe they can't see me, but I can see them and I'm tired of looking at their ugly faces." Gallick pulled his pants up with a jump, his deep, resonating voice contrasting with his childish actions.

Dragick smiled at his friend. The dwarves were brothers in every way except blood. They shared blue eyes with flattish noses and huge ears that stuck out beyond long brown hair. Their thick brown beards were identical in texture and length. The only way to tell the two apart was height. Gallick was a full loaf of bread shorter.

"When are they going to leave?" bemoaned the shorter dwarf. He collapsed onto a stone bench lining the wall opposite the fake door. "I'm ready to go hunting again."

"They have to be close. The group won't be able to stand the inactivity for much longer." Dragick peeked through a viewing hole. "They're starting to bicker."

The bald, muscular human sat on the back of the wagon, whining to the skinny brunette with the shoulder bag. Dragick couldn't quite make out what he was saying, but he clearly saw the girl roll her eyes. A curvy human—much more attractive in Dragick's opinion—sat cross-legged on the ground, scouring through a burgundy-covered book. Dragick had witnessed humans searching through books during previous excursions but never to this level of dedication.

"Though their determination might send them to one of the other, harder-to-reach entrances. They certainly seem focused on getting in."

"I don't care where they go as long as they leave my jurisdiction." Gallick stretched his arms over his head and yawned. His stomach growled. "I say we storm out, scare them away, and bring home a delicious buck for dinner."

"Did you forget to grab your lunch again?" Dragick asked, turning to his friend, amused. "You can't have mine this time. Debranim made me a meat pie from last night's leftovers."

"Your wife is the best cook around. It's undwarf of you not to share your good luck with your best friend."

"Nice try. Debranim got the recipe from *your* wife last time we were at your house." Dragick sat on the bench, taking his break.

Gallick retrieved his spear and dutifully took over peering out the spy hole.

"Polarin refuses to make my lunch anymore," grumbled Gallick.

"You insulted her again, didn't you? Sometimes I wonder about you."

"Hey, it's not my fault her skin is as thin as a moon mushroom's. I didn't mean anything by it."

"What did you say this time?" Dragick was almost afraid to hear the answer. Last time the two fought, Gallick had slept in Dragick's living room until Debranim finally convinced Polarin to give him a second chance. Since then, his friend had been on his best behavior.

"She was trying on a new dress and I pointed out that... " Gallick stopped mid-sentence. "Dragick, come look at this."

Dragick thought Gallick was stalling until the flickering candlelight showed the color drained from the shorter dwarf's face. The resting guard jumped to his feet and took his partner's place. The skinny brunette with the shoulder bag held a limb with cottony seeds peeking out of a pod framed by green, heart-shaped leaves. Any trained guard would recognize that branch.

It was Aspen.

"Go get the priest. Now!"

Gallick dropped his spear, and sprinted down the torchlit entryway. Dragick had never seen his lazy friend's legs move so fleetly.

"LUNCH IS SERVED!" Gregor announced, mustering as much cheer as he could.

"Thank you, Gregor." Talia accepted a bowl of vegetable soup with salted cod. "And thank you for taking lunch today. I know it's not been fun to twiddle our thumbs and hope for a miracle."

Ial patted Talia on the shoulder. "If we're meant to enter, we will."

The husbandry guardian always managed to calm Talia when she was on the verge of panic. She wondered if it was a trick he used with the horses. The thought made Talia consider being offended.

"But when do we know to move on?" Gregor asked.

"Maybe Tanin already breached the door and the Krimmel won't let anyone else in?" Talia postulated.

"Maybe there are no Krimmel. No one has seen or interacted with the fractured dwarven people in centuries." Naul poured himself a bowl of soup from the cauldron over the fire.

"The aspen has to have something to do with it. Rebekka said we need it for the next leg of our journey. This is the next leg, right?" Nyna took the bowl Gregor offered. She set it on the wagon, contents untouched.

Dew slammed the book shut and tried to stand. Her legs had apparently fallen asleep, making for a precarious ascent. Gregor grabbed her arm to steady her before handing her a bowl of soup. "The book doesn't say anything about aspen trees or branches of any sort for the Holy Diamond. The book says that gem is still held at the old dwarven kingdom. My guess is no one updated it after the Dwarven Civil War."

"I don't know why we should believe anything your crazy sister claimed." Naul added his opinion from the fire, where he filled his own bowl. "She almost killed Talia. Who knows what following her advice could lead to?"

"Take that back!" yelled Dew.

Talia pinched her forehead, making a pleading face at Ial. Her husbandry guardian reluctantly set down his lunch to intervene in Dew and Naul's argument. Oblivious to the bickering, as anyone who grew up in a family with twelve siblings would be, Nyna took the branch she held to the door. Talia followed. The guardian held it up like an offering. Nothing happened.

"Maybe you have to do it. Rebekka said the trees chose you." Nyna handed the branch to Talia.

The wood felt so cold, separated from the warmth of the mother tree. She felt a bit silly, but Talia had nothing to lose at this point. The princess held the branch above her head and looked respectfully down at the ground as if she offered a sacrifice to a god. Nothing happened.

"Maybe the door doesn't eat aspen. I could get you a few pine cones?" Gregor offered, sipping on his soup.

Talia dropped her arms, resisting the urge to throw the sacred thing at the noble. She spun around, tossing him a dirty look instead.

"Talia, listen." Nyna held her hands flat on the wall with an ear pressed against one of the carvings. "I think I hear... breathing."

Handing the branch to Gregor, Talia mirrored her companion's stance. She heard nothing, though she felt a slight breeze on her abdomen. Talia dropped to her knees and searched for the source. She found a hole the diameter of her pinky finger and peered inside. The princess fell over backward in shock. "There's an eyeball looking back at me!"

"What?" Gregor knelt beside her and found the hole. "I don't see anything. It's pitch black."

"I swear I saw an eyeball." Talia stared into the hole again. Nothing was there.

"Ummm, Talia?" Ial attracted her attention.

The sudden quiet of the camp spooked Talia as she turned south toward Ial's voice. Seven dwarves stood in a semicircle on the edge of the clearing.

At least, Talia thought they were dwarves. The figures on each end looked like the ones Talia was accustomed to. Stocky features, thick, wiry beards, full heads of unruly hair were all standard traits. The four likely guards of some sort wore clay-red uniforms with deep gray accents. All had brown hair and blue eyes and carried long, menacing spears.

What was beyond Talia's experience were the three central men. About the height of an average nine-year-old human, these figures were willowy, with long, thin fingers and pronounced necks. The silver robes draped over their delicate forms were adorned with constellations. She wondered how often the dwarves left their indoor kingdom to observe the stars.

Most shocking of all, these dwarves were completely clean shaven—no beard, no head hair, no arm hair. The princess had worked with dwarves for years, through trade in the kingdom and at the Defense School. She had never seen an adult male dwarf without facial hair. The beard was such an essential part of an Eckerd's maleness that if one was unable to grow a full beard, he would buy a toupee for his face.

The clean-shaven dwarves held their heads high, garnering respect from the guards trailing them. Talia stood flabbergasted, surprise preventing her from making the first move.

The thinnest dwarf shook his robe and said, "Who received the sacred seed branch from the entwined aspens?"

"I did." Talia held up her hand as if she were answering a question for a teacher. The dwarf who spoke focused on her. Gregor cradled the aspen into her grip.

"Come forward," the silver-robed dwarf ordered.

Talia walked toward the commanding dwarf, trying to calculate her next move. Her guardians fell in line around her, ready with their sheathed weapons. The princess relied on her training. She pushed her shoulders back and held the branch out. She lengthened her stride, showing it was her choice to come forward. The lead dwarf held his hands up to accept the offering. Talia chose to bend her knees to place it gently in his arms instead of bowing before the stranger.

"It is a beautiful specimen. Unseen in these mountains for millennia." The dwarf's blue eyes glittered with fanatical glee. "Prophecy says the bearer of the aspen branch is to be allowed into the kingdom for a fortnight. Is this your wish?"

"Yes, please," Talia pleaded. "We seek an item of great importance to our people."

"I know what you seek. And it is important to our people as well." The dwarf turned, grasping the branch tightly. "Though the king will be tough to convince."

Talia didn't know what that meant, but she'd made it this far. With a look at her companions to make sure they followed, she joined the odd dwarf. The guardians formed two lines on either side of Talia.

The dwarf who had spoken stopped. "Only the bearer may enter."

"These men and women are my royal guardians, bound to me by an unbreakable oath. Two must accompany me at all times to retain their honor." There were other consequences for failure, but Talia didn't feel the need to enumerate them. "The tradition was established centuries ago to protect the bloodline of Tarbin's royalty."

"Unbreakable oath?" The dwarf's eyes squinted. Talia could almost see the thoughts running through his mind, digesting the new information. "What are you called?"

"I am Princess Talia Winterlaus of Tarbin." Talia stood tall, trying to look as regal as possible.

"I am afraid only the bearer of the branch is allowed to enter. As the superior priest, I cannot defy the orders of the prophecy."

"Then we'll take it back, thank you." Gregor snatched the branch from the priest. He held it over his head like a big brother teasing his younger siblings.

The superior priest glared at him. The guards drew their weapons, advancing on the disrespectful human. Talia's guardians drew their own swords and assumed defensive posts around Talia and Gregor.

"Stop!" shouted Talia and the priest in harmony.

"Sheathe your weapons," ordered Talia.

Her companions hesitated before the threat of the dwarven guards.

Talia's face pinched in anger. "Now!"

The superior priest threw his hands down at his guards. The smooth sound of metal on leather filled the clearing, veiling the threat, not diminishing it. Talia seized the abused aspen branch from Gregor. She presented the prize to the priest once more. He pushed his guards aside to regain the sacred relic.

"This is not how I wanted relations between our peoples to begin. Please forgive the misplaced enthusiasm of my traveling companion." She threw a disapproving glare at the lordling, emphasizing her point. "He understands how vital our task is and wishes only for a successful outcome. I've been sent on a sacred mission to prove my worthiness to rule my kingdom."

One of the other bald-headed dwarves, likely a priest of a lower rank, whispered in the lead dwarf's ear. The superior priest nodded once. He handed the precious object to the younger dwarf, who eyed Gregor warily.

"There is one more test." The superior priest reached into his glittery robes and pulled out a needle. As the dwarf reached for it, Talia noticed the large ring on the mature dwarf's index finger. The band of the ring twisted around his finger, like the ivy on a tree, reaching up to grasp a purplish-blue crystal. Except for the color of the stone, Talia thought the piece of jewelry looked identical to the ring High Priestess Nomyra wore—and maybe like that mysterious ring from the Royal Forest.

"There is a legend whispered through the caverns. The telling differs depending on family history and the sobriety of the speaker, but there are a few things they all have in common. When the blood of the descendant touches Argo, he will recognize one of his own."

He removed the ring and held it between his fingers, gemstone up. Talia realized he meant the ring was Argo. The superior priest pricked his finger with the needle and spread his blood on the gem. The gem's color darkened with the smear on its surface.

"Though most of us have never seen a human, the rumor persists that the bloodline lives in one. This individual will bring about the Recharging. As my young assistant points out, the timing would be perfect."

The dwarf wiped his blood off the gem with the jacket of one of the guards. The heavily bearded guard's face paled. Talia couldn't tell if it was from embarrassment or disgust.

The superior priest held up the needle and the gem. His raised eyebrows and steady stare told Talia he waited to test her blood.

"The blood of the True Heir will determine the champion of the quest," Dew whispered in Talia's ear, repeating the high priestess's words.

Before she could change her mind, Talia grabbed the needle and poked it into her finger a little too enthusiastically. Pain shot through her hand as blood spilled freely from the puncture. She held her hand over the proffered ring, allowing it to drip onto the surface.

As soon as her blood came into contact with the gem, the liquid was absorbed, like water poured onto sand. Talia's mind flared at a recent memory of something similar. From deep inside the crystal, a blue-tinged glow emanated. It brightened with each subsequent drop, until the clearing lit with an unnatural light. Maybe she hadn't imagined it the first time.

A collective gasp echoed off the granite wall, emitted by human and dwarf alike. Talia yanked her hand away. She sucked on her finger to stop the bleeding. The glow was exactly like the emerald she had found in the leaves of the Royal Forest. Could they be connected?

"It is true." The superior priest fell to his knees, mirrored by the rest of his party. Tears of religious fervor flowed from his eyes. He tore his gaze away from the ring as the light faded. "You are the human of legend, Princess Talia Winterlaus of Tarbin. You must come immediately. Bring your entire party."

"Let's go," said Talia before the dwarf could change his mind.

For having sat unproductively for three days, the companions found themselves unready to break down camp. Ial unhooked the horses from the wagon. They could come back for the extra supplies. After they attached as many supply bags to the horses as possible, the human party faced the granite door, waiting to gain admittance.

"Uh, where'd he go?" Naul asked. "Isn't this the door?"

"Was no one watching them?" Talia rubbed her forehead.

While everyone was packing, the dwarven party had slipped away through the woods.

"Maybe they have to open it up from the inside?" guessed Nyna.

"If that were true, then how are the dwarves getting in?" asked Gregor. "Come to think of it, where did they come from in the first place?"

"Are you coming?" One of the guards, tall for the dwarves Talia was accustomed to, stepped out of the tree line.

"Yes, yes, we are," replied Talia. She shrugged at her companions and started south along the granite wall, following the bearded dwarf.

They followed him through the underbrush, horses in tow, to another expanse of cleared granite. The stone held no outline of a door or an opening or even a crack. One of the guards climbed a tree adjacent to the wall. He jumped onto a pillar twice as tall as a human. The guard who guided the companions to this part of the mountain repeated the actions onto a similar structure about three carts away. The two dwarves jumped up and down in perfect synchronicity, each set of feet hitting the pillar at the same time.

Talia felt the ground tremble. The distinct sound of stone

scraping stone resonated from under her feet. She instinctively took a few steps back, staring down. A huge rectangle of grass, big enough to fit two horses side by side, rose out of the ground as if hinged on the granite mountain. As the earth opened up, Talia saw a torchlit tunnel. The smell of mildew wafted from the opening.

"By the Light." Nyna summed up the collective emotions of the group.

Bits of dirt fell from the huge piece of sod that had been hoisted out of the ground. A massive net held the soil in place around the framework forming the earthen door. When the door had risen to a forty-five-degree angle, the second set of dwarven guards levered two boulders onto the pillars to hold them flush against the ground.

"No wonder we couldn't break the code on the door. It's a fake," Dew declared.

"Don't feel as dumb now?" asked Ial, peering into the darkness. Talia knew nothing frustrated Dew more than not being able to solve a mystery.

"Maybe we should feel *really* dumb because we never figured out the door was fake," Naul teased.

Dew swatted him with the reins of her horse. Talia saw the dwarven priests observing the playful behavior.

"That's enough. We could be the first humans to enter the Krimmel Kingdom in recorded history," Talia rebuked her guardians. "Maybe we could show a little dignity at the monumental occasion."

The silver-robed dwarves walked down the ramp into the tunnel. Talia soothed Ruix. She understood why the horse acted skittish. Entering a dark cave felt very much like entering her grave. The princess took a deep breath and followed the priests.

CHAPTER NINETEEN

The companions trudged single file through the underground passageway. The meager torches the dwarf guards carried failed to illuminate farther than the lead priest's footfalls. The horses had to be blindfolded to walk at all. Ial tied their reins to each other's tails to lead them in one long line through the tunnel.

"Those animals are not fit to be traveling the caves," the superior priest observed. "You are lucky these tunnels were built especially large to allow carts through for trade."

"You still trade with other nations?" asked Gregor from behind Talia.

"Not for centuries." The priest's voice echoed on the stone.

Talia was surprised she could hear anyone speak at all. The clop of the horse's hooves bounced around the tunnel like an invading army. The smell of horse and unwashed people amplified in the close quarters. All Talia's senses were compromised in the underground environment. She couldn't understand how the dwarves functioned down here.

"Halt!" commanded one of the dwarven guards.

The party stopped. The sudden silence sent a shiver down Talia's spine. Everything felt unnatural. She stretched her neck to peer around Naul. The light from the lead guard's torch reflected off a stone wall. She repressed a groan.

"Please don't tell me we've been going the wrong way the whole time." Naul rubbed his bald head.

"Silence!" demanded the same guard.

Talia was about to add her own complaints when she thought she heard tapping, originating from the other side of the stone wall. The guard used the butt of his long spear to tap out a complicated rhythm on the ground. This time, Talia was sure she heard a faint answer in a different rhythm. The lead guard scratched the door with the spearhead. Talia cringed at the screech.

The sound of stone on stone, similar to that of the entrance opening, filled the tunnel. The horses pranced about nervously. She heard Ial attempt to soothe their panic.

Bright light flooded the dark tunnel, blinding Talia. She shielded her eyes with her left hand, blinking. The party moved forward into the sunlit chamber.

"Is that clover?" asked Nyna.

Ial brought the horses around. Dew helped him separate the nervous creatures.

After the light, the fragrance of the dome cave hit Talia. Behind the fresh woody scent lurked a musty, goat-like odor. Taking advantage of the extra space to fan out a bit, Talia moved beside Naul. The path on the right side was bordered by grasses and clover and some sort of yellow flower. On the left lay a corral full of furry four-legged creatures about the size of sheep. The domesticated animals were unlike anything Talia had ever seen. The odd creatures had small, pointed ears like a cat and long twisted horns like a goat.

"What in the heck are those?" Talia watched one use its long, furless snout to carry bits of greenery out of a trough to its mouth, which was full of flat, squarish teeth.

"Procapras." One of the young priests seemed to think the name explained everything.

Ial reached out his hand to pat one on the head, careful not to touch the horns. The animal's blank eyes looked at him without changing the rhythm of his chewing. "They're one of the common farm animals of ancient times. Master Gravis gave an entire lecture on the relationship of the procapras to the other domesticated ungulates."

"Are they good to eat?" Naul rubbed his stomach.

Dew smacked the reins in her hands in the large companion's direction. She missed, swatting a horse instead. The blindfolded animal reared up before Ial was able to settle it down. The commotion sent the other horses teetering, pulling on their reins in agitation. The procapras didn't move.

While her guardians calmed the mounts, Talia watched the superior priest send two of the guards and the other two priests sprinting to a tunnel on the other side of the cavern. Talia didn't know if she should be worried or not.

"Procapras are okay for eating, but they're much better for carrying gear on trips." The resonating voice of one of the remaining guards surprised Talia. "They can haul more than four times their own weight."

His face scrunched in disapproval, the taller guard elbowed the talkative one. Talia thought his eyes said, *Don't talk to the outsiders.*

The companions walked through a cavern larger than Talia would have thought possible without the mountain coming down on them. The far corners were lost in shadow, but the middle area with the fields and animals was infused with light.

"Look at the holes in the ceiling!" Gregor pointed from behind Talia. "It looks like the dwarves made openings to let the light in."

"I see them. But they're small and way up there. How can they let in so much light?" Talia searched the cavern.

"Those cisterns leading to the troughs and barrels below must be to collect rain water. I'd think they'd block most of the light," Naul observed.

"What is he doing?" Nyna pointed at a dwarf hanging from the ceiling on a pulley. He looked to be manipulating some sort of device hanging from the wall.

"He's going to fall and break his skull." Naul shivered.

"He is an anglist. He specializes in directing the light," the loquacious dwarf explained, ignoring the other guard.

The hanging dwarf adjusted the object toward the right wall. A beam of light illuminated an area surrounding a pillar. The greens sticking out of the ground looked like feathery carrot stalks.

"They're mirrors!" Gregor exclaimed. "They must use mirrors to focus the light. Brilliant!"

"That's clever." Talia picked out more ropes and ladders attached to almost every surface of the cave ceilings and walls. More dwarves climbing through the maze to align each mirror depending on which field needed light.

"I wish we could take a few minutes to sketch it," Gregor lamented. "We could use this technique in large castles that are densely constructed and allow very little light to find its way indoors."

Two dwarves dressed in dirt-colored jumpers bowed before the superior priest. They exchanged words in a heavy language Talia hadn't heard before. She raised an eyebrow at Dew. The linguist shrugged.

"You may leave your horses tied to the fence. The herders will see to their care." When the group hesitated to obey, the priest sighed. "The tunnels ahead are a tighter fit than the previous journey. Your skittish mounts are unlikely to leave us unharmed if we drag them through such close quarters."

The husbandry guardian moved around the group and handed his reins to one of the dwarf herders. "The procapras look healthy. The horses will be fine," Ial offered.

The herder was so dirty his skin, hair, and jumper all appeared to be the same dull brown. Ial, not a whole foot taller than the dwarf, bowed his head. The dwarf repeated the gesture. Talia thought the two animal trainers exchanged an understanding. The rest of them trusted Ial, so they tied their horses to the fence as requested.

The companions followed the dwarves along the main path through the center of the cavern. In front of Talia lay diverging pathways. Mushrooms the size of small dogs grew on the walls of one. She wondered what they would taste like. Her stomach rumbled, reminding her lunch had been cut short. Talia glanced back at Naul. Now she knew why he had asked if the procapras were good eating. If she was hungry, he must be starving.

The group entered the tunnel on the other side of the cavern. Talia snuck one more glimpse into the light behind her before entering the darkness again.

The companions traveled in silence. The dwarves brought no torches at all this time. They must have been intimately familiar with the route or could see much better than the humans could in the faint light.

Talia fought panic. The deep shadows might hide pits and dangerous protrusions. Her worries seemed to rub off onto her guardians, who stayed closer than normal. Dew held her hand on one side, Ial on the other. Naul and Nyna walked ahead and practically dragged their feet to test the path. Gregor trailed behind.

A sharp turn blocked the meager light from the farming cavern. Talia froze in the complete darkness. She heard the grumbling of the guards at her hesitation. Low light was dangerous enough. She wasn't going to move another step until she could see again.

As Talia's eyes adjusted to the absence of light, a faint glow emanated from the walls. Tiny mushrooms lined the earthen tunnel. Each one let out a dim light, but in the complete darkness, it was better than nothing.

The only dwarves Talia and her people came into contact with were the Eckerd in the east. That society preferred to live in homes carved out of the mountain side, but they still spent most of their time above ground. Talia wondered how long it had taken the Krimmel to grow accustomed to completely underground living.

To be so far from the Light's Blessing would be torture to the princess. She found herself grateful she was not a dwarf.

CHAPTER TWENTY

The dark tunnel finally emptied onto a street. Judging by the worn stone paving and multiple businesses, it was the busy part of town. Yet, Talia didn't see another living soul outside of the party. The quiet gave Talia goosebumps. She wanted to say something but felt it would be disrespectful to break the eerie silence.

Woven homes, constructed from a sort of vine or root, lined the walkway. The princess heard twittering coming from above her head. She caught a glimpse of a figure ducking out of view on a roof top. Talia postulated most of the population hid while trying to catch sight of the humans. How odd it must be to have a species not seen for eight hundred years reappear out of nowhere.

The companions entered another much shorter passageway that lead them to massive homes carved directly into the walls of the cave. A few dwarves in colored clothing peeked through window coverings at the procession. Talia had spent enough of her life in noble homes to realize they were in the rich part of town. She wondered if this was the entire Krimmel Kingdom in one area or if it represented one city among many.

As the group took yet another turn, Talia felt a bit more comfortable with her surroundings. She had not seen any crevices or unsafe footing. Wherever the priest had to take her was obviously along a well-worn path.

The last tunnel ended at a huge audience chamber. Steps chiseled out of the granite climbed down onto a center stage. The flight the companions took was one of six scattered around the circular room. Between the sets of stairs were stone seats. The quartz in the granite shimmered as the torchlight bounced off its surface, like fairies dancing in a ring. Talia smiled to herself. Fairies. Now that would be an adventure.

Around the center stage were stools too short for most human children. In the middle of the raised platform was a tall dais that held a chair. The seat back was higher than the highest row of stone seats. The border of the velvety red upholstery sparkled with precious gems. A large torch was mounted on each side of the rectangular dais.

"If you will please choose your seat, we will begin." The priest indicated the stools surrounding the center stage.

Talia had seen this kind of grandstanding before. The king would take the throne on high, demanding his subjects look up at his grandeur. The light from underneath would shadow the ruler, making him seem mysterious and otherworldly.

Talia smiled. Finally, something her training as a princess prepared her for. She sat in the stool immediately in front of the throne. She needed to befriend him if she had a chance of discovering the diamond.

Her companions sat beside and behind their charge. The priest's assistant pulled down a lever attached to the stage. The now familiar sound of moving stone filled the chamber. Doors slid into the floor at the top of each set of stairs. Hundreds of dwarves stomped into the chamber, the sudden racket shocking after the almost noiseless trip through the underground kingdom.

As the audience filled the seats, Talia covered her nose with her sleeve. The onslaught of cologned dwarves mixed with sweating dwarves in the closed chamber assaulted her senses. She dropped her hand at a look from Dew. She had to consider the proper decorum for a meeting between two royals.

She studied the audience to glean what information she could. Dwarves clothed in brightly colored, tailored tunics and slacks took the seats closest to the top. They must have been the nobility, for they weren't required to look so far up at their king. The middle layer of dwarves, by far the most numerous, wore tunics and pants and hats in muted colors. They whispered to each other excitedly. The words echoed off the stone walls, garbling them into an unintelligible buzz. The last group to filter in were dressed in the dirt-colored overalls of the farmers they'd already met.

Talia raised an eyebrow at the similarity between this set up and gatherings in Tarbinulus. After centuries of separation, the dwarves had established social classes like the humans. She wondered what else they had in common. Maybe she would have the chance to reason with the king of the Krimmel to help her with her quest.

The superior priest stepped onto the stage, below one of the torches. He held his hands up. His silver robes shimmered from the flickering fire. The audience stopped fidgeting, blanketing the chamber in complete silence.

"The greatest king to sit upon the throne since the Krimmel carved the kingdom out of limestone and granite, King Greleck Stoneworth deems you worthy to look upon his glory." The clean-shaven dwarf twisted his wrists and then dropped his hands to his sides.

The slap of his thighs was followed by a minor explosion. Talia tried to jump to her feet, but the low stool made springing difficult. Instead, she fell to her knees, arms flailing. Naul caught an arm and set her back up on her wooden peg. A whiff of sulfur assaulted her senses as a plume of circular smoke rose from the stage to cover the dais. The audience gasped.

Through the dissipating smoke, she could see a stout figure sitting on the throne. The smoke bomb had hidden his entrance well. Talia was glad High Priestess Nomyra hadn't discovered this trick. The Great Hall would be filled with smoke on a regular basis.

King Greleck sat tall in his elevated throne, glaring at his subjects. Talia had a hard time making out his features. The torches from below threw his face into shadow. His dark beard moved slightly on his face, as if his mouth clenched and unclenched. With what emotion, Talia could only guess. He wore a tall crown, almost as tall as his torso, which glittered with precious gems like the throne. In his right hand, he held a petite scepter mounted with a huge diamond.

Talia felt a pull in her stomach. Her anxiety made itself known. The large crystal rock could be the Holy Diamond.

"Why has access to my kingdom been granted to these... humans?" King Greleck spit the word out like sour beer.

"They came bearing the aspen branch of legend." The superior priest received the seed-laden limb from the younger silver-robed dwarf.

"Does not the legend establish that only the branch-bearer is to gain entry?" The king was obviously not satisfied with the priest's explanation. "I see six humans before me. More than have been permitted entry in eight centuries!"

"It is extreme, oh great King." The priest's tone sounded more like a teacher addressing a student than a subject addressing a ruler. "However, the human princess met the prophecy in the Ancient Tome."

Talia thought she saw the king clutch his scepter more tightly. He knew what the prophecy meant and looked unwilling to part with his symbol of power.

"Is it true?" A dwarf hung his head over the edge of a landing above the throne.

He broke the illusion of a smooth ceiling when he peeked over the side. Otherwise, Talia would never have spotted it.

"Get back up there, Aleck. You're supposed to be observing, not participating." King Greleck spoke through clenched teeth.

"But, Father, if the priest speaks true, it's time to open our doors. Our isolation ends." The dwarf the king had called Aleck flipped over the edge onto a hidden ladder on the back of the tall throne. The young man was spry for a dwarf. He slid down and landed on the dais to join the superior priest.

"Get back up there, Aleck." The king's angry whisper carried across the chamber.

The dwarf ignored his father. His eyes sparkled like the quartz in the surrounding granite. He put his hands on his hips as he addressed the superior priest. "Please, Jurick. Recite the Ancient Tome prophecy these humans met."

"I would be honored, Prince Aleck." The superior priest stepped forward and stood stiffly. He spoke in a trance-like voice:

"The Holy Diamond shall be protected
By the King of the Dwarves
Until the blood of the True Heir
Shines through the Darkness,
Calling the Holy Gemstones home,
The Reunion of Blood, Holy Gemstones, and Key
Will bring the Recharging,
Opening all doors
And awakening the ancients."

Talia frowned at the mention of the Recharging again. The princess wanted to control her own destiny, but she wasn't anxious to be responsible for revitalizing the entire planet. All the talk of planets and blood and destiny gave her a headache.

"Beautifully recited, Superior Priest Jurick." The prince clapped his hands appreciatively. "Which one is the True Heir?"

"The central female figure, Prince Aleck. Her companion's call her Princess Talia Winterlaus of Tarbin."

The king scoffed upon his throne. "A girl? How can a girl be the True Heir?"

Talia rolled her eyes. Was every king the same?

"The blood cannot lie, my King," said the superior priest.

"Does she talk?" the prince asked.

"Yes, Prince Aleck, I speak." Talia couldn't hold back in silence any longer. "I'm on a quest to collect the Holy Gemstones lost from the Tarbin crown a millennium ago."

"Sounds like you're on a grand adventure! I've never left the inside of this mountain." Prince Aleck rubbed his hands on his knees. "Can I see your blood?"

"It looks like normal blood." Talia shrugged apologetically. She somehow didn't want to disappoint this lively dwarf.

"You see!" The king pointed at the princess. "She claims to be ordinary, as no True Heir would. She is not the one. Escort the intruders out before I decide to make an example of them."

"Oh, Father. They are not intruders. The superior priest invited them in." Aleck turned back to Talia. "Can I please see your blood? I want to know what has ole Jurick excited enough to call a Grand Hall Conclave. We haven't been together like this in years."

The dwarf audience mumbled in deep baritones, too muddled to make out any words. Many of the audience members sat on the edge of their seats. She wondered if she should be worried.

"She hesitates." The king stood on the edge of his throne, clutching the scepter close to his chest. His left hand balanced the awkwardly tall crown on his head. "She fooled the superior priest and tricked her way into our kingdom."

"I did no such thing." Talia forgot royal decorum as her temper flared. The king's accusations brought out her frustration from the past weeks. She pricked a fresh finger with her belt dagger, holding her hand to the prince. "Here."

"She is correct. It looks to be normal, red blood." Aleck's quieter tone gave away his disappointment.

The superior priest stepped off the stage with his ring in hand. After a nod from Talia, he gripped her wrist, allowing a good view from the audience as well as the dais. He squeezed a drop onto the gem of his ring.

As in the clearing, the stone absorbed it and emitted a blue glow.

The small light flashed through the cave, sending the stoic dwarves into panicked discussion. Talia accepted a handkerchief from Naul to wrap around her finger.

"Outrageous!" shouted the king. He was so upset he forgot to straighten the crown, which leaned precariously to the right. "The blood has to come from a dwarf. Humans only destroy in this world. Dwarves create. Why would Almighty Thoretick give the gift to humankind?"

"It is not our place to question what is," admonished the superior priest.

"Well, it is my place. My kingdom depends on me to protect it. I will not relinquish the Holy Diamond to a human girl who can perform a cheap parlor trick."

"Can I see the ring?" Aleck's calm curiosity was a complete contrast to his father's rage.

The superior priest handed it to him.

"It's warm." The prince held out his other hand to Talia without taking his eye off the ring. "May I borrow your blade?"

Talia handed it to him, ignoring Naul as he scooted closer to her.

"I am the heir to the Krimmel Kingdom, Father." Prince Aleck scratched his index finger and dripped the blood on the gem. He held the ring up for the chamber to see. "Nothing is happening. If not me, Father, then who? Humans and dwarves lived and worked together for thousands of years. Maybe it is time to revisit the old ways."

The king climbed off the dais, reaching the stage with almost the same grace his son had used. Aleck caught the slipping crown before it hit the ground, putting it back on his father's head.

"The Holy Diamond must decide." The king held the scepter before his son. "It will choose you."

The son obeyed his father. He squeezed his finger enough to get a couple more drops to splash on the flawless diamond. The king gripped the handle fiercely. Talia knew if the king's will was strong enough the gem would shine.

"The Holy Diamond doesn't choose me, my King." The prince

gently pried the older dwarf's fingers from the scepter, never losing eye contact.

Prince Aleck held the scepter before Princess Talia. She remembered High Priestess Nomyra shattering an identical-looking piece at her Forging Ceremony. She took her dagger and, once more, cut the skin on a third finger. The sharp pain made Talia consider another body part to bleed.

She dripped on the proffered gem. As the deep red liquid fell onto the diamond, Talia wondered how many scars she would have if her blood was required to test every piece of jewelry.

Aleck's eye grew as his hands trembled. Talia couldn't tell if the shudder originated as an emotional reaction or something internal to the gem. A force from the diamond pulled Talia to its surface and held on. She gasped in shock and tried to remove her finger from the jewel. It was as if her warm flesh and the cold stone were one.

"She dares touch the diamond." The king accused Talia in a voice as if she'd just killed his first born.

King Greleck's voice came to Talia through a filter, as her consciousness was pulled into the gem.

A female voice filled her mind. A mist swirled around her, white and opaque. "Maitliin... don't... how can it be... not possible." A male voice chanting in a language Talia didn't recognize sent shivers down her spine.

"Let go of me!" Talia ordered the inanimate object. It released her, sending her stumbling backward. Naul caught the princess before she could trip. Aleck shot the other way, falling hard on his backside with the scepter still in his hands. Before he could gain his footing, a blue beam of light shot from the Holy Diamond. It hit the granite ceiling and bounced around the chamber. Dwarves hit the floor, trying to avoid the unknown threat.

If she hadn't known any better, Talia thought the diamond had obeyed her command to let her go.

The princess almost tripped over the prone dwarf clutching the scepter. Her companions covered their eyes to ward off the brightness Talia was immune to. "Stop," she said.

The light immediately extinguished. Aleck dropped the scepter. Talia caught it before it could hit the ground.

"What an exciting life you must lead." The prince bounced to his feet. The rest of his subjects shakily looked up. "Come on out. It's over, unfortunately."

"Talia, are you okay?"

She blinked at Gregor, uncomprehending at first. Those haunting voices still ran around, familiar yet foreign.

"She is the True Heir." From the dais, Superior Priest Jurick addressed the audience. "The Holy Diamond responded to her blood and obeyed her commands. I vote for Princess Talia Winterlaus of Tarbin to take possession of the Holy Diamond until such time as the Recharging has passed and the world is no longer in need of it."

"Then it will return to Krimmel where it belongs," the king insisted.

"Agreed," said Talia, realizing the dwarves might let her take the jewel with her.

"All who say aye?" The king took over the vote.

A deep-voiced roar echoed the dwarves' acceptance. The wide-eyed fear Talia witnessed on the dimly lit faces probably had something to do with their willingness to rid themselves of the Holy Diamond they had thought only ceremonial.

Talia could not get the vision of mist and voices out of her mind. Who was Maitliin? What did he have to do with the jewels from the Tarbin crown? What was the odd language they had spoken? Once again, Talia found herself with more questions than answers.

CHAPTER TWENTY-ONE

TALIA COULD SEE the light at the end of the tunnel. For almost a month, three priests had led the humans through dark chambers and pathways to get to the other side of the Krimmel Kingdom. The educated group had acted as translators for the deeper communities of dwarves who didn't speak Common. The king had assigned the two guards who first spotted the humans to protect the Holy Diamond until the priceless gem returned to its home in the mountain. Talia wondered if the dwarves were being rewarded or punished.

Talia missed her pony, Ruix. The companions had had to squeeze through tiny crevices in the more isolated parts of the cave system. The horses and wagon would've never made it to the other side. Aleck had insisted the king allow Talia to take a pack of procapras as trade for her horses and wagon. After much grumbling, he had agreed. Talia had shaken hands with him after she negotiated the loan. She loved Ruix too much to abandon him.

The king had thrown in a shepherd to herd the procapras. The rural dwarf remained quiet and kept to himself for the entire trip. Talia assumed he was better with animals than people.

As the sunlight bounced off the quartz in the granite mountain, Talia was eager to leave the land of eternal night and winter chill. She restrained herself from running toward the opening. She recalled the tale of a shipwrecked sailor who had been saved after one week in the open water. The first thing the man had done was kiss the solid ground. Talia finally understood his motivation. Rolling around in the grass and soaking up the warmth from the Light's Daughter sounded as close to paradise as she could imagine.

"That looks wide open. Is this part of your kingdom completely accessible?" Gregor noticed the anomaly first. Talia was too happy to see the outside again to question its presence.

"It is an open cave, but those who don't know the way cannot enter." Priest Trulick refused to elaborate. "You will see. Do not go ahead of me from this moment on."

Priests Trulick and Reinum led the way, followed by Dew, Gregor, and Nyna. The scepter's dwarf guards, Dragick and Gallick, stuck by Talia's side closer than her own guardians. The scepter wasn't leaving their sight. She considered handing it over to someone else to give herself some breathing room. Naul, Ial, and Priest Trinum walked behind, with the shepherd and gear bringing up the rear.

Trulick turned down a small tunnel to the left of their current path. Talia hadn't noticed the branching tunnel until the priest's torch lit up the tight quarters. She thought about the hidden ledge above King Greleck's throne.

Talia eyed the straight, wide path leading to the end of the cavern. Fresh air from the outside brushed past the companions. So close. Moving away from the light into a smaller, darker space felt like torture.

"Don't even consider it. The easy path leads to death," Priest Trinum warned.

The companions exchanged worried looks.

Talia had to duck to squeeze into the side tunnel. The party shifted into single file.

"I don't think I'm going to make it through the opening." Naul's shoulders were too wide.

"Suck it in, big guy." Ial smacked him on the shoulder. The smaller guardian walked through without ducking.

Priest Trulick bent down and picked up a loose rock. She threw the reddish-gray object, the size of her fist, as far as she could toward the light. Through random holes in the wall, Talia watched the dark object arch up and then down.

"Did you hear the rock hit?"

"Shhh." Trinum hushed Ial before he could finish.

The stone had been out of the priest's hand for many seconds when Talia heard a faint splash. A fierce battle erupted below the surface. Splashing and growling and slapping echoed from below. Talia's eyes grew as she imagined how large the creature must be to make so much noise over a tiny splash.

"What is that?" whispered Nyna, pressed tightly against the wall.

"The troglo salamanders. They slumber until awoken. Once conscious, their appetite is insatiable."

"Hold on. You just woke up a vicious predator to prove a point?" Dew's hands clenched as she froze in the tunnel.

"Your friend looked in need of motivation." Priest Trinum shrugged. "We should depart before the salamanders decide to make the long climb to investigate further."

Cursing under his breath, Naul scrunched his shoulders in and bent in half to fit into the cave. It might have been easier if he crawled, the muscled man looked so uncomfortable.

Luckily, the side tunnel wasn't that long. It ended close enough to the entrance to see needles on tree branches swaying in the breeze. Talia smelled sticky sweet pine. The chill in the air told her they were still high up in the mountains. It should have been warmer this time of year. That narrowed down the possible routes to take to the Elven Forest.

The companions fell out of the close quarters like spores popping out of a mushroom. Naul practically rolled, unable to straighten his back after the awkward angle he'd struck. The companions stumbled toward the opening, heedless of any order.

"Wait," said Priest Trulick.

Talia froze, half expecting a man-sized salamander to jump out from the dark.

"You must cross exactly along this granite beam to the opposite side, then hug the wall to the exit."

"Sounds easy enough." Ial followed immediately behind the robed dwarf to the outside world. He arrived unharmed. "Just don't look down."

"Don't look down?" Talia was puzzled. The ground was solid all the way around the granite beam. She dipped a foot off to the right of the inches thick beam and encountered nothing but air. The illusion now broken, the steep drop so cleverly cut into the path to make it look like flat ground popped into Talia's reality. The temporary blindness from staring at the sunlight above ground made it difficult to see anything. It was brilliant.

"How do they do that?" asked Nyna beside her.

"I don't know. They've obviously learned a lot dwelling in a cave for centuries."

Talia held her breath and crossed as quickly as she could. She reached the outside with a deep breath. The crisp air smelled new and inviting. The temperature was no colder than in the cave, but the movement sent a shiver down her spine. What an odd thing to miss, a breeze. She caught a whiff of her companions and realized it had been a week since they bathed. First on her priority list was to find a stream to wash the grime and sweat off.

Talia watched the rest of the party cross the bridge from the darkness.

"What about the procapras?" Her high-pitched voice gave away her nervousness.

"Don't worry, Princess," assured Guard Dragick. "They have been domesticated from a species that climbs thin, rocky ledges on the most severe mountains. The edge is large for them."

The shepherd herded the procapras to the stone crossing. A whiff of fetid moisture, so strong Talia could smell it from outside, seeped from the cavern. The procapras hesitated. Talia had never seen the animals blink, let alone stutter on the path. A thump shook the granite bridge, followed by a grumbling growl foreign to Talia.

The procapras panicked. They ran along the edge. Most of the animals reached the far side, hit the wall, and then turned to the left to the outside. One animal ran in the wrong direction in its panic. It avoided a fall by climbing on meager footing along the far wall. It leaped across the last gap, heading back into the darkness. Talia prayed to the Light the animal didn't carry anything essential. The last pack animal ran into the rear of the procapra ahead of it. It jumped to the right, missed the ledge, and fell off, screaming, into the darkness. The shepherd dived forward, grabbing the back leg of the flailing ungulate. He used the momentum of the fall to swing the beast back onto the edge. The procapra's legs didn't stop moving until it reached safety.

Unable to correct his balance, the shepherd's arms wind-milled as his center of gravity shifted precariously over the edge. The guards ran back into the cave and grabbed the shepherd before he could fall. The bridge shook again. A scraping sound, like the guard's spear on stone, filled the entrance. The three fell to their knees and crawled to the wall leading out.

"Watch out!" yelled Ial, retrieving his bow and an arrow from his quiver. Reaching out of the darkness, a webbed lizard foot gripped the granite bridge. A salamander head the size of a horse's, with bright red markings, followed.

An arrow hit the salamander square on the snout. It roared with an unnatural sound, shaking its head from side to side. More salamanders joined its complaint. They didn't sound too far behind. Ial nocked an arrow for a second assault.

"Move it!" Talia shouted to the guards, pulling out her sword to protect the fleeing dwarves.

"Don't worry. They won't come into the light," the shepherd huffed, trying to catch his breath.

The salamander, with an arrow shaft sticking out of its head, pulled its torso onto the bridge. Talia saw her reflection in the big green eyes. The salamander arched its head back, then used one foot to shield his eyes.

The shepherd fell onto the grass, throwing his head up to breathe in as deeply as possible. "The salamanders have no eyelids. The light is extremely painful." With his head tilted back, his hood slipped off. He tried to grab the cloth, but it was too late.

"My Prince?" Both Guards Dragick and Gallick bowed simultaneously. The three young priests stood frozen, unsure how to proceed.

"Prince Aleck?" Talia asked.

"Well, I guess now is as good a time as any to reveal myself. There's no going back after that." The Prince of the Krimmel gained his feet and tossed aside his shepherd's cloak.

"My Prince, you have deceived us." All the color faded from Priest Trulick's face. "Your father will be furious. We will be punished."

"No, you won't," reassured the prince. "I tucked a detailed note into his crown. When he dons it for audience day, he will know my plan. It's time for us to open our doors. We are stagnating under that mountain. No better than those troglo salamanders, unable to enter the world of Light. We might be people of stone, but we don't have to always be surrounded by Darkness. The Light loves us too."

"You have to go back, Prince Aleck." Talia tried reasoning with the dwarf. She had enough to worry about. She didn't want to add the protection of foreign royalty to the list. "We're not even sure where we're going next. I can't guarantee your safety. I don't want relations between our peoples to begin with a princess from my world responsible for the death of a prince from yours."

"But the prophecy is about to be fulfilled. We will open our doors and none of my people have any knowledge of other modern cultures. We are sorely unprepared. I will act as a liaison for my subjects." Aleck gathered the procapras into a tight circle.

Talia smiled. He must have played shepherd too long to ignore his duties. She really liked Aleck. He seemed to know much more about the Recharging and the history of the Holy Gemstones. Maybe he could be an asset on her journey.

Besides, the prince seemed determined to come along. Who was Talia to tell a member of a foreign royal family what he was or was not allowed to do?

"I guess you're welcome to come," Talia concluded.

"I, Gregor Rivenwood of Kenia, land of the wheat fields, would like to begin trade with the Krimmel." Gregor held out his hand in friendship. "I would be honored to be your first human business partner."

"I accept." Aleck looked at Gregor's extended hand, then at his own. He held up his left hand.

Gregor nodded to the dwarf's other one. Aleck switched and held it out steadily. Gregor encircled his long fingers around the dwarf's stout ones.

"Then it's official." Gregor shook the grip up and down.

"Please, Your Highness," pleaded Priest Trulick, rubbing his chin where his beard should have been. "You must accompany us back to your duties. It is not safe out here."

"You can send representatives to the human world as soon as we return." Priest Trinum tried to persuade Aleck. "You don't have your honor guard. The best future you can offer is continued existence."

"What about these two guards? They have performed admirably on this trip. And they've already saved my life once." Prince Aleck referred to Guards Dragick and Gallick.

"They are not trained in personal defense," protested Priest Trinum.

"They protect an entire kingdom. I think they can handle one little prince." Aleck made it clear he wasn't going back into the cave.

Dragick and Gallick straightened their backs and tapped their spears on the ground in unison.

The priests admitted defeat. They said their goodbyes to traverse back through the kingdom and report to the king.

"So, where to now?" asked Aleck.

The exuberance pouring off the dwarf was contagious.

"We have to decide our next move," Talia said.

"Maybe this will help." Aleck produced a full color map from an inside pocket of the robes he had tossed aside earlier.

"By the Light, it's beautiful." Nyna helped Aleck unfold the parchment.

"Let me find the tome." Dew, with Ial's help, isolated the procapra that carried her books. She leaned over the map displayed on the grass. "Thanks to the Light, these didn't disappear with the fleeing procapra."

"We have come out here." Aleck pointed to the western side of the Krimmel Mountain Range.

"This map isn't accurate. I'm not sure we can trust it." Talia pointed to the center of the continent. "It has a large city and forested landscape south of the Eckerd Mountain Range. There's nothing but desert and roaming tribes in that area."

"It has Tarbin as the name of the entire continent instead of our kingdom in the northeast. We call the land mass the Renquist Continent," Dew pointed out.

"Look at all those roads." Nyna traced one that followed a river in what was now Gandariul in the south. "It's like a twisty basket of yarn. They go everywhere."

Aleck flipped the map over. "The map isn't false. It's old. My ancestors used this map as they sought out a new place to live after the Civil War." A cave system drawn in three pieces representing different levels filled the back. "This was used to establish our first cities under the mountain seven hundred years ago."

He traced a finger along an underground river. "The water's flow has shifted south, running through a ravine, from when this map was made. The entrance to our kingdom in the north has since collapsed. We don't go to that section of the mountain at all."

"The older the better for our purposes. Our modern knowledge hasn't helped on this journey yet." Dew flipped the pages of the tome to the introduction.

Talia helped Aleck turn the map back to the world view. "Weren't the mermaids one of the civilizations mentioned? This map has them near the frozen islands in the Southern Sea as well as a smaller location in the Ngaro Ocean to the north."

"Mermaids." Dew ran her finger along one of the descriptions in the book. "Yes. It says the mermaids protected the Holy Black Opal."

Naul rubbed his bald head. "Looks like we need a boat."

"Which is going to be difficult without the gold." Ial pointed toward the cave. "The procapra that panicked had the gold trunk on him."

"Curse the Dark." Talia clenched her fists and walked in a circle, thinking.

Gregor swallowed hard. "The point is moot anyway."

Talia turned to him, her eyebrows raised. "What are you talking about?"

"Prince Tanin booked a ship out of Tarbinulus heading directly to the Kiwa Islands. By now, he should already have the Holy Black Opal."

Naul gripped the hilt of his sword. Talia put a hand on his arm without looking away from the lordling.

"How do you know this?"

Every eye in the group watched Gregor's response. "He told me his travel plans the day before the Forging Ceremony. He bragged that the Holy Diamond would be delivered to him at the port. I told him I wasn't sure it was the Holy Diamond, but he wouldn't listen. I had to know if I was right."

"So you wormed your way into my party with only the vaguest notion of a legend and the connection of an old friend?" Talia's anger simmered. Her arms shook. Her lips paled.

"Are you spying for him?" Naul accused, his grip tightening on his weapon.

Dew stood and closed her book. Nyna and Ial flanked Gregor. Aleck gasped at the human conflict like he was watching a play. The dwarf guards backed their prince away from the group.

"No, of course not." Gregor kept his hands out, away from his sword belt. "I just had to know."

"Know what?" Talia's tone warned the lordling to explain himself well.

"I had to know if Master Overstone was a madman or a prophet. He told me my family, the Rivenwoods, are an ancient family of protectors. I must aid the True Heir in his quest to find the Holy Gemstones. He told me all of this when I was at school, but I brushed it off. It wasn't until Prince Tanin talked about his quest that I started to believe the old dwarf."

"That's what Old Stoney was referring to when he talked about *your* destiny." Talia crossed her arms. At least that was one question answered.

"At the Forging Ceremony, when you were permitted to participate, I took a chance. I've always felt I was meant for something more than ruling over farmers like my father." Gregor pleaded with Talia. "This might be the only way to find out."

Talia studied the ground. She understood that nagging feeling. It had haunted her most of her life. She thought it was the unfairness of being the firstborn and not being allowed to be the heir. After the incident with her blood on the Holy Diamond, Talia knew her instincts were right and she was destined for something great. How could she deny Gregor the same discovery?

Dew asked what Talia should have. "Who do you think is the True Heir?"

Talia raised an eyebrow, waiting for his answer. Gregor blinked at Dew, then Talia, then back again.

"I—I don't know. I thought for sure it was Tanin. He's the heir apparent, right?" He nodded to Naul for support.

The defense guardian's face reddened. Talia felt the heat pouring off his body. She needed to settle this before Naul crushed the lordling. Unless she *wanted* to let him resort to violence. She hadn't quite decided yet.

"According to the *Articles of Royal Deference*, the royal child of age who completes the Forging Quest successfully is the heir. I've never seen True Heir defined." Dew held the tome to her chest. She appeared calm, but she stood lightly on her feet, prepared for action.

"The True Heir is a prophecy, not a royal title." Prince Aleck spoke from the sidelines. Dragick stopped him from moving forward.

"Okay. Fine. I have no idea who the True Heir is, but I want to find out," Gregor acquiesced.

"Where does that leave me?" Talia asked. "I can't trust you. How do I know you're not going to give the Holy Diamond to Tanin as soon as you see him?"

"These strong guards would have something to say about that." Gregor gestured to the burly dwarves. Both nodded their heads and crossed their arms.

"Do you know where Prince Tanin was heading next?" Nyna sat down next to the map on the grass.

"No."

"Then what good are you?" Talia felt her ears go red. She resisted the urge to punch the lordling. That's what her brother would do. She vowed to rule more sensibly.

"I do know he planned to dock at Port Thelioma in the south and meet the ship back in Darvis at the capital port." Gregor rolled his shoulders. "I might have overheard Rory finalize the shipping schedule with the captain when I was leaving Tanin's chambers."

"So he's traveling by land from the south to the northwest." Nyna dragged her finger along a northern path.

Aleck shrugged off his guards.

"He will probably stop at the nadph. They are one of the ancient races." Aleck knelt by the map. He pointed to Naddle Swamp, slightly north of Port Thelioma.

Talia turned her back on Gregor. She'd deal with him later. "We'll never beat him to that one. Where do you think he's going next?"

Dew folded the map to focus on their location. "The Elven Forest is to the northwest of us. Depending on how long the prince spends getting the Holy Black Opal and Holy Emerald, we might be able to beat him to the Holy Sapphire."

Nyna shifted her pack over her shoulder. "They say it's guarded by the ghosts of the extinct elves."

"We have the bulk of the mountain range to cross to get far enough west. It might look shorter, but it's slow going. Tanin only has to travel north through the plains. He'll beat us." Talia tapped her foot. Why were there so many obstacles?

"We could go to the Krimmel Aviary and borrow some giant eagles." Ial pointed to a spot next to a modest crater lake. "I've been there once. I should be able to find it again."

Gregor spoke, forgetting everyone was mad at him. "It looks like the aviary is only a few days away. Then a two-day flight to the Elven Forest."

The companions glared at him. The lordling backed away and offered no further suggestions.

"Flying? That sounds exciting!" Aleck clapped his hands together. "We have to do that."

Talia concurred with the unanimous vote. Gregor walked in front of her as the party headed west. She had to decide what to do with the lordling. She certainly couldn't trust him. Maybe she'd leave him at the aviary to make his own way home. Talia understood his need to find his own path, instead of the one set out by his father. It was the reason she was on this crazy quest. But she had never lied or cheated to get where she was. How far was Gregor willing to go to escape his future and fulfill his destiny? Talia would have to keep a close eye on him.

CHAPTER TWENTY-TWO

THE OUTSKIRTS of the swamp looked more homogeneous than Tanin expected. The species of naddle filling it resembled the one in the Royal Forest of Tarbinulus. The lowest branches hung fifteen feet up. Unlike the single specimen he was used to, every branch was bare as far as Tanin could see. The lack of leaves made him uncomfortable.

"Only naddle trees? I've never seen an entire forest made up of one species." Kettlor touched the bark, tracing the rough patterns with his fingers.

"Maybe they only look the same because the leaves have fallen," Rory postulated.

"I don't see any debris on the ground." Orui peered through the tree trunks. "The naddle tree in the garden never loses its leaves."

"I don't care about the foliage. Does the lore warn us about anything before we enter?" Tanin focused on Tyler.

"It says only the invited are allowed in." The cultural guardian still favored his leg but was able to walk with the help of a cane.

"Well, good thing I'm invited. No one will turn away the heir of Tarbin." Tanin picked off bits of grass from his tunic. The week he'd spent on horseback to arrive at his next destination had left his clothes in need of a good cleaning. "Hopefully, there's no dress code."

Kettlor adjusted a saddle bag over his horse's flank. Tanin watched the container sway with the bulbous pearl the husbandry guardian had begged to keep. Tanin's lip twitched at his failure to obtain the Holy Black Opal. Clinging to the leather pouch around his neck with the Holy Diamond, Tanin stared into the forest. If the Holy Emerald was not there, Nomyra would be exiled for her complete incompetence.

"It is midday. Why don't we stop for a quick meal while we study the map?" suggested Rory.

Without speaking, Tanin dismounted and led his horse into the tree line. He smiled as his guardians scrambled to dismount and follow their charge. Keep your servants on their toes, his father always said.

Who needs lunch? I'm on a vital quest.

The swampy smell overwhelmed Tanin as soon as he passed into shadow. Despite the dead appearance of the barren trees, the strong odor of decaying vegetation showed the true health of the wetlands. The ambient light dulled until the companions walked in complete darkness. Tanin's horse pulled on his reins, fear causing him to fidget and stomp his front legs.

"Everyone, stop!" Rory ordered.

Orui's deep voice came from over Tanin's left shoulder, but he couldn't see him. "How did it get so dark? The bare branches wouldn't block the light so completely, would they?"

Prince Tanin's voice reverberated in the silence. "No stopping. We must continue to the center of the swamp and talk with the Naddle Council."

A glowing object, no bigger than a man's fist, flashed in front of Tanin's vision. He shook his head, ignoring the illusion. The men walked a few more steps and found themselves outside the forest again.

"What was that ball of light?" Rory rubbed his eyes against the sudden brightness.

"You saw that, too?" Tanin tossed his head to get his bangs out of his eyes.

"Fairies," Tyler whispered as if speaking loudly would call the magical creatures down upon them.

Rory focused on the cultural guardian. "What did you say?"

"Fairies," Tyler repeated. "The naddle supposedly have fairies as companions."

Tanin scoffed at the idea. "What? Magic? Now you've lost your mind."

"Did we just walk in a circle?" asked Orui.

"Not without our horses." Kettlor pointed out the absence of the four-legged companions.

Tanin whistled for his gelding. He routinely summoned the trained warhorse from the deep forest at home that way. This time, no sound of cantering hoofbeats reached his ears.

"They must be lost in the dark as well." Tanin scowled at the dead trees. "High Priestess Nomyra said all paths lead to the center. We need only find a path."

Tanin stalked the perimeter, searching for a path or any sign of his horse. After an hour of walking, no path or animal showed itself.

"Enough. I'm heading in again." Tanin abruptly turned on his heel and breached the tree line.

The stench washed over the group.

"Why do we only smell decay when we cross into the trees?" Orui held his shirt collar over his nose.

Again, the swamp fell to complete darkness a few feet in.

"Maybe we haven't been invited? I'll see if I missed an invitation request." The sound of flipping pages came from Tanin's right. He shook his head, waiting for Tyler to realize his mistake. "I can't see."

"By the Light, we are heading deeper in and I don't want to hear another word of dissension." Tanin clutched the Holy Diamond around his neck.

A flash of light flitted in front of the men.

"There it is again." Tanin lifted his hand to try and grasp the glowing ball amid the deep darkness. He walked toward the vibrating light. "This way."

The prince's next step fell on soft grass outside the perimeter. He stomped on the ground, barely missing Rory's foot. He waved his fists at the midday sun. "You cannot stop me. It is my destiny."

"Ah!" Tyler held up a wax-sealed envelope with feminine handwriting on the outside. "I forgot the props."

Tanin grabbed the envelope from his cultural guardian. He whacked Tyler on the back of the head to shake up his scattered brains. The outside said: *To gain audience with the Naddle Council.*

Peeling off the wax seal, Tanin dumped five rings into his hand.

He put one on his right index finger and handed the rest to his guardians. Tanin stared at the golden jewelry, styled like leafy vines entwined together.

"This had better work." He marched forward, mustering all the confidence of an heir apparent.

Rory and Kettlor were at his side, with Orui and Tyler taking up the rear.

At the spot where the complete darkness engulfed the companions, the rings glowed. A crackling sound, like paper crumpling, flowed through the black. Tanin tracked the sound with his head. Following behind the odd noise, the swamp appeared.

The companions stepped into the inner part of the wetlands. Bare naddle trees dominated the herbage of the living swamp. A multitude of plant species filled the in-betweens of the green and brown swampland. A path of wooden planks opened up before the companions, beckoning them deeper into the wood.

"All paths lead to the center," whispered Tyler.

Tanin stepped onto the damp wood. His wide stride forced Rory to jog to get in front of him.

Tanin hadn't noticed the silence of the perimeter until they crossed into the inner section. Frogs croaked from one side of the path to the other, growing silent as the men got too close. Small birds jumped from branch to branch over their heads, twittering at the strangers in their sanctuary.

"Do you get the feeling these animals aren't used to visitors?" Kettlor asked.

"If no one can get into this forest, can anyone get out?" Tyler held up his hand with the ring. It sat on his finger like any ordinary piece of jewelry.

Kettlor surveyed the surroundings. "At least there are more trees than just naddles like the border suggested. This is much more what I expect from a wetland habitat."

Tanin rolled his eyes. He couldn't care less what kind of trees lived here as long as he retrieved the Holy Emerald.

"Did you see that?" asked Orui, pointing to yellow trumpet-shaped flowers on a vine climbing up a cypress tree.

"See what?" asked Rory.

"That flower moved." The medicinal guardian stared wide-eyed at his disbelieving companion. "I swear I saw it move."

"You probably saw a lizard or something. Plants don't move." Kettlor dismissed the claim.

Orui punched him in the shoulder. "Right. And forests don't go pitch black and kick you out either."

"Point taken," Kettlor conceded.

"More walking and less talking. We wasted enough time trying to get in." Tanin increased his pace, hoping his guardians would have too little breath to keep jabbering.

After a few hours of marching through the swamp, Tanin didn't notice the smell at all. Either it had faded or it didn't bother him anymore. His pace slowed as fatigue overtook his initial enthusiasm.

"I'm starving."

Tanin flipped a dismissive hand at the medicinal guardian. "I know, Orui. Everyone knows."

Orui's growling stomach had annoyed Tanin for the last hour while the companions followed the seemingly straight line. The deeper water under the wooden planks had moved farther away somewhere along the route. They were now surrounded by slimy mud, with the occasional slithering beast leaving behind a long trail.

"We should have eaten before we plunged into the forest." Kettlor took a large swig from his water bladder.

"I need to relieve myself." Tyler stopped at the side of the path and reached for his waist band.

"What are you doing?" Rory admonished the cultural guardian.

Tanin almost ran into Rory as he crossed in front of his prince to yell at the cultural guardian.

Tyler apologized profusely as he moved off the protected path. The mud made a sucking sound as he laboriously pulled his boots out of the sticky substance to keep moving forward. His limp more distinct through the rough terrain.

Rory turned to Prince Tanin. "I apologize, my Prince. Our surroundings are making us forget our manners."

"I couldn't care less if he wet himself. I need to get to the center of the forest and claim the Holy Emerald." Tanin glared at Rory for not understanding the urgency of his mission. "It'll take him much longer to traverse the terrain than to simply pee into a bush from here."

As if to prove his point, Tyler's panicked voice yelped, "Let go of me. Help!"

Tanin scowled at Rory. "See?"

"Stay with the prince," Rory ordered Kettlor and Orui as he plunged into the forest after Tyler.

Tanin leaped over a bush after his guardian, ignoring Kettlor's pleas to stay on the path. If they had to be delayed, Tanin wasn't going to miss any action. The walking with no discernible progress was eating at his soul.

The cultural guardian hacked at a red-flowered vine by his feet with his dagger. A back swing almost slashed Rory's arm.

"Why are you attacking the underbrush?" Rory's voice rang angry.

"It won't let go!" Tyler lost his balance and fell to the ground. He screamed.

Tanin saw the vine with spade-shaped leaves twisted around Tyler's bad leg. The vines dragged the guardian a foot deeper into the woods. Kettlor grabbed Tyler's hands and dug his feet into the mud. Rory chopped at the woody vines, trying to find the one around the cultural guardian's leg.

A roar echoed from deeper in the trees. Orui stood with his staff in front of the prince. Tanin looked up from the shaking ground. A vine-covered form rose out of the mud. Tentacles made of green ivy undulated around the cottage-sized beast. The angry howl reverberated from a large opening that had to be a mouth.

"Kettlor, we need your bow." Rory frantically slashed at the vines holding Tyler's leg.

Tyler clung to a cypress knee as Kettlor pulled out his bow and arrows. Another vine encircled Rory's ankle and knocked him off his feet.

Kettlor jumped onto a nearby rock. The archer shot arrows like hail at the attacking beast. Orui managed to grab Rory's arm before he could be swept into the growling mouth. Kettlor hit the beast three times in succession in the center of the mouth. The plant's roar quivered the red flowers bordering his jaw. It released its prey.

"Run!" Orui grabbed Tanin's elbow and drug him toward the path.

Over his shoulder, the prince saw Rory help Tyler to his feet. Kettlor and Rory took an arm each and carried the exhausted cultural guardian back to the path.

"What in the Darkness was that?" Orui swore, as he forced his feet through the mud.

"I don't know. I've never seen anything like it." Kettlor puffed along with his footfalls.

"Wait," Prince Tanin ordered, a few yards down the trail. "I don't hear or see anything behind us."

The men stopped running. Kettlor bent in half, putting his hands on his knees. "I haven't sprinted like that since we raided Professor Whitetop's herb cabinet."

"What happened to 'plants don't move?'" Orui punched the husbandry guardian on the arm.

"Plants don't move." Kettlor defended his statement. "Apparently, something that very much resembles a plant does."

"And eats people," added Tyler.

"From now on, we stay on the trail." Tanin waited for Rory to nod his assent.

CHAPTER TWENTY-THREE

"THERE'S STILL no sign of the horses." Kettlor sat cross-legged, surveying the surrounding swampland.

Tanin kicked at one of the walkway's wooden planks, impatient to keep going. His guardians had insisted on a break after walking for another hour after the vine creature attack. Orui complained about his scarred arm aching from his staff smacking the stiff vines. The swelling in Tyler's already injured leg had worsened.

The refusal of the center to show itself frustrated Tanin into a temper.

"Are we sure this is the right way? How do we know we've arrived if we don't know where we're going?" Orui had gotten more and more irritated as the endless walking continued.

"All paths lead to the center," Tyler repeated, though with less enthusiasm than at the start.

Tanin grew annoyed at the cultural guardian's faith in the high priestess's words. That woman had failed Tanin again. She would pay when he returned.

"We'll never get anywhere if we don't keep going." Tanin swept his hands in front of his body.

Rory and Kettlor stood, joints crackling. The uninjured two helped their ailing comrades to their feet.

Kettlor adjusted his bow. "How do we now we didn't pass the center two hours back?"

As if he had called it into existence, the wooden path ended in a pristine grassy field. There was no gradual change from wetlands to dry forest. The mud simply disappeared.

Orui crossed his good arm over his bandaged one. "I'm getting a bit tired of impossible things happening."

"Look at the trees." Ignoring the medicinal guardian's complaints, Kettlor stood on the edge of the path, pointing straight ahead.

A dozen naddle trees were planted in a circle around the perimeter of the field. Unlike their leafless brethren, these trees bore full branches of tear-shaped, serrated leaves. Jade-colored stone slabs of different sizes and thicknesses were stacked twice as high as a man in the center of the circle.

"Should we step off the path?" Tyler eyed the grass.

"I don't know if that's a good idea." Rory blocked Tanin's forward stride.

Tanin scoffed at his guardians. "So, we should stand all day on the edge, afraid to step into the unknown?" He pushed Rory aside and strolled into the clearing. "If we weren't supposed to be here, the Stars would not have sent us."

Rory gripped his sword hilt and followed his prince into the circle of naddle trees.

"Someone must be maintaining this lawn." Kettlor felt the blades with his hands. "I don't see a single weed."

"These trees are so healthy. The royal gardener would be impressed." Orui brushed his hand along the rough bark. "Nyna is going to be mad she missed this."

Tanin balled his fists at the mention of one of his sister's guardians. His journey was going poorly enough. He didn't need a reminder that it was also a competition.

Rory stood beside Prince Tanin while Kettlor and Orui inspected their surroundings, looking for traps or dangers of any sort. The group hadn't been on many adventures together, but they had visited keeps of varying friendliness toward Tarbin royalty.

"I have the instructions for the formal plea to borrow the Holy Emerald from the Naddle Council." Tyler flipped open his notes.

"Are they supposed to show up or do we summon them?" Tanin inspected the pedestal made of slabs of streaked jasper in greens and golds. The opaque stone displayed unique striped patterns that melted into each other as they traveled along the piece. Tanin reached out to touch it.

"The glowing orb!" Orui shouted.

Tanin cringed as he braced to be sent back to the outside of the forest. When nothing happened, he rotated on his heels, surveying his surroundings. There was indeed a light hovering over Orui. More flew from the surrounding woods. The orbs danced around the travelers.

"Hey!" Rory protested when one of them flew into his bag. He batted it away.

Dozens more flew out of the woods. One pulled Tanin's shirt. His hair was tied in a knot before he could swat the light. He grew dizzy at their erratic flight.

Rory's voice pitched in anger. "Giggling? Are they giggling?"

The persistent pests dived in, attacking Tanin and his guardians at once. They weren't hurting Tanin, but every part of his body was poked and prodded. For a single moment, a tiny, nude woman with four wings like a dragonfly landed on his upraised arm.

Tanin couldn't believe what he was seeing. Yet, how could he deny the evidence of his eyes? "Fairy."

"I thought we decided there was no such things as fairies?" Kettlor stood to the left of Tanin.

Orui yelled at Kettlor through clenched teeth and joined his prince on the other side. "You keep saying things aren't real that are trying to kill us."

Without warning, the fairies cleared the circle, disappearing among the naddle trees.

"My ring's gone." Rory held his empty finger for Tanin to inspect. A small drop of blood welled from the indentation.

The prince spread the fingers of his right hand. His ring was gone too, replaced by a small cut. A quick exchange of glances from his companions affirmed everyone's was missing.

"Come back here, you little pickpockets." Tanin turned in circles under the trees, threatening the fairies. In a moment of fear, he clutched the Holy Diamond around his neck. It was there.

"Quit giggling. It's not funny." Orui shot rude hand gestures at the tree dwellers.

A deep voice reverberated around the clearing. "It's pointless to yell at fairies. They are immune to reprimands. We should know."

"Who speaks?" Tanin demanded.

"I." The voice seemed to be coming from behind a tree.

"Come into the clearing so we can see you." Tanin moved back to the center.

"It has been a long time since we talked to humans." The bark on one of the naddle trees shifted. In the middle, a three-dimensional triangular shape formed. An oval hole opened below the nose-like projection. It moved up and down revealing the smooth skin under the rough bark. Above the nose, two eyes, complete with pupils, formed from the bark. "We'd forgotten you like to interact with a face."

Tanin, protected by Rory, stood tall in front of the talking naddle. He tried to hide his shock with anger. "How dare you sit and watch us without making yourself known."

"How dare you enter our sanctuary without a formal invitation." The tree reacted quickly for an inanimate object.

"Our naddle doesn't make a face out of bark or talk." Kettlor's arms hung at his side.

Orui punched the husbandry guardian's shoulder.

"I assure you he does." The bark mouth moved with the words.

"Your pets took our rings." Orui's cheeks shone bright red as he addressed the naddle.

"And were none too gentle about it either." Rory sucked a drop of blood from his tiny wound.

A cherry-sized nut shot out of the talking tree's highest branches. It hit Orui square on the forehead. Giggling erupted in the branches. The foliage bounced up and down jovially. Tyler laughed. Orui's glare hushed him.

"They don't take kindly to being called pets. The fairies and the nadph have been partners in this swamp for millennia. Though our number has dropped considerably in the last few centuries." His branches drooped.

Tanin glared at the wooden face. He was ready to collect the Holy Emerald and get out of there. "I am Prince Tanin Winterlaus, heir to the Tarbin throne. I have been sent on a quest to retrieve the Holy Gemstones to be reunited on the Tarbin crown. I am the True Heir decreed by the Stars."

"Your blood tells a different tale than your lineage." The face started to fade into the background. "Only the blood counts."

Tanin looked at his clotting finger. *What was this mad tree talking about?*

"What if he is the True Heir?" asked a voice, not quite as deep as the first.

Tanin turned on his heel as another naddle spoke. A third came to life on his right. The trees showed creativity as each bark face was uniquely structured. One had an exceptionally large nose. Another's eyes were close together. One after another, the naddle trees brought their faces to the front.

"This cannot be real." Kettlor rubbed his eyes. "We must have breathed in some sort of hallucinogenic vapor from the bog."

"And we all happen to be having the same hallucination? I don't think so." Orui turned in circles, calculating the danger.

Tyler sketched the Naddle Council as quickly as he could. Tanin scowled, annoyed with his enthusiasm.

The trees continued their debate, ignoring the humans.

"We were told to give it to the girl. I see no girl." The first naddle tree defended his decision.

"What girl?" asked Tanin.

"The Recharging looms," said a much higher-pitched voice. "How long do we wait?"

"He did have the rings. The astropriests were to give those only to the True Heir."

"The astropriests are human. Their memory is short."

"One of the humans *is* of the blood."

The deep-voiced tree seemed to be the head of the naddle, but not the king. The royal court would never argue with King Roland this way. Council was a good name for them. This was why Tanin would never allow a council of any power in his kingdom. Decisions took too long and required too much compromise.

"They carry the Holy Black Opal too," added the high-pitched voice.

Tanin froze at the mention. Were they still talking about him?

"We should give him the Holy Emerald. We won't make it another millennium."

"Our numbers have dropped more quickly than we anticipated," said a fourth voice from the right.

"We were told to give it to the *girl!*" shouted the original voice.

His trembling branches sent the fairies skittering into other trees. The companions took a step back at the naddle's ire. The other trees seemed unfazed.

"He has lived among the humans for too long."

"He does not see the slow death of our brethren."

"We must protect our future from the past."

"This human may be our only hope."

"We should give him the Holy Emerald."

"He could be an emissary."

"Are we in agreement?" The first tree questioned the rest.

The clearing grew quiet. Tanin couldn't tell what they had agreed on.

"We are agreed," responded the rest of the trees in unison.

Tanin moved to the side as the ground around the giant naddle tree groaned. Cracks formed in the pristinely manicured lawn. The fairies took flight excitedly. His roots sent dirt into the air as they tore the ground asunder. Tanin's guardians surrounded him.

"I have not moved in centuries." The old tree chuckled, sending a few leaves floating to the ground. He walked on his roots in a rhythmic pattern, keeping most of the knotty wood on the ground at any one time. "It feels good to stretch the roots."

"Our naddle tree doesn't do that," repeated Kettlor.

Orui punched him harder this time.

How the tree could "see" where he was going intrigued Tanin. If his face was a manifestation for the humans, where were his sensors? Tanin realized the naddle tree in the Royal Forest could do this as well. Maybe he'd have it burned to the ground. Who knew what information it had gathered over the years?

The council leader stopped within branch-reach of the pile in the center of the clearing. A swarm of fairies encircled it. The naddle removed the topmost piece of jasper with two limbs. Since the branches stood above his face, it looked like he was using his hair.

"Four millennia ago, the Brachian Volcano erupted, engulfing an ancestral cemetery with its molten lava. By studying the grave markers that survived the cataclysmic eruption, we found the site to be the final resting place of the originators of our species." He removed a second stone and placed it beside the first.

"As the digging continued, the largest bog jaspers ever found were uncovered. We recognized them as the remains of our revered ancestors who forged the path toward our society." Another striated piece joined the first two. The naddle handled the pieces like cherished children.

"After the Sundering, almost a thousand years ago, we were tasked with protecting the Holy Emerald." The deep-voiced tree removed a small piece from the top of the pedestal. "Who better to protect it than the spirits of those who made it possible for us to exist?"

The naddle held a goose-egg-sized emerald in his branches. The swarm of fairies circled the stone, their glow magnified by the faceted gem. Tanin blocked his eyes from the blinding green. The tree moved his facial façade lower on his trunk, placing his "eyes" at the same height as Tanin's. The prince locked his knees, uncomfortable but unwilling to show weakness.

"My brethren want me to give this to you because they are desperate, not because they trust you." Tanin felt air brush by his hair, as if the tree had sighed. "Know that I give you the stone because I am bowing to their need, not your power."

Tanin bristled at the insult. He held out his hand to accept the gem. "I will find all the Holy Gemstones and remount them on the crown, their proper home."

"The fairies will return you to your horses." The naddle tree dismissed the humans as he replaced the bog jasper at the top of the pedestal.

"Do we need the rings?" asked Tyler.

"You need not return."

The fairies, returning to balls of light, flew in circles around the group of humans. The clearing fell to blackness outside the group of humans. Tanin blinked once and found himself back at the perimeter of the swamp, staring at his missing gelding. The rest of the party stood stunned round him.

Prince Tanin held up the green stone in his hand. Rory handed him another pouch from his pack. The prince tucked the gem into the leather and put it around his neck with the Holy Diamond.

"Two down." Orui grabbed a snack of venison jerky from his saddlebag.

"Now burn it," Tanin ordered as he checked the straps on his saddle.

"I'm sorry, my Prince?" Rory paused with one foot in a stirrup. "Burn what?"

"It." Tanin motioned at the trees behind him.

"You want us to set the swamp on fire?" Tyler's mouth dropped open as he held onto his horse for support.

"Those trees on the outskirts are fairly dry. It will catch." Tanin tossed a torch from his pack to Kettlor.

"It's not an issue of whether it will burn or not." Rory waved his arms around in uncharacteristic animation. "My Prince, what about the naddle? Do they not deserve to live?"

"He insulted me. Which means he insulted Tarbin. I will not start my reign with enemies lurking behind my back." Tanin growled his command. "Now burn it. That's an order."

Tanin glared at his guardians. How dare they question his orders.

Orui pulled a torch from his bag and held it straight for Rory to light. "Hopefully, it will get those pesky fairies too."

He held the hot end to the lowest branch he could reach until it flashed into flame. He continued to another tree. Kettlor followed his lead with his own burning torch. Before long, the fire jumped from tree to tree without assistance.

Tanin caught tears in Tyler's eyes. When the cultural guardian noticed his prince staring, he wiped his face. Rory helped Tyler mount his horse before Tanin could reprimand him for his weakness.

"Now we depart." Tanin watched the flames burn through the withered branches. Most of them were dead already. He refused to feel guilty for cleaning up dead wood. New trees, normal ones, would sprout soon enough.

"We have a three-week journey north to the Elven Forest." Tyler pulled out his map as the rest of the guardians mounted up.

"My Prince, it will be tough to discern landmarks as night falls." Rory rode beside Tanin.

"Rory, you worry too much." Tanin looked up at the sky. "The Stars will guide us to the Holy Sapphire."

"Of course, my Prince."

CHAPTER TWENTY-FOUR

"Did the illusion work?" The head nadph of the council addressed a fairy as soon as she flew into his presence.

The fairy twittered in a high-pitched voice at remarkable speed.

"The humans attempted to set fire to our sleeping brethren?"

"We should not have given them the Holy Emerald."

"Only a subordinate was of the blood."

"Do not fret for our sleeping brethren. Emelda and Espyn spied on their actions to protect us. When they saw torches, they conjured the image of a great blaze engulfing our home."

"The humans did not notice the lack of heat?"

"Truly an inferior species to be fooled so easily."

"How do we retrieve the Holy Gemstones? The Recharging cannot be delayed."

"It is time to trust our brother in the Ancient Garden." The animated tree placed a stone onto the green grass by his roots.

"The Holy Emerald? You still possess it."

"We agreed to give it to the humans. You have disobeyed the will of the council."

"I will accept your gratitude on a later date." His tone left no room for debate. Two fairies swept out of his upper branches. "It is time to visit your sister."

The fairies held hands, hovering over the stone.

"You send the Holy Gemstones to the human stronghold?"

"We have not discussed the proper action."

"He knows the True Heir. We will leave it to him."

Spell complete, one fairy scooped up the jewel, now the size of her palm.

"Guard this as if the world depends on it, because *ours* does."

The bickering faces faded into the trunks, replaced by vertical bark.

CHAPTER TWENTY-FIVE

Talia admired the reds and oranges of the sun setting behind the mountain peaks. The temperature dropped only slightly. She was grateful to be in the depths of the mountains during summer, not the middle of winter. The transition from day to night happened remarkably fast.

Talia watched the reflection of the Krimmel Aviary waver in and out of focus on the surface of Tranquility Lake. The four-story building, which had what looked like wrap-around porches on the top three levels, bulged from the side of a cliff. Each level had its own roof that stood out far enough to shade the porch below. The corners flared, as if ready to catch snow instead of shedding it. The entire structure resembled four perfectly constructed houses stacked one on top of the other.

The cliff jutted from the center of the lake as if a giant had plucked a small mountain from its base and plopped it down where he fancied. The gray, jagged granite had many overhangs as bits broke off during the winter. In at least half a dozen of those crevices, huge nests of interwoven branches clung to the side. Giant Eagles built their homes in precarious locations.

Tomorrow, Talia would scour the lakeshore, looking for a way up. The exhaustion of her party had made her realize the group needed a break after the grueling climb to their current location. The air was much thinner than any of them were used to and the humans tired easily. The dwarves seemed to be traveling without any strain.

As she reclined on a cart-sized boulder, her body appreciated the call for rest. Her mind, however, continued to churn with her next move. Was it wise to hope she could acquire Giant Eagles to cut the journey's time? Should she have forged on ahead and hoped that Tanin was having as little luck as she was?

Talia had no power on this side of the world. She hoped the trainers would accept the urgency of their quest, but no treaty said they had to. King Roland bought his GEs from the Northshore Aviary. Talia could offer a deal to use the Krimmel one as well.

Prince Aleck and Lordling Gregor stoked the fire while Nyna prepared dinner. The two dwarven guards insisted on helping with the meal prep. They claimed the dwarf prince was their responsibility, and they would make sure he was fed. Talia suspected they didn't trust the humans completely. After the bickering with Gregor, she didn't blame them for being cautious.

The lordling sat beside Aleck by the fire. Naul sharpened the party's swords, exchanging tales with the prince. The defense guardian ignored Gregor when they would usually have bantered back and forth. Talia felt the same pain Naul did. She knew a lordling and a princess could never be together romantically, but she had looked forward to a lifelong friendship. Now, it was impossible.

Talia changed her focus to Ial, who scanned the area, munching on berries Dew had found on the path. The cultural guardian rested at the base of the massive stone, studying the tome left with them by Librarian Feltwith.

Talia crossed her legs, wishing she could read her guardian. Dew scrounged through the book for the hundredth time since the companions had left the Krimmel Kingdom. She had discovered the recommended method for retrieving the Holy Sapphire involved a formal ceremony with the Head of the Elven Council. Considering the elves were extinct, Talia doubted the text would be helpful. She hoped the Holy Gemstone was mounted on a large piece of jewelry or a scepter, like the Holy Diamond. If she was lucky, the ornament would have been highly venerated and placed in a prominent location in the elven capital.

Ial bolted upright. "Did you see that? A shadow passed overhead."

"I didn't hear anything." Guard Dragick sat up straight with one hand on the sword by his side.

"You shouldn't." Talia searched the sky for a shape that would block the stars. "The Giant Eagle flies silently so as not to warn her prey."

Prince Aleck's voice filled with wonder, rather than fear. "They think of us as prey?" He stood on his tip toes as if that added any height advantage to his viewpoint.

"Perhaps we should find shelter, Your Majesty." Dragick guided Aleck off the rock by his elbow.

"These are trained GEs. They won't attack us," Dew assured the nervous guard.

"I wonder why they waited so long to check us out?" Talia blocked the firelight with her hand to see the darkened sky more clearly. The reality of her limited time to complete her quest loomed before her.

"The darkness gives them more coverage." Naul stepped outside the fire circle.

Ial stepped beside his muscular companion, using his mass to block the firelight. "Exactly, Naul. I didn't know you knew so much about Giant Eagles."

"Our tactician at the Defense School had a thing for aerial fights. He used to pit the GEs against the dragons."

"He used to have some interesting philosophies on dragons, didn't he? The old dwarf had a bit of dementia, I think." Gregor tilted his head.

"He thought dragons were real. That's more than dementia," Naul scoffed.

"Dragons are real," Aleck replied, still searching the sky for the Giant Eagle.

"Why do you say that?" Talia perked up a bit. Before she began this journey, she would have dismissed the dwarf's claim as superstitious. After all she had seen, her mind had opened up to the impossible.

"Because they are. It's an entire class. I always thought it queer that we're taught about all the living creatures, magical and mundane, on our planet, but we're not allowed to interact with them."

"Have you seen one?" asked Nyna.

"Oh, I'd love to see a real fire-breathing dragon." Aleck focused on the party.

"If you haven't seen one, how are you certain dragons are real?" asked Talia.

"Princess." Ial brought Talia's attention to the lakeshore, where a Giant Eagle had landed, almost noiselessly, on a boulder.

The raptor's body was ten feet tall with a wingspan of twenty-five feet, marking it as an adult female. A male would be much smaller. A human, who had been mounted on a flat saddle on the back of the bird, slid down to straddle the tail. He jumped from the boulder and approached the fire circle.

"Lain?" Ial spoke first.

"Ial?" The rider embraced the husbandry guardian.

"Why did you get assigned to the isolated Eagle's Nest?"

Lain pushed his goggles onto his head, revealing brilliant blue eyes. His petite stature put him only a bit taller than Dragick. He moved his wiry arms vigorously when he talked. "I requested it."

"Scallina."

"She broke my heart. What can I say? I needed some time as far away as I could get." He indicated the isolated mountain peak. "This seemed like the perfect location."

"Are you going to introduce us?" Talia asked, coming up beside Ial.

"Of course, I'm sorry. Lain of Garvil." Ial indicated the GE rider, whose nose imitated the beak of his mount. "This is Princess Talia Winterlaus of Tarbin."

Talia nodded to the rider, who bowed deeply before her. "It is an honor to meet a friend of Ial's."

Lain met her eyes while still bent in his bow. "The pleasure is mine, Princess."

Talia continued with the introductions of her other guardians, then turned to the dwarf. "This is Prince Aleck Stoneworth of the Krimmel Dwarves." Talia watched Lain's face as her words sank in.

Prince Aleck confidently put out his left hand and Lain shook it vigorously. "Krimmel Dwarves? I thought your people were sealed in, never to play with others."

"The Recharging is soon. It is time to learn how to 'play with others,' as you say. Now I'll go first." Aleck walked fearlessly toward the GE on the boulder.

The bird screeched and ruffled her feathers as the unfamiliar person approached. Gallick and Dragick stepped in front of their prince.

"Whoa, Your Highness," said Lain. "Aquila doesn't take kindly to strangers without me. Which leads me to the reason I am here." He turned to Talia. "Are you passing through, or did you come for a visit?"

Talia stated her request as if it couldn't be refused. "We're here to borrow some of your stock to reach the next destination on the Forging Quest for Tarbin royalty."

"I'll let the warden know." Lain bounded back on top of the granite. "'Til the morn."

Lain climbed onto the back of the GE and grabbed the reins. The bird launched straight up. A gust of air buffeted the party. Talia protected her eyes from small stones kicked up from the shore. When she could safely drop her arm, she saw no sign of the mount or rider in the pitch-black night.

"So, was that a yes?" asked Talia.

"That was an 'I'll ask the boss.'" Dew interpreted.

"They wouldn't refuse the princess of Tarbin, would they?" Gregor was shocked by the treatment.

"The Krimmel Aviary is not under Tarbin rule. They're completely independent and follow their own guidelines." Ial shivered as a cold breeze blew off the lake.

"What will we do with the procapras?" Aleck scratched one of the goat-like ungulates between the horns.

"The GEs will grip them in their talons and fly them with us." Ial's explanation caused Aleck's face to pale.

Talia had watched the GEs transport lots of goods, living and static, when she was at the husbandry school. "Don't worry. They'll be gentle. The birds are trained not to eat anything that has human scent on it. Otherwise, our horses would be easy pickings."

"How do they feed?" asked the curious prince.

"Questions, questions, so many questions." Naul put away his weapon-cleaning equipment. "It's like having a toddler."

"A lively toddler that keeps us entertained." Nyna giggled.

At first light, the Giant Eagles came. Prince Aleck ran to the shore to watch the birds fly in. Their golden-brown feathers and bright gold beaks and feet reflected the low light. Even with their legs tucked into their torsos, Talia could see the claws on the ends of their talons. One of the Giant Eagles had a rider; the other five had empty flat leather saddles. As the birds got closer, Talia could see the reins wrapped around the outside of their beaks with the ends tied around the saddles.

Ial whistled.

Lain landed first. The rest of the feathered mounts followed. Two on the left nudged each other affectionately.

"Young ones. They'll need a firmer hand." Ial winked at Prince Aleck. "Want to ride?"

"Hold on." Lain stopped the companions from moving toward the birds. "I have a couple messages to deliver from Head Trainer Marcus Ropar. First, you are welcome to visit the aviary, but you can't borrow any birds."

"But we need them for our royal mission. It's not like we're going on a picnic." Talia had a difficult time holding in her frustration. Sometimes, all the group hit were roadblocks.

"I'm just the messenger." Lain placated the princess with his hands held out. "Head Trainer will explain his reasons. Secondly, I assign the riders to the birds, no questions asked."

"What about our pack animals?" asked Dragick.

"This tea will calm them for the flight." Lain produced two bladders from Aquila's saddle.

"They won't need it." Aleck swatted one on the back of the haunch. The procapra jumped but never stopped chewing on its breakfast.

"Bless the Light! Are those procapras? We thought they were extinct." Lain sat on the ground in front of one of the long-nosed ungulates. He ran his fingers through the short gray fur. "The ears are much pointier than in our old books. And that nose." Lain traced the elephant-like protrusion with a finger.

The procapra blinked.

"In the dark, I thought they were goats." Lain gained his feet. "They're so calm in front of the GEs. Are they always this steady?"

"Most of the time." Dragick sounded proud at his beast's bravery.

"They get exceptionally restless at feeding time. They make a weird buzzing, bleating sound when they're hungry. Kind of like the big guy." Gallick shot a thumb in Naul's direction.

"Very funny." Naul clapped the dwarf on the shoulder, almost knocking him off his feet.

Aleck bounced from foot to foot. His enthusiasm for a ride was contagious. Talia couldn't wait either. It had been a few years since she finished her stint at the Husbandry School. The thrill of freedom as she soared through the skies had uplifted her spirit. She could use some uplifting right about now.

Lain jumped up from the ground and wiped his hands on his pants. "Let's go!"

The GE rider divided the group by height and weight. Talia and Aleck were to ride together regardless of the arguments from their guards. Naul received his own mount, adding to the man's fears. Gregor rode with Dragick. Ial took Gallick on one of the young birds. Dew and Nyna rode the last bird. Talia was relieved to see a huge smile on Dew's face for the first time since they'd left her village.

Lain mounted his bird and shouted a command Talia didn't recognize. Lain's Giant Eagle bent her mighty legs and leaped off the ground, not opening her wings until she started to fall. The bird flapped three forceful times before gliding in a gentle zigzag pattern overhead.

The rest of the Giant Eagles launched into the air at once. Talia gripped the reins a little tighter than needed at the sudden movement. The birds fell into a predetermined order behind the lead animal.

Lain swooped over the shoreline and ordered his mount to pick up a procapra. Again, the other five birds followed suit, each on picking up one procapra. The ungulates barely noticed. Talia watched the four-legged animal clutched in the claws of the predator flying in front of her. He blinked blankly and gnawed his teeth together as if still chewing on grass.

Aleck was pressed against the back of the bird with Talia flayed on top of him in a most undignified manner. Straps tied around their waists secured them to the saddle. Yet Talia knew they were more for mental security. If the bird flipped on its back or took a quick turn without the riders bracing for it, both would tumble into the water.

Tranquility Lake shrank as the Giant Eagle train made slow circles to climb the height to the aviary.

Talia relaxed and enjoyed the ride. As they rose above the tree-tops, a cold breeze chafed her face and back. Saltwater hit Talia's cheek. Confused for a moment, she noticed the prince crying.

Talia yelled over the wind, "Are you all right?"

Aleck didn't attempt to wipe his face. "I've never seen anything so beautiful."

She squeezed the dwarf's shoulder. Talia remembered how she had felt the first time she took to the air. It looked like she and Aleck had something in common.

Their bird flew high enough that she could see the Randoian mountain peak to the east. The Light's Daughter reflected off its craggy rock so far away. Sometimes, she felt like the party hadn't gone anywhere in the months they'd been on the road. Up this high, the true vastness of the mountain range they had traversed hit home. The traveling might be slow, but she was definitely getting somewhere.

Talia blinked as their Giant Eagle made its final sweep to the top of the mountain cliff. The sublime architecture of the aviary impressed her. She had never seen anything like it. Huge tree trunks spanned the inside of the enclosure for the birds to perch. A ladder lead straight from the top layer to the second layer. The wrap-around porches were more impressive up close.

The bottom layer was completely closed in. She couldn't see anything in that part of the building. The line of birds circled back around to the far side. Sheep scurried about, trying to hide underneath one another as the birds got close.

Lain's Aquila dropped—if not gently, accurately—her procapra into an empty pen. The line of GEs behind the experienced rider followed suit.

Talia jumped at a loud squawk from behind her. She looked over her shoulder. Ial's young bird had been distracted by the sheep and forgot it was holding another animal. The GE swooped down on the sheep, sending the skittish animals to the corners of the pen. Ial wrangled the bird under control. It looked like Gallick was squeezing him for dear life with his eyes closed and buried in his shoulder. Ial had the bird release the procapra with the sheep.

Better safe with sheep than over the edge of the cliff, thought Talia.

She lost sight of the pair as her mount landed gracefully on a raised platform close to the building. Talia disconnected herself and Aleck from the saddle. They both walked down the steps to the companions who had landed safely before them.

"Does Ial need help?" asked Talia as Lain jumped up to the platform to remove the saddle from her Giant Eagle.

"He's got her under control." Lain dismissed Talia's concerns. "Ornatus particularly enjoys fresh sheep."

Dragick climbed down the stairs. "I thought they wouldn't eat anything that smelled like humans."

"We don't handle the sheep at all. We throw them hay and change their water. The sheep are food for when the lake freezes up and the birds can't find enough fish to fill their bellies." Lain tossed the saddle down to a colleague. He pulled a trout out of a large bucket and tossed it to Talia's Giant Eagle.

The bird extended its wings and made a giant leap. With two mighty flaps, the raptor made it to the top porch, securely landing on the upturned corner. Talia heard a loud screech from inside the building. The GE hopped, deceivingly softly for such a large creature, into the enclosure and disappeared.

Ial and Gallick finally landed safe and sound. Naul helped the shaken dwarf down the steps. It looked like they both could use a drink. Talia hoped they weren't scarred for life on flying. They had a two-day journey ahead of them, if she could change the warden's mind about lending her some mounts.

Dew held her hand over her nose. "What is that smell?"

Talia looked puzzled. She hadn't noticed anything. "What smell?" She took a great whiff, then doubled over, gagging. "Oh, my Light, what died?"

"Nothing." Lain gestured to his mates. "Do you get anything?"

The riders shook their heads in the negative.

"The fine odor you are experiencing is the buildup of Giant Eagle droppings. The ammonia can be strong until the rain washes through." A man wearing a full-length light leather jacket stepped out of the shadows. Talia inspected his legs, certain he was on stilts. He stood at least a head taller than Naul. His short tan hair stuck out at every angle as if he had just climbed out of bed.

"Hey, Ial." The man addressed the companion like an old buddy. He gave the much shorter youth a hug with his long, thin arms. Talia thought he might be able to wrap them all the way around Ial back to his own shoulders.

"Princess Talia Winterlaus of Tarbin meet Head Trainer Marcus Ropar." Lain offered the introduction.

Talia held out her hand. The head trainer bowed with great flourish. She couldn't tell if he was being overly cautious with her royal leanings or if he was making fun of her. She dropped her hand and returned the bow with a modest one of her own.

"Prince Aleck Stoneworth of Krimmel meet Head Trainer Marcus Ropar." Lain emphasized the word "Krimmel" as he introduced the dwarf.

Before Marcus could respond, Aleck imitated the human's dramatic bow, scraping the ground with his beard in his excitement. The trainer laughed heartily, his huge smile taking up his face.

"We are practically neighbors, and I have yet to see any of your fellow dwarves." Marcus had a twinkle in his eye, as if he were keeping a secret. "Well, not with you knowing we saw you anyway."

Guard Dragick blustered. "Impossible." His self-righteous stature bespoke his belief that nothing would get past his fellow guards.

"A side effect of living underground for centuries." Marcus chuckled. "You never look up."

Dragick's face turned red, but Aleck laughed with the human. "We do tend to look at our feet a lot. It's dark. We don't want to trip."

The pair laughed harder. Marcus put his hand on the prince's head affably. The dichotomy of the extremely tall human having fun with the extremely short dwarf was mind-boggling.

"Anyone else reminded of a bad joke?" asked Naul.

Talia shot the defense guardian a warning look. She felt the dislike from Marcus but didn't know why. There was something about her he didn't like. She shook her head. She was being too sensitive.

"Let's adjourn to the dining hall and share a meal." The trainer looked over the heads of the gathered party. He walked toward the building with Prince Aleck, who had to jog to keep up. "You never truly know someone until you've seen them eat... and drink."

Guard Gallick perked up at the last words. He took Dragick by the shoulders and led him inside.

Talia smiled at the dwarves who were quickly becoming friends. Hopefully, she could also make friends with the warden and beat her brother to the next stone.

CHAPTER TWENTY-SIX

Talia took in the number of young boys and girls running around
the property, tending to the birds and sheep. "Why do you keep the
bird droppings, instead of washing them down the mountain? You
apparently have plenty of help?"

"What do you think we trade with the desert people?" Lain
asked.

"Fertilizer," guessed Ial.

"Exactly, my friend." Marcus joined the conversation behind
him. "We're particular about who buys our birds. But anyone can buy
the bird shit. It opens up our trade routes to exotic markets. The more
money we can bring in, the more stable and independent we
become."

"You trade with the desert?" Gregor quickened his pace to catch
up with the trainer. "We've been trying to contact them for years. All
our expeditions come back empty-handed, if they come back at all."

"If your men identified themselves as Tarbinians, it is clear why
they don't have any luck."

Ire emanated from the man again. Talia was positive this time she
didn't imagine it. Dew looked at her sideways. She had picked up on

the grudge as well. Persuasion was going to be harder than Talia had hoped.

The companions passed into the building's first floor. Talia realized how much bigger the building was than she had first calculated. Each of the four stories was at least twenty feet tall, including the bottom level the companions had entered.

Marcus led the party straight ahead through a large set of double doors. Inside stood the dining hall with three long tables set and ready for the afternoon meal. The party spread out at the same table. Talia sat across from Marcus, intent on getting him to address her without grimacing. Prince Aleck sat beside the trainer. The dwarf's head was even with his chest.

"You are so tall. Is that normal for humans?" Aleck loudly whispered to Marcus. The dwarf looked furtively at Talia. She got the impression he thought he was accompanying a small-stature race of humans.

"Oh, no." Lain smacked the trainer on the shoulder as he walked by to get his seat. "Marcus grew that tall by sheer force of will and moved to the top of a mountain so the Stars would tuck him in at night."

"That's not at all what happened," scoffed Marcus. "My mother wanted a son so tall, he could clean the roof without a ladder. So she made me change from the side of the mountain until the pull of the world stretched me out."

"Lies!" yelled a woman from the kitchen, where the delicious aroma of smoked sausage originated.

The children placing pitchers of milk and sweet wine on the table jumped as a group. The servants delivered loaves of steaming bread accompanied by mounds of freshly churned butter to the tables. A plump older woman, wiping her hands on her soiled apron, followed them out.

"Are you speaking ill of me before I've been introduced?" The woman smacked Marcus on the back of the head.

"Ow, Mom." The obnoxious adult Marcus turned into a bashful

child. "I was telling my joke about you making me hang from the mountain."

"Well, that's true. But it was to clean the old bird nests, not make you taller. My name is Penelope Ropar, and I'm the warden of the Krimmel Aviary." Penelope focused her sharp eyes on Talia. "And you are?"

"I am Princess Talia Winterlaus of Tarbin." She rose from her seat at the bench. The warden's focus made her uncomfortable. It was like she already knew who the princess was but wanted her to confirm it. "And my friends here are my guardians."

Prince Aleck rose from his seat and imitated Marcus's overdramatic bow to the warden. He held out his hand for good measure. "I am Prince Aleck Stoneworth of Krimmel. These are my guardians."

"I see my son has already been a bad influence on our guests." Reaching high up, she smacked Marcus on the back of his head again. Then she heartily shook Aleck's hand. The older woman's beefy one completely enclosed the dwarf's. "We need to talk, Prince Aleck. We've been wanting to set up trade with your people for some time now. Contacting you has proven difficult."

"I am exploring the world as a representative of my people. I would be honored to talk about what Krimmel Aviary has to offer us." Aleck smoothed his beard, like his father had done when negotiating with Talia.

The princess watched Nyna stifle a giggle.

"No time like the present." Penelope tapped her son on his shoulder to make him give up his seat.

"Drincall, get out the good stuff for my friends." The warden snapped her fingers at one of the teenage boys who was ordering the other servants about.

"You have a lot of child servants. Where are their parents?" Nyna ruffled the hair of one of the little boys, who did not look kindly on her affection.

"There are many unwanted children in this world. We have a lot of work here. It all evens out."

"My kingdom would also be interested in trading with the Krimmel Aviary." Talia sat directly across from Penelope. The woman hadn't given her a second glance after the intense stare at their meeting. Talia didn't know what to think of the woman ignoring her.

"So, Prince Aleck, what is your main export?" The warden acted like she hadn't heard Talia. Penelope piled food onto hers and Aleck's plates.

"We don't export anything outside the mountain. Yet." Aleck dived into his plate with abandon. "This is delicious! Why is no one else eating?"

"Good question." Penelope looked under her eyebrows at Talia and pushed a platter of roasted vegetables closer to her plate.

Talia kept the woman's gaze as she put a spoonful on her plate, and passed the platter to Gregor. The rest of the group followed suit, though Talia could tell her guardians were alert. They must have felt the same tension she did. Talia took a calming breath to stop herself from screaming at the woman for her disrespect.

"My kingdom would love to negotiate trade with Krimmel Aviary." Talia hoped persistence would gain her an audience. How was she to convince this woman to lend the party Giant Eagles if she wouldn't even talk to her?

"My family does *not* do business with Tarbin."

Before Talia could ask why, a dozen or so riders entered the dining hall. They spread out on the last two tables. Marcus looked relieved to be able to join his mates. Servants rushed to supply the hungry crowd with food and drink. Ial begged Talia with his eyes to be released to join the riders. Talia nodded her permission. Maybe he'd have more luck than she.

"We have need of good riding, GEs. I bet Gregor's grand estate could use the fertilizer for his wheat fields." Talia elbowed the noble, who was distracted by a blonde at the rider's table winking at him.

"Ab-absolutely," Gregor stammered, refocusing on the task at hand. "We would gladly exchange the rich fertilizer for wheat in the fall and cherries in the spring."

"It has been a while since I've tasted cherry pie." The warden took a large draft of her beer. "But can't, sorry."

Talia swallowed, trying to keep her temper. "Madam Ropar, if I may be so bold. Why did you allow us up here if you had no interest in anything we had to offer?"

The warden sat up straight on the bench and wiped her mouth with her apron. The whole time, she remained focused on the princess, Talia didn't waver.

"No one from the Tarbin royal family has dared set foot in these mountains in decades. To actually ask for an audience with the aviary?" Penelope whistled. "That takes courage. I wanted to meet that person."

"Princess Talia is on a very important quest." Aleck talked through a mouthful of potatoes. He turned to Talia. "Show her the Holy Diamond."

Talia shot him a warning glare too late. Penelope was treating her with such animosity Talia wasn't sure if she should show her full hand.

"Diamond?" Penelope's interest was piqued.

Talia held her hand out to Naul. He pulled out the scepter from his bag. The room fell into quiet whispers. The riders from the other two tables must have heard what was going on. Talia unfolded the cloth covering the dwarven scepter. She held the gem high.

"It *is* the Holy Diamond, isn't it?" Penelope's fingers opened and closed, as if she wanted to touch it.

"Why does everyone know about this thing except us?" Nyna whispered to Dew.

"The Holy Gemstones were the reason we cut connections with your people. I was a member of the astropriests many years ago. I, and a few others, abandoned the order as the hierarchy refused to see the Recharging as a unifying event for the world. Too many wanted to keep the energy for humans alone. When High

Priestess Giddeona refused to send a team to repair the Machine, I knew it would all happen again. One race is not meant to have all that power. The Light prevented it a millennium ago. Why would they think the Light had changed her mind?" The warden pulled off the band holding her hair piled on her hand. Her thin blonde hair tumbled around her shoulders, making her look ten years younger.

Talia had no idea what Penelope was talking about. But she couldn't acknowledge her ignorance. She didn't want to do anything that would make the warden ignore her again.

"I wouldn't stay and watch hope die for the resurrection of the lost races. My friends and I left." Penelope held her hands up to encompass the building around her. "I came home to continue the family business. My sisters and brothers of the true faith spread out across the world. Without the chance to correct our ancestor's mistake, what was there left to worship?"

Dew pulled out the leather-bound book she had studied with such dedication on the trip. "Giddeona Feltwith is the librarian at Tarbin Castle. She sent us on this quest and gave us this book as a guide."

"Giddeona resigned?" A spark lit up Penelope's face. "May I?"

Talia nodded at Dew, who gave Penelope the book with only a minor twinge.

The warden opened it reverently. "She gave you the lore book. She does want you to succeed. If she still wanted the power, the old coot would've told you how to get the Holy Gemstones and nothing else. Miracles do happen."

Talia gained Penelope's attention again. She seemed to be warming up to the party. "Librarian Feltwith defied High Priestess Nomyra to include me in the quest. I don't know what the ultimate goal is for either of them. I wish only to complete my quest and serve my people as the True Heir my birthright foretold."

"Are you of the blood? Have you been tested?"

"I'm not sure if I know what that means." Talia looked warily down at the faceted stone. "But the Holy Diamond does respond to me."

Penelope crossed her hands on the table. "May I see?"

"Here?" Talia needed the warden's cooperation if she was going to have a chance to get to the Elven Forest before the end of her allotted time, but she wasn't sure she wanted to hear any phantom voices.

"Here is fine. I have no secrets from my riders," said Penelope.

"A sample then. I don't want to frighten the GEs."

Talia unsheathed her knife from her belt. The metal had seen her own blood more often than any other, not exactly the use she had imagined for the handy tool. She slashed her left pinky finger. Careful not to touch the diamond lest the gem pull her in again, Talia dripped her blood onto the clear jewel.

The Holy Diamond absorbed the fluid and radiated a blue shine. The riders from adjacent tables fell over themselves trying to get a glimpse over the shoulders of the sitting guests. Talia smiled at their enthusiasm. In a world where magic was constantly spoken of but never seen, to actually view a bit of unexplained phenomenon sparked the imagination.

The gem faded as quickly as it had lit.

"You truly are the one." The ire disappeared from Penelope's gaze. "You truly are antagonistic to Nomyra's goals?"

"She fought tooth and nail to stop me from going on this quest."

"Then anything you need from me is yours." The warden stood and spoke to the entire room. "Princess Talia and her guardians—"

"And Prince Aleck," added Talia.

"And Prince Aleck and his guards are welcome guests from this day forward. Any assistance they require, they will get. Am I understood?"

"Yes, Warden Ropar," the riders and servants replied in unison.

"You will be heading to the Elven Forest next, yes?" she asked Talia.

She nodded.

"Good. You will get there in two days. I will supplement any food you need. Marcus will set you up with birds."

Marcus stood behind his mother. "You should keep the procapras here. They'll only slow you down."

"What is this nonsense you speak of?" The older woman stuck her hands on her hips. "Procapras are extinct."

"They are very boring animals. You can have them." Prince Aleck struck mugs with Gallick.

The warden headed out to the yards.

Marcus wore a winning grin on his face. "I knew that would get her. The woman has a soft spot for exotic animals."

The companions left their unfinished dinner and followed the older woman outside.

The procapras nibbled on the weeds in their enclosure, completely unbothered by the predators flying overhead.

"I've only seen drawings of this species. They used to roam wild all over the mountains." Penelope leaned over the fence to pet the hairless, proboscis-like nose. "I thought you said you had nothing to trade, Prince Aleck?"

"I didn't know you would be interested in our working animals." Aleck put an arm around the shoulder of each dwarf guard. "You see! It is a good thing I joined the adventure. We'll be ready for the world after the Recharging."

Penelope addressed the riders gawking at the unknown ungulates in the old sheep enclosure. "These beauties can sniff out the most difficult-to-find herbs in the forest. The Medicinal School used to keep a trained herd for that exact purpose. These could provide a third market for us, boys."

She practically glowed as her hair flipped around her face in the wind.

"Let's get you saddled up, Princess," She said. "It's time to bring the old order back."

CHAPTER TWENTY-SEVEN

Talia watched the last of the mountains fade underneath her. Her Giant Eagle, Accipitri, gained altitude as he hit a thermal rising from the warm field below. Talia's cheeks were red with chill. Being sandwiched between the GE and Nyna kept the rest of her toasty warm.

A giggle interrupted her internal thoughts. Looking over her shoulder, Talia saw Aleck with an ear-to-ear grin so big she could see his teeth through his beard. His Giant Eagle had found the same thermal and was floating in gentle arcs. Guard Dragick, sharing the GE with his prince, clung for dear life to the saddle. His deathly pale face remained stony in controlled fear. Talia marveled at the contrast between their reactions.

The rest of her companions followed close behind. Somehow, she had thought the birds would fly in perfect Vs like migrating geese. Apparently, the GEs were much more independent. The birds of prey scattered across the sky, seemingly unconcerned with the location of their fellow flyers. Talia knew they were alert though. Whenever a kettle of vultures took to the air or a wild giant eagle got close, the aviary birds closed ranks in an intimate formation.

Below the princess lay swaths of grassy land bordered by trees.

She thought the rectangles looked like Kenia wheat fields if they'd been abandoned for years. Talia squinted ahead, looking for a line of dense tree growth signaling the border of the Elven Forest.

Penelope had warned the group they'd have to circle down as soon as they spotted the tree line. The birds routinely flew west to visit Naplion, a small farming community and trading partner of the aviary. The traveling parties were forced to the south because no one could convince the birds to fly through or above the forest.

Matriarch Penelope Ropar insisted the forest was the ancient home of the elves. Her lore verified the location on Aleck's map. Talia wondered if the GEs could sense the extinct status of a once-great people. Rumors persisted in the area that anyone who entered never returned. Talia quickly dismissed any such superstition. Tales of that sort flowed from village to village describing any dense forest to keep the children from roaming about and getting lost.

"Ho!" yelled Lain into his cupped hands, getting the sound to travel to Talia. She followed his indication to a seemingly solid line of green and reddish-brown ahead.

The princess moved her hand in a circular motion above her head. She watched the signal pass between her companions. Then she guided her bird down, balancing carefully with Nyna on her back. The two leaned to the left, making a lazy circle toward the mountains. At a lower elevation a few yards above the tree line, they turned toward the forest again. They were low enough now that Talia could clearly see the overgrown fields. They contained more barley than expected for the wild but not enough to look cultivated. The locals probably used to farm the grain in these fields. Their mountain caves would make great places to ferment beer. She wondered if hops were grown in the same fields or if they were imported.

As the companions cleared the fallow land, the large redwoods filled Talia's vision. Still high enough to fly above the trees, she wished they could continue to the waterfall where the elven capital was supposedly located. If the map was accurate, the group had an entire day's hike ahead of them. She was about to signal the group to circle down a second elevation when a tingling sensation tickled her gut. Nyna shook her shoulder and pointed at the ground.

Galloping horses headed for the forest. She angled the GE dramatically to get a closer look. The rider in the lead looked straight at her and threw a rude gesture over his head.

"Tanin!" shouted Talia. "Where did he come from?"

Seeing her brother sent her heart pumping. First, it validated they were headed in the correct direction. Now she had to beat him to the Holy Sapphire. After everything they'd been through, she wouldn't let her twin beat her in this quest. Talia decided to risk flying over the forest.

"Hold tight!" Talia shouted to Nyna behind her.

Talia felt her guardian tighten her grip. Talia focused on flying straight. She dove toward the perimeter, immediately over Tanin's head. Accipitri passed the horses with a screech. The rest of the birds lagged behind as Talia pushed hers, hoping the momentum would prevent him from balking.

She was wrong. Immediately before he would have passed the first trunk, Accipitri banked sharply to the left. Talia managed to grasp his neck as she slipped to the side. Nyna was not as lucky. She flew over the GE's shoulder, unable to hold on with the unexpected change in direction. The guardian's safety strap snapped taut, preventing her from a great fall but completely throwing Accipitri off-balance. As he was trained to do if ever a rider was unseated, he descended as quickly as he could manage. The three crashed to the hard earth. The crunch from Nyna hitting the packed grass sank Talia's stomach. She dismounted and collapsed over her medicinal guardian.

What had she been thinking? She had been warned, but she rushed at the trees anyway. Now Nyna paid the price for her ambition and reckless behavior.

"Nyna, are you all right? Can you hear me?" Talia held the medicinal guardian's head in her arms. She was breathing, but unresponsive. A red blot soaked into her right sleeve. Her arm was bent in an unnatural fashion.

Before Talia realized the other birds had landed, Dew and Ial rushed over to help. Talia backed up to get out of the way. She knew she should be strong, but she couldn't stop the tears from rolling down her cheeks.

"Looks like the Dark has other plans for you," her brother taunted as he galloped past the group.

Tanin kicked his gelding's flanks, forcing his mount to stay on course. The horse threw his head up, fighting the commands.

"Looks like the horses don't like it either," Gregor observed.

The other horses in the group slowed. Tanin's mount was forced ahead by sheer will. Only Rory's horse still followed. Kettlor struggled to stay on his mare as she reared in protest. Orui laid on the ground, having been bucked off. Tyler sat on his calm mare, not attempting to move forward.

Tanin's steed hit the shadows and came to a dead stop. Tanin flew over his head. Rory's horse smashed into the back of the chestnut. The defense guardian managed to dismount like he performed such acrobatics routinely. Rory bent over his charge.

Talia found no pleasure in her brother's pain. She was too worried about Nyna to gloat. Gregor put an arm around Talia's shoulders. She glared at him. He quickly removed it.

"Get me a splint from the kit," Ial ordered Dew as he pulled a thin knife from Nyna's medicinal bag. "I want to set her arm before she wakes up."

Talia bent down and took the tool from the husbandry guardian. She wanted to help. Watching and crying were not characteristics of the leader who deserved to rule her people. Brushing her tears from her cheeks, Talia sliced the sleeve of Nyna's tunic. The guardian's willowy arm twisted so her palm and elbow were both facing up. One of the thin bones in the forearm penetrated the skin. Deep red blood seeped from the wound. Talia blanched.

"I can take care of this, Talia," Ial insisted. "Nyna might be our resident medical expert, but I've seen worse wounds than this on animals."

"Nyna is my responsibility. I'm helping." Talia's authoritative voice left no room for interjection.

"Of course," Ial acquiesced. "Naul, I might need you to hold her still."

The large man lost all color from his face. "If I can do it with my eyes closed."

"Please. I don't need two patients."

Dew handed the splint and tie cloths to Ial. "Here. I'm sorry it took so long. I forgot which GE we tied it to."

"Lain?" Ial pulled out a packet of herbs from Nyna's bag. "Mix the ointment for the external wound please. It should be the same consistency as the mask for a GE's beak."

Lain nodded his understanding.

"I will help." Prince Aleck's playful demeanor quieted under the serious circumstances.

"Talia, hold her upper arm perfectly still. Ready?" Ial surveyed Naul bracing Nyna's shoulders while Dew and Gregor held down her legs. The injured companion remained unconscious.

Ial pulled Nyna's forearm out and twisted it to the proper shape. An uncontrollable shiver ran down Talia's spine at the crunch of the bones as they scraped one another. Nyna's eyes shot open with an agonized scream. She convulsed and tried to rip her arm away from the pain. The bleeding increased, filling the air with a metallic odor. Naul gagged and turned his head. Talia hoped he could hold it until Nyna was properly tended to.

"Nyna." Talia leaned her face close to her guardian's. "Nyna." She repeated the phrase until the guardian focused through the pain and looked into Talia's blue eyes. "You need to lay still so Ial can set your arm. If you're ever going to learn to use that bow properly, you'll need full use of both your arms."

Talia watched her words sink in. Nyna stopped struggling against her bondage. The disciplined woman set her mouth and stared up at the clear sky as Ial carefully spread the herb mixture on her wound.

"It burns." Nyna winced in pain, tightening her muscles. She screamed and grabbed her ribs with her left arm.

"I was afraid of that." Lain came back with a cup of steaming liquid. Talia recognized the pungent odor of willow bark tea. "I think you broke a couple ribs too. Here, sweet girl. Drink some of this. It will ease your pain."

Ial lifted Nyna's shirt to reveal swollen lumps on her ribs. "Those are going to be the prettiest shades of purple in a few hours."

While Lain fed Nyna tea, Ial put the splints on either side of the wounded arm. Talia held them in place while Ial tied the torn cloth securely around the arm.

Naul helped Nyna sit up.

"I am so sorry, my friend. I saw Tanin and panicked. I didn't see any reason for Accipitri to refuse the flight." Talia stammered, guilt pouring out with her tears. "I thought he would fly through for me. I don't..."

"I still don't see any reason for the GE to have refused to fly over. There's nothing there." Nyna stared directly into Talia's eyes. "You didn't do anything wrong. We can't control everything our animals do."

"Can you stand?" asked Ial.

"If I can have more of that tea." Nyna reached for the mug with her uninjured arm. "You might have missed your calling, Lain. You mix like a Medicinal School alumnus."

The husbandry graduate handed her the cup, which she drank in one big drag.

"Looks like Tanin is okay," reported Naul, looking anywhere except the red-smeared grass.

Talia cringed as her brother stood and yelled at his horse. A ruffle of feathers distracted her from her twin. The dwarves and Lain had unpacked the birds while she had dealt with her injured guardian.

Lain bowed to Talia with his hand over his heart. "I must be off, Princess. I will send word to Naplion of your impending arrival."

Penelope had assured the companions if they followed the river out of the Elven Forest, they would arrive at Naplion in a few days. She had assigned Lain to set up their supplies and secure new horses before he returned home with the Giant Eagles. The princess was grateful for the assistance and would have to find a way to thank the Krimmel Aviary when she completed her quest.

"We're ready." Prince Aleck wore a full traveling pack on his back.

Talia wondered what she would do to get him injured. "I don't suppose there is any way I can convince you and your guards to fly to Naplion is there? This trip is becoming dangerous, and I don't want to risk your safety."

"And miss the adventure?" Aleck looked shocked at the suggestion.

"We cannot leave the prince," said Guard Dragick.

"Or the Holy Diamond," added Guard Gallick.

"As I cannot give orders to a sovereign prince, we will travel together." Talia waved Lain off. "May the Light guide your journey."

Lain nodded his head. "And may the Dark sleep through yours."

Talia and her party bid the rider farewell. Then she gathered her companions and their supplies to confront her brother.

"Nice flying, sis," taunted Tanin as soon as Talia was close enough to hear him.

"Nyna will recover just fine." Talia glared. "How is your Forging Quest going? Have you been hit with enough hammers, or should I help?"

Tanin didn't flinch at her disrespect. "All goes as planned."

"So, you haven't found any Holy Gemstones?"

Tanin swung around with clenched fists. A heated blanket of anger rolled off him. "I have two. And I'm heading for number three now. I assume you are here for the Holy Sapphire as well."

Talia nodded. He had two, and she had only managed to find one? "Two?"

"Yes, sister. I am the rightful ruler of Tarbin. By blood, by ability, and by decree of the Stars." Tanin straightened his shoulders and raised his arms to the sky as if he lifted the Stars himself. "They have brought me the Holy Diamond and the Holy Emerald."

"Diamond? The princess has the Holy Diamond." Gregor pointed at the bag flung over Talia's shoulder.

"I see where your allegiances lie, my friend." Bile fell from Tanin's lips as his eyes penetrated Gregor. Talia could see him stifle a growl, like a caged animal. "What you say is impossible. The dwarves gave it to me freely. Why would they deal with a powerless girl and her puppy dog?"

"Tanin," Gregor's voice was pleading.

Talia studied their interaction. She still didn't know if she could trust Gregor. She needed to glean anything she could from their interactions. Maybe she could leave the lordling with her brother. Then again, that would give Tanin all the information she had discovered independently. She'd be better off keeping Gregor close so she could watch him.

"You may address me as Prince Tanin or Your Highness, but you have lost any privilege to greet me as a friend. You crossed the line when you chose to aid my enemy." He tossed a hand in Talia's direction.

Talia pulled the scepter from her bag. "I am not your enemy. I am your sister. And I do have the Holy Diamond."

"Impossible." The word fell out of Tanin's mouth. He stepped forward aggressively to take a closer look. Naul stepped in front of Talia, preventing the prince from accosting the princess. Rory stepped in front of the prince to balance the power. Naul stood head and shoulders taller than Rory, but Talia had seen Rory's sword arms and wouldn't want to see those two battle.

Tanin pulled out a leather pouch tucked into his shirt while remaining focused on the diamond in Talia's hand. The prince retrieved a diamond that appeared identical to the one mounted on the scepter. If the two had been switched, Talia wouldn't have been able to choose the correct one by looks alone.

"Are there two? How is that possible?" Talia switched her gaze between the jewel in her hand and the identically cut and sized jewel in her brother's.

"Mine came directly from the Eckerd, who have protected it for centuries until it was time to hand it over to the True Heir." Tanin emphasized the last word. "Where did you get yours?"

"From the Krimmel, who took the genuine Holy Diamond during the Dwarven Civil War. They've been protecting it. The Eckerd held a copy."

"Impossible! I tested the diamond. It scratches glass and doesn't break against stone. I hold the one and only Holy Diamond."

"Does it glow with the Blood?" Prince Aleck surprised Talia from behind. "Only the Holy Diamond responds to the Blood. All others are mere imitations."

"And who are you, dwarf? Tanin held his head high, looking down his nose.

"I am Prince Aleck, heir to the throne of the Krimmel Kingdom." The dwarf held out his left hand, as cheerful as ever.

"What is this nonsense? The Krimmel are holed up in their mountain kingdom, never to interact with anyone, let alone some second-hand princess on a stolen mission." Tanin's face reddened more as he ignored the dwarf's hand. Talia thought he was starting to resemble a turnip.

Aleck put his hand down, eyebrows knit together in the face of Tanin's anger. Talia sighed. Her brother required a demonstration. She proffered a healed finger to Naul, but his face immediately blanched. She sighed and shifted to Gregor. He raised his eyebrows, making sure she wanted him to do it. She nodded her acquiescence. Gregor pulled a dagger from his belt.

Rory unsheathed his sword halfway and spread his legs, ready to attack.

Gregor rolled his eyes at the guardian's paranoia. "The knife is not for your charge."

He gripped her petite hand in his muscular one. Gently, he made a thin slice across the meaty part of the princess's right hand. Naul's face blanched slightly. Talia didn't flinch. She held her dripping hand over the diamond. The jewel soaked up the blood. As regular as this sight was becoming, Talia still felt awe when observing it.

She held the Holy Diamond up to give a clear view to Tanin and his guardians standing behind him. The Holy Gemstone soaked up the last of the offered blood and then released a modest blue glow. Though not impressive to Talia's party, who first witnessed the effect on a massive scale inside a cave, Tanin and his guardians oohed and aahed at the sight.

"Yes, of course." Tyler ignored the invisible line between the two parties, getting a close look at the fading light on the scepter. "The Blood of the True Heir will command the Holy Gemstones. High Priestess Nomyra told me to ignore that part of the lore. But if everything else is correct, why wouldn't the blood be?"

"What do you mean 'the Blood of the True Heir'? I'm the *True Heir*!" Tanin clenched his fists. Talia feared he would throttle his own guardian.

"We're twins," Talia spoke through a tight jaw. "We have the same blood."

Tanin's anger returned to pre-explosion level. "There can't be two *True* Heirs."

"The prophecy can't predict everything. Maybe the writer didn't consider the possibility of twins." Tyler wrote notes in the margin of the book he held. "We should test your diamond to see if it glows."

Tanin pulled a knife from his belt and cut his hand.

Talia tried to warn her brother. "Don't put your hand on the gem. It practically dragged me into the stone, the pull was so intense."

He placed the wound directly on his diamond, sneering at his sister. He easily pulled his hand on and off. "I must be stronger than a bit of sticky blood."

"A fake diamond won't react to the Blood of the True Heir. There is only *one* Holy Diamond," Aleck explained again. The puzzlement on the dwarf's face bespoke his belief that maybe the human prince was a bit slow.

Talia hoped Tanin didn't notice the tone. He removed his hand from the diamond and held the gem on display. Tanin focused on Talia, pride in his infallibility shining on his smug face.

Nothing happened.

His eyebrow met each other as he scowled at the nonreactive jewel. Blood dripped down the opaque surface to pool in his palm. The diamond didn't absorb the fluid like Talia's. No glow emanated from the rock.

Tanin grabbed the diamond and threw it as far as he could. The rock sailed over the heads of his companions and fell at the base of a giant redwood. His explosion of rage caused Talia to hand the scepter to Naul, who tucked it into his tunic. No one would be able to get that from him while he was alive.

"The lore doesn't speak of the Holy Diamond switching hands between the dwarven kingdoms." Tyler sounded interested instead of upset. "I must amend the notations."

"The lore doesn't say anything about two dwarven kingdoms," added Dew. "The literature was written before the Dwarven Civil War. At least, the books we were given."

Tanin threw down the cloth he had used to wipe his cut and crossed his arms, closing the discussion.

"So, you have one and I have one." Talia smirked at her brother, more confident in her chances. "Assuming the Holy Emerald you have is the correct one."

Tanin fumed. "Of course, it is. We walked into Naddle Swamp and received it directly from the council."

Talia put her hands up. She wasn't going to fight with him. Plus, she had no idea what council he referred to. "Okay, fine. We can travel together to acquire the Holy Sapphire. After all, I don't see what choice we have."

"Fine." Tanin exchanged a look with Rory that Talia couldn't interpret, but she was sure it didn't bode well for her. "I will wrap up plans with my guardians, and then we can set off."

Talia nodded, surprised at her brother's sudden turn to reason. He was up to something. She would have to tread lightly.

Talia checked the sword on her hip and the dagger in her belt. She shouldered her pack with sufficient food and water for this leg of the trip. The remainder of her party silently checked their supplies and weapons as well. Naul picked up Nyna's load. No one knew what waited for them in the forest or how Tanin's presence would complicate matters. Talia smiled reassuringly to her trusted group and headed into the trees.

CHAPTER TWENTY-EIGHT

LIGHT FILTERED through the tree branches of the great forest. Thilphiliari sat on the warming ground next to one of the sacred trees. The elf lord held his wife's hand against his protruding cheek bone, gently caressing his skin with hers.

"My darling, they come. I can feel their approach. Our wait is almost over."

His wife remained silent as the elven lord kissed her silky, almost translucent skin.

"I will restore our people to their height of glory. We will work the great Machine and recharge that which deserves the power." A scowl wrinkled the elf's features. "The humans will know the pain and suffering that has plagued our people for a millennium."

His wife stood quietly, her hand limp in his grasp.

"Now, my darling, I know you do not approve." Thilphiliari kissed her hand again. "Your heart is too caring. The humans do not deserve your affection."

With no response from his companion, the elf continued, "I feel the Holy Diamond and the Holy Black Opal. With the Holy Sapphire safe in my hands, I am halfway to the goal."

The elven lord stood, reluctantly releasing the hand of his beloved. "I must prepare for their arrival."

He brushed the dark hair from the face of his beautiful mate. "You will see, my darling. Our children will be avenged with the corpses of the entire dwarven race and the enslavement of the humans. I am ready and cannot fail."

Thilphiliari kissed her forehead. His robe scraped the ground as he walked to the palace to prepare. "Our sacrifice will not have been in vain. The prophecy will be fulfilled by me, the True Heir."

CHAPTER TWENTY-NINE

"Are you ready?" Talia asked her brother.

"More than you. I've been preparing for this quest for a year. I know exactly what awaits us." Tanin marched into the forest.

Rory and Orui rushed to get in front. Everyone else followed.

Talia analyzed her brother and his guardians. Something had changed between them. Tyler walked with a definite limp, and Orui favored his right arm. Talia glanced at Nyna, who walked slowly but surely with Ial's help. Talia wondered what toll the Dark required to allow them to complete this quest. She hoped it was worth it.

Talia asked, "Anything we should know?"

"Asks the girl who wishes to steal my throne." Tanin's words dripped with anger.

"Steal?" Prince Aleck scurried to the lead of the group. His short legs pumped twice as fast as the human's as he tried to keep pace.

"Has she not told you the truth of her cause, Prince of the Krimmel?" Tanin's voice took on the polite tone he used for foreign dignitaries. "My dear sister has been given every privilege a girl of royal blood could wish for. She has received the best education, been awarded lands as a dowry to her future husband, dressed in the most extravagant attire. All these advantages and more have come with no responsibilities on her sweet little head. And yet, she wishes to take my place on the throne."

Talia's face flushed. Is that how he saw her actions? "I was first born. I only desire to fulfill my duty as determined by the Stars themselves."

"Of course, she has one duty." Tanin put his hands through the straps of his backpack, ignoring his sister's comment. "Talia's only responsibility is to marry Lord Bello Hilderamn of Darvis. Her life of privilege will continue as her union strengthens her kingdom, uniting the entire northern half of the continent."

"Life of privilege? How can you say such a thing?" The words fell out of Talia's mouth in a torrent.

"Do you hear the disdain in her voice when I mention her duty?" Tanin's voice darkened as he nodded his head toward his sister. "Instead of obeying her father, the king, she chooses to try and usurp *my* duty as heir of Tarbin by thwarting *my* efforts to successfully complete *my* quest."

A shadow passed over Aleck's face. "Sometimes, fathers are wrong."

"My only duty is to my people," retaliated Talia. "Allying with Lord Bello is not the right move. I don't know what his plans are, but I think it has more to do with earning my royal name than it does with uniting kingdoms."

"Can we, please, just find the Golden Palace?" asked Tanin, as if he were the sensible one. "I'm sure we can continue our bickering when we find the Holy Sapphire."

Tanin winked at Aleck as if sharing a secret. Fuming, Talia jogged ahead of the group with Dew and Naul immediately behind her. Gregor jogged to catch up, giving Tanin a wide berth.

"How could you have been friends with him for so many years?" Dew questioned the lordling.

"I'm starting to ask myself that same question."

"What are we following?" Naul pointed to the packed soil underfoot.

Talia didn't remember finding a path. A moment ago, she was stepping around shrubbery that pulled at her pants. Now, she walked along with enough room for a cart to pass unharmed.

"It looks like an animal trail." Ial bent down to get a closer look. "I don't see any hoof prints, but the soil is so solidly compacted they might not show."

"It's too large to be deer," Gregor added.

Talia raised her voice to carry through the party. "You would know better than any of us. What do you think made it?"

Ial replied, "I want to say horse, but I don't see any other evidence."

"It doesn't smell like horse." Gregor took a whiff of the air. "Though there is something."

The air was thick with the fishy smell of the aviary with a touch of muskiness.

"What is that?" Orui wrinkled his nose.

"Incredible!" Prince Aleck held up a gray-and-white feather with both hands. The feather was as long as the dwarf was tall. "I thought Giant Eagles didn't come into the forest."

Nyna touched her sling with her good arm. "They don't. I have proof."

Talia swallowed. The guilt over Nyna's injury clouded her thoughts.

Ial offered Nyna a sip of water. "I've never seen a gray GE either."

"Actually, this forest hosts groups of... " Tyler coughed as Orui elbowed him in the chest.

Tanin glowered at his cultural guardian. Talia frowned. They knew something, but weren't about to share.

"Could the birds have made this path?" Naul scratched the rock-like dirt with his heel.

"Nah." Ial helped Nyna to a fallen tree.

"Do you hear that?" Rory spoke for the first time. "The river?"

The sloshing sounds of rushing water greeted the group. The soft slapping against its banks bounced off the tree trunks and echoed along the path.

"The Ingiris River," Tyler said, though he still rubbed his chest from his earlier attempt. "If we are approaching the quiet end of the river, which it sounds like we are, then we're too far west. We need to follow the river upstream to the waterfall and rapids. At the peak of the waterfall sits the Golden Palace."

Dew consulted the map Aleck had given them. She nodded to Talia in agreement and tucked the map back into the tome.

"Wait. What was that?" Talia flipped back a couple pages before Dew closed the book. An odd creature with the combined features of an eagle and lion was sketched in a corner. "Ial, could this be what dropped the feather?"

Dew read the inscription under the picture. "Griffin."

Kettlor blanched.

Ial scoffed. "They don't exist."

Gregor took two steps back and rammed into Talia. "Or it could be standing in front of us?"

As Gregor stepped to the side, Talia saw an enormous animal almost the width of the trail. Its raptor head, resplendent with gray-and-white feathers, almost touched the lowest branch on the redwoods. The feathers flowed down to the middle of its back, where the bird form changed drastically to that of a feline predator. The tawny color and muscular back legs looked like they belonged to the lions of the Renquist Desert. The long cord of a tail, tipped with a fluff of brown fur, whipped back and forth. She recalled a barn cat who used to flick hers in exactly the same way when she was irritated. Where the bird met the cat in the middle of the animal's back, a pair of folded wings fidgeted. The griffin scraped its razor-sharp talons on the packed dirt.

"Oh, how beautiful!" Aleck weaved his way around the companions, moving before the creature.

The griffin angled a yellow eye at the dwarf. It let out a vicious screech, opening its wings to their full eighteen feet. Its pink tongue looked large enough to grab Aleck. Naul picked up the curious dwarf by his collar and pushed him aside as the griffin attacked.

"To the trees!" yelled Talia.

She hoped the dense foliage would slow the beast down, allowing the companions to escape. Unfortunately, the dense undergrowth also slowed down the dwarves.

Aleck tripped a mere foot into the understory. The griffin reared, ready to attack. Guard Dragick shielded his prince with his body while Guard Gallick swatted the beast on a back haunch. The animal pivoted easily for such a huge beast in such tight quarters. Naul dropped his pack and unsheathed his sword. Talia, Ial, and Gregor joined him. The group encircled the beast. Each took turns distracting it from its chosen target.

"I'm guessing he is the reason the GEs and horses wouldn't breach the forest." Gregor skidded backward, avoiding a claw.

Nyna stood in the tree line with Dew. They scanned the page describing the mythical creature.

"Anything helpful in there?" Talia ducked as the griffin swung around, its wing barely missing her head.

"I'm translating as quickly as I can." Dew squeezed her eyes together, ignoring the commotion around her. "*Odium—*"

"Dislikes." Nyna snapped the fingers of her good hand.

"Good. Now what does *transpassare* mean. I can't remember."

A talon shot out at Dew. Naul reached it first. His sword batted the barrel-sized leg aside.

The scratch on the foreleg enraged the griffin into a frenzy. He gave his wings a mighty flap, gaining feet in seconds. Dead leaves blew across the trail around the tree trunks. The debris assaulted the companions, obstructing their view. Dew clutched the book to her chest, trying to keep her page.

"Are you just going to stand there?" Talia swore at her brother who watched the action from afar.

Rory stood one step in front of his prince, gripping the hilt of his sword with such force the veins stood out in his neck. Tanin held his hand on his chest with his sword still in its sheath, as if he were enjoying a sporting event, not watching his sister and her companions fighting for their lives.

"It's okay. You can join the fight. We don't mind," Gregor taunted Tanin's party.

"You do not aid your kin?" Aleck gained his feet, his sword, the size of Naul's dagger, drawn. The dwarf questioned Tanin's inaction. "What kind of ruler will you be?"

"She's not in real danger, Prince Aleck." Tanin cracked his knuckles as he tormented his sister. "She simply didn't do the proper research before setting off on this journey."

Tanin accepted a pendant on a gold chain from Tyler. A creamy gem mounted in the center reflected the filtered sunlight as he held it over his head. "Calm, Mighty Griffin!"

Tanin's vibrato was so strong Talia felt it in her chest.

The griffin stopped its thrashing attacks. The beast released a screech higher in pitch than its earlier complaints. It focused on the pendant. One mighty flap propelled it toward Tanin. Landing gracefully in front of the prince, the calm animal bent a knee before the human. Its forward-facing eyes never left the gem, as if caught in its gleam.

"You see, Prince Aleck of the Krimmel." Tanin boldly scratched the feathered cap of the animal. His hand was no bigger than one of the beast's eyes. "You must always adventure with the proper tools. I knew there were griffins in this forest, and I brought along the pendant to control them."

"Ooh, can I try it?" The dwarf ran toward the human prince. He tripped over a tree root. Aleck's momentum threw him into the griffin's feathered side. Though not enough to move the massive beast, the collision caused the large eyes to blink twice, and the griffin shook its head.

Tanin stepped back as the griffin snapped at him. Rory maneuvered himself to the side of the griffin's feathered neck. At his prince's nod, the defense guardian severed its head from its body. Blood gushed from the wound as if a dam had ruptured. The lifeless body collapsed on top of Aleck.

"Prince Aleck!" shouted Guard Dragick.

Kettlor and Orui pushed the body onto its side. The dwarven guards dragged out their charge.

"Why did you kill it?" Aleck stared wide-eyed at the corpse of the magical creature. His guards pulled him back before the blood could flood his shoes.

"It was going to kill you, Your Highness. We must protect our allies." Tanin spoke as he circled to the back of the creature. He sliced off the tail and tossed it to Orui. The companion wrapped it in a piece of leather and stowed it in his pack.

Tears fell down Nyna's cheeks.

Naul put his arm around her, his mass acting as a comforting blanket. "It tried to tear us to pieces, you know."

"I know." Nyna let the tears drip down her face to the front of her shirt. "It was so majestic. It might have been the last one. I'm starting to think I don't know anything about our world."

The deep red blood flowed along the path toward Talia. The ebb and flow was so much like water, but with an unnatural thickness. Talia gagged as the salty-sweet smell of death flooded her senses.

"We should go before any of his friends show up." Her words broke the spell.

The party moved forward, this time with Tanin in the lead, his gait cocky and self-assured. Talia felt a new loathing for her brother. Something had changed in him. Or maybe, something had changed in her and she saw him differently.

CHAPTER THIRTY

"ANY IDEAS on how we get in?" Talia stood before the stunning Elven Palace.

Dew sat on a boulder of the river bank with the ancient tome in her lap. "I'm looking for some kind of schematic or something."

From downriver, the palace had looked like it was gilded in gold. Talia felt disappointed as the party got closer. Yellow-flowered vines covered the entirety of the structure, producing the illusion of gold. The acceptance of the truth did nothing to diminish the grandeur of the building. If Talia hadn't known it was built by sentients, she might have believed it had grown out of the forest naturally. The leaf-topped turrets lacked symmetry. They seemed to pop up wherever they wanted without serving any kind of military advantage.

"I see what you mean, Prince Aleck." Gregor joined the dwarves studying the palace. "A dwarf would never have designed a building this whimsical."

"The elves crafted all their own buildings." Aleck nodded his head.

"How do we find the entrance?" Talia asked. No openings or glasswork were visible.

Nyna pulled on a vine. "Maybe this plant grew over the windows and doors. I wonder what kind it is."

"It's possible." Aleck scratched his beard as he studied the structure. "But the elven stronghold has been called the Golden Palace for millennia, which makes me think the flowered vines were always here."

"Go ahead, Sister. Ladies first." Tanin jumped down from the uneven end of the stone bridge the companions had crossed to get to the palace.

"Why are you behind, Tanin? Afraid to take the lead?"

Her brother's lip curled, showing his upper teeth like an aggravated dog. "The trip has been long and boring. I like watching you struggle. It amuses me."

It was Talia's turn to curl her lip. Most of the time, there was very little similarity between the twins. When they faced off like this, their twin status was unmistakable.

"Fine. When I find the Holy Sapphire, I'll be in the lead." Talia dragged her foot through the sand. "Naul? Dew? Dig around and see if you can find another one of these?"

Talia sneezed from the sand particles floating in the air.

"Here's another one," Dew called.

"And here." Gregor had found one as well.

The shaped slate seemed to make up a path. Talia followed it to a section of the castle that contained an arch of rope-like vines that looked extra twisted. Ial and Naul flanked her as she reached up to push the woody parts aside.

"The plant." Orui shared a fearful look with Tyler.

The cultural guardian swallowed. "The flowers aren't red, though."

Tanin shushed his guardians before they could say another word. Talia wondered why her brother's group stood so far back from the palace, barely over the edge of the stone bridge. Before Talia could make a snide remark, a muffled booming filled the clearing. Tanin's party jumped, their tension snapped by the unexpected sound.

Talia pulled her sword and scanned the sky.

"Where did that come from?" Naul crouched low to the ground. "Another griffin?"

"Talia, you have to come see this." Prince Aleck stuck his head through a curtain of green vegetation. "There's a door in here with a big knocker." He dropped the vines, completely disappearing behind the foliage.

The muffled booming repeated two more times. Talia heard Aleck say something else but couldn't make out the words. Dragick and Gallick pulled back the green coverage in front of the door.

Aleck vibrated with excitement as he caressed the knocker like a long-lost pet. "This was definitely made by a dwarf."

"Dwarves and elves working together?" Gallick snorted.

"Maybe they stole it from us?" Dragick sneezed. "I don't know how anyone could breathe with all this pollen."

Talia noticed the heavy floral scent at the entrance.

"This door couldn't have been stolen. The opening is irregular with the wooden sides perfectly squeezed into the gaps." Aleck traced the edge of the solid piece of wood. It looked like the cross section of an enormous redwood. "The tree had to have been as wide as an elf is tall."

"Maybe the building was constructed around the door, not the other way around." Gregor lifted the aspen-leaf-shaped door knocker, which sparkled in the filtered light. "It looks and feels like solid bronze, but it's as shiny as if it were brand new."

"Aspen again? Coincidence?" Talia looked at Dew.

The cultural guardian shrugged her shoulders, eyebrows up. "Your guess is as good as mine."

"Obviously, it's not attacking. Let me through." Tanin pushed through his guardians, who were holding him back from the building.

"What's not attacking? You've had a long trip, my Prince." Gregor used a more formal tone than normal with Tanin.

His former friend ignored him.

Tyler hobbled forward, leaning heavily on a walking stick he had found in the woods. "In Naddle Swamp, an animated plant with red flowers tried to... " The cultural guardian grew silent as Orui threatened Tyler with his elbow.

Gregor struggled with his habit of brotherly teasing. Talia realized what he had sacrificed by helping her in her quest. Talia had watcher her brother stomp on more than one enemy for lesser reasons than treason. Maybe she'd have to give Gregor another chance. The lordling noticed her looking at him and smiled. Talia scowled, her anger still hot. Maybe later.

Aleck slammed the door knocker, startling Talia. With the plants pulled back, the deep, metallic sound vibrated through the clearing, echoing along the river. Aleck clapped his hands in glee. Gregor laughed with Naul. The dwarf's enthusiasm was contagious.

"Okay. If we're done playing with the toys, can we find a way in? I don't see a knob." Talia leaned toward the door as a tingling in her core pulled her toward the wood.

The door swung open on silent hinges. Talia flapped her arms in an attempt to not fall on her face. Dew grabbed her hand as a counterbalance.

A man as tall as Naul but as thin as Nyna stepped out of the shadow inside the opening. He held out his branch-like arms, palms up, in supplication. His willowy stance belied the aura of strength surrounding him. His pale, smooth skin contrasted with the deep brown of his waist-length, straight hair. A tiara of twisted branches and gems held the mane back from his face and his ears.

His pointed ears.

"An elf," Dew whispered. Her knees bent as if she would curtsy before him.

Talia bowed her head in respect, eyes to the ground, right hand on her heart. Her companions followed her lead.

"The elves are extinct," Tanin said emphatically, as if the more force he put behind his words, the truer they would become.

Talia ignored her brother, though she took comfort in the proof that he didn't know everything about this quest. She had a chance after all.

"I am Lord Thilphiliari. I welcome you to the Elven Kingdom." He spoke slowly and carefully, as if out of practice. His voice brought to mind images of swaying leaves and gentle rain. "Please, come inside to wash the road from your weary feet. The evening meal is being prepared to soothe your hunger."

As if his voice had conjured the aroma, the smell of roasting meat and steaming vegetables wafted through the door. Naul and Gallick groaned with wanting. Talia's mouth watered. The party hadn't stopped for lunch. The emotional angst of the day had killed any appetite. The delicious smells coming from inside the Golden Palace reawakened Talia's stomach.

Lord Thilphiliari stepped out of the doorway with one arm extended inside. He bowed his head at Talia and Tanin. She couldn't shake the impression that the elf lord only addressed the royal twins.

Tanin pushed through everyone to get to the front. "I am Prince Tanin Winterlaus, future king of Tarbin. I am honored to meet a living elf. We were falsely informed of the extinction of your race."

Talia stepped forward to introduce herself.

"This is my sister, Princess Talia." Tanin relegated her to subordinate status with one sentence. "I will speak for Tarbin in any negotiation. We welcome your hospitality and hope to begin a mutually beneficial friendship."

Talia bit her tongue. She didn't want the elf's first impression of her to be one of a bitter, spoiled child, which is exactly what she'd sound like if she said what she was thinking.

Unblinking, Thilphiliari stared at Tanin. His jaw tensed and then relaxed so quickly Talia thought she had imagined it. The elf bowed again in seeming acceptance of Tanin's speech. The prince returned the bow as he passed through the doorway. His guardians followed close at his heels, each one nodding in respect as he passed the willowy elf.

"It is a pleasure to meet you, Lord Thilphiliari. I look forward to learning of your people." As Talia spoke, the elf's focus slowly turned to her. Talia bowed as much to break eye contact as to show respect. She couldn't shake the pull inside her toward this foreign creature.

Naul and Gregor entered the doorway first. Talia followed with the dwarves on her heels. The elf glided with unexpected speed between Prince Aleck and Talia. His hair swished sideways like the tail of an angry beast. Dragick and Gallick unsheathed their swords at the obvious threat.

"No dwarf will set foot over this threshold while I am responsible for its safety." Lord Thilphiliari tilted his head back, staring straight down his nose at the dwarves.

"The princess does not go in without us." Guard Dragick's stance said he was intent on sticking with Talia.

She was relieved he had the sense not to mention the Holy Diamond.

"Excuse me, Lord Thilphiliari. May I please confer with my companions?" Talia might have asked a question, but her voice and posture made it clear, she was making a demand. She raised an eyebrow at Naul, who followed her.

"Naul, give me the scepter with your back to the door." Talia held out her hand as the defense guardian complied. Talia handed the Holy Diamond to Prince Aleck. "I don't know that I trust Lord Thilphiliari, but I have to try to get the Holy Sapphire."

"Of course, Talia. We want to help." Aleck handed the scepter to Guard Dragick, who secured it to a bag around his waist.

"The elf is apparently not going to allow you entrance, but you three can look around the perimeter of the Golden Palace to search for clues. I will send Naul and Dew out to help as soon as we can get away." Talia hoped her handing over the Holy Diamond without it being demanded would convey her allegiance with the dwarves.

"I would like to see the inside of that magnificent structure." Aleck sighed as he took in the palace behind Talia. "But I will do my duty first. There might be an adventure waiting for us out here."

"And I'll sneak dinner out somehow." Naul winked at Gallick, who rubbed his belly subconsciously.

Talia patted Naul, glad he was able to lighten the mood. She headed back to the entrance where Dew and Gregor held open the vines. Thilphiliari's deep black eyes never wavered from the princess. A shiver ran down Talia's spine as she realized the elf's pupils had no white around them.

"The contingent from Krimmel have agreed to wait for us outside. I will confer with them intermittently and send out a companion to bring them food."

"As you wish." The elf showed his full set of white teeth as he smiled.

Though shaped identically to a human's, Talia's imagination put sharp tips on the end of each tooth. Talia shook her head to clear the vision. There was something about this elf that pulled her toward him, yet simultaneously repelled her.

The door closed. She blinked her eyes a few times, adjusting to the darker interior. Talia hadn't realized how loud the rumble of the river was until it was blocked by the building.

She walked behind her silent host. His hands moved gently, as if he were carrying on a conversation with himself. Talia wondered if the elf was alone in this forest. If so, for how long?

"My dear sister, did you get lost in the few steps from the doorway to here? Maybe I should keep a closer eye on you." Tanin tapped his foot and crossed his arms. "I apologize for her ineptitude."

Talia's fists clenched against her thighs. Otherwise, she might have taken a swing at her brother.

Gregor broke the tension with a quiet observation. "That dividing door in front of us looks like it was carved out of the same vines that blanket the Golden Palace."

Thilphiliari felt along the side of the door. The elf closed his eyes with his palm on the chosen tentacle-like carving. He whispered in a soft flowing language that brought about the peaceful feeling of rustling leaves and quiet rain Talia had experienced earlier.

"Elvish," Nyna gasped. She exchanged a look with Dew. "I've never heard it spoken by a native speaker. No one alive has."

"It's beautiful," agreed Dew.

The vegetation slithered up to the ceiling thirty feet above the visitors. Their movement was unorganized but rampant, as the many roots seemed to be pulled up by countless hands.

Kettlor jumped back, face pale. "You can control them?"

"The forest and all its creatures obey my command." Thilphiliari stepped forward into a brightly lit room that temporarily blinded his guests. "You are the first humans to set foot in the Golden Palace in over six hundred years."

Lord Thilphiliari waited with his arms raised and his back to the humans. The overly dramatic pause gave the guests time to soak in the grandeur of their unfamiliar surroundings.

Talia marveled at the ingenuity of the construction. The typical straight wooden beams or stone columns of a structure this size had been replaced by living trees. The brown-specked bark flowed in graceful arches to a stunning height; Talia estimated they were eighty feet. The thin, flexible trunks had to be stronger than they looked, for they supported an explosion of leaf-covered branches at their peak. The branches of each tree twisted with the branches of its neighbor, as if woven together to provide a water-tight seal. Any gaps along the sides or between the treetops were covered with the same yellow-flowered plant that draped the exterior.

Talia now understood the randomness of the exterior design. The trees were groomed as structural elements based on where they naturally grew. The elves must have manipulated their surroundings, instead of tearing everything down and building anew.

Lord Thilphiliari clapped his hands twice, the sound echoing through the furniture-less chamber. Two creatures, about half the height of the elf, scurried out of the shadows.

The elven lord addressed his guests. "You must be weary after your trek. Zinni and Mari will show you to your rooms so you can freshen up before we discuss why you have traveled so far to visit me."

"Are those what I think they are?" Nyna asked. "If only Professor Clade were here to witness this."

Thilphiliari's servants stood on pale green roots splayed beneath a fibrous stalk. One stalk had two layers of long, pointed leaves facing opposite directions from one another. The flower's head consisted of three layers of fuchsia petals, with a yellow circlet of stamens crowning the center. A puff of closely knit reddish-orange served as the head for the second flower, whose leaves were thin and jagged.

"Plants moving on their own again. Professor Clade is going to have to come up with new categories for everything we're discovering," Orui agreed.

"You've seen this before?" Nyna's curiosity was piqued.

"In Naddle Swamp—" Tyler groaned as Tanin smacked his guardian on the back of the head.

Tyler shut his mouth and moved away from Nyna. Talia smirked. Apparently, fraternizing with the enemy was forbidden. That explained why Tanin's group had been so quiet through the forest.

"Please accept our hospitality for as long as you need." Thilphiliari bowed, his hands extended in either direction.

Talia didn't want to rest. She wanted to talk about why they were here and move on. The lord's complete dismissal left no room for her to intercede without looking petulant.

Each flower chose one direction. Their roots scurried along the ground in a rhythm similar to a centipede's.

"Shall we?" Tanin followed the fuchsia flower, Zinni. He paused with his guardians beside him, waiting for Talia to follow suit.

"A clean face would be refreshing. Thank you, Lord Thilphiliari." Talia addressed the lord directly, ignoring her brother. "When do you want us to join you for dinner?"

"Zinni and Mari will lead you back when the table is set, Princess Talia." The elf's dark, unblinking eyes focused on her.

Talia nodded, unable to do much else as the creepiness of the lord overtook her confidence.

"We are following a walking marigold that is as tall as Prince Aleck." Gregor seemed mesmerized by the swaying petals. "What has happened to our world?"

"Whatever it is, we're going to go along with it until I get the Holy Sapphire."

"Shhh." Dew nodded her head at the walking plant.

"It doesn't have ears," Naul observed, pulling at his own.

"It doesn't have eyes either, and it hasn't missed a turn yet," Ial pointed out.

Talia flicked her fingers. "Maybe we should hold any discussion until we're behind closed doors."

"Or lowered vines?" In front of the party, Gregor indicated the same sort of tendrils reaching to the floor that the elf had raised when they'd entered the Great Hall.

Mari pulled on one hung separately from the others, which acted as a door. The tendrils pulled themselves toward the upper canopy of the Golden Palace.

Talia hesitated at the opening. "What if we go in and it won't let us back out?"

Mari entered the chamber and pointed with its jagged leaf. A vine hung down to the right of the opening. The reddish-orange flower wrapped its leaves around the branch and pulled. The brownish tendrils extended over the doorway as if someone had lowered each one individually at slightly varying speeds.

"No ears, but it did hear us." Dew stuck her tongue out at Naul.

"Or Lord Thilphiliari can hear everything we're saying and told Mari what to do." The situation became odder and odder to Talia.

The runners climbed to the ceiling again revealing Mari, who released the vine it had pulled when the tendrils covered the doorway. The flower bowed with limbs bent, the puff of petals brushing the ground.

Talia straightened her back and walked into the chamber. When all the companions were inside, Mari scurried on its roots to a terra-cotta pot sitting outside the chamber.

"Talia." Ial put his hand on her shoulder. Talia turned to observe the flower.

Mari sunk its roots into the pot, straightened its stalk, and extended its leaves. As if they had awaited the flower's arrival, a couple of branches above the large pot parted, letting in sunlight. Talia swore Mari sighed in satisfaction as the warm light surrounded the plant.

"Naul, please." Talia indicated the woody limb that seemed to act as some kind of switch.

Naul gripped the vine with both hands. He pulled gently, as if afraid of yanking on it too hard. When nothing happened, he gave it a stronger tug. The living door descended as it had for Mari. Naul held it until the last tendril touched the ground.

"Hopefully, we can have some privacy in here." Talia sat on a pillow that looked like it was covered in lichen. She pet the soft algae absentmindedly as she would a dog in her lap. "At least we can discuss what to do with Tanin. It's the first time we've been far enough away from him to talk."

Before any real conversation, a blood-curdling scream filtered through the layers of vegetation.

CHAPTER THIRTY-ONE

At first, Talia thought the scream was an alarm. Gregor pulled the vine opener, sending the living. door up.

Talia eyed the still plant to see if Mari had made that horrific noise. The flower continued to sway gently as if in a deep sleep. The yell sounded again.

"This way, Princess." Naul started down the corridor.

Talia ran after him. The group skidded to a halt in the main room, almost running into Tanin and his guardians.

Another scream, higher pitched than the first two, echoed in the large room. This time, Talia sensed the sound came from outside, behind the palace.

"Where are Orui and Kettlor?" Dew noticed the missing guardians first.

"They went to... " Tyler doubled over with an elbow in the gut from Rory.

"None of your business." Prince Tanin crossed his arms solidly, though he jumped when another cry rent the air.

"Prince Aleck." Talia identified the dwarf's voice. She marched up to her brother, stopping inches from his nose. On her tiptoes, she lowered her voice threateningly. "If your men have harmed our friends... "

Tanin leaned aggressively toward his sister. "Maybe you should've held onto your one victory, instead of stashing it with your diminutive allies." Their guardians closed in, ready for a confrontation.

Another shriek broke the tension.

The group abandoned their fight and ran toward the voice. Around the corner, a large door opened onto a vast stone patio decorated with a long table laden with food. Talia spotted Prince Aleck and his guards staring at the forest beyond the stone floor. Prince Aleck turned at her appearance and ran toward his friend, babbling and pointing.

"Was that you screaming?" Talia took the dwarf's shoulders in her arms, bringing her face down to his. Tears streaked down his cheeks, but no blood or bruising was evident. "What happened? You don't look hurt?"

"We have to get out of here now." Guard Gallick's hand shook on his sword hilt.

His pale face and wide eyes alarmed Talia. She had never seen him so serious. Guard Dragick's whiskers quivered. Both dwarves were on high alert, their weapons drawn.

Kettlor and Orui slid to a stop on the stone flooring, weapons drawn. Breathing heavily, they shook their head at the prince. Tanin stomped a paver with his boot.

"By the Stars in the sky," Dew gasped from the edge of the patio, distracting Talia from her brother.

Talia followed her gaze beyond the paved patio. The trees seen from the front of the Golden Palace were mostly redwoods, like the rest of the forest. The white bark and heart-shaped leaves of these trees had become all too familiar to Talia: aspen.

"At least we know why the door knocker was an aspen leaf." Nyna leaned heavily on Ial.

Tanin sniffed the air. "Do you smell something off?"

Orui wiped his nose with his hand. "Probably a dead animal in the underbrush."

Ial nodded in agreement. Talia identified a whiff of decay from the trees.

Guard Dragick gestured over his shoulder without turning around. "Look closer."

Curious, Talia walked into the shadows of the trees.

"I was trying to find a way in. I didn't want to miss out." Words poured from Aleck as he followed Talia, looking only at his feet. "I came around back and saw hundreds of the sacred tree. I ran to behold the miracle. And then... "

Talia was close enough for the taller branches to filter the sunlight, allowing her to see into the darkness. She suppressed a scream with her hand as she found the source of the stench. She froze mid-step, causing Aleck to bump into her.

Corpses of varying degrees of decay stuck out from the bark of a dozen aspens. It looked like the bodies were somehow blended with the trunks and had died as they tried to free themselves. An arm bone and two femurs protruded from one aspen, a pile of dust and bone pieces at its base. Another held a desiccated body, more mummy than rotting corpse. A pile of bleached hair hung over the face. A touch of pointed ear peaked through the strands. Talia lost control of her stomach at the grotesque sight of maggots filling the half-interred, half-exposed chest of an elf.

"Elves. They're all dead elves." Aleck held his hand on Talia's back in shared disgust. "The elves and dwarves might have their differences, but this?"

Talia wiped her mouth with her sleeve, the acidic taste adding to her disgust. "Whoever did this must answer for it."

"This one's alive!" Nyna held the hand of an elf maiden firmly embedded in the white bark of an aspen.

Talia rushed to her side, eager to save someone amid the carnage. One hand protruded from the trunk, adorned with a white gold twisted ring. The flawless skin of her pale face contrasted with the rough, speckled bark surrounding it just in front of where her ears should have been. With her eyes closed and pink lips pressed in peace, it looked like a mask had been attached to the tree instead of an elf lady stuck within its depths.

"How do you know she's alive?" Tanin asked from the patio where he hadn't moved.

"Her hand is warm." Ial held it in both of his.

"Someone's been taking care of her. There's makeup on her face." Nyna held up her finger after rubbing the sleeping elf's cheek.

"Can we get her out of there?" Talia proposed. A tingling sensation traveled along her skin.

"Do not touch my wife!" Lord Thilphiliari's voice boomed from the center of the patio. Tanin backed up at his surprise appearance. The elf wore deep blue pants that flared at the end, obscuring his feet. His tunic, of the same color, had strands of white metal sewn into the shape of a branch full of aspen leaves. Around his waist, a white leather belt held a gleaming silver scabbard with a sheathed long sword.

"Talia." Gregor tapped his own sword hilt and then nodded at the formally dressed lord.

Mounted on the hilt of his long sword, Talia saw a goose-egg-sized jewel shimmering in the deepest blue. Her instincts told her that was the Holy Sapphire. She nodded at Gregor. Talia caught her brother whispering to Rory and holding his own hilt in his hand. Tanin had come to the same conclusion.

Nyna spoke to Thilphiliari. "We want to help her."

Talia felt guilty for forgetting the distressed young elf.

"You could not begin to understand how to help her." The lord seemed to grow six inches as he straightened to his full height. He looked down his nose at his guests.

Prince Aleck stepped out from behind Talia. His horror turned to anger at the atrocity he had witnessed. "What happened to your people? Were you not to protect them while they slept?"

"Protect?" Thilphiliari's voice quivered with emotion. "For six centuries, I have done nothing but protect my people. I alone."

Almost a millennium of isolation must have drove the elf to insanity.

Gregor nodded his head at the mutilated elven bodies. "Funny way to protect them."

"The griffins invaded and started to build their nests in the sacred aspens. They would have destroyed the trees and hence my people sleeping within." The lord focused on his hands, brushing imaginary dirt from them. "My magic was weak from the war and staying alive. I could not prevent their takeover." He ground his teeth and looked into Talia's eyes, as if searching for understanding, maybe forgiveness. "I had to sacrifice a few of my comrades to save the population. Their magic allowed me to drive off the griffins and place a shield around the aspen forest to keep them out."

"Why are your people in the trees to begin with?" Talia didn't understand what was happening or how she should act.

"Without the Recharging, sustaining our numbers proved difficult. There was simply not enough magic left in the world to keep our entire civilization alive. We had to find another solution."

"That's why your people sleep." Nyna caressed the bark of the partially extracted female.

"Like bears," Kettlor added.

"Bears? You know nothing of our plight." Lord Thilphiliari's lip curled. His fingers twitched. "My people were created by the Stars themselves to spread magic upon this world. We were here before dwarves and humans. We ruled this continent before the nadph spoke their first words. The *elves* are the true progenitors."

Gregor and Dew moved behind Thilphiliari as his lecture wove on. Talia feared the elf would explode at any moment.

"What do you mean, 'progenitors?'" Talia kept the elf's focus on the forest, giving Gregor time to position himself by the sword. Tanin moved beside the lordling, a grin on his face full of threat instead of mirth.

Aleck stepped another foot forward. "According to the lore, only humans have the proper blood to catalyze the Recharging. Her blood." He motioned to Talia. "You can't save your people without her. She is the True Heir."

"I'm the True Heir." Tanin glared at his sister.

"Enough!" shouted Thilphiliari. "I will show you how much I need you."

The elf raised his long-fingered hands over his head and spoke a few words Talia didn't understand. He slammed his hands toward the ground. Talia fell, plastered against the damp grass. She managed to twist her head to witness her companions, as well as Tanin's, stuck in the same position.

"I will take the Holy Gemstones now. You have no need of them." Thilphiliari mimed his hands pulling a rope, mumbling under his breath. Talia felt herself lifted off the ground. Her brother was similarly elevated to her left. Unable to control their movement, the twins floated toward the elf. His eyes were so big, Talia could see the forest reflected in their black depths.

"You mean this gem?" Prince Aleck's arm shook as he struggled to hold up the Holy Diamond for the elf lord to see.

The distraction caused Thilphiliari to drop the humans. "You do not keep the precious stones on your person at all times? Sacrilege." He lunged toward the dwarf.

Talia hit the paved surface, which knocked the breath out of her. She spied her brother trying to catch his own. Unwilling to give Tanin the upper hand, she swallowed her discomfort and rolled toward the elf. Unnoticed from behind, Gregor cut Thilphiliari's belt just as Talia reached for the scabbard. She bounded to her feet and unsheathed the sword, studying the Holy Sapphire.

Thilphiliari whipped around with an angry growl. Talia jumped back several times, putting distance between her and the deranged elf. Naul and Dew stepped in front of her.

The elf lord raised his closed fists. "Always a nuisance! After I recharge the world and awaken my people, we will end your scourge on the planet."

The powerful magic user spread his fingers. A glow surrounded Talia, and her body levitated off the ground. Her guardians, surrounded by a similar shimmer, couldn't move. Talia flailed her arms, trying to maintain some control of her elevation. The elf cackled as he twisted one hand. Talia brought her hand up to her throat. She couldn't breathe, but she refused to relinquish the sword.

Tanin ran to her, reaching up to claim his prize. Thilphiliari stomped on a paver. The stone swallowed Tanin's feet. The prince fell hard on the ground with a snap and a moan.

"I will take my sword back now." Lord Thilphiliari bent his elbows, magically propelling Talia toward his position.

Wind rushed through Talia's hair as she flew toward the waiting lord. At the last moment, she raised the silver sword. The sharpened metal impaled Thilphiliari to the hilt. The elf remained standing for a few seconds as if held upright by his own magic. Then he collapsed like an abandoned puppet.

Talia fell to her knees, hands flat on the ground, panting for breath. She knelt by the fallen elf. She'd never killed anyone before. She knew intellectually she had had no choice, but her heart ached with what she had been forced to do. She brushed off her self-doubt as her brother rushed toward her. She grabbed the sword and yanked it from the body.

"Give it to me. I have a mission to complete." Tanin held his hand out expectantly.

His guardians pulled their weapons. Talia's party matched their aggressive stance.

"It is in my possession. Why should I give it to you?" Talia protected the sword against her chest, moving her foot to avoid blood dripping on it. The jewel hummed against her skin. It had to be the Holy Sapphire.

Tanin took a step toward her. The tension in the clearing rose higher than it had been when the elf attacked. Talia knew that focus. Tanin was going to attack.

The dwarves added their support to Talia. Her group had more sword arms than Tanin's. She felt good about her odds but didn't want to see any more bloodshed today.

"Please, Brother. Why can't we work together? I don't want your throne. I only want to serve Tarbin in a greater way than through a marriage bed."

"A Dark Curse on you, Sister. Father has always favored you, though I am his son and heir apparent. I will prove to him he has adored the wrong twin." Tanin's words were bold, but his eyes scanned Talia's greater numbers.

Rory whispered in Tanin's ear.

Whatever he said caused Tanin to put away his weapon, motioning for his guardians to do the same. "The Stars will make all final decisions. I can wait."

He smiled at Talia. Far from comforting her, the predatory expression put her more on edge.

Without a farewell, Tanin strode around the Golden Palace, heading toward the river with his companions in tow. Tyler looked over his shoulder at the fallen elf before he disappeared around the corner.

Talia found herself suddenly exhausted as the adrenaline from the fight wore off. She jumped at an unexpected tug on her sleeve.

"Here." Aleck closed Talia's fingers over the dwarf scepter. "The Stars have already deemed you worthy of this Holy Gemstone."

Guards Dragick and Gallick nodded their approval.

"Should we bury him?" Gregor stared down at Lord Thilphiliari's bloodied body. The lordling knelt next to the pool of congealing blood. "It doesn't feel right to leave him here."

"He was only trying to protect his people, at least at first." Dew put a hand on Gregor's shoulder. "Being alone for centuries would drive anyone mad."

"We should bury him next to his wife." Leaning next to the hibernating elf, Talia whispered, "I'm sorry. He left me no choice." The elf lady looked pristine and peaceful. Talia hoped the inside mirrored the outside. Being locked inside a tree for centuries sounded as close to Forever Darkness as she could imagine.

Nyna poked the dirt by Talia's feet. "The soil seems soft enough." With her one good hand, she awkwardly stuck her scabbard into the ground.

Talia buckled the Holy Sapphire sword to her belt and used her hands to help Nyna. The rest of her party used what they could find to speed the process along.

By the time Lord Thilphiliari lay safely under a fresh pile of soil, the companions were sweaty and covered in deep dark soil. The turned earth overwhelmed the metallic smell of fresh blood, a sort of cleansing. Dew picked enough yellow flowers from the Golden Palace to cover the grave. Talia was relieved the digging had been easier than she had imagined. It was like the tree roots loosened the dirt for her, eager to accept one of their own.

Talia knelt beside the grave, flattening both hands on the flowered surface. "I will make sure your people are awakened at the proper time. Whatever that time might be."

"You had no choice." Nyna knelt beside her charge and put an arm around her shoulders. "He was going to kill everyone. You saved us."

"In the process, I condemned an entire race to perpetual hibernation." Talia shrugged her arm off and stood.

"After the Recharging, there will be enough magic to awaken them. Thilphiliari, in his arrogance, wouldn't listen to reason. Without the blood, the Machine will not work. By killing him, you gave his people a chance. I doubt they'll survive another millennium." Prince Aleck tried to comfort Talia.

She stomped across the pavement, heading toward the river. "I might have some sort of magical blood, but I don't know what that means. Up to a few months ago, I thought magic was a trick of jesters. And if I have this special blood, I'm not the *only* one. The royal family has many branches. How do we know that I've actually been chosen? That I'm the True Heir." Her breathing became labored and her footing unsure on the slick stones near the water's edge. "Because I'm the firstborn of a set of twins that could have gone either way by the fluke of the midwife. And how am I supposed to know what I'm to do? And why does it seem like I'm the center of some sort of event I've never heard of?" Talia yelled across the waterfall, her frustration carried down the rapids.

Gregor placed a hand on Talia's shaking shoulder. "You're not alone."

Dew placed hers on Talia's other shoulder. "We're with you."

Aleck grasped her soft hand with his rough one. One by one, the dwarves and the humans gathered around Talia, each one making their presence known. A soothing aura calmed the princess's nerves. A single tear trailed down her cheek.

Naul's stomach growled. Talia laughed. Her release of tension allowed the rest of her party to join in. Before long, they were a mess of giggling children.

Talia wiped the tears from her eyes and took a breath. "We should head out. My brother has a significant lead since he still has horses."

"Could we grab some of the prepared food and eat on the road?" Naul rubbed his upset stomach.

Talia nodded. "Of course, grab what you can. We'll quiet our grumbling bellies on our way to Naplion to get the horses Lain should have reserved for us."

Talia sat cross-legged on the edge of the waterfall while her guardians packed up supplies. She could do this. She had to.

CHAPTER THIRTY-TWO

Hours after the intruders departed, the yellow, trumpet-shaped flowers covering the fresh grave moved gently. Some fell off the mound, tumbling down the fresh soil. A pale hand, caked in dried blood, pierced the surface. Finding the rough bark of the aspen, the hand crept upward, searching. With the hand exposed and groping, more of the loosely packed dirt shifted, revealing the bloodless face of Lord Thilphiliari. His mouth moved, but no sound escaped. His fingers found the hand of his wife, frozen half in and half out of the trunk. He gripped with all the strength he could muster.

The eyes of the mask sticking out of the tree shot open. Colors rippled through the bark, an entire rainbow of energy. The woman struggled to free her hand from the death grip. Having freshly awakened, she didn't have enough strength to fight herself loose.

"Forgive me, my love. After all these years, I thought I had sacrificed enough." He sat up easily, displacing the layer of soil over his shallow grave. "Alas, I must have your magic if I am to complete my quest and save our people."

Tears ran down the elf lord's face as his beloved spouse was torn piece by piece from her protective home. The upper branches swung violently, producing a localized windstorm. No sound assaulted his ears beyond the rending of the bark and the groaning of the tree. But in his head, he could hear her screaming.

Her eyes focused for an instant on her husband's face. Still gripping her hand, Thilphiliari stood before his silent confidante. One tear ran down her cheek. Her expression pleaded with him to stop. He held up her chin with his free hand and kissed her with all the passion he had felt when he first laid eyes on her centuries ago. The parts of her body she had managed to wrench from the tree convulsed as the last bit of magic drained into Lord Thilphiliari.

The tree now stood still, silent witness to the slaughter. Lord Thilphiliari stretched as his cells returned to full strength. He released his dead wife's hand with a vow. "The humans will pay for what they have done to you. I will control the Machine, and the world will lie at my feet."

The mad elf snapped his fingers and disappeared.

CHAPTER THIRTY-THREE

TALIA'S PARTY stayed in Naplion long enough to set the port city of Darvis as their next destination. Though the home of Lord Bello Hilderamn, Talia's betrothed, it was also the closest place to charter a ship. The next logical gem to go after was the Holy Ruby rumored to be guarded by the mythical dragons of the volcanic islands in the Ngaro Sea. Though Tanin had a significant lead over her, Talia had to try. He didn't have the Holy Diamond. Or the Holy Sapphire. She still had a chance.

The three weeks it took to travel from Naplion to Darvis had allowed Talia to experience the change from summer to autumn in slow motion. The green leaves of the warm months had changed to reds and browns as their elevation lowered and time progressed. Now the salty air of the port city perked Talia's senses. She looked forward to a fresh platter of fish and vegetables, along with the tart lime pie the region was famous for. The fall weather in the northern town felt much warmer than it usually did in her home of Tarbinulus.

The bedraggled companions entered Darvis City's gates as the sun rose on the horizon. Anxious to get to a real bed and freshly prepared food, they hadn't stopped to rest for the last night of their journey. The horses Lain had purchased in Naplion dragged their hooves on the cobbled roads. The normally energetic clip-clop had drained to a dull one hoof in front of the other. Talia missed her Ruix. For the first time in weeks, she wondered how the dwarves were treating her horse.

She tried to silence the nagging fear eating at the back of her mind. King Vanderlae and King Roland were bitter enemies. After the death of Princess Grace years ago, the Tarbin royal family hadn't returned. The strained relations between the two kingdoms had led Talia's father to seek other powerful allies within Darvis, such as Lord Bello Hilderamn. Knowing she walked the streets run by the man she had gone on this quest to avoid put Talia on edge.

"We should stay at an inn on the west side of town." Talia wanted to avoid the high-class buildings where her family used to stay when on diplomatic visits. "We should keep as low a profile as possible."

"Agreed." Gregor nodded. "I don't like the way Prince Tanin so graciously relinquished his claim on the Holy Gemstones."

"I've been wondering what Rory whispered in his ear to get him to simmer down." Dew dismounted to give her legs a stretch.

The rest of the companions dismounted. The streets grew more crowded as the sun woke the city's inhabitants. It was easier to lead the horses than to ride them through the foot traffic. The noise of merchants shouting for the sale of their wares grew in volume as they passed the market on the way to the west side of town. They boarded their mounts at a stable attached to a modest inn.

"Hmmm, I smell spiced potatoes and bacon." Naul led his friends to a long table with enough seats for everyone. He flagged down a waitress and ordered food before Talia had even sat.

Guard Gallick breathed in deeply. "What is this bacon you speak of?"

"You have never eaten bacon?" Naul hugged his shorter companion. "You are about to taste a little bit of Light-Blessed perfection."

"So what's the plan?" Gregor took a seat beside Talia.

"Sleep. Does sleep count as a plan?" Nyna sat her head down, gingerly protecting her broken arm under the table.

Talia smiled at her guardian. "If only. We'll sleep on the ship. We should get out of Darvis as soon as we can. And no one call me princess, please."

The customers weren't the sort found in Talia's normal circle. Salt seeped from their skin, wrinkled and deeply tanned from years at sea. The only females in the restaurant were waitresses by day, barmaids by night. Talia had heard tales of places like this but had never visited one. She pictured any one of them turning her in to Lord Bello for the reward.

One of the waitresses, who had large breasts and thin legs, carried eight mugs to the companions. Talia was impressed by her strength and flexibility as she wove around the other customers. Another girl, daughter or younger sister judging by the similar features, dropped two large skillets of spicy potatoes onto the table. Their pale complexions contrasted with the leather look of their customers. Talia smiled at the women, who ignored her. The girl turned to fulfill other demands while the older waitress held out her hand.

Luckily, the silver sword—after the Holy Sapphire had been pried loose—had sold for a hefty purse. Naul put pieces in the server's hand. The woman slowly tucked the coins into her bodice and aimed a crooked smile at Gregor.

"Are there no women immune to your charms?" Talia watched the waitress look over her shoulder as she left the table.

Gregor winked at the princess. "You, apparently."

Talia switched her focus to her guardians before he made her blush. She longed to go back to the bantering, but she wasn't ready yet.

The party was a little battered and bruised, but their spirits were still high. Talia might not always make the correct decisions in her life, but these four guardians had been well chosen. When she had selected these particular students out of the dozens available, she had hoped for loyal and capable guardians. Instead, she gained unexpected friendship.

For the next hour, they ate and drank in silence, having shared all their stories on the road. Talia stretched into the back of her chair. She drained her mug of the famous Darvis herbed mead. The sweet and earthy blend pleasantly trickled down her throat.

The sensation reminded her of the last conversation with her father. His inability to see her as anything but a result of his manhood, a pawn to move on the board to acquire more power, infuriated Talia. She signaled to her companions it was time to get down to business. Years of living and working together trained her guardians to immediately focus on her.

Prince Aleck had drifted to another table, where he was teaching some of the sailors a bawdy dwarf drinking song. Guard Dragick directed his charge back to the party.

"Sailors are fun." Aleck swayed slightly as he fell into the seat offered by Guard Gallick. "I've never met anyone who spent so much time on top of the water."

"I'm sure they've never met a Krimmel dwarf, either." Naul raised his mug in salute.

The cheerful Aleck lifted his full mug with both hands, encouraging the whole table to do the same. "To new friends and high adventure." The group clunked their wooden mugs together, sloshing a bit.

Talia wiped her mouth with her sleeve. She could get used to this free style of living. "Dew, review where we're going so we can make sure to get the proper supplies and ship."

"According to the book and Pri... " Dew stopped herself from saying "prince." She placed her delicate hand on the dwarf's substantial one to ask forgiveness for her forwardness. "Er, Aleck, we need to head to the volcanic islands to the north. Tarbinians have called it the Dragon's Breath Archipelago due to the active lava flow and regularly exploding volcanoes. But the book and Aleck say it is the ancient home of actual dragons."

"If you had made that statement a few months ago, I would have laughed until I couldn't talk." Ial shook his head around a mouthful of potatoes, finishing off the skillet.

"Because normally you're so loquacious." Gregor laughed.

Ial shrugged.

"I've always wanted to see the Dragon's Breath region." Gregor wiped his forehead with his sleeve.

"Ial and Dew, you charter the ship to the islands. The rest of us will head to the market to get supplies for the trip." Talia circled her fingers as if drawing a mental picture of the city. "We want to avoid the high-profile charters. Have everything delivered to the south dock. We'll meet in two hours." She looked at Ial and Dew. "Get the vessel leaving as soon as possible. Tanin's probably already out there. We need to catch up."

"We're on it," Dew spoke, and Ial nodded.

Talia rose. "Let's go."

CHAPTER THIRTY-FOUR

Morning started early in the fish market. The timing worked perfectly for Talia and her companions.

"Can you have the rations delivered to the dock under the name... " Talia's eyes grew large as she realized she didn't want to use her real name and hadn't thought to come up with an alias.

. "Lordling Gregorius Winslet." Gregor stepped in to hide her stammering. "I apologize for my companion. It's been a long trip, and we still have a ways to go."

The merchant looked at Gregor knowingly. The pudgy man offered a yellow daisy from his display to Talia. "The strains of the road are too much for any woman, especially one as lovely as you."

Talia scowled at the absurd statement. She opened her mouth to defend her gender.

"Take the flower, my darling." Gregor put the stem in her hand and guided her away from the stand before she could explode. "One battle at a time," he whispered in her ear as he winked over his shoulder at the merchant.

She pushed him off. He might be right, but that didn't give him the privilege to stand so close.

"That was the last of the purchases." Nyna adjusted her new sling. The group had taken the time to visit a Medicinal School-sanctioned shop to get her arm properly cleaned and set. After days of healing on its own, resetting the break had been impossible. The graduate on premise had sold the group extra herb mixes for the pain and infection.

"Looks like we're ready to meet Dew and Ial. Where are Aleck and Dragick?"

"He took off while I was haggling. Something about the fishy odor. I thought he came back to find you." Naul turned to look into the crowd. Being a head taller than most of the people in the market, he could easily scan for the dwarves.

"They'll meet us at the entrance. Prince Aleck wanted to buy a souvenir for his father, the king." Guard Gallick had stayed with Talia, who carried the scepter in her shoulder bag.

"I haven't seen any dwarves since we entered Darvis. They should be easy to spot." Gregor climbed a low brick wall bordering the yard of a house on the outskirts of the market. He pointed to Naul's right. "I see him."

Talia led the group through the crowd to the wooden cart Gregor indicated. A huge man, the roundest she'd ever seen, rested an arm over one of the three barrels. His other hand, as big as Talia's head, held a mug of beer he sloshed around as he spoke. Prince Aleck, perched atop a stool he must have climbed to sit on, held the same size mug with both hands. The dwarf sipped it appreciatively and laughed at the brewer's jokes.

"Talia." Aleck waved as he saw the princess separate from the other shoppers. "You have to try this. It's different from anything I've ever tasted. Randall crafts these unique beers by using different kinds of barley and hops. Randall, you must pour Talia a taste."

Aleck swayed slightly as he held out his drink, throwing his balance on the stool too far forward. Guard Dragick grabbed his charge's belt loop, preventing an unroyal-like spill. He took the mug from Aleck as the prince tried to take another sip. Aleck's lips followed the beer, uncertain why it kept getting farther away.

"Please have a sample, m'lady." Randall bowed low before the new potential customers. "The sample is free. If you like it, tell your local barkeep to send orders to Randall the Brewer from Darvis."

The man grabbed a small wooden cup and poured a bit from the barrel he was leaning on. "This one is my favorite: strongly bitter with hints of orange in the end. It finishes clean, so you're ready for your next sip." He offered the sample to Gregor. "I even have a sweeter variety with blueberries added in the end. The sweet and sour overtones are favorites of the ladies." Randall winked at Dew as he reached for another sample.

"I am sure your beer is wonderful, Mr. Randall, but we must be on our way." Talia took the cup from Gregor and handed it back to the brewer. Before the professional salesman could stop her, she headed toward the exit of the market.

"This place is fascinating," said Aleck as his guards took one elbow each to guide him through the crowd behind the humans. "I tried some sort of fried bread and a battered green vegetable I've never seen. Lots of hats. Do you like my new hat?"

Aleck's new headwear flopped to one side of his head, looking more like a wet sack than a fancy hat. The dark green color made his eyes appear muddy, and the one sad feather drooped, forcing him to constantly blow it out of his face.

The eager look on Aleck's face softened Talia's rebuke for the choice. "It looks very fashionable."

Despite her urgency, Talia's heart lightened at the dwarf's return to his jovial nature. Since the grotesque scene behind the Golden Palace, Aleck had been more subdued. The somber demeanor seemed against his nature. Talia found hope in his enjoyment of this new experience.

"Oh, it is. The milliner said it was the latest style." Aleck tripped on an uneven paver, sending his hat over his eyes. Gallick straightened it for him. "Look at the puppies! Have you ever seen anything so cute?"

Prince Aleck reached down to pet one no bigger than his hand. The boy holding the baby was as tall as the dwarf. The lad's face flushed in shock as the dog he held licked Aleck's face. Talia guessed he'd never seen a dwarf before. The race wasn't nearly as common in Darvis as they were in Tarbinulus.

The princess reached the exit to the market and almost ran into her brother. Naul put his arm in front of her to avoid the collision. Tanin's guardians glared at Talia, daring them to start a fight.

"Ah, my dear sister. It took you long enough to get here. We've prepared a welcome party for you." Tanin took a step back, his arms outstretched. Rory made a whistling sound. A circle of armed Darvis guards surrounded her and her companions. Talia saw Aleck distracted by the puppy, oblivious to the peril they were in.

Her heart raced as she tried to calculate her next move. "Shouldn't you be on your way to the next Holy Gemstone, or do you just like me beating you?"

Tanin laughed so hard, it frightened Talia. Anything he was that happy about couldn't be good for her.

Out of the corner of her eye, Talia saw Prince Aleck look up. He took a step forward to join the party. Dragick stomped his spear on the ground and shook his head. The guards moved closer to the spear-toting dwarf but didn't look beyond the circle. Aleck hesitated.

"Drop your weapons immediately, or my guards will have to do their job."

Talia recognized the sneer in the deep voice. Stepping down from a carriage in front of the market gate, the robust form of Lord Bello filled her vision. Talia's eyes locked onto the one person she had wanted to avoid.

"Did he get uglier, or is that just me?" Gregor asked over Talia's shoulder.

Lord Bello's hovering eyebrows clouded his face like a brewing storm. Shivers overtook the princess's body, but she ground her teeth, refusing to show any outward sign of weakness. She found comfort in her hand resting on her sword hilt. "You have no right to give orders to the Princess of Tarbin."

"Maybe not." Lord Bello entered the circle of guards, stopping close enough to the princess to be able to look down at her. "But I do have the right to escort my bride to her marital home at the castle."

Her knees shook, but she didn't look away. "We have to drop our weapons because...?"

"King's orders, Princess Talia." A man wearing full armor with a red scarf tied around his neck stepped forward. His thin frame was barely big enough to hold the heavy metal, yet he moved with a quiet ease. "As captain of the guard, I am required to bring all guests to the castle unarmed."

The captain hooked his thumbs in his sword belt. His eyes flicked to the rooftops. Talia saw archers with arrows nocked. She frowned at the captain. She well knew they wouldn't hurt her, but they would take down everyone else.

"Where is that annoying dwarf? The one that asks all the questions." Orui twisted his staff threateningly.

"Prince Aleck of Krimmel was called home on business," Guard Gallick spoke up, emphasizing the word "prince."

Guard Dragick said something in the guttural dwarven language, which Talia didn't speak. Prince Aleck, still outside the circle with the boy and his puppy, backed away. Talia hoped he had the good sense to escape.

"There!" yelled one of the archers on the other side of the plaza.

Prince Aleck sprinted into the crowd. Talia couldn't see him as he disappeared, but she traced his path as people scooted out of the way. The captain of the guard nodded his head at the archer. The man took aim and released his arrow.

"No!" Dragick dove toward a space between the circled guards. One grabbed him by the back of his collar, tossing him to the ground.

Talia saw a human bystander fall to the arrow. The crowd shook their fists and yelled at the archer.

"Stop!" commanded Talia, loud enough for the onlookers to hear.

She unbuckled her sword belt and handed it to the captain of the guard. He sighed in relief as he accepted the weapon. Talia stepped back and tilted her head at her companions. They understood and obeyed, handing over their swords.

"And I will take the Holy Diamond and the Holy Sapphire." Tanin reached for Talia's shoulder bag, yanking the strap over her head. "You won't need it in your role as wife." He spat the word out like venom.

Talia grabbed the strap and wrapped it around her wrists. "You have to earn them for the victory." She tugged her bag, pulling Tanin off balance.

"Actually, dear sister." Tanin clutched his teeth and yanked back, legs spread for balance. "You have to obtain the gemstones any way you can. The method is *not* scrutinized."

Rory stepped around Tanin and sliced through the strap with one smooth arc of his sword. Talia stumbled backward. Naul steadied her before she could tumble to the ground.

Dragick and Gallick confronted Prince Tanin, weaponless but seething with hostility.

"The Holy Diamond belongs to our people. You have no claim."

"Wait!" Talia warned.

Two guards grabbed their heads from behind and slit their bearded throats. Blood gushed as the dwarves dropped to their knees almost in unison. They looked at each other and fell, one over the other.

Talia stared, the horror more than she could take. Her heart drained with the lifeblood of her allies.

"Why?" Nyna cried.

The medicinal guardian fell to her knees by the dwarves. Talia grasped her shoulders and helped her up before the deep red liquid reached Nyna. With Nyna safely in Naul's arms, Talia glared at her brother.

Gregor beat her to it. He shouted at Tanin, his fury overtaking his common sense. Rory stepped in front of the prince, ready to take down the unarmed man. Talia blocked Gregor's aggressive movement. She took his cheeks in her hands and forced his eyes down to focus on her. His face was so red, it looked like someone had painted it with cherry juice.

"I will not lose another friend today." Talia demanded his compliance with her whispered words. "Rory won't hesitate to add your body to the pile. Then you would never avenge their deaths."

The word "avenge" made its way through Gregor's fury. Talia felt his jaw relax and his arms surround her waist. For a moment, she felt they were the only two people in the world. She wanted to collapse into his arms, seeking and giving comfort.

"That's quite enough manhandling of my fiancée." Lord Bello yanked Talia away from Gregor.

The lordling's face reddened to crimson, threatening another rash move. Talia held up a restraining hand, her eyes begging him and her tense guardians to back down.

"I will not be harmed. He needs me alive."

Lord Bello stuffed her into his carriage, snickering at her confidence.

"I must be off, Sister. I am saddened to miss your wedding, but I do have an important quest to complete and a kingdom to rule." Tanin pulled the scepter from her bag and placed it gingerly into his own. He tucked the sapphire into a pouch around his neck. He tossed her empty bag into the carriage. "I'll return in a year or so to meet my nephew. I'm sure he will be fat and strong like his father."

Lord Bello bowed at Prince Tanin. "I will send you a formal invite for his naming ceremony."

Tanin tilted his head in acknowledgment. He set off toward the dock, guardians in tow.

"What do I do with them?" The captain of the guard asked Lord Bello, his sword pointed at Gregor's throat. The steel in his eyes revealed his intention to have their bodies join the dead dwarf guards."

"Killing a guardian is a treasonous act and will be met with total destruction," Talia threatened from the carriage window. She thought the guard's sword arm wavered.

"Toss them in the dungeon. We'll deal with them later." The carriage leaned dangerously to the side as Bello's large frame climbed the steps.

"And these?" The captain kicked the dead dwarves with the toe of his boot.

"Throw them into the sea. And find the missing dwarf and two guardians. We wouldn't want them to miss the wedding."

CHAPTER THIRTY-FIVE

Talia paced her chambers. Her wedding dress swished across the floor as she changed directions. The room in the Darvis castle was as opulent as Talia had been taught to expect. But she felt no more at home than she was sure her guardians felt in the dungeon below the castle. Her guardians, her friends. The absence of the four people who were closer to her than blood relatives made the overly dressed bride feel naked. The last time she had been without at least one of their company, she was nine years old. Now she was about to be married to a nightmare of a man in a foreign kingdom unfriendly to her native land. For once in her life, Talia wished her mother was there.

"Princess Talia, please, let us finish your hair. We have only plaited one side." An elderly woman introduced as Madam Hillard sat on a stool next to Talia's dressing table. The woman had soft hands, which bespoke her privileged upbringing. Her kind gray eyes begged the bride to take her seat. Talia wondered how much of today's happenings the old woman understood. Not for the first time that afternoon, Talia wished for her sword back. She could take out the guards at the door and make her escape.

"Please," Madam Hillard begged again, patting the cushioned chair with one hand.

Talia took pity on the woman. She didn't know what cruel fate awaited the servant if the princess wasn't presentable by the allotted time. As she took her seat, two handmaidens spread the lace train carefully around Talia to prevent any wrinkles from marring the multicolored silk fabric. Talia thought she heard a sigh of relief from the seamstress as she bent down to finish hemming the bottom of the dress. Madam Hillard began her detailed braid on the right side of Talia's head.

From her seat, all Talia could see was her reflection in the vanity mirror and that of the ladies fluttering around her. Most girls dreamed of their wedding day. She remembered classmates who had sketches of their dresses and feasts and flower arrangements in their school books. Even though her father and brother had beaten her future betrothal into her adolescent mind, Talia had believed she would avoid the fate somehow.

How naïve she had been. She couldn't look at her reflection any longer. She tried to rise. The young handmaidens, who had straightened her dress, pushed Talia back onto the cushion before the braid could fall out of Madam Hillard's hand.

"Now, my dear, I know you are nervous. I remember my wedding day like it was yesterday." The old woman continued to braid.

"Oh, did it resemble mine?" She was done being nice. "Were you married with a sword to the throat of your loved ones in a land hostile to your home?"

Hillard ignored her temper tantrum. "My fiancé, Lord Dwendel Tuloon, was a powerful merchant on the south side. He did most of his business with Tarbin, my dear. And he owned many of the buildings south of the docks."

"You saw his masculine figure," one of the handmaidens embellished the story.

"And his hefty treasury." The older of the two servants giggled.

"Quite the contrary." Madam Hillard motioned for one of the

handmaidens to hold up a cup of water, allowing her to tame a bit of wild hair. "I did not lay eyes on my betrothed until my veil was lifted at the end of the aisle. My parents had arranged the whole thing for a hefty dowry of one city block."

"But when you finally saw his smiling visage on your wedding day, your heart belonged to him forever after."

"Oh, by the Stars, no." The old woman heaved her shoulders in a silent chuckle. "I was a mere fifteen years old, and Lord Dwendel Tuloon was over forty. I felt like I was attending my funeral. My first look at the man whose bed I would share made my insides become my outsides all over the altar."

"You did not!" Talia stomped her foot in disbelief.

The seamstress stabbed her with a needle.

"Ouch!"

"Oh, excuse me, Princess. Your sudden movement unsteadied my stitch."

Talia thought she heard a note of sarcasm under the woman's words but chose to ignore it. Her constant pacing was certainly not making the woman's job any easier.

"I did." Madam Hillard continued without losing a beat. "My parents were mortified. My bridegroom didn't react at all, but he looked at me with darkness, one lip curled. His hands twitched. I could feel the heat pouring from his body as if he was burning up inside."

Talia's foot tapped nervously as the old lady droned on. She knew the woman meant to be comforting, but Talia felt like a trapped ewe waiting to be fed to a Giant Eagle. She needed to escape. Even if she managed to pass the two guards at the door, how would she free her guardians from the dungeons? Though they were charged with protecting her, Talia couldn't bear the thought of her friends' execution due to her cowardice in the face of a future with Lord Bello.

"Yes, yes, and eventually you found love and lived happily ever after."

"Hardly, my dear child." Madam Hillard pulled Talia's hair a bit too aggressively. "He came to me when he felt the need and draped me over his arm at client dinners like a fancy painting he had acquired. We never shared anything akin to love, not even after his children were born." She finished the braid and accepted small white flowers from a handmaiden to tuck into the plaits.

"After the children, he left you alone and you found peace," Talia interjected, wanting the lecture to end so she could think.

"No." Madam Hillard jammed a reinforced stem into Talia's scalp. The princess winced. "He lost everything when the trade routes between Darvis and Tarbin were shut down."

Talia didn't know what to say. She felt bad for being so selfish. She remembered the turbulent times when Princess Grace perished at sea. The angry voices of her father and the king of Darvis was one of her most vivid memories. She had seen her father upset, but never with righteous anger.

"We had nothing to do with the sinking of Princess Grace's ship. The tragedy of her loss was felt in my kingdom as well." Her father's words echoed in her mind.

"So my husband claimed. No one knew your people better than he. Lord Bello convinced the king otherwise." The old woman sighed. "After losing everything, I was forced to take work in my doddering years in the castle advising other young, foolish women."

Madam Hillard rose from her stool. Her knee popped as she stretched to her full height. Talia reached out reflexively to catch her.

"Hands back, young lady. I'm not that feeble, though my body might make a few complaints." She tottered to the wash basin, where she took a dollop of fragrant cream into her palm. She rubbed the cream into her old, age-marked skin. Gathering another dollop, she shooed away the seamstress as she took Talia's hands. Rubbing gently, the delicate smell of lavender and vanilla wafted from the cream. "This will keep him calm tonight, my dear. The first night is always the scariest."

Madam Hillard lifted Talia's hands, encouraging the princess to rise. She stared, a breath away from Talia. "Do not fight. Do not complain. Once your husband is happy and satisfied, he will leave you alone."

Talia opened her mouth to protest. The old woman squeezed her hand tightly, almost painfully. "Women have no power in this world. Be happy you at least will never need to worry about feeding yourself or your children. Most have it much worse."

Talia's mind swirled with her complete disagreement. The kind look in Madam Hillard's eyes gave her pause. She remained silent in respect of the old woman who was only trying to comfort a terrified girl on her wedding day. Yet, Talia's ambition refused to allow her to settle for a well-fed life.

Outside her chamber, Talia heard a commotion. The guards were yelling at someone to leave the vicinity. A girl responded to their orders. Talia thought she recognized that voice. The princess dropped the old woman's hands, gathered her dress, and ran to open the door.

In the torchlit hallway, a girl in a shimmering performance leotard with the bright colors traditional to a Darvis wedding bounced up and down on her toes. The two guards brandished their weapons at the performer as if she were a wild animal intent on breaking into the suite. Talia pushed one of the guards aside. The crown of golden curls gave away Dew. Aleck must have found her at the docks. Talia stopped herself from shouting her guardian's name, but the huge smile across her face was impossible to suppress.

The handmaidens crowded behind the bride, trying to see what all the excitement was about.

"Oh, Princess Talia, I've always wanted to meet a real princess." Dew teetered like a little school girl, back and forth on her toes as if she had to use the chamber pot. "I brought these especially for you. I wanted to grace your wedding with the white dwarf calla lily, the traditional flower for Tarbin weddings."

"By the night sky, gentlemen, does this child threaten your post with her admiration for royalty?" Talia scowled at the guards. The men abashedly lowered their weapons. Talia stood her tallest with her chin in the air. "Come forward, girl. My handmaiden will accept your gift."

Dew giggled as she presented herself to the princess. Talia wished she could read her guardian's mind. One of the handmaidens accepted the bouquet of long-stemmed white flowers tied together with a large white ribbon. Dew bowed low before Talia. The princess reached down and raised her with one hand. The two women stood eye-to-eye. Dew's green irises twinkled, filling Talia with hope she had all but abandoned. She might not be able to read her guardian's mind, but she knew there was a way out.

"I look forward to your performance at the wedding."

"We will not disappoint. Everyone has been rehearsing endlessly for this day." Dew giggled again and looked away, as if too shy to keep eye contact with royalty.

"Okay, that's enough. Back to your troupe." The dark-haired guard used his pike to separate the princess and her fan.

Dew ran around the corner of the hallway, looking back once and giggling with her hand over her mouth as if she just met her idol.

Talia took the bouquet from the handmaiden. "I am as beautified as I can be. You are all dismissed."

"But?" One of the handmaidens resisted being sent away.

"No point in arguing with royalty, young one." Madam Hillard gathered the handmaidens as she would a herd of sheep. "We will see you at the wedding, Princess Talia."

Talia closed the door behind the servants. She pulled the ribbon from the bouquet. Nothing was written on the inside. She plied the inside of the flowers, pushing aside the long stamens. Yellow dust covered her lotion-coated hands. The tiny particles made her sneeze, dislodging a strand of blonde hair.

"By the ever-present Light," Talia cursed.

She couldn't find a note from her guardians, and now she was destroying the coif Madam Hillard had put so much energy into. Talia plopped in front of the mirror, placing the lilies on the vanity.

She tried to tuck the loose hair back into a braid and secure it with one of the flowers.

In the reflection, she noticed a slit above a long, flat leaf on one of the calla lilies. Talia dropped her hair to pry open the stem. Inside, she found a note written in Dew's handwriting. Talia held the paper to her chest. Tears formed in her eyes. She flicked them away, then began to read.

CHAPTER THIRTY-SIX

THE CENTURIES-OLD CATHEDRAL was decorated for the first royal wedding in over four decades. The stone building, enclosed within the castle walls, remained separate from the main residence.

The ceiling, constructed from huge timbers that held up the wooden roof, displayed the antiquated architecture. Most modern public buildings were assembled using arched stone roofs to keep the fire hazard low. Talia stared at the wooden beams two hundred fifty feet above her head. Dark navy banners depicting various constellations covered the walls. The pillars of ancient redwoods had been faced with limestone decades ago. Brightly colored fabric twisted around each one and bordered each aisle.

Talia frowned. The performance atmosphere with serious constellation astrology mixed Darvis and Tarbin traditions. She wasn't sure she liked the contrast. Of course, nothing would please her on this particular day.

The bride's corner was curtained off from the rest of the main room. She knew the opposite end held her bridegroom, Lord Bello Hilderamn. Talia awaited her cue to walk down the outside aisle to the altar and take vows she had no intention of honoring.

A vision of Lordling Gregor invaded her thoughts. She pushed it aside. These feelings for a man she wasn't even sure she could trust bothered her. The sensation of his strong arms wrapped around her waist came upon her like an unwanted haunting. Her blushing cheeks betrayed her growing desire.

The sound of hoofbeats vibrated through the stone wall next to Talia. She thought of Ial making the horses perform. She couldn't hear the dancers, but she knew Dew was part of the troupe outside. She took a moment to ask the Light to guide and protect her guardians and herself as they made their escape attempt. Though her brother had an impressive head start, the quest was not over yet. She wouldn't give up.

Talia stood at the curtain opening, clapping the bouquet delivered to her a few minutes ago. Madam Hillard sat on a stool rubbing her hands to keep them warm. Talia wondered if the old noblewoman was supposed to make sure the bride remained presentable or to make sure she remained present.

"I am glad you took my advice, Princess. Your future will be as the Stars have written. The constant pacing and nervous twitching will bring you no comfort."

"Yes, Madam. I'm sure everything will work out the way the Light intended." The old woman didn't realize Talia's calm stemmed from the dagger hilt she held in the middle of her wedding bouquet. She was not getting married today.

The orchestra struck up the first notes of the wedding duet. The crowd quieted. Though Talia couldn't see them, she sensed all eyes turn to the cordoned-off rooms in the back of the cathedral.

"It is time." Madam Hillard placed her hat back on her head. She held the curtain open and bowed as Talia exited along the wall.

The audience gasped. She stole a glimpse at the opposite wall where Lord Bello's giant form walked with surprising grace. Talia focused straight ahead. Her knuckles whitened as she held onto the dagger hilt for dear life. She found herself wishing there was a Plan B just in case Plan A failed miserably. That beast of a man would never lay a hand on her.

A female and a male voice joined the orchestra. The soprano sang the part of the virtuous young girl eager to leave behind childish dreams to serve her husband and bear many heirs. The tenor's voice lamented the loss of youthful freedom but gloried in the honor of continuing the family name. The bride and groom marched to the beat of the duet, giving the audience plenty of time to admire their formal dress. Talia ignored their whispers and concentrated on the stage.

The front of the cathedral had been retrofitted with astropriest regalia. A tapestry featuring Talia's birth constellation hung on the left side of the stage while another constellation Talia assumed was Bello's hung on the right. The altar, covered in a deep purple cloth, didn't blend with the hexagon shape of the stage. The ancient purpose of the building must have been quite different from the modern usage. On the table, Talia caught flashes of the flickering flames of candelabras. An astropriest, dressed in the traditional yellow-trimmed, stark-white robe of the high priest, stood center stage with his hands held wide. He stared at the ceiling as if he could see through to the sky above.

A pivotal ceremony in the middle of the day was unnatural to the Tarbin native, though she understood the change. Torches would offer more of a hazard than a repellant of the dark, considering the flammable wooden ceiling. A circular stained-glass window embedded in the wall at the back of the stage was the only light source.

Talia snarled as she caught the visage of King Vanderlae under the decorative window. The angle of the sun caused its light to fall beyond the throne, leaving the king in shadows. His complete lack of movement gave her no clue to what he was thinking. She wondered how Lord Bello had talked the king into sanctioning the union between his most trusted adviser and his archenemy's daughter. The Darvis ruler had always been envious of her father and his position over the most powerful kingdom on the continent. That's why he started the guardian tradition for his royal line, making Princess Grace the first of Darvis royal blood to receive four guardians from the four schools as the tradition demanded in Tarbin.

The astropriests were a new sight as well. Previously, Darvis had practiced Filial Veneration, a religion based on honoring one's ancestors and the strength of family ties. The brightly colored clothes and circus-like celebration outside were a throwback to the more traditional Darvis wedding. The somber, formal elements were wholly Tarbin in origin. Talia didn't know what had made King Vanderlae snap and convert his entire country to Astrology.

The crowd shifted from foot to foot, hands tucked into armpits to keep warm. A few had wool gloves and colorful scarfs. With pitchers of mulled wine for the guests' comfort, guards and servants created three aisles, one through the middle and two more on the outside walls.

The guests looked like a swarm of contained insects. The colors and twittering of the crowd, along with the heat of all the bodies, caused Talia to swoon. A servant stepped forward and caught her before she could tumble onto the wooden floor. Falling on the dagger tucked into her bouquet was one way to get out of this marriage, but not the direction she wanted. She offered a grateful smile to the strong servant. Naul winked back.

Talia sprung out of his arms and took a few quick steps to catch up with Bello across the room. She focused ahead and forced a serious expression onto her face. Her heart, however, beat faster in elation. Naul had broken out of prison, which meant that Nyna and Gregor had too. He would never have left them. Talia was so relieved to know her entire party was safe. Well, "safe" assuming they could pull off the revolt.

The last notes of the duet echoed in the rafters as Talia and Bello reached the bottom of the steps and faced each other. Talia no longer felt helpless, knowing Bello had no leverage over her with her companions free. The high priest lowered his head and arms and addressed the couple.

"Princess Talia Winterlaus of Tarbin and Lord Bello Hilderamn of Darvis." The thin man with a bulbous nose paused until the bride and groom had focused on him. "Behind me are the constellations of your birth. The Light and the Dark determined your destiny before sending your soul to this world. Please step forward and ask the deities to aid in your journey as your paths intersect and continue as one."

Talia and Bello walked forward until they were an arm's length apart. Talia's hand twitched on the dagger. She could pounce on him now and end this. Yet, Lord Bello's guards would stop her before she got in a single swipe of the blade. The couple walked up the four steps and knelt in front of the high priest. The officiant turned his back to the couple to address the king.

"Now!" yelled the female soloist. She drew her weapon and attacked one of Bello's guards.

Talia backed up against the table. Next time, Dew had to leave a more detailed letter. She wasn't expecting the attack to begin on the stage behind her. And who was the vocalist turned commander?

The front doors whipped open. A rush of cold wind blew into the crowded chamber. The audience moaned with the attack on their gathered warmth. The astropriest pivoted so quickly the sleeves of his robe smacked Bello in the face. The crowd's relief turned to fear as the performing horses stampeded into the packed building. The audience ran in all directions, overwhelming the guards who tried to keep order. Servants tossed aside wine pitchers and pulled out hidden weapons. They attacked the guards, who were distracted by the fleeing guests and wild horses.

The king stood, shouting something Talia couldn't make out in the noise. Lord Bello gained his feet, tossing his cumbersome outer coat onto the ground to get to his sword hilt.

Squinting at the soloist, Talia swore she looked familiar. A beat later, as the woman swung her sword in a wide, aggressive arch Talia remembered from her childhood, she realized the soloist was the Princess of Darvis. "Grace, you're alive! How is that possible?"

Bello growled as he headed across the stairs toward the not-dead princess. Talia kicked the back of his knees. He dropped his sword to catch himself before bashing his head into a step. Talia jumped on his back, her dagger at his throat. She'd recently killed for the first time and didn't know if she could handle more guilt. She hesitated. The large man flipped her over his shoulder. Her head hit a stone step, hard.

She lay there, looking at the ceiling. Small hairs flew in the air. The smell of hay filled her nose. She managed to turn her head in Lord Bello's direction. Heat seemed to radiate around his body from his seething anger.

Princess Grace ran full speed at Bello, face distorted in battle rage. Grace raised her sword to cut him down. The much larger man used her momentum against her. He slid his shoulder low and tossed the smaller woman behind him. She crashed into the stone stage.

"Princess!" Rube, Grace's cultural guardian who had acted as the tenor in the duet, tried to come to her aid.

"And so she comes back from the dead." Bello loomed over Princess Grace. "Jealous I'm wedding another?"

Talia rolled onto her side. She attempted to stand. Nyna and Gregor were by her side. She didn't remember them getting there.

Bello pulled a knife from his boot. He laughed the most gut-wrenching sound Talia had ever heard. King Vanderlae's shout echoed as if he were in a far-off chamber. Lord Bello lifted the knife over his head. Grace attempted to roll onto her side as Gregor bounded to her aide. He wouldn't make it on time.

A short figure darted from under the purple tablecloth covering the altar.

"Aleck." Talia pushed against the floor to stand. Her hand slipped. She realized her head was bleeding.

The dwarf didn't change his course. He shoved the astropriest out of the way. His rough hand scooped up Talia's dagger. Aleck's powerful legs launched him into the air. He rammed into the surprised lord.

"For my brothers." Aleck's words were spoken through clenched teeth.

The dwarf prince drove the dagger to the hilt into Lord Bello's heart. The huge man dropped the knife he held over his head. He tossed the dwarf aside like an annoying pest and ripped the dagger from his chest. Lord Bello watched his bright green shirt darken, as his lifeblood drained.

"Not... yet... " were the bridegroom's final words as he collapsed to the floor.

Princess Grace managed to roll out of the way before his massive weight could crush her. She clasped hands with Rube, who pulled her to her feet. She mounted the table and shouted above the fray.

"Bello is dead!" Her voice carried across the room, bouncing off the columns.

Talia stood while Nyna held a piece of torn dress to the princess's head. They met with Gregor, who was checking on the crumpled form of Prince Aleck. Naul and Dew joined their party a moment later.

"Ial's coming," Dew assured Talia.

Talia paused at a piercing whistle from the main entrance. The horses stopped galloping around the building and headed straight for the doors. The hall fell quiet without the aggressive hoofbeats on the wooden floors. The guests looked around, wide-eyed, for lost loved ones. The skirmishes between rebels and guards ceased at the awkward silence.

"Bello Hilderamn is dead. Princess Grace Vanderlae, your future ruler, is alive. Decide now where your loyalties lie."

The guests muttered to each other for no more than a couple seconds before they fell to their knees. The guards loyal to the Hilderamn house followed the trend and fell to their knees. The rebels cheered.

"Is it really you?" King Ernest Vanderlae leaned on the altar, staring up at his daughter.

"Yes, Father, it's me." Princess Grace jumped off the table and took her father's hands in her own. She stood a good four inches taller than her progenitor. "Please forgive my cruel trick. I tried to talk to you, but you wouldn't listen."

"My darling Grace? You are alive?" The king hugged his little girl so forcibly, Talia wondered how she could breathe. "I was so stubborn. Please forgive me. I only wanted what was best for you." Tears ran down the old man's cheeks.

"What's best for me is to take care of myself and my people." Grace held her father close, as if she were the parent and he the child. "We need to make some changes."

Talia succumbed to her emotions. Could a reunion like that be possible with her father?

Ial finally joined the party onstage. "I always cry at weddings too."

The companions looked at each other. Ial and Dew wore obnoxious sequined costumes. Nyna, Naul, and Gregor wore servant clothes. Princess Talia led the ludicrous outfits with her brightly colored flowing skirt with rivulets of her own blood down one side. The companions laughed until their sides hurt. The tension drained from the group as they realized they were once again free.

"There is a spectacular feast set up in the Great Hall. I don't see any reason to waste all that food." Princess Grace stood at the top of the stairs with her four guardians surrounding her.

The people cheered their agreement.

Her most loyal followers hoisted her above their heads and carried her out of the cathedral chanting her name.

"I could eat," Gregor said as he put an arm around Aleck's shoulders.

The dwarf pushed him off.

"Do you think they have any of that sweet bread?" Naul asked.

"Without the henbane, of course," Nyna added.

"Henbane?" the princess asked.

"That's how we got out of the dungeon. Kori, Princess Grace's medicinal guardian, drugged the guards with henbane treats." Nyna squeezed Talia's elbow with her good hand. "Can you believe they're alive?"

Talia stared at Princess Grace on the shoulders of her people. "No, I can't. It's a miracle."

"I'm dying to find out what happened." Gregor threw his servant cape to the ground.

Talia resisted the urge to fall into his arms. She wasn't mad at him anymore, but she still wasn't certain she could fully trust him. Though if he were working for Tanin, it was odd he had stayed with her instead of fleeing with her brother.

"Maybe we should take care of this wound first."

Talia flinched as Dew parted her braided hair to get a better look at her scalp.

"The bleeding has slowed, but I'd like to get it cleaned up to see if you need stitches," Nyna agreed.

"And I could use a change of clothes." Ial held his manure-stained slacks above his darkened boots.

Talia searched the remaining crowd. "Let's grab a servant and see what we can find."

On the stage, over the body of Lord Bello Hilderamn, Aleck sobbed uncontrollably. Talia swallowed hard. His guards had looked after him during the entire trip up to this point. She'd forgotten he was now alone.

Talia motioned Ial and Nyna to get supplies. The rest of the companions climbed the few steps to stand next to the grieving dwarf. Dew placed her hand on his shoulder.

Talia knelt beside the dwarf. "You saved me and Princess Grace. You have honored your people and provided a great service to mine. You, Prince Aleck Stoneworth, are what every royal strives to be."

Aleck collapsed on her lap. His tears soaked through the layers of her gown. Talia held the young prince, uncertain what else to do.

CHAPTER THIRTY-SEVEN

Prince Tanin Winterlaus sat at a desk in his cabin on the ship. He was grateful High Priestess Nomyra had warned him what he was likely to find on the island. Even with the knowledge, the actual sight caused the uninitiated sailors to swim back to the ship and leave Tanin's party to row on their own.

With the fourth gemstone in hand, Tanin headed home with as much alacrity as the sails could muster. Captain Sonacevontes complained under his breath about the dangerous waters and possibility of pirates, but Tanin was too impatient to be home to worry about such matters. The Tarbin royal crest flew. No one would dare attack his official vessel.

Staring at his prize seated upon the desktop, Tanin tried to calculate its worth. The value of the gemstones on the open market was nothing compared to the completion of his quest. The stones, dull in the shadow of the lower-deck cabin, ensured his crowning as the future King of Tarbin. High Priestess Nomyra had promised him so much more than being ruler of one modest kingdom. She had filled his head with visions of a united continent with Tanin as supreme ruler.

The High Priestess's teachings had come true thus far except for the Holy Black Opal. Tanin had followed her directions precisely. It was Nomyra's fault he didn't have that one in his possession. Tanin had grown more and more frustrated with the High Priestess along the trip. He couldn't wait to replace her when he returned. Maybe he would send her off to the frigid regions to find the Dark-cursed gem. If she were gone, it would make the transition much easier.

Without Talia around to complain about everything, his whole life would be easier. He laughed at the thought of his bratty twin sister wedded to Lord Bello Hilderamn. Surely Bello had claimed her as his own by now. If Tanin was truly lucky, Talia would be fat with child before he had finished celebrating his victorious return. Those babies would be the ugliest children in the history of the royal blood. Tanin laughed again.

"Are you hungry, my Prince?" Rory's head peeked through the door to check on his charge.

"No, no, no. I will call for you when I need something." Tanin dismissed his guardian without looking up from the gems. Rory seemed to interrupt him every few minutes. The prince grew weary of his doting presence.

As the door closed, Tanin scoffed to himself. They thought he didn't hear them, but he did. Those men who were supposed to be the most loyal to him in the kingdom. They swore to devote their life to his protection and well-being. Without any familial obligations or outside responsibilities, those highly trained men were tasked with protecting Tanin's interests and good health. Behind closed doors, those conspirators gossiped.

His guardians didn't understand his confusion, and he dared not confess. He picked up the stained knife from his desk and nicked a finger. He squeezed drops of blood onto each stone and waited. Nothing. Why did the stones glow for Talia, but not for him? Maybe there was something wrong with her and the glow was a warning?

Tanin couldn't shake the feeling that something was wrong. His guardians could mumble all they wanted. It was Tanin's responsibility to protect Tarbin and conquer the rest of Renquist. Nomyra had assured the prince that magic was the key to his success. The high priestess, or the new high priest, would know how to get the stones to obey. Tanin would have to be patient.

Patience was one trait he'd never quite mastered.

"Sir." Rory tentatively knocked on the door.

"What?" Tanin tried to sound as irritated as possible. He threw a cloth over the bloody stones.

"The captain asks for your presence on deck."

"Fine. I'll be right up."

Another couple of weeks at sea and a week on the road. Tanin was almost home. He was ready to don his crown and change a few things.

TANIN SHADED his eyes with his hand to lessen the blinding sun. The cabins below didn't feel dark until the glaring sunlight of the deck proved how lightless they were. Tanin focused down until his eyes adjusted.

Kettlor sat on a bench around the main mast. He rubbed the bulbous pearl from the Kiwa Island with chamois leather to coax a shine. The undulations along the surface looked like a hat sitting on a severed head. Already in a foul mood, Tanin's temper was stoked by the proof of his failure out in the open for everyone to judge. He considered ordering the husbandry guardian to put the pearl away. He couldn't bear to disappoint his father. The king adored Talia and ignored Tanin, though he was to be the future ruler. The dichotomy in treatment baffled the prince. He deserved to be honored beyond his twin.

Prince Tanin winced as First Officer Maritoss approached with the ship's navigator in tow. The fop's cologne, out of place on the ocean vessel, made Tanin sneeze. Rory climbed the ladder to join him.

"Sire, may I have a word?" Maritoss bowed to the prince.

"Only if you've found a way to speed our journey as I requested." Tanin looped his thumbs in his belt.

"I think if we stay on course, it will take five weeks to reach North Port."

Tanin looked at the navigator for confirmation. The nervous man nodded his head once.

"If we steer north to catch the jet stream, the only place you'll be headin' is straight to the afterlife!" The captain popped up from below decks. He breathed heavily from the exertion, his foul breath overwhelming Maritoss's cologne.

"May I make a suggestion?" asked the first officer in his oily voice.

"Is that not why I stand here?" Tanin's visceral dislike of the man seeped from his pores.

"Last season, I served with the Tarbin trading ship, *Krakatoa*. We stopped at Darvis City and then went straight to Thurrelrun." Maritoss motioned toward the navigator's charts. "May I?"

The navigator gladly moved out of the way, giving the first officer the focus of the powerful men. The captain and prince followed Maritoss's finger as he traced out a path into deeper water. Tanin hadn't paid much attention to navigation. To him, going farther north away from land would make the journey take longer.

"One of our crew, a Ngaro defect from a fishing village not far from here, knew a quicker route. He led us north. With no deadline to meet, we went along for the ride, curiosity ruling our decision making. We fought... " Maritoss cringed at the irritation written on the prince's face. The first officer talked faster. "To our surprise, when we reached the deeper water, our speed increased. Some current carried us much faster than the unpredictable winds close to shore. We landed at North Port and backtracked a day to Thurrelrun. Even with the backtracking west, we cut two weeks off our projected route."

"That's too close to Ngaro waters. It's not safe," argued Captain Sonacevontes.

"This sea is owned by no one. We have as much right to travel it as do the Ngaro." Maritoss stood straight, exuding confidence.

"How long will it take us to make port if we go your way?" asked Tanin.

"Three weeks."

The captain puffed out his chest. "Why did you not mention this passage during the planning?"

"I didn't know how vital the prince's mission was. The southern route is definitely safer, but time-consuming."

"It would be three weeks, Captain. I checked the calculations myself." The navigator wiped his sweaty brow with his sleeve.

"Shall I prepare the leadsman?" asked Maritoss.

"Our mission is sanctioned by High Priestess Nomyra and King Roland Winterlaus. The Light is on our side. We will be successful." Tanin pushed the importance of his mission. If Sonacevontes didn't approve the orders, Tanin would toss him overboard and put the first officer in charge.

The captain pulled his hat on and off twice, staring at the water. "All right, we'll try your way, Maritoss. But if a single barnacle on my ship hits anything, we're reversing and heading south."

"Yes, sir." Maritoss saluted the officer and left the deck to brief the leadsman.

The navigator looked relieved as he relayed the new course to the helmsman.

"If my ship or crew are damaged—"

"My father, the king, will reimburse you for any trouble." Tanin dismissed the captain with a wave of his hand.

Rory followed Tanin off the bridge. Tanin passed Kettlor caressing the grotesque pearl.

"Put that disgusting thing away before I throw it overboard," he ordered.

"Yes, my Prince." Kettlor tucked it into a leather bag hung from his belt. The bag swung back and forth, as though it contained a decapitated head.

CHAPTER THIRTY-EIGHT

A week into the voyage, Tanin had grown tired of nothing but blue sea and blue sky. He almost longed for a storm to break the tedium.

A crosswind whipped the sails causing the ship to sway to the starboard side. The captain ordered the crew to correct the cloth to maintain their current momentum. The old sailor seemed as anxious as the prince to be done with this part of the voyage. The officer's demeanor had darkened over the last week. He barked at his crew instead of casually relaying orders.

Tanin glanced back at the dolphins playing in the choppy wake. Behind the frolicking animals, the prince saw a shadowed shape.

"Rory, do you see that?" Tanin pointed to the object on the water, which was approaching at an alarming rate. "It's a big ocean. Why are they following us?"

"Captain!" Rory yelled up to the bridge.

Sonacevontes wrinkled his nose in annoyance. The old man shot a look over his shoulder. He froze, mouth open. Grabbing the spyglass from its holder beside the wheel, he studied the oncoming vessel.

The captain twisted around, face flushed under his beard. "Pirates," he whispered.

"Pirates!" yelled the helmsman to the crew below.

Rory drew his swords. His arm back to normal, Orui swung his staff in a circle. The two guardians positioned themselves alongside the prince.

Rory took charge. "We need to get you belowdecks, my Prince."

"I haven't been in a good fight in ages. I'm not leaving."

Rory stood agape as his charge refused to choose the safe route.

"I respect your need to join the fight. All this time aboard ship, staring at nothing but water, has me itching to bloody my staff too," Orui agreed. "But our duty is to keep you safe, my Prince."

"Please, Prince Tanin, let us take you belowdecks," Rory pleaded.

"Your duty is to serve me." Tanin unsheathed his sword in a wide arc, forcing his guardians to stand back or get sliced. "Which means you will stand beside me as I battle the nasty pirates who think they can attack the prince of Tarbin."

Rory and Orui exchanged worried looks Tanin refused to acknowledge.

He surveyed the ship for Kettlor and Tyler. The husbandry guardian was climbing the main mast, the large pearl swinging from his waist. With a permanent limp from the squid attack, Tyler's leg moved awkwardly. Unarmed except for a small dagger tucked in his belt, Tyler's hand-to-hand training would be tested today.

"Five hundred yards and closing," Kettlor yelled from overhead as he strung his bow.

The officers had their swords in hand and were making sure the rest of the crew manned their stations.

"Two hundred yards!" Kettlor yelled. Two more bowmen joined the guardian in the crow's nest.

"We're not going to outrun them," Rory pointed out.

"Don't worry." Maritoss waltzed to the railing. "They'll ask for our surrender first. We can bribe our way out of it."

"Maybe they'll take the mutated pearl off our hands." Orui elbowed Tanin.

"I will not negotiate with marauding barbarians. As soon as I am king, the first thing we will do is squash the Ngaro permanently for supporting such thievery." Tanin's grip tightened on his sword hilt.

The pirate ship tacked to port. A heart-stopping boom magnified over the water. Two cannonballs shot through the main sail. A third skirted the top of the deck. The flying metal ball snapped both sides of the railing. A fourth cannonball smacked the water before the ship, sending a wave onto the deck. The ship tilted precariously.

Orui caught Tanin as he lost his footing. They grabbed the railing to steady themselves. Smoke filled the air with the smell of sulfur.

"Cannons? Pirates have cannon-mounted ships? We haven't figured out how to do that yet." Tanin gawked at the square openings below the deck of the attacking vessel. Dark holes encased in iron thrust through half of them.

The pirate ship fired again at closer range. The projectiles exploded on the deck, sending debris flying. Another ripped through the port hull.

Tanin heard a man screaming. He looked over the side in time to see the bloody mass of a body tangled in wooden shards. The gore in the opening reminded Tanin of the giant clam, torn asunder. Maybe the sea was seeking its vengeance.

The captain barked orders that Tanin couldn't make out above the ringing in his ears.

The pirate ship flew past the injured merchant vessel. While the attacking ship tacked to come around again, Tanin grabbed Maritoss by the front of his lace shirt.

"How do they have cannons and we don't? Why did you have us come this way? Did you set us up to be obliterated?" Tanin's spit covered the face of the terrified first officer.

Before the man could do more than stutter, a third round of explosions struck the wooden ship. Tanin lost his grip on Maritoss. The first officer fell to the vibrating deck.

"My Prince!" Tyler shouted a warning.

One of the cannons had struck the foremast. The massive wooden log cracked. It fell toward Tanin. Rory dropped one of his swords and grabbed his charge. The two dove to the side. The mast landed heavily, sending splinters into the air. Protected by Rory's body, Tanin felt wind pass over his head.

"I'm stuck." The mast piece wedged Tyler's injured leg against the deck.

"Your clumsiness causes nothing but problems." Tanin considered leaving his guardian under the beam, out of the way.

Rory tried to defend Tyler. "My Prince, he warned you of its trajectory."

Rory and Orui lifted the beam high enough for the cultural guardian to wiggle free.

"Can you stand?" Orui tore Tyler's pants leg to survey the injury.

"It's the same leg the squid got. Must not be my lucky side." Tyler tried to put weight on his foot but collapsed.

"Grappling hooks!" Kettlor warned from the crow's nest.

The crew on the pirate ship threw the roped hooks onto the deck. They dug into the wood. The enemy crew released the mainsail. The Ngaro sailors pushed the boom hard against the wind. The ship slowed, parallel with Tanin.

"Cut the ropes!" yelled the captain.

The Tarbin sailors jumped to the starboard side with knives in hand. The crew on the enemy ship adjusted their sails to match the speed of their captured prey. The two vessels groaned against each other like giant wrestling beasts. Tanin rushed to that side of the ship with Rory close behind.

As two pirates crossed the ropes, they fell into the sea, their lines cut by Sonacevontes's crew. Two more fell to arrows from the bowmen in the crow's nest. Six managed to make it to the deck unharmed. Rory disarmed a Ngaro, claiming the man's sword as his own. The defense guardian's dancing sword cut down two more. Tanin stabbed one before the pirate could bring his weapon up. With

Tanin's sword stuck in the body, another assailant jumped onto his back. Rory tore the man off and tossed him overboard in one movement.

The second group of pirates rushed over immediately after the first. Sonacevontes's crew fought with impressive skill. The men pouring off the enemy ship reminded Tanin of a disturbed ant nest. They streamed out, as from an endless supply.

A few marauders crossed the first line of defenders. Orui took a man out with an expertly thrown dagger. Tyler tripped a rushing pirate from Orui's flank. The Tarbinians defeated three men for every one the pirates felled. But Tanin realized they would soon be overwhelmed. The prince glimpsed the first officer slinking belowdecks. Tanin promised to punish Maritoss for his cowardice.

"I'm out of arrows." Kettlor tossed his bow over his shoulder to shimmy down the main mast. The pearl on his belt threw off his balance. He crashed to the deck below. One foot fell through the damaged decking. An attacker slashed at his torso. The misaimed swipe scraped the pouch. The bulbous pearl fell out and rolled awkwardly across the deck.

The keel of the merchant ship hit something in the water. The vessel careened steeply to port. The broken foremast rolled, crushing Kettlor's assailant.

"No!" Kettlor yelled. The giant wooden rolling pin smashed the giant pearl.

"Forget the ugly thing and help us," ordered Tanin. He fought another pirate who was a bit tougher than the first couple he'd killed. The enemy exposed his right side, allowing Tanin to slice through his rib cage. "I think they're sending in the good fighters now. That one took me all of a minute to defeat."

Rory smashed the skull of the next man, who ran at Tanin while he bragged. Kettlor joined his charge, protecting the prince's flank. The enemies appeared to be coming from everywhere.

"My Prince?" Tanin barely heard Tyler's voice over the ships scraping and swords clashing. "It rolled right to me."

Tanin glanced back to see the guardian holding a palm-sized black opal.

The ship grew still for Tanin. All sound was replaced with a rush in his ears. All movement slowed to a dull pulse. Orui fought a Ngaro, keeping him away from the prone Tyler.

"Inside the pearl? It was inside the pearl." Kettlor's voice came from a tunnel, far away.

"Behind you!" Rory's shout in his ear snapped Tanin back to real time.

As a Ngaro rushed Orui, Tanin pushed his way to his guardian, but he didn't forget the black opal. "Get the stone," Tanin ordered his men.

Tyler's gaze followed the enemy aimed at Orui. He dropped the Holy Gemstone.

"No!" the prince growled.

The cultural guardian grabbed a broken plank. He smacked the rushing pirate's knee. The man tripped into a controlled roll and regained his feet. He pounced on Tyler more quickly than the guardian could counter. His dagger plunged into the linguist's lung, right below his heart.

"Tyler." Kettlor's anguished voice broke Orui's concentration.

As he pivoted, the medicinal guardian slipped on the bloodied deck, but that didn't prevent him from defending his fellow. Orui wrapped his good arm around the pirate's neck and fell backward from Tyler. His momentum dragged the large man off.

Orui twisted the neck of the marauder, then rolled the dead man off his body.

"Where's the Holy Black Opal?" Tanin searched the deck near his two guardians.

Orui crawled to Tyler while the others fought off attackers. He examined the wound.

"I have it, my Prince. It came back to me." Tyler clenched the fist-sized stone against his bleeding chest.

Tears streamed down his face. Orui shook his head once at Tanin.

The medicinal guardian pulled the dagger out of Tyler's chest. Tyler coughed up fluid but kept hold of the black opal. His lifeblood poured from his wound, covering the gem and the deck below.

Orui screamed a war cry and went into a battle rage, his staff taking down one pirate after another. Kettlor backed him up as the two butchered their way through all possible attackers. Rory stood guard over the prince and his fallen companion.

Tanin focused on his dying guardian. He reached down with a trembling hand.

"It was in the pearl the whole time." Tanin breathed the words like a prayer. He tried to take the Holy Gemstone, but it wouldn't budge. "Give me the opal."

"It's yours, my Prince." Tyler gargled the words.

Tanin tore the gem from Tyler while the guardian choked on his own blood. Aware of nothing else, Tanin held the blood-soaked stone aloft. "I have the Holy Black Opal."

"My Prince." Rory pushed back a lock of Tyler's hair. "Tyler is dying."

"He protected the Holy Black Opal. He served his prince well."

As Tanin cooed over the stone, the gem soaked up its blanket of blood. A pulse from deep within the Holy Gemstones reflected in Tanin's eyes.

"Maybe I should hold that for you, my Prince." Rory reached for the gem, afraid of its unstone-like behavior.

Tanin held his guardian back with an outstretched arm. "The gem is meant for me and only me. I will keep it safe."

The pulsing grew to a blast of blue light that shot out in all directions. The eerie light covered the surface of both ships, easily seen in the afternoon sun.

All fighting stopped. The Tarbin sailors covered their eyes. The pirates fell to their knees, hands up in submission to the glowing stone.

"The sign of the True Heir, as foretold. We leave you to your quest." The voice originated from the captain of the attacking vessel.

The tremble in his voice echoed the fervent awe of his kneeling men. The Ngaro stood and departed.

Arms slack at their sides, Sonacevontes's crew watched the enemy ship release their vessel and sail away. The shocked men switched focus to Prince Tanin. One by one, the Tarbinian crew backed away from the unnatural light.

"The voice. Make it stop. Please let me be at peace," Tyler mumbled.

The light faded. Tanin blinked his eyes. Everything looked so dull. Tanin cradled the gem in both hands like a baby bird. He knew he was the True Heir. He knew his blood would make the jewels shine. Talia couldn't have a gift that he did not. Relief flooded through Tanin, overwhelming the adrenaline from the battle.

Tanin heard Rory's sword slide into its sheath. Looking at his feet, he witnessed his companions gathered around their mortally injured comrade. Tanin watched a play, unable to connect emotionally.

Rory squeezed Tyler's hand. The cultural guardian's eyes were filled with fear. He grasped and released his shirt over his mortal wound.

"When the Stars wish you well, they give you health. When the Stars wish you happy, they give you love. When the Stars wish you home, they call to you. The Light calls to you now, Tyler. Go home."

The grip on Rory's hand tightened and then released. Tyler's eyes glazed over. His raspy breathing stopped. One tear rolled down Rory's cheek.

Outside the circle mourning the loss of one of their own, Prince Tanin admired the Holy Black Opal. His destiny was ensured.

CHAPTER THIRTY-NINE

Princess Talia Winterlaus leaned against the main mast of the *Darvis Renegade*. Despite the urgency of her time limit, Talia had stayed in the city for an extra couple of weeks to mend relations with the neighboring kingdom. Talia had enjoyed the time to catch up with Princess Grace. The very much alive royal had explained she had had to fake her death to save her kingdom. King Vanderlae had refused to listen to his daughter about Bello's conspiring to usurp the throne. She had been forced to build an insurgent army to free her father from the manipulative merchant's clutches. Talia's wedding had provided the perfect cover for her coup.

Princess Grace repeatedly apologized for Tarbin taking the blame for her death. She had failed to see how far Bello would go to find someone of royal blood to marry. Talia understood the frustration of not being able to control everything her decisions impacted. While she and her guardians had recovered in the port city, Nyna's arm had had a chance to heal. Talia felt a twinge of guilt that she had been injured at all. Somehow, Talia needed to learn to think ahead better. People depended on her to keep them safe.

Now, the cool ocean breeze whipped through Talia's hair,

bringing with it a sense of peace. Though she had little to feel peaceful about. Her mission was drawing to an end, and she had nothing to show for it. Her brother was probably almost home with four Holy Gemstones. He might have stolen two of the jewels from her, but she knew he was right. Her father wouldn't care how Tanin had come to possess the quest pieces. Dew couldn't find anything in the tome that forbid any method, including cheating, to complete the quest.

Her happy mood faded. She caught sight of Ial and Nyna leaning over the railing, watching the dolphins play in the wake of the ship. Her scowl softened. When they had first entered the warmer northern waters, Talia had had to use all her persuasive powers to prevent Ial from jumping in to find a manta ray. What he was going to do with a wild one, she never figured out. The husbandry guardian's ocean roots ran deep. On the way home, the ship would pass his home town of Thurrelrun, a peninsula on the northern tip of Tarbin.

Gregor joined Talia by the main mast. "Contemplating your next move?"

"I'm not sure there is a next move. We're heading to the volcanic islands, but I don't know what I expect to find there. Tanin has been a step or two ahead of us the whole time." Talia pulled her hair out of her face and held it back with one hand.

"If your travel plans had been personally arranged by the High Priestess, you would have known exactly where to go and what to do as well." Gregor lifted her chin, catching her breath in his deep brown eyes. "Of course, the Holy Diamond would still be hidden. That means High Priestess Nomyra doesn't know it all, regardless of the airs she puts on."

Talia blinked. She removed his hand and turned toward the bow. Her heart sped up and her body temperature rose every time she saw Gregor. Something had changed in Darvis. She had to finish the mission quickly before she did something she would regret.

Talia looked for the dwarf prince. Aleck sat on the railings, legs draped on either side of the rigging. He had barely spoken since the wedding day.

"Maybe it would have been better if we had never entered Krimmel. Left the dwarves and their diamond at peace."

"After all you've seen on this journey, how can you say that? You helped free a kingdom from a usurper and watched a princess become queen." Gregor blushed at the memory of Grace Vanderlae.

"I could have watched a close friend become king." Talia rocked her hip into the lordling's. "Grace certainly pulled out all the stops to woo you."

"My heart is already taken." Gregor's expression turned serious.

Talia looked away, wanting him to stop talking now.

"Lady Arabelle floated about the Tarbin court and stole my attention. Her curves and winning personality haunt my dreams." Gregor's teasing voice lightened the mood.

Talia elbowed the uncouth lordling. She couldn't understand how Gregor cheered her up so easily.

"Land ho!" warned the sailor in the crow's nest.

Talia and Gregor hurried to the bow to catch a glimpse of the volcanic islands. Aleck stood on the edge of the railing, holding onto the rigging for balance. A wide stream of light gray smoke rose out of the water. Smaller puffs of white joined the larger stream. As the ship approached, dark gray smoke filled in the center of the clouds. The drift dissipated as it rose in the sky. The closer the ship got, the more the blue was obscured by gray.

Aleck spoke the first words he'd uttered since starting the ocean voyage. "It looks like it's coming right out of the water."

Talia was relieved to hear his voice again. She couldn't imagine what he was going through and had no idea how to comfort him. Princess Grace had offered to have the dwarf escorted home. Aleck had refused. He had to retrieve the Holy Diamond before he could face Gallick's and Dragick's families. Their death would not be meaningless.

"Some of it probably does seep from the sea," Captain Gruin explained from immediately behind the onlookers.

Talia jumped. The captain's deep voice had startled her. He seemed to come out of nowhere without squeaking a single deck board. "The volcanoes are under the water?" she asked.

"The volcanic islands are a chain. Some of the activity still takes place underwater. The white smoke indicates hot spots, while the black smoke warns of an impending explosion. Or at the very least, a constant slow burning."

Talia saw why the captain called them a chain. The islands seemed to be linked by an unknown force with the land sticking up at almost regular intervals on a slightly curving line. Each island was a different size, however, with varying shapes and heights.

"I can see rock." Aleck's voice picked up a bit of his usual child-like excitement. "Land in the middle of water. It's such a foreign concept."

"How do we know which one to explore?" Nyna asked.

"I couldn't find any hints in the book the librarian gave us. There are some disturbing drawings of dragons, though." Dew joined the party from below deck.

"I wouldn't worry about flying lizards." The captain laughed, obviously considering the concept absurd. "Ancient peoples made up stories to explain the burning earth and poisonous gases rising from the ground. What else could be powerful enough to cause such chaos except fictional beasts aimed at our destruction? But it's really a natural part of the world, independent of any beast."

"A year ago, I would have been just as skeptical, Captain." Dew folded her arms. "After what we've seen in the last few months, I'm ready to believe anything."

Talia scrutinized the islands as each came into view. The one farthest west had slow-sloping sides with steam rising from its center. The entire surface was bright green. She judged it big enough for a small town. The next couple were little more than black fingers sticking slightly above the water, as if a giant swimmer begged for help. The next sizable island blew black smoke from its interior. The sides of the island rose at a steep incline. She couldn't see above the vegetation covered cliff face. The green was dotted with white from the hundreds of birds nested along the wall. The next two land masses were gray and black with steam gently swaying in the wind as it lifted from the surface. The final island above the water had dark black pebbly beaches leading to soft green pasture-like land. Large brown animals Talia guessed were seals laid along the shore just out of reach of the crashing surf.

Talia felt a pull, as if something were calling to her. She'd felt the same sensation when she entered the Krimmel Mountain and the Elven Forest. "The middle island. The Holy Ruby is on that one."

"Of course it is." Naul scratched his stubbly head. The long days at sea had made it difficult to keep a smooth shave. "It couldn't be the nicely sloping one or the one with the scenic beach. No. We have to scale the cliff face to complete our quest."

"I'm starting to think quests are overrated." Gregor grumbled. "How do you know it's there?"

"I can't explain it." Talia loosened her grip on the railing as her hands started to go numb. "I just know that's where the Holy Gemstone is."

"If we pull the ship in close, we might be able to launch a rope to the top of the cliff and shorten our climb," Ial offered.

"No such luck, I'm afraid. We're not getting any closer than we have to. The underwater hazards are always changing and not always visible. I won't risk the safety of my ship to make your climb easier." The captain shouted orders to get the landing boats ready to launch.

Talia clenched her fists, prepared to order the captain to obey her. Nyna put a soft hand over her fingers. Talia took a deep breath. Her kindness had worked better than her anger so far on this journey. She gave the captain the benefit of the doubt. He knew these waters and his ship better than anyone else.

As the crewmen readied the boats, the first officer pulled the captain aside and whispered in his ear.

"It seems your talk of dragons has invaded my ship's crew." The man slapped Dew on the shoulder, almost sending the petite girl to her knees. "They are refusing to row you. You're on your own. We'll wait here."

The captain headed back to the bridge before any protests could reach his ears.

Talia watched him walk away. "What's new?"

CHAPTER FORTY

Talia was having trouble catching her breath. The rowing had taken twice as long as the captain had estimated when he sent the party off. The huge cliff had made landing almost impossible. The group had paddled around the island until they found a bit of pebbly beach, no more than a few feet deep. The steep face on that side was not as daunting as the opposite. Talia decided they should land there.

Aleck had suggested the party climb the incline with a zigzag path to make the angle less of an obstacle. Talia was glad he was participating again and took his extensive cave experience into account.

Talia collapsed beside the dwarf at the crest of the cliff face. Looking down the way they had come, she couldn't believe they had actually made it this far. "Let's rest for a minute."

"What is that smell?" Naul complained as he removed a boot to empty out a rock.

"Sulfur," Aleck explained matter-of-factly. "We have a few hot springs on the far south side of Krimmel. They are all heated by the melted earth. The smell of sulfur permeates the caverns on that end."

Dew and Aleck walked to the edge of the cliff facing the interior of the island.

"Oh, Talia. You have to see this." Dew stood in awe.

"Incredible." Aleck captured the view in one word.

Nyna groaned as she accepted Gregor's hand and begrudgingly regained her feet. The princess laughed at her companion until she put weight on her own feet and pain shot up to her shoulders.

"When we get home, can we sleep for a week?" Nyna stretched her back and then walked with Talia to Dew and Aleck.

"At least," Talia agreed.

"But we'll miss out on the partying and the... " Gregor stopped midsentence.

All seven companions stood on the edge of a crater the size of Tarbinulus. Out of the center of the indentation rose another growth of land with a cauldron in the middle. Light gray smoke rose from the hill, which was not as tall as the surrounding cliff face. Shades of green covered every surface. The panoramic view instilled awe in each onlooker. Tears streamed down Dew's face. Aleck almost looked like his old self with the curious twinkle in his eye.

"Now I understand why they call it a breathtaking view," Ial whispered to Nyna, who blushed at his proximity.

Something about this island was making them all a little emotional, thought Talia.

"Keep an eye out to locate any signs of Tanin having been here. There's no way we could have beaten him, but he might have left empty-handed." Talia headed down. She didn't want to tell her companions she knew her brother had left without the Holy Ruby because she could sense its presence. They had already looked at her as if she were crazy when she had insisted she knew where to start.

"At least this side of the cliff isn't trying to kill us." Naul walked with a steadier pace down than he had up.

"What is that?" Aleck pointed to a large, rounded object resting at the bottom of the central hill. Its shiny red surface sparkled in the sunlight.

"Lava stone?" Talia offered.

"Lava Stone is deep black, like the pebbles from the beach." Gregor shook his head. "And I've never seen one that big. They're much too brittle to be stable at such a large size."

"Could it be lava?" Ial carefully watched where he put his next step. "I don't want to step into liquid rocks."

"There's no steam or smoke coming from it. It can't be that hot." Dew thought for a moment. "Plus, if the volcano was spewing lava now, the vegetation would be cooked."

"So what is it?" Nyna asked.

"Only one way to find out." Talia headed straight for the object.

The flat part of the cauldron was home to an endless mesh of intertwined shrubbery. Talia and her companions fought for every step they took through the jungle. Talia kept her sights on the hill in the center to prevent them from wandering around in circles. The closer she got to the hill, the more she hoped they didn't have to scale its sides to reach the ruby. They were completely vertical like a castle wall.

The party had been in such a hurry to complete this leg of the mission, they had forgotten to bring any kind of provisions. The group was dreadfully thirsty. At this point, Talia didn't know how they would manage to row their way back to the boat.

"The sulfur is really strong down here." Dew put a finger under her nose to try and block the odor.

"Smells like vacation." Aleck took in a deep breath.

Talia pushed aside the last row of overgrown bushes, exposing the relatively vegetation-free zone close to the cauldron.

"Where did the red object go?" Aleck strode unbidden into the clearing, stroking his beard.

"We could have gotten off course somewhere in the labyrinth of greenery." Gregor walked the perimeter of the hill, everyone else trudging behind him.

He stopped abruptly as he came around an outcropping formed from collapsed lava gravel. Aleck bumped into his behind. Talia walked around the frozen lordling and stopped in her tracks. The unidentified red object was a massive statue of a dragon. Its scales were the color of fresh dripping blood, the edge of each piece meticulously scalloped. The dragon's spiked tail was curled around the house-sized body, its head resting on the end. Its wings were folded peacefully along its spine. The details in the face made the beast look life-like. Majestic horns twisted from the peak of its head. They looked more like long braids than deadly weapons.

"Has to be the same artist who carved our dragon," Talia whispered. She wasn't sure why she spoke so softly, but it seemed appropriate.

"But our dragon is fierce." Dew took a couple steps toward the statue. "This one is at peace."

"Do you think the ruby is part of the dragon somewhere?" Naul fingered his sword hilt.

"Anyone else have an odd sense of danger?" Nyna stood half a step back from the group, cradling her shoulder bag.

Naul gripped his sword hilt. "Maybe."

Aleck slipped under Gregor's outstretched arm and headed straight for the statue. "How wonderful! Dwarf hands didn't make this masterpiece. I wonder who did."

The humans stood frozen while the prince caressed the curving tail. Gregor attempted to squeak out something, but Talia didn't understand him. She couldn't seem to move her legs.

"I've never seen this stone before. It's nice and warm from the sun. These look like real scales. I'd hate to meet the fish they came from in the open water." Aleck laid his hand flat on one. His fingers didn't reach the edges. He knocked on the surface with a fist.

Gregor jumped at the noise. Nyna took another step backward. Ial joined Aleck at the dragon. He placed one hand above the statue's back haunch, below the wing tip. His eyebrows rose as he exchanged a look with Talia.

Her sense of dread grew. "Aleck, maybe you should take a few steps back." There was something wrong with the statue, but she couldn't put her finger on what.

"It's breathing." The words escaped Gregor's lips.

Talia squinted at the dragon's chest. She watched it expand ever so subtly. If Gregor hadn't pointed it out, Talia wouldn't have noticed, at least consciously. "That's impossible."

Aleck caressed the dragon's snout, unhindered by any other observations. The dragon's eyes, as big as the dwarf's head, popped open. The vertical pupils were surrounded by deep red irises the same shade as the ruby in the statue at the Tarbin royal gardens. The dragon narrowed its focus to the dwarf.

"Fascinating." Aleck closed in on the staring eyes, mere inches away from the dragon. "Dwarven statues don't move."

"Neither do human ones." Ial grabbed the dwarf's collar and dragged him back to the rest of the companions.

"Are you going to try to pry my eyes out as well?" The dragon lifted its head, blinking its eyes a couple times.

"Did you hear that?" Gregor still hadn't moved.

"I didn't know dragons could talk," Dew responded.

"I didn't know dragons were real," Talia countered.

"Shouldn't we be running away?" Nyna asked.

"If you leave now, you won't get what you seek." The dragon's voice fell over the companions like a warm breeze. "I assume you seek something, or why would you disturb my sleep? You know the old saying: 'Never wake a sleeping dragon.'"

"We say 'Never wake a sleeping baby,'" Dew corrected the dragon.

Talia elbowed her to be quiet.

"A sleeping baby? Humans have such short memories. What can an infant do but spit up on you? A dragon... "

The beast unfurled its spiked tail and pushed up its enormous body on its front haunches. It took in a long deep breath, causing the vegetation to draw into the clearing. The beast extended its shimmering neck into the sky and exhaled. A fountain of fire shot from the dragon's mouth. A wave of heat engulfed the companions. Both humans and dwarf hit the ground and covered their heads.

"Ah, that felt good. I really needed to clear my throat." The dragon smacked its jaws a couple of times. It looked back at the companions. "You can rise. I shan't eat you. You haven't given me cause, yet."

A light grumbling arose from the dragon as its sides vibrated.

"Is it growling or laughing?" Gregor asked Talia as he extended a hand to pull her to her feet.

"Laughing?" Talia didn't know which it was, but laughing left a better outcome for her friends. She squeezed Gregor's hand and then straightened to her most regal posture. She took two steps into the clearing. "I am Princess Talia Winterlaus of Tarbin. I am on a mission to retrieve the Holy Gemstones to restore the crown."

"So said the human boy, but he knew not of the real mission." The dragon opened and closed its talons on the rocky ground.

"She is of the blood." Aleck raised a finger like he'd made a discovery.

The dragon ducked its head in front of Talia. Its snake-like movement sent a shiver down Talia's spine. Ial and Dew stepped in front of the princess. The dragon ignored them. It took a deep breath. For a moment, Talia feared it would incinerate her where she stood.

Instead, the dragon straightened. "You are of the blood."

The dragon bent its body close to the ground. It launched itself into the air with such force, the ground shook. The jump alone propelled the beast sixty feet into the air. It unfurled its wings, the span of which was triple the length of the body. The dragon circled the cauldron and then disappeared into its depths.

A tear trailed down Talia's cheek at the beauty of the majestic beast. She realized what she had felt earlier was not fear, but longing. Something about the dragon called to her.

The dragon glided back to the clearing in soft circles. It landed with more grace than Talia would have expected from such a huge creature. The dragon emptied a sack in front of the princess.

"You must choose. The boy human chose incorrectly." The dragon sat back on its haunches and waited.

"Tanin was here then?"

"He was not of the blood, but one of his party was. I thought that close enough to attempt a choosing."

Talia sat on the ground in front of the rubies. They were all the correct size to fit into the crown. She noticed that tugging feeling in her chest that had brought her to the island in the first place. The sensation pushed her toward the ruby second from the left. Without thinking, she picked up the red gem and studied it. How did she know for sure this was the correct one? She looked at the dragon. It didn't offer any advice. The beast had allowed her brother to leave the island without telling him he had the wrong one.

Gregor pulled a dagger from his belt and offered it to Talia. She accepted the blade, instantly realizing what Gregor was suggesting. With the jewel in her lap, Talia drew in a breath and pricked her middle finger. She dripped blood onto the ruby. A wave of wonder filled her mind as it soaked into the stone. That part hadn't gotten old. She stuck her finger in her mouth and watched the gem. After the last drop was absorbed, the ruby shone with a deep inner light.

"This is the Holy Ruby." Talia stood, holding up the glowing gem for the dragon to see.

"You chose wisely." The dragon nodded its head like a venerable teacher proud of its student. "Though I should eat the dark one for helping."

Gregor stepped behind Talia and grabbed his sword hilt.

Talia shook her head at the lordling. "How do I thank you? I don't even know what you are called?"

"I have many names. I don't know which would fit your perception." The dragon laid down and curled its tail around its body again.

"Ragaropina the Patient." Aleck stepped up to the dragon. "The mother of the next generation of dragons."

"That name is as good as any. I am surprised the dwarves

remember it. They were unconcerned with magical needs during my time."

"Most of my people are still unconcerned with anything outside the mountain." Aleck hung his head. "I aim to change that."

"I wish you luck, young one." The dragon yawned dramatically, exposing pointed teeth the size of Talia's arm. "I must rest. My children will awaken soon. And hatchlings require an enormous amount of energy."

"Ragaropina the Patient, thank you for the ruby." Talia tucked the precious gem into her pouch. She turned to her companions. "We have one."

"Can we go home now?" Naul scratched his arm where welts had popped up from insect bites.

"Are we going to make it on time?" Nyna pulled a salve from her bag and rubbed the creamy mixture on Naul's rash.

"We should be back to the ship by nightfall. Then off to Tarbin." Gregor calculated the course. "The trade winds are on our side. We should be there in four weeks."

Talia crossed her arms, staring at the ground. "And Tanin is four weeks ahead of us already."

Her companions grew quiet.

"We only have one gemstone anyway. Does it matter if we return on time?" Ial tried to see the upside.

"And Bello is out of the picture. At least you won't end up with him," Gregor added.

"My father will find someone just as horrible, and I will have just as little say in the matter." Talia straightened her shoulders and set off into the underbrush. "I am the firstborn. If I had been born male, there wouldn't even be a question of my worth."

"We have to try to make it. We could make a case that Prince Tanin didn't acquire the Holy Gemstones himself," Gregor offered.

"If we can plant a seed of doubt, maybe enough of the lords will choose your side." Dew started to see the political angle.

"Then what?" Talia's voice deepened in anger. "Civil war? Look what that did to Darvis. I don't want to do that to my people simply because I don't wish to marry."

"Excuse me. I couldn't help but overhear." Ragaropina tilted her head to the side. "The human boy not of the blood has the other Holy Gemstones?"

"Yes, ma'am," Talia answered. She didn't know why she felt guilty.

"This cannot stand. He will be unable to work the Machine. My children need the Recharging."

The dragon took another dramatic leap into the cauldron. She returned with a wooden container as big as a dinghy. She opened the lid and pulled out a large flap of leather.

"A saddle?" Ial's curiosity overcame his hesitation. He shook the edges of the large piece of leather. "Here is the buckle for the girth, but I'm not sure what these smaller straps on top are for."

"If you wish to stay on, tie them tightly," the dragon offered as an explanation.

"Ah, those are our seats. No stirrups. Which makes sense, because I don't think any of us could reach far enough to make stir-rups useful." Ial climbed the side of the wooden box to see if anything was left inside. "No bridle either."

"I go where I wish. You ride if I let you." Ragaropina winked at the husbandry guardian.

Ial laughed at what would have been a terrifying sight to a sane person.

"I've never seen him speak so many words at once." Gregor's shock shown clearly on his face.

"It's certainly not a common sight," Talia agreed. She couldn't help but catch some of Ial's enthusiasm. "Ragaropina the Patient, are you offering us a ride home?"

"I haven't left the island for centuries. My children will be safe for a short trip." The dragon stretched her back and legs like an athlete getting ready for a competition. "I can get you to Tarbinulus in a few days."

"I love flying!" Aleck was on board with the plan immediately.

"A dwarf who wishes to leave the ground. You are an unusual one. We will get to know each other during the flight." The dragon spread herself flat on the ground with her wings tightly folded against her back. "Now allow me to guide you through tacking a dragon."

CHAPTER FORTY-ONE

The dirt road leading from North Port to Tarbinulus transitioned to paved road a couple miles from the city walls. The sun warmed the chill air from the last bluster of winter.

"Halt!" Prince Tanin shouted from the window of his carriage, the lead in a train of five. After months of traveling by sea and on horseback, he wanted a more relaxing ride from the port to home.

Rory sat across from Tanin. "Is something wrong, my Prince? We'll be home in a turn of the corner."

Tanin noticed wrinkles on Rory's forehead. His guardians looked to have aged much more than a year on their trip. He considered it a weakness to allow stress to manifest on his features. Tanin would scope out the other schools when he interviewed a replacement for Tyler. Maybe he'd start a new tradition. If a royal loses a guardian, the other three must be replaced. If they failed to protect one of their own, how could they be expected to protect the king?

Besides, Rory seemed to question every decision Tanin made. He didn't know how much longer he could tolerate such interference from a servant.

"I wish to make a grand entrance." Tanin climbed out of the small window. Standing on the frame of the door, he pulled his lithe form to the roof.

With a couple weeks to spare, Tanin had gone on a shopping spree. He hadn't had time or space to purchase souvenirs for his friends and family while on his quest. His guardians had scoured the markets in North Port to gather exotic gifts. It would be easy enough to convince the receivers that Tanin had thought of them while on his grand adventure.

Tanin lay flat on his belly on the roof of the carriage. He held on to the tie-down railings.

"My Prince, it's not safe on the roof. The road is bumpy and the tree branches low hanging." Rory prepared to climb up with Tanin.

"Quit worrying so much. You're worse than my mother. I'll be fine. And the people will talk about my triumphant return for generations." Tanin had never felt more confident. He nodded to Kettlor, who was holding the horses' reins. "Let's go home."

"Take it easy," Rory ordered the husbandry guardian.

Kettlor gave him an acknowledging nod. Orui, beside Kettlor on the bench seat, lifted his eyebrow at Tanin on the roof. Kettlor snapped the reins, sending the horses forward.

As soon as the horses had reached a steady trot, Tanin got on his knees and released the railings. The whipping wind filled him with exhilaration. The walls of the city were around the next corner. Tanin had sent a messenger ahead to spread the news of his imminent return. He had better have spread the word widely. Tanin expected a welcome home worthy of his rank and the mission he'd completed. He gained his full footing, one leg in front of the other and his arms out for balance.

The carriage turned the corner, and the city walls erupted with cheers. Townspeople lined the streets, jumping and cheering.

"Look at them, Rory. I am everything they want in a king. My people welcome me home."

Rory sat on the windowsill on the left side of the carriage. His hands balanced on the roof. Orui rested on his knees, facing his prince. Tanin feigned to his right precariously. Orui dashed forward to steady his leaning charge. Rory tensed and started to pull himself up to the roof.

Tanin laughed at his guardians. "Quit worrying, you two. The Stars want me to rule. They wouldn't let me fall now. Relax and enjoy the rewards poured upon you for being my guardians."

Orui turned around in a huff and planted his butt on the bench seat. "Fall to your death. See if I care," the medicinal guardian muttered under his breath, arms crossed.

Rory threw a pillow from the carriage at Orui's head. The pouting youth exchanged an angry glare with the defense guardian. Rory's tight-lipped shake of his head caused Orui to roll his eyes. The guardian reluctantly reclaimed his place as protector of the right side of the carriage.

"We are close to the gate, my Prince. Please be careful of you head." Kettlor warned as he slowed the horses to a walk to avoid trampling the crowd building at the gate.

Tanin flattened against the roof as the carriage passed under the portcullis.

On the other side of the gate, Tanin bounced to his feet, legs shoulder-length apart and hands on his hips. Tanin felt like a conquering ruler entering the city of a vanquished tyrant. The people crowded the streets, so close together they looked like a many headed beast undulating with rapture. Voices rose above the clopping of the horses' hooves on the paved road. "Prince Tanin! Prince Tanin! Prince Tanin!"

He soaked in the adoration like a starving man. His face lit up as an idea came to him.

"Rory, hand me my money pouch." Tanin knelt on the carriage roof to better reach his guardian.

"There's not much left after the shopping spree, my Prince." He slowly handed the bag over.

With the roar of the adoring crowd in his ears, Tanin chose to ignore his guardian. He threw coins to the gathered masses and the people went wild. The enthusiasm crescendoed until the buildings lining the road vibrated. Tanin laughed and laughed, relishing the attention.

Kettlor whipped the horses to keep them walking as the people overwhelmed the guards and spilled into the road. Orui palmed his throwing knives, ready to cull the number of onlookers.

"Maybe you should use your staff." Kettlor motioned to the less lethal weapon sitting beside him.

Orui nodded, though a disappointed look crossed his face. Tanin pushed the guardian with his big toe, giving him an approving wink. Maybe he would keep Orui. They shared many of the same views.

The medicinal guardian made his way in front of the carriage. He swung his staff around himself and the area in front of the horses, whacking stray hands or shoulders of overenthusiastic fans.

When Tanin ran out of coins, he decided to toss the empty purse into the crowd. They still wanted more. He took off his hat and brandished it suggestively. Screams from ladies in the crowd encouraged Tanin to put on a show of strength. Rory's face reddened at Tanin's maneuvers atop the moving vehicle as the hands of screaming fans reached up to touch him. Tanin tossed his hat and watched a group of teenage girls wrestle over it.

The carriage approached the curtain wall of the castle. Tanin looked to the battlements where King Roland waved enthusiastically. The king gestured to the guards at the gate.

A dozen armored men marched through as the portcullis rose. They blocked the crowd from entering the castle grounds as the train of carriages rolled into the courtyard. Tanin jumped onto the bench seat instead of flattening against the roof. The vehicles circled around so they could all fit within the courtyard as the gate came back down.

Tanin caught sight of High Priestess Nomyra high in her tower above the fray. Her long hair whipped in the wind. Her dark navy robe moved as if alive. The image of the stunning beauty disrobed on stage flashed through Tanin's mind.

"My son." King Roland huffed heavily from scaling the stairs up and down the battlements. "My age is catching up with me. I'm relieved to have a successful son ready to take over after the Light calls me home."

"That time is still quite a ways off." Tanin squeezed his father affectionately, comforting the older man.

King Roland released his son. "At least, I assume you return in triumph with that crowd so happy to see you."

Tanin's nose crinkled at his father's lack of confidence in him. "Of course, I return successful. All five gems are home and ready to be mounted on the Tarbin crown."

"Rory!" Tanin called to his companion. The guardian brought a long, flat, cloth-wrapped object to his prince.

"This, Father, is a scabbard made from griffin hide and bejeweled with precious stones from the Dwarven Kingdom."

"Griffin? But I thought they were extinct? How did you get this?" King Roland held the leather up to the light, where the stones created mini-rainbows.

"We came upon many wondrous things in our travels. This mission was the most dangerous ever undertaken. The winner is indeed worthy to rule the legendary kingdom of Tarbin." He flung his arm over the older man's meaty shoulder. Finally, he would receive the attention he deserved. "Let's enjoy some mead while I regale you with the entire adventure."

"Where's Tyler?" King Roland's cultural guardian noticed the companion's absence.

Rory lifted the urn for the other guardians to see.

"We will prepare the ceremony immediately." Two of the king's guardians marched into the castle.

"Dear Tyler. He will be missed." King Roland buckled the new scabbard to his belt. "I'll send for a sampling of young ones from the Cultural School as a replacement."

"He will have plenty of time to learn his trade while I await my turn on the throne." Tanin walked with his father to the castle entrance.

Tanin watched Rory give orders to servants to unpack. Then he rushed to catch up with Tanin, holding the trunk containing the Holy Gemstones.

"Have you seen your sister in your travels?" King Roland didn't look directly at Tanin.

Tanin's neck tightened as he resisted the urge to shake his father out of his adoration for his spoiled little girl. When would the old man see she was useless, a spare? Tanin was all Roland needed to continue his legacy.

"That is one of the things I must tell you about. By the time I arrived in Darvis City, after months of grueling travel acquiring four of the Holy Gemstones, Bello and Talia were off on their honeymoon."

"She was married without me? I was supposed to be at the ceremony." King Roland stopped mid stride and turned Tanin to face him. "What happened? Tell me everything."

"Father, there are things you must know about our high priestess. She kept many details of the mission from me," Tanin whispered into the king's ear.

"It seems High Priestess Nomyra was so furious with Talia for interrupting her plans she gave her false information. My poor innocent sister went straight to Darvis, almost beating Lord Bello home. A letter arrived from you authorizing Hilderamn to claim his bride now, because you wouldn't be able to make the journey due to poor health." Tanin recited the story he had concocted on his long trip home. He bit his tongue to prevent himself from spoiling the act with a giggle. "I have my suspicions on where that letter came from."

King Roland's eyes flew back and forth. He pivoted toward the castle and marched purposely toward his wing.

Tanin patted Rory on the back. "It's too easy sometimes."

CHAPTER FORTY-TWO

Long after Tanin had returned, High Priestess Nomyra sat by the fire in her antechamber. The flickering flames chased off the chill. Her fingers stroked her chin until the skin was raw. Prince Tanin never came to visit. He was supposed to report to her as soon as he freed himself from his father. Her experience with court intrigue had her instincts buzzing. Something was happening beyond her control. This was a new experience for the expert manipulator.

Nomyra stood, flustered with anger as much as the heat of the fire. She bundled her long hair atop her head, putting a wooden rod through the center to hold it up out of the way. On her desk, she unrolled a mat with Elvish words scrolled in a spiral from the center to the edges. If the spoiled brat refused to bring the Holy Gemstones to the powerful woman, she would fetch them herself.

Turning Krag's stone to the inside of her palm, Nomyra pressed her hands together. She pictured the chest holding the jewels. Her mind outlined every detail. After years of discipline and practice, she could recall every sharp corner of the wood and crack in the leather binding. Her hands tingled as magic flowed from the ring to surround her body. As she pressed her eyes closed, a green aura surrounded her. The humming drowned out all other sound. She opened her hands and pressed her palms to the mat. The glow of her body flowed into the flattened scroll.

She held her arms out at shoulder height, concentrating on the black-painted wood of the chest. When she had every detail captured in her mind, she clapped her hands as hard as she could. The ring bit into her flesh. A wave of energy exploded horizontally, pushing Nomyra back one step.

Nomyra kept her eyes shut for a moment as she enjoyed the pleasant tingling in her flesh from the released power. When she opened her eyes, the summoned box sat on her desk. Since it was a bit warm to the touch, Nomyra flung the lid open with her fingertips. She lifted the leather padding to reveal five goose-egg-sized jewels, an unmatched collection tucked into wooden slots lined with black silk. Nomyra traced the facets of the ruby with her finger. The larger version of the rock in Krag held sentimental value for her.

Her finger felt nothing from the touch. Odd. The high priestess hadn't told Tanin about the reaction his blood would have with the Holy Gemstones. The conceited child would have proved impossible to control if he knew the true power that flowed through his being. Nomyra might not be the heir, but she was of the Blood. The Holy Gemstones should react to her lifeblood in the same manner as any in her line.

The high priestess pulled out the wooden insert protecting the five gems and laid it in front of the box. She retrieved a small dagger from the nightstand. As she reentered her antechamber, the flickering fire danced off the Holy Gemstones, filling the room with a moving rainbow. Nomyra saw the light as a sign she was following the correct path.

Nomyra's dramatic flair never left her, even when she was alone. She held her hand over the line of jewels, dagger point pressed against her index finger. "Please, oh Holy Light, guide me to your will. Bring me to my destiny."

She pushed her finger against the dagger, creating a cut deep enough to bleed freely. The high priestess dripped healthy drops onto all five stones. The diamond soaked up the deep red liquid and flowed with a warm blue light. The sapphire and black opal repeated the process. The blood on the ruby and emerald, however, streamed down their surfaces. The liquid snaked across the silk and soaked into the tablecloth.

"You must be thirstier." Nomyra squeezed extra onto the ruby.

Nothing happened.

She slashed her palm and held the emerald against the wound. Blood dripped down her arm, staining her robes.

Still, no reaction.

"No, no, no, no, *no!*" Her voice crescendoed until her body vibrated with the violence. "Why do we have a thousand years to plan for something and still run out of time? Damn this short human life! Damn the ignorance of the populace! Damn my ancestors for leaving it all to me!"

She grabbed the fake gems to fling them into the fire. Nomyra froze mid-swing. The gems fell from her blood-slicked hand and landed with a soft thud on the rug under the table. The high priestess had a ceremony to perform the night after tomorrow. If she didn't have the real Holy Gemstones, she would need the fake ones to stand in for now.

She wiped the ruby and the emerald on her already stained robes. With the fakes snug in their slots, she put the wooden insert back into the travel box. She closed the lid and clapped her hands once more. The box winked off her desk. Tanin would never know she had seen the stones.

Inhaling slowly, Nomyra calmed her heart and relaxed her muscles. She wrapped her robe sleeve around her bleeding hand and regained her seat by the fire. She needed to plan. Her mind swirled with the details of the ceremony. This was not the first time Nomyra had to break from the script. She would complete the ceremony and then find the missing Holy Gemstones. She had a little over a year. Nomyra would not fail. The world counted on her.

Nomyra woke with a start. The embers of the fire emitted warm red light, but little heat. She wasn't sure how long she'd been out. At least a few hours. The woman started as she heard thumping on her door. Shes unfolded her legs from beneath her, shaking them to encourage circulation.

"High Priestess," a voice on the other side of the door insisted. "High Priestess Nomyra, you must wake up."

Nomyra pulled on the handle to silence the obnoxious noise so early in the morning. "What do you require at this hour?"

The young servant girl screamed at the sight of her mistress. The high priestess remembered her blood-soaked robe and imagined the frightful image she must portray.

"I cut myself on a broken bottle yesterday. I'm fine. Calm yourself." She tugged the cloth of her robe from the cut on her palm. The wound reopened, flowing gently. "Why do you disturb me, child? Speak!"

"A dragon has been spotted over the city." The girl's face lit up with excitement. "It's *huge*, red, and headed toward the castle."

The high priestess slammed the door shut. She ran to the other side of her antechamber to a set of stairs. The middle-aged woman gripped her robe and raised it well above her knees. She jumped the stone steps two at a time to get to her observatory as quickly as possible.

Clearing the last step without taking a breath, Nomyra leaned on the balustrade, her chest heaving. The chill in the air went unnoticed as she traveled along the perimeter of her tower. Nomyra scanned the skies as she often did. This time she looked for a dragon. A glint of red flashed over her head, aiming for the trees behind the castle. As the proper red dragon turned a spiral circle to lose altitude, Nomyra picked out people riding in a saddle.

"Talia. It has to be." The mesmerized woman watched as the creature gracefully landed in the Royal Forest.

Nomyra knew the old ones would be awakening with the Recharging so close. The dragon's presence might simplify Nomyra's problem. She needed the ruby, and the dragons had been placed in charge of guarding it. For some reason, Tanin had been given a false gemstone. The dragon must be here to fix the error. After all, the beast needed the Machine to function to rescue her race.

Nomyra walked back to her chambers to clean up. Thoughts of the guards eager to attack caused her to hurry her movements. She had to make it to the forest before the guards drove. off the dragon.

Dropping her robe, she sponged the dried blood from her arms and hands. She grabbed a clean robe, leaving her soiled one on the floor. As she pulled the rod from her hair, her white tresses fell in gentle waves below her shoulders. She dragged a comb through the ends and left the rest free. She ran out the door, slipping clean white gloves onto her hands to hide her fresh wounds.

Nomyra smiled as a plan came to her. She could still salvage her life's work and that of her family for endless generations. The astro-priests would rule the world again as the Stars demanded.

CHAPTER FORTY-THREE

RAGAROPINA LANDED with incredible grace for a creature of such mass carrying passengers. Still shivering, Talia climbed from the dragon.

"Next time I ride a dragon, I'm dressing warmer. And bringing a blanket or two." Talia basked in the warmth of the morning sun peeking over the walls.

Dew jumped down beside her charge. "I found the crisp air refreshing." The women stepped over the streaming water surrounding the landing ground.

"I wasn't born in a mountain town with snow up to my chin in the spring." Talia retorted as they moved to give thanks to the dragon for the ride.

Aleck was already talking with Ragaropina.

"Dragick and Gallick." The dragon rolled her tongue behind her sharp teeth. "I like the feel of the words. Your Friends' sacrifices shall be remembered. Two of my children will share their names."

Tears sprang to Aleck's eyes. He hugged Ragaropina's neck, his dwarven arms unable to encircle the entire circumference. "Their families will be honored."

"She has good aim, doesn't she?" Gregor's voice came from the other side of the dragon.

Talia looked up and saw the head of the black dragon statue over Ragaropina's back. The inanimate stone sent shivers down her spine, but all fear was extinguished.

"This is not my first visit to the Tarbinulus Citadel. I remember the city as much bigger though. Most of the land we flew over looked vastly different from the last time my brethren and I filled the skies. The disaster affected all creatures, magic and mundane. You would do well to remember that lesson, Princess." The dragon bent her scaled head to Talia's level, her unblinking eyes focused on the human.

Talia felt the desperation in the old one's voice. She nodded, straightening her face to show her seriousness.

A large commotion echoed along the hedges. A group of guards, shouting and brandishing weapons, jumped into the clearing. Talia spotted the captain, who wore a large, domed hat to disguise the fact that he was a head shorter than the tallest guard. Talia's stomach churned more violently than it had when the dragon had taken flight the first time.

"I don't feel well." She gripped Dew's shoulder for support.

"A regiment of guards surprising us *for no reason* will do that to you." Dew's voice carried over the blustering of the uniformed men.

The captain pushed his men behind him instead of taking a step closer to the beast. "Dragon! We demand you surrender."

"And how do you imagine you will make her obey your command?" Naul laughed so hard, he gripped his sides.

Gregor slapped him on the shoulder in shared appreciation.

Talia saw everything happening but couldn't concentrate on it. A humming in her ears stilled any other sound. An invisible force pulled at her insides, urging her deeper into the forest. She was drawn to her tree, the single naddle.

"That is the Holy Emerald you hear, Princess." Ragaropina's

voice broke through Talia's sensory block. "The time draws near, and the stones are anxious to be reunited."

"I order you to stand down." Talia put her hands on her hips, her most commanding pose. "Ragaropina the Patient is with me. She is to be treated as an honored guest."

The captain stared at the princess, mouth agape. Before he could react, High Priestess Nomyra slid into the clearing. Immediately behind her ran Tanin and his guardians.

The dragon turned on her haunches at the high priestess's entrance. "You know he is not of the blood, do you not?"

"Of course, he is. I checked the ancestry carefully." Nomyra straightened her back, defending against the sudden attack. "I have done my part. But you have not done yours. Where is the Holy Ruby?"

"Here." Talia held up the gem.

Her companions closed ranks around her. The air dripped with tension. Talia wasn't sure who would take the first shot.

"But I was there first. You gave the ruby to me." Tanin stepped up beside Nomyra, demanding answers from the towering beast.

"He is not of the Blood. The Machine will not obey him." Ragaropina ignored the petulant boy, speaking only to Nomyra.

The high priestess narrowed her eyes at the princess. Talia felt as though the woman looked directly into her soul. Talia looked away first.

High Priestess Nomyra bowed acquiescence to the dragon. "I will complete my mission. Do you know where the Holy Emerald is?"

"I do not. But she of the blood does."

Ragaropina turned her back on Nomyra. The dragon flicked her spiked tail dangerously close to Tanin, causing the prince to leap back. The dragon used her talons to pry apart two scales at the base of her neck. She puffed out a bit of smoke at the irritation, filling the area with the smell of sulfur, ever present on her island. Holding it pinned between two sharp talons, Ragaropina presented Talia with a red dragon charm on a golden chain. Talia held the exquisite jewelry in her palm. The details cast into the charm, no bigger than a human thumb, made the metal look alive.

"If you are in need, squeeze the dragon and think of me. I will come." Ragaropina stood on her back haunches. The humans ducked as she spread her wings, flexing her muscles. "Goodbye, my friends. We shall meet again soon."

With her parting words, the dragon launched herself into the air. She circled the garden twice and then headed north.

Talia sniffed. "You can go now," she told the captain of the guards, her disdain evident.

The guards looked to their boss, waiting for orders. Some had sheathed their swords already. Others stared at the sky as if the beast would shower raining fire at any moment.

"I need to confer with the king." The captain stalked off, pushing a guard who stood in his way. The rest of his men melted into the shrubbery from whence they'd come.

Tanin confronted his sister with his characteristic swagger back in place. "I'll take the Holy Ruby now. It was kind of you to fetch it for me. Don't you have a husband waiting for you?"

"No." Talia crossed her arms, moving her weight to one hip. She lifted an eyebrow and waited for Tanin to have his temper tantrum.

"What do you mean no?"

"Bello kneels before the Darkness to answer for his crimes," Aleck explained from beside the princess.

"You killed him?" Nomyra sounded more proud than shocked.

Talia placed a quieting hand on Aleck's shoulder. "Not I. Turns. Out Princess Grace is alive. She led a rebellion to free her kingdom from the villainous influence of Lord Bello. Her timing freed me to continue my quest."

"Impossible," Tanin muttered.

"Incredible," Nomyra countered.

Gregor interrupted the staring contest between the three. "Princess?"

Her companions' sunburned faces contrasted with the dark circles under their eyes. Talia's exhaustion mirrored their expressions. She addressed them, as a dismissal to her brother and the high priestess. "Let's head to our quarters for food and rest. Lordling Gregor and Prince Aleck, we will set you up with adjacent rooms for your comfort."

The forest called to her. *I will return when jealous eyes are not watching,* she thought.

Her stomach pain loosened. She took a deep breath. The naddle tree understood. Such an odd statement. Her world had changed drastically since she had last visited the Royal Forest. Talia wondered what else had changed.

CHAPTER FORTY-FOUR

Nomyra focused on the shiny desk in front of the king. The large alabaster slab mounted atop a carved naddle tree trunk took up half the chancery. Roland held office behind the imposing desk when he wished to look powerful and literate. The façade didn't fool the high priestess. The king's secretary, Herman, who managed the ins and outs of running the castle and who transcribed all the official correspondence, doubled as one of Nomyra's oldest informants.

Though technically independent of the royal families, the astro-priests lived on a precarious line between divine and secular. Nomyra had the education and experience to read the signs of the Stars, which granted her special rights. The king had the power to take or leave her advice. If King Roland were to turn on Nomyra, she wouldn't have the power to stop him. The high priestess didn't care about the king's opinion, only the prince's cooperation.

Though if Tanin was not of the Blood, none of them mattered.

The middle-aged woman veiled her seething fury with forced humility by avoiding eye contact with the king.

"Where does your scheming lead, Priestess?" King Roland leaned toward Nomyra, his knuckles pressed against the cold stone. "My son claims that you briefed him on his quest you left out a few details."

"I told him what the Stars told me," Nomyra said quietly, trying to sound demure. It wasn't an easy task for her. "And the details I gleaned from the old books."

Tanin, surrounded by Rory and Orui, stomped his foot against the floor. "Are you saying, Priestess, the Stars didn't know the Krimmel had the Holy Diamond?" Tanin spat at her feet. "Or, Priestess, the fact that the Holy Black Opal was hidden inside an ugly pearl? Or the fact that a crazy elf guarded the Holy Sapphire? Maybe, Priestess, the Light refused to speak to you because you were unworthy."

Nomyra shot an icy look at the petulant prince. The child didn't have a clue.

"The Stars reveal what they wish. Some challenges must be overcome by the quester. The Light wishes us to prove our worthiness. And the ancient literature cannot predict the changes in societies over millennia, especially when we have stopped communicating with many of these people."

"I can forgive a few lapses in knowledge with the information being so difficult to obtain, Priestess." The twinkle in the king's eye had a "but" written all over it. "What I cannot forgive is your willingness to put my crown on the head my daughter. She can't handle the responsibility or criticism that comes with the title. How dare you burden her with such matters."

"My King, I have no intention… "

Roland held up his hand to silence her. His face flushed as he motioned with his other hand to someone in the shadows. Nomyra met his eyes, sensing the danger within.

A guard shoved a tied and gagged Herman into the torchlight. Nomyra's eyes widened at the appearance of her spy, bruised and beaten. The king must know everything. The high priestess saw her meticulous plans going up in smoke due to one spy she had kept on for too long.

"Most of all, Priestess, you cannot be forgiven for spying on the sovereign of Tarbin, over whom you have no authority."

The last words shot at Nomyra like daggers. "Your Majesty, I have no idea what you're referring to. I have no more than a passing acquaintance with your secretary." Nomyra's head spun as she tried to conceive of a way out of her predicament.

"Of course, the torture only produced lies. I can no longer trust him."

King Roland nodded to the guard holding the bound servant. Herman squirmed, trying to free himself, his eyes popping out of his head. He screamed through his gag words that no one understood. The stony-faced guard slid a knife across his throat. The helpless man's blood splashed the scrolls on the walls that represented his life's work. Nomyra shot a hand to her mouth, unable to hide her shock. Her fear morphed to anger.

"How dare you slaughter a man in my presence without a viewing of his Star Chart. That man's soul won't know how to cross over."

The guard dragged Herman's body back into the shadows, where Nomyra heard a door open and close. She stared at the blood trail. Nomyra's fury cleared her mind, turning her to another observation.

"And I am high priestess, not priestess. I earned my place decades ago and expect to be treated with the respect I am due."

"You were right, High Priest Seamus. Your aunt noticed the change in title." King Roland smirked at Nomyra as her nephew appeared out of the shadows on the other side of the desk.

"It took her much longer than I thought it would, Your Majesty." Seamus held his official robe above the blood smeared along the floor as he moved to stand beside the king. "It's tough growing old."

"Good thing she's been placed in retirement by the Tower." Tanin practically jumped up and down as he handed a scroll to Nomyra. "Father said I could give you the monition."

Nomyra's hand shook as she accepted the rolled parchment. The Tower's seal held the paper together. She broke the wax, tearing the paper in her need to see the words herself. "The elders cannot make a decision like this without bringing me in for a formal inquiry. This is not legal." She brandished the scroll like a weapon. Which it was, a deadly weapon against her. "And I have the right to choose my successor."

"Exactly. Which is why we consulted your nephew, who assured us he would be your chosen. High Priest Seamus has had the advantage of learning from the best there was. How could we desire any other replacement?" King Roland threw his arm around Seamus's shoulders as if they were old friends.

"I know your desire has always been to bequeath me your position as royal adviser. You groomed me to take over, as King Roland has done for Prince Tanin."

Tanin added his own barb. "I hope she hasn't led you astray as much as she has me."

"My aunt and I have no *secrets* from each other, my Prince." The way Seamus emphasized "secrets" warned Nomyra to quiet her remonstrations.

The fool didn't understand blackmailing her with the truth of the twin's conception would seal his fate as well as hers.

"Do not worry, Auntie. I share your vision and will make sure the kingdom is properly informed of all the Light's demands to ensure the return to the glorious legendary kingdom." Seamus straightened his robe as the king removed his arm and sat at his desk.

"You are to empty your rooms so your nephew can move his stuff in. The steward is preparing your new quarters as we speak." The king unrolled a scroll, as if Nomyra was no more important than a servant who had a question about the linens.

"I am expected to stay in the castle, then?" Nomyra needed only this night.

"We're going to keep an eye on you," Tanin sneered. Rory shared a laugh with him.

Nomyra caught the worry etched on Rory's face. She wondered if

she could find the source and use it against the prince. The king shuffled through a basket of scrolls on the table.

"Stupid paperwork. That's why I had a secretary to begin with."
The king yelled for his chamberlain, "Cort, come in here!"

"Am I then invited to the conclusion of the Forging Ceremony
tomorrow night?" Nomyra twirled Krag around her finger, trying to
contain her fury. The power in the stone could turn everyone in the
room to dust, including her nephew. She waited on his answer before
deciding whether to unleash her wrath. Nomyra would not allow her
destiny to be corrupted.

"Yes, Auntie. We want you there. You started the ball rolling, and
you should see how it all ends." Seamus walked around the side of
the desk. He kissed her hands in feigned reverence. It took all of
Nomyra's will not to snatch her hand away and slap the boy for his
insolence. "I think you will be surprised."

Tanin yanked her left arm behind her back and held her still.
The king ignored the commotion from across his desk. For a split
second, she thought Tanin was going to slit her throat and drop her
body like Herman's. The truth turned out to be much worse. High
Priest Seamus ripped the ruby ring from her finger. All she could do
was scream.

Seamus slipped Krag on his finger. "This symbol belongs with the
High Priest of Tarbin. Which is me."

Tanin groped Nomyra through her robe as he released her arm.
His violation didn't register in the weakened state she experienced
without her ring.

"You don't realize what you've done." Heat radiated from
Nomyra as she completely lost her composure and dove after
Seamus, prepared to rip his arm off to get her ring back.

Rory and Orui pulled her off her nephew. Seamus ducked
behind his sovereign, as far away from his aunt as possible.

"Enough!" King Roland slammed his fists against his desk,
making the entire stone top bounce. "You have chosen your own

path, woman. Accept the consequences, or you will not be allowed into the ceremony."

The strong-willed pair stared at each other, teeth bared. Nomyra shook her arms away from the two men holding her and straightened her back. She bowed to King Roland and then left without being dismissed.

"You can't turn your back on the king." Tanin tried to grab her shoulder, but Nomyra deftly dodged his attempt.

"Let her go. Her time is over," King Roland ordered as the door closed behind her.

We'll see whose time is over after the ceremony. Nomyra had to find Talia. It was time to throw her cards on the table. Most of them anyway. The grand finale to the prophecy would be her greatest achievement. No one in the royal family—or her own—would stop her from fulfilling her destiny.

CHAPTER FORTY-FIVE

THE FOREST LOOKED so different in Dark's reign, but Talia knew her way around instinctively. The humming in her ears she had heard at the dragon landing returned. She closed her eyes and concentrated on the source. Definitely the naddle.

"This way," she instructed her guardians as she took off at a run.

Talia sprinted around the bushes, ignoring the low branches pulling at her hair. Her shoes hit a puddle of sludge, but she kept her pace. Naul cursed behind her as he hit the same patch.

All night, Talia had tossed and turned. A voice haunted her dreams, calling to her. When she'd awoken a little after moon rise, the only thing she could think about was finding the source. The urgency pulled at her very soul. After the not-extinct dragon, the mysterious elf, the hidden dwarf kingdom, and the glowing stones, her guardians believe her story without question. Gregor and Aleck had distracted the guards watching the princess's wing so the rest of their party could escape unnoticed.

As she reached the naddle tree's clearing, Talia froze. Her mud-soaked shoes caused her to slide to a stop. Dew bumped into her back. Naul dodged the girls, ending up in the mud on the side of the path. Nyna gave Naul a hand out of the muck, while Ial and Dew stood close to Talia. They all looked to their charge for the next move.

Yesterday, her mother had expressed gratitude Talia had made it back safely. Talia's hair had been flattened to her skull from the constant petting. Her father had shown no interest in hearing her side of the story. As Talia had guessed, the king saw a male heir as the future ruler of Tarbin, regardless of birth order. Even to Talia, complaining that her brother had stolen the gems from her sounded like whining. Roland had shaken his head and insisted that challenges plagued any reign. The man in charge had to be prepared to make tough decisions to do what was best for his people. Roland had hugged Talia and promised to find another man to take care of her.

Talia had never expected to reign. Now that it had been floated in front of her as a possibility, and then away, Talia felt cheated. It almost would have been better to never have had that hope to begin with.

Talia's chest heaved as she remembered to breathe. The naddle tree rose high, casting an eerie shadow on the low foliage. "Of course."

Talia looked at the faded scar on her hand from the knife cut she'd earned after cleaning the buck a lifetime ago. With everything that had happened since then, she had completely forgotten the out-of-place emerald she'd found in the leaves at the base of the tree. It had been the first time she'd seen a gem soak in her blood and glow. She'd dismissed it too readily. What would her journey have been like if she'd stopped to consider the importance of such a discovery?

Dew pointed to a floating orb near the naddle tree. "What is that?"

"Were we followed?" Nyna whispered.

"I don't think so. But we did rush in here with little caution." Naul scraped his boots against an exposed root, trying to remove some of the odiferous mud.

Talia ignored her guardian's discomfort. The light was definitely moving. That could be the mysterious flying orb she was certain had taken the emerald. She rushed the tree to keep an eye on the light. She wouldn't lose it this time.

In a blink, the ball of light flew within an inch of Talia's nose. She jumped back, eyes wide at the intrusion. The flickering light circumvented her head and then flew around each of her companions. When the erratic, glowing ball hovered in front of ther for a second, Talia saw two sets of wings, laid out like a dragonfly's, on the back of a tiny woman with long, wavy green hair.

"A fairy?" Dew gasped from behind Talia's shoulder.

Talia reached up to touch the magical creature. A puff of air washed over her face as the fairy flew off into the brush surrounding the naddle. On her way, she passed two torches stuck into the ground. They erupted into light at the touch.

"Don't mind Philomena." The muffled voice came from the woods. "She's used to working behind the scenes. She was so happy you came, she wanted to welcome you."

"Who is that? Show yourself," Naul ordered, his sword in his hand. The other guardians followed his lead, taking up stances around the princess.

"I apologize. I've been silent for so long. I've forgotten my manners."

The rough vertical bark around the thick trunk of the naddle tree started to shift. The smooth surface underneath remained unmarred. The companions backed up two steps. Talia expected the trunk to open like a door, revealing a secret compartment. Instead, a horizontal opening broke through the bark. Two oval-like shapes formed above the new opening.

"Is this better?" the naddle tree asked the companions.

The horizontal break in the bark moved like a mouth as the voice resonated over the path. Talia realized the circles above the "mouth" were supposed to represent eyes. Ial rubbed his nose self-consciously. As if on cue, more bark moved, stacking one piece on top of another and forming a rough cylinder between the eyes.

"I forgot about the nose. Humans feel better when a face has a nose. Oddly, elves don't seem to mind one way or the other."

"You'd think nothing would surprise me anymore." Talia felt mesmerized by the moving bark mouth.

Naul's sword arm hung limply by his side. "Prince Aleck is going to be upset he missed out on a talking naddle tree."

"We prefer to be called nadph. Your short human lifespan tends to modify words over time. Nadph became nadep, which became nadle with a long *a,* which became the current naddle."

"Have you been calling me?" Talia didn't know a more fitting term for the sensation.

"Not I." A thin, flexible branch reached into a cavity in a denser section. The branch presented a bundle wrapped in dark green leaves to Talia. "This called to you, child of the blood."

Talia held out her hand. The nadph unfolded its leaves and gave the Holy Emerald to Talia. Questions flooded her mind. "Why can I sense their presence when no one else can?"

"Only humans of the Blood can sense the Holy Gemstones. You are not the only one, but you are one of few."

"Is that why these stones respond to my blood?"

"Yes, child. Long before I walked the earth—"

"You can walk?" Nyna couldn't stop herself from muttering her shock out loud.

The ancient tree ignored the interruption. "Your ancestor, the Great Wizard Reloian, invented the Machine to capture most of the magic supplied by the Great Conjunction and funnel it into our planet. Your many greats-grandfather wanted the world to shine with magic. His discovery changed the world. The populations of magical creatures, elves, and dragons and a few others, grew with the surplus of magical energy. The excess magic found homes in new species: the nadph and the mermaids. Magical and mundane creatures prospered together, populating every land mass and ocean in the world. This continent possessed the only kingdom with all major superpowers represented: nadph, humans, elves, dwarves, dragons, and mermaids."

"The legendary nation High Priestess Nomyra referred to when she sent us on our mission." Talia soaked in everything the nadph said.

"Yes, Princess. We prospered for centuries, until a human wizard, another of your ancestors, decided to siphon the energy for his own use. The Machine exploded and the Recharging did not occur. Without the influx of energy, the magical creatures couldn't survive at such numbers for another thousand years, when the next Great Conjunction would occur." The tree scratched his trunk around the moving bark face. "We need wait only fourteen more months."

"I still don't see how I am a part of this. I have no magical ability. I've never heard of the Machine you talk of. My blood reacts with the gems, but all they do is glow. I am not an astropriest and am completely unable to predict the conjunction." Talia's old angry self reared its head.

"The prophecy names you, the True Heir, as the descendant who will reunite the Holy Gemstones with your blood to power the Machine. You will save the magical people of this realm." The face shifted to the side of the trunk. "Is that not accurate, Priestess?"

"It is true the prophecy calls out the True Heir as the wielder of the Blood and Holy Gemstones." Nomyra stepped onto the path, the torches lighting her face. Her skin so pale, it seemed to produce its own light rather than reflect the flame of the torches. "But it does not make you heir of what you think."

Tanin jumped out from the other side of the path. "Since I am the heir, the prophecy refers to me, not my twin."

"It has not been determined who the heir is yet, brother." Talia's face flushed with anger at her brother's continued intrusion. "The ceremony is tomorrow night. I will make my case that you stole the gems. You did not win them."

"Add this beauty to your list of complaints." Tanin held up the ruby, its facets sparkling red in the flickering light.

Talia's stomach sank. "Where are Lordling Gregor and Prince Aleck?" She'd left the ruby with them for safekeeping in case Tanin found her outside her room.

"They're taking a tour of our lower levels." Tanin tossed the gem into the air and caught it. "Now hand over the Holy Emerald."

Castle guards poured out of the shrubbery, swords drawn. They wore only leather armor, which explained how Talia hadn't heard clanging as they were surrounded.

"We are not in a foreign kingdom, Tanin. This is my home too. You can't lock up my friends and steal my property." Talia fingered her sword hilt. Her muscles shook with adrenaline. "It wouldn't be the first time I beat you in a fight in this forest."

"You can argue as you see fit with Father, who will preside over the proceedings tomorrow." Tanin shoved Nomyra into Talia.

The surprised woman slammed into Talia, causing both of them to hit the ground. The guards rushed forward and disarmed Talia's companions before they could react. As the women struggled to untangle themselves from each other, Tanin pried the Holy Gemstone from Talia's hand.

"And then there were five."

Talia grabbed a dagger out of her boot and jumped to her feet. Nomyra tripped her before she could take a second step.

Tanin leisurely strolled down the path toward the castle, Rory holding a torch for him. He juggled the two priceless gems. "I wonder if I could juggle five? We'll have to test my skills in my quarters. Surely something must be a challenge. Everything else I am tasked with is so simple."

Having completed their role, the guards released Talia's guardians and left after Prince Tanin.

Dew offered a hand to Talia, but she was much too angry to notice the offer of assistance.

"What just happened?" asked Nyna.

"Apparently, King Roland and Prince Tanin have taken over the ceremony tomorrow." Nomyra dusted dirt from her robes. She seemed calm, but Talia sensed her anger bubbling beneath the surface.

"Why did you stop me?" Talia screamed at the older woman, the dagger still clutched in her hand.

"If you had managed to get through your brother's guardians, what would you have done? Injured your brother, resulting in your imprisonment? I'm sure it would be a very nice prison with a soft mattress and regular meals." Nomyra focused on Talia with her calculating eyes. "But a prison, nevertheless, where you would have been more powerless than you have ever perceived yourself to be."

"That was my choice to make, not yours," Talia retaliated, but she lowered her weapon.

Nomyra ignored her childish outburst. The woman bowed to the nadph. "How is she of the Blood, but not her twin. How is that possible?"

"We tested them, as you should have done. Their father's are not the same. You should not assume your scheming flows as you intend. The Light and Dark have their own plans." The ancient tree's deep voice soothed the mood of the group.

"I understand, ancient one." Nomyra bowed again. She focused on Talia, as if she had never seen her before. "I must make plans for tomorrow."

The priestess headed down the path with a confident stride.

Dew crossed her arms over her chest. "I don't know that we can trust her."

"We could free Gregor and Aleck and head back to Darvis?" Nyna offered, shifting her shoulder bag.

"And then what? Live as permanent outcasts? Go to war with my homeland? Watch my brother destroy Tarbin and be powerless to prevent it?" Talia returned to her habitual pacing. Though one thing said tonight kept returning to her thoughts: *Their fathers are not the same.* What did that mean?

"We should read the prophecy." Dew's voice broke through

Talia's tension. "If the Light and Dark have plans for you, we should know what they are before we make any decisions."

Talia stopped in front of Dew. She gave her a tight hug. "Thank you."

"It could be in the book from the librarian. I didn't look for a prophecy in my translation. I was concentrating on the location of the Holy Gemstones." Dew pulled the book from Nyna's bag.

Philomena flew from behind the nadph. Her slight form landed atop the burgundy cover. The fairy flapped her wings, elevating herself high enough to allow the pages to turn freely. She moved her hands in an intricate pattern. The book flopped open, and the pages flipped independently.

"I should be used to this by now, but it still sets me on edge every time," Naul whispered to Nyna. She nodded, her eyes wide.

"If the nadph's claims are true, then we should all get used to it," Talia observed.

"Indeed," the talking tree agreed.

The tome settled at a page near the back of the manuscript. The fairy flew around Dew's head once and then took off for the shelter of the nadph's branches, turning into a ball of light again with her speed.

"All this practice has my Elvish much improved. Let's see what this says." Dew moved closer to one of the torches, illuminating the prophecy.

"*As the planets meet in the Darkness,*
Their once-a-millennium dance,
The key and stones,
Divided as the world cracked,
Will call the firstborn.
And so the Holy Gemstones will unite
With the key of gold and the blood of the Heir.
The union seals with the blessing of Light.
The Machine obeys the Bright One,
For the Blood knows its own.

The progeny of Maitliin will correct his mistake.
The cycle will renew."

"They're just words on an ancient piece of paper. How do we know they pertain to me?" Talia couldn't see how these few words spelled out her destiny and the destiny of her kingdom.

"The Holy Gemstones chose you. They beg for you to bring them home." The nadph's face straightened into serious lines. "The prophecy could have referred to anyone of the Blood until the stones chose. Now you are the only one who can save us all."

Talia sighed, feeling the weight on her shoulders. Somehow, she knew the tree was right. She had to correct what her ancestor had ruined with his greed. The magical creatures deserved life as much as she did. But how did she and Tanin not have the same ancestors? She had so many questions.

"What do we do now? The gems might call to me, but I do not possess them."

"Go to the priestess. Her interests align with yours for the moment. She wishes the Machine to be successful." The tree scratched his nose, loosening a dusting of bark. "Though I would be cautious. Her full motives are not clear."

"Thank you, ancient one." Talia bowed deeply.

CHAPTER FORTY-SIX

<hr>

THE MOLDY AIR of the dungeon made Talia sneeze. Her fingers brushed the slimy brick walls. She pulled her hand back in revulsion. She'd insisted on heading straight to free Gregor and Aleck. Though she knew that was the correct decision, her senses argued with her as she tried not to slip on the steps. Naul had insisted on going first with Nyna. Ial and Dew walked behind their charge. No one was sure how friendly the guards would be to Talia's orders.

Dew folded her arms over her chest. "I've not been down here."

"Father brought Tanin and me when we were very young. Or I should say he brought Tanin, and I tagged along." Talia wiped her hand on her breeches, having accidentally touched the wall again. "He told us about the king's duty to protect his people. Sometimes, that job had unpleasant responsibilities, such as locking up criminals and interrogating enemies. There's an entire room down here with unspeakable tools for human mutilation."

Nyna shook her head in disgust. "Sometimes, I wonder how you are related to those two."

"It's very different from the one in Darvis. It's all stacked stones, instead of carved out of the limestone." Naul reached the end of the flight and pushed on one of the prison doors. "It looks just as solid, though."

"I'm hoping we won't have to bust them out." Talia straightened her hair and shirt and stood tall. "The guards will release Gregor and Aleck because I order them to."

"The guards will what?" A pair of grimy individuals, wearing full soldier uniforms that couldn't have been washed for months, walked out of the shadows of the corridor. "Who are you, and what are you doing down here?"

"You will address me with respect, or my guardians will have new dummies for target practice." Talia glared at the dungeon guards, trying to breathe steadily and hide the fact that the two had surprised her.

"And you are?" the older guard asked again, tilting his head to the right as if he couldn't quite hear her.

Talia glared at the man. She surreptitiously nudged Dew with her foot. Dew stumbled forward. Her face lit up as she realized what Talia wanted.

"This is Princess Talia Winterlaus. How dare you not recognize your sovereign's daughter! We will report this immediately!" Dew pivoted on her heels, the other companions following her lead.

The guards' faces paled, if that was even possible.

"Wait," Talia ordered in her severest voice. Her guardians froze. Nyna's shoulders shuttered slightly. Talia hoped her guardian could manage to hold off her giggle. These guards were on the edge as it was. They wouldn't obey the princess unless they believed her authority.

"I am fair. It is very dark in this dank level of the castle. Maybe these dutiful guards could not see me properly."

"Yes, my Princess." The thinner guard bowed deeply, almost hitting the ground with his forehead. "Please forgive us."

"Yes, my Princess. I have a hard time hearing, and my seeing is not much better." The bald guard proclaimed, bowing only his head.

His belly prevented more bending. "Please don't report us to the king. We wish only to serve."

"As I suspected." Talia's lips thinned into a tight smile, one she had often seen on Nomyra. "Release my friends, Lordling Gregor of Kenia and Prince Aleck of Krimmel."

Both guards froze as they were rising from their bows and exchanged glances.

The thin one pulled at his fingers. "But they were sent here by Prince Tanin with orders they weren't to be looked at."

"Of course they were, but Prince Tanin is busy preparing for the conclusion of the Forging Ceremony. He asked me if I would be so kind as to get the two prisoners ready for the performance tonight. He plans on proving the might of our beloved Tarbin to the dissenters. They will convey his message to their fathers." Talia moved Naul and Dew aside and walked right up to the guards. "Now, release Lordling Gregor and Prince Aleck immediately."

"Yes, my Princess." Both men marched down the corridor, the bald one holding a set of keys to a torch to search for the correct one.

Naul and Ial touched fists behind Talia's back. Nyna smiled outright but had managed to keep the giggling to herself. Talia had only seen her nervous a handful of times, but every time, the girl couldn't stop laughing.

"What's going on? I demand to see Princess Talia." Gregor's angry voice carried down the corridor.

"Hold your horses. I'm coming," the short older guard called.

The keys clanked loudly as he held them up to the door lock. With a turn, the door swung outward. Gregor grabbed the guard, ready to take him out and make his escape.

"Lordling Gregor. Unhand that man. He was only following orders." Talia admonished her friend, making sure her voice reached his ears.

"Talia?" Gregor let go of the small man's tunic. The younger guard gave him a piercing look. "Ahem, I mean, my Princess? What are you doing down here?"

"You have no right to question me. Gather your dwarf friend and come with me. The prince wishes you prepared for the ceremony this evening." Talia turned on her heels and started for the stairs.

The second guard opened Prince Aleck's door. The dwarf shook the surprised man's hand.

"Thank you for your hospitality. Though next time, I'd prefer to sleep in a room upstairs." Aleck stretched his back as he joined Gregor. "The conditions are inviting. Reminds me of home, but the bed left much to be desired."

"I'd hardly call the pile of hay a bed," Gregor retorted as the two joined Talia's party.

"Well, a fresh pile would have been gladly received. Hey, Talia." Prince Aleck hugged her.

Talia chanced a look at the motley pair of guards who stared after the party with doubt in their eyes. She believed they couldn't stop them at this point, but any attempt on their part would eat into the companion's planning time.

"Move along, gentlemen. My brother awaits," Talia ordered as she ushered the recent prisoners up the stairs ahead of herself.

"How many times do we have to stage a prison break?" Naul asked once the companions were safely up the stairs.

"Maybe we need to leave Lordling Gregor at home. His international dungeon tour is cutting into our questing time." Dew playfully pushed him up a step.

"Hey, this is no joke. I will carve my name on the wall of every prison on our continent," Gregor defended himself. "My father always said I had to have goals."

"My father always said to take the trash out before going to bed," Aleck added wisely. "But I usually forgot."

Gregor squeezed the dwarf's shoulders as they mounted the last steps to the main castle. "Maybe our fathers could get together and work out better advice."

"How about we work on one father at a time?" Talia recommended. "Mine's first."

No one argued with her.

Nomyra walked out in front of the companions from a branching corridor. "Princess Talia, I've been searching for you."

Talia reached for her weapon a split second after her guardians.

"I have no ears for you, High Priestess." Talia tried to go around her.

Nomyra stepped in front, blocking her escape. "Please, hear me out. I'm on your side. I was wrong all these years thinking Tanin was the True Heir. Only men have ruled in Tarbin. It was an honest mistake." Nomyra tossed her hair over her shoulder as she pleaded with Talia to listen. "Can we go somewhere more private?"

"So you can poison me, discredit me, or restrain me? I don't think so." Talia feigned left then looped around Nomyra, heading toward her quarters.

Nomyra shouted at the backs of the companions, "The king has replaced me as high priestess. My nephew will be officiating the conclusion of the Forging Ceremony."

Talia froze.

"I only desire the Recharging to be successful. If you are the twin with the Blood, you are the True Heir and the only one who can make the Machine function. Regardless of what your brother or your father say, it must be so."

Nomyra stood in front of Talia again. She grasped her shoulders. Naul moved forward to defend his charge, but Talia waved him off.

She released a great sigh. "I'm listening."

CHAPTER FORTY-SEVEN

ONCE AGAIN, Talia found herself in the Great Hall, awaiting the beginning of another monumental ceremony that would change her life forever. She brushed imaginary dust from her tunic and leggings, the same ones she'd worn at the beginning of the Forging Ceremony. Hopefully, she would be as lucky at the conclusion as she had been almost a year ago.

Princess Talia sat on the stage a few feet from Prince Tanin. The royal children had two guardians standing behind them as formal protection. They both happened to also make a statement. Talia had chosen Dew and Nyna to show that women were as capable as men of defending the heir to the throne. Naul and Ial sat quietly in the first row beside Priestess Nomyra.

Tanin had Rory, who never seemed to be more than a couple feet away from him, and his new cultural guardian, Hodan. The ten-year-old's official swearing in ceremony had been postponed. Tanin was showing he had nothing to fear by choosing an untested child as his second. Orui and Kettlor bore scowls at the edge of the stage, obviously not happy about being replaced in the main performance by a little boy. Talia felt a moment of pity for the child, who was sure to have one hell of a hazing ahead of him.

Talia's knees bounced as the audience filed in. The crowd was oddly quiet. Somehow, they managed to reflect the tension in the room without knowing the details. Nyna put her hand on the fidgeting princess's shoulder. Everything was going as planned. Talia tried to remain calm.

On the other side of the stage, King Roland sat on his grand throne. His substantial stomach reached to the tips of his fingers where they rested on the padded arms. On his head sat the jewel-less crown. Two of his guardians stood behind him. One was an eighteen-year-old replacement who had served the king for eight years after his original defense guardian died of an illness. Talia didn't miss the reflection of an experienced guardian alongside a new guardian protecting her brother and her father. King Roland displayed his solidarity with his son, while showing that losing a companion had no reflection on your skills as a leader. Her father's choice of successor could not be clearer.

King Roland's last two men carried in a covered tray and placed it on a table in the center of the stage. Even if Talia hadn't been able to see the five protrusions in the cloth, she would have been able to sense their presence. She was growing accustomed to the soft humming in her chest. The royal guardians took their places on either side of the two already behind the king.

The attendants at the back of the room closed the doors to the hall. Talia straightened her shoulders and flattened her feet to still their bouncing. She curled and uncurled her fingers and then laid them flat against her thighs. She took one more glance at the audience. Naul winked at her before the oil lamps along the wall were dimmed. Talia thought of Gregor and Aleck, who waited for their cue.

The stage lights brightened with extra torches. The crowd aahed at a flash of light and thick smoke behind the central table. Nomyra's nephew had inherited her dramatic flair. Talia wondered if his performance would end with him disrobing as well.

The new high priest seemed to the audience to come out of nowhere. Talia's angle allowed her to see the trapdoor he had climbed from. The forty year old stepped in front of the dissipating smoke, his hands held high. His scarlet robe glimmered in the reflected stage lighting. Talia was surprised to see such an untraditional color on a first appearance. She'd only seen deep blues and purples, with the occasional white, on Nomyra. Visiting astropriests typically stuck with black and white. The princess wondered what the crimson robe signified.

The audience gasped, either from awe at this entrance or from surprise that the officiant was new. One way or another, Seamus was definitely separating himself from his aunt.

"The Forging Quest. One of the oldest and most revered traditions in Tarbin culture. My aunt, Priestess Nomyra, assigned the quest to the royal Winterlaus twins, Tanin and Talia."

He left out that Talia had included herself in the Quest against Nomyra's wishes. She started to fidget again, wondering if trusting the same woman was the wisest idea.

"I, High Priest Seamus, am honored to fulfill my first official role as astropriest to the king by announcing the True Heir of Tarbin." Seamus pulled the cloth up and then down in quick movements, exposing the five Holy Gemstones to the light.

The crowd oohed on cue. The high priest's eyes twinkled with the power he had over the emotions of his audience. The cloth disappeared under the table. Then Seamus bowed in front of King Roland. The older gentleman stood and removed his crown.

"This symbol unites the old kingdoms into one powerful identity." The king handed the golden circlet to the younger man. "I trust the Stars to use this crown to choose the sovereign fit to rule our great kingdom."

A few guests clapped. The awkwardness of the sound within the silence made them stop abruptly.

Seamus brought the headwear to the table. He picked up the fist-sized diamond. "Prince Tanin Winterlaus brought us the Holy Diamond." He paused, daring Talia to intercede.

Nomyra's plan called for her to be patient. When the princess sat without complaint, the high priest continued.

"The jewel was graciously guarded by the Dwarven Kingdom until the crown was ready to receive its glory. As you can see, this gem is genuine."

Seamus smacked the diamond on the table, hard enough to make the other jewels bounce. Talia flinched, knowing Aleck was listening to the ceremony. Hopefully, he wouldn't react to his homeland's greatest treasure being treated with such disrespect.

"If the gemstone fits on the royal crown, Prince Tanin Winterlaus receives credit for completing the first of the five tasks of the quest."

Seamus touched the diamond below one of the five ridges on the crown. The diamond snapped into the metal with a magical grip. At first, Talia thought Seamus had performed another illusion. The shock on the man's face told her otherwise.

"The crown accepts the diamond as the original." He flourished the mounted jewel for the light to dance in its facets.

The audience remained completely silent.

Seamus reverently set the crown on the table and picked up the black opal. "Prince Tanin Winterlaus brought us the Holy Black Opal. The jewel was graciously guarded by the Kiwa islanders until the crown was ready to receive its glory."

The high priest placed the second precious stone on the turret next to the diamond. Talia saw the man hesitate before getting close enough for the jewel to bond with the metal. The effect awed the audience once again.

Seamus repeated the procedure three more times until the crown had all five Holy Gemstones mounted around its circumference. Not once did he mention Princess Talia's role in obtaining the precious stones, nor Prince Tanin's treachery during the quest. Though not surprised, Talia found her stomach aching with disappointment. If the truth had surfaced about her success in obtaining four out of the five gemstones, the rest of Nomyra's plan wouldn't be necessary.

"The Forging Quest is complete. Prince Tanin and Princess Talia, please come forward to hear the ruling."

The twins stepped away from their guardians and knelt on two embroidered pillows in front of the table.

High Priest Seamus held the crown high. For a moment, Talia thought he was going to place it on his own head. She was so tired of surprises, she didn't know if she could handle one more. Instead, the man walked in front of his king and presented the bejeweled headwear.

"Two royal children were sent on the Forging Quest with equal parameters. One returned with five gemstones, while one came home with none. The Light has clearly chosen the True Heir of Tarbin."

"I accept your interpretation, High Priest." King Roland reached out to reclaim his priceless crown.

The floor-to-ceiling double doors shot open, slamming against the wall on either side. The king jumped, dropping the crown. Seamus caught the headwear before it hit the ground. He cradled it close to his chest. All four of Tanin's guardians ran to the prince's side, Orui dragging the new kid. Talia's guardians rushed to protect her. They were not worried about the intruder but rather the powerful men onstage.

The nadph from the Royal Forest pushed through the chamber. The middle aisle was not big enough for the tree's trunk, forcing him to slide benches out of the way as he approached the stage. The scraping of the furniture contrasted with the softer padding of his roots moving him along. The seated guests in his vicinity rushed out of the way, crowding against the far walls. Talia smiled when she spotted Prince Aleck sitting on a branch on the right side of the nadph's bark-formed face. She was grateful the old tree had decided to form his face before entering.

"Look, Talia, eyebrows. I made him put on eyebrows. He can do more expressions now. Watch!" Aleck shouted over the screaming audience.

Talia hoped her family had missed him mentioning her name. She didn't want them to think this was a trick. Judging by Tanin's glare in her direction, her hopes were pointless. King Roland stood in a broad stance at the edge of the stage, staring at the unnatural phenomenon. Talia admired her father's bravery, while at the same time hating his stubbornness.

The king swung a torch threateningly. A ball of light flew from a twisted branch toward him. The remaining audience gasped. Philomena, the fairy, flew a spiral circle around the flame of the torch. Water coalesced around the fire as if trapped in a bubble. Steam erupted from the perfect sphere in all directions, scalding the king. He yelled and dropped the doused wood. Talia stopped herself from running to make sure her father was uninjured as the smell of wet embers permeated the stage.

Tanin glared at Talia. "What are you doing?" His hand flexed on his sword hilt.

Her brother wouldn't attack her onstage in front of all these witnesses. She shrugged her shoulders and shook her head, asserting her innocence. Before she could defend herself, the nadph's deep voice filled the hall like a storm:

"And so the Holy Gemstones will unite
With the key of gold and the Blood of the Heir.
The union will seal with the blessing of Light."

The nadph towered over the people, its uppermost branches brushing the ceiling. Small green leaves rained onto the stage. The nadph's bulk blocked the light from the audience chamber. The sight was intimidating, only countered by the friendly, grandfatherly expression on the tree. "You must test the Blood to determine the Heir. The prophecy cannot be denied."

Talia caught Aleck's attention and made her face look stern. The dwarf nodded and whispered to the fairy. She danced around the branches. The nadph apparently received the message, for his eyebrows moved to form a stern V. His eyes squinted, removing the welcoming oval shape, and his mouth tightened into a frown. The transformation had an immediate effect. The handful of people who had remained out of curiosity exited the room as unobtrusively as they could manage. No one seemed to want that face turned toward them. Only a few pockets of people too afraid to move remained in the hall.

The king took a few steps back, putting his guardians between himself and the angry walking tree. He patted his face with his royal cape. Tanin didn't seem to be afraid. His face looked as intimidating as the ancient tree's. He shrugged off Rory's attempts to back him away from the edge of the stage where the nadph loomed.

"I am the True Heir, and I will *not* open a vein for a walking piece of fire wood." Tanin pointed to the dwarf in the branches. "You are supposed to be in the dungeon. You've proved yourself, and hence your people, a supporter of an insurgent force in my kingdom. The punishment is death. You first, then your people."

"Tanin, you can't do that. He is my guest." Talia looked to the king, desperate for support. "Father?"

"Talia, I have defended you and protected you every step of the way. You've gone too far. If he is your guest, you share in his guilt. Consider your words, my daughter." King Roland spoke coldly, without taking his eyes off the nadph. "Take the dwarf out, my son. He is working some sort of dark magic to control your sister."

A knife flew high. It missed Aleck and lodged in an upper branch. A flash of light erupted from within the nadph's branches. Orui fell to his back. Ial offered Tanin's guardian a hand up. Orui lunged at the smaller guardian. Ial dodged to the left, and Orui missed him completely. Ial whacked his attacker on the back of the head with his sword hilt. The medicinal guardian hit the floor, motionless.

Chaos erupted onstage.

CHAPTER FORTY-EIGHT

As the groups attacked each other, two of the king's guardians stepped in on Tanin's side. His face bright red, Tanin lunged at Talia. She blocked his ferocious swing with the sheath of her sword. The leather cracked with a resounding snap.

Talia yelled over the noise, "The crown!"

The king and his two remaining guardians flattened to the ground as the nadph stretched an enormous branch over their heads. The thin leafy end wrapped around the fleeing high priest. The clinging branch dragged him back to center stage. Seamus shook violently, sweat pouring from his face, but he still clutched the crown to his chest.

"Enough!" Nomyra's commanding voice resonated through the chaos.

The skirmishes halted as the participants searched for the source of the new threat. Nomyra climbed the stairs, holding her ceremonial robes up so as not to trip on them. Her stomping footsteps echoed throughout the Great Hall. She stopped in front of her nephew, her pale face framed by her wild white hair.

"The Light does not speak to you." With the tree branch

restraining the shaking man, Nomyra slipped the ring off his finger. She put it back on her hand with a visible sigh. "And never will."

She directed her next words at Prince Tanin. "The ancient one is correct. The Blood must be tested for the quest to be completed. The demands of the Light cannot be avoided."

Nomyra held out her hands to Seamus. He clutched the crown closer to his chest.

"You cannot claim it," the king intervened. "That crown belongs to Tarbin, not the astropriests."

Another branch blocked the blustering king from taking his crown.

"You know so little, old man. Try putting down your ale and picking up a book." Nomyra tapped the wooden arm restraining Seamus.

It squeezed until the man dropped the bejeweled headwear in favor of breathing. She caught it and turned around, flipping her hair and robe.

The king lunged at the woman. The nadph pushed him backward. Two of his guardians raised their swords to hack at the offending branch. Fairies flew around the armed men, completely disorienting them. One's sword fell and hit his foot. The second lost his grip on his weapon. The blade sunk into the stage a few inches from the king's hand. The three men backed away from the magical pests.

"Prince Tanin Winterlaus and Princess Talia Winterlaus, please step forward."

Tanin was as likely to run Talia through as obey the priestess.

"You are twins, my Prince. You have the same blood. What do you fear?" Nomyra held the crown on her palms, chest high. "You are this close."

Tanin glared back and forth between Talia and Nomyra.

"Claim your crown, son. You are and always have been my heir," King Roland assured the prince from the other side of the stage.

Tanin sheathed his sword and walked forward, Rory behind him.

Talia dropped her broken scabbard before matching his pace. She would have to trust her guardians to defend her if something went wrong.

"Prince Tanin and Princess Talia, the Light requires a sample of your blood." Nomyra stood, waiting.

Tanin held out his hand to Rory for his dagger. Talia looked at Naul. He grabbed his belt sheepishly.

"I threw it at Kettlor earlier. I'm sorry," the defense guardian whispered.

Talia looked at Tanin.

"You're not using mine," her twin scoffed.

"Here, Talia. Use mine." Prince Aleck stood beside the princess. Talia had missed him climbing down from the tree in the midst of the skirmish onstage.

"Thank you, my friend." Talia accepted the smaller dagger and sliced her right palm before she could change her mind.

Tanin sliced his left palm. They both held up their hands near the side of the crown. Talia watched the blood drip down her arm and that of her brother. It looked exactly the same to her. The slight metallic odor wafted from both wounds. Nomyra nodded her head. The twins simultaneously placed their bleeding hands against the metal.

A flash threw Tanin into Rory. The force tossed them both to the other side of the room. The two became entangled in the hanging curtains.

The crown grabbed onto Talia's hand as the diamond had the first time she touched it. The demanding force pulled her in deeper than the one gem alone had had the power to do. She fell into the crown, becoming part of it.

The stage disappeared. She was surrounded by a swirling mist, the color of gemstones. Whispering. The same voice from the Krimmel display whispered in her ear. The words were more distinct this time. But she couldn't grasp them. Language. The language was one she couldn't understand. What was the voice trying to tell her? A warning? Praise? Direction? Without a face attached to the words, Talia couldn't identify the tone of the mutterings.

Nomyra's voice floated out of the mist, gray color among the bright rainbow. "Can you see him?"

Talia attempted to put her hands out in front of her to feel where she was. Her right hand wouldn't obey the command. "I can't see anything."

"Don't move," Nomyra warned. "Can you hear him?"

"Yes. But I don't understand."

"You will. I'm going to cut the connection for now. The Key is pulling too much energy too quickly."

Talia squinted into the mist. "Wait. I think I see him."

A figure materialized. The gas flowed around it like a rock in a river. The slender form had shoulder-length bright-white hair. He looked to be wearing a robe, but the swirling gases made the lines of the clothing tough to distinguish. His hair moved with the gas as if he were standing there, not an image formed by the mist. He slowly turned. His lips moved, but not in time with the whispering. He seemed to be chanting independently. He opened his eyes. Black. No pupil. No iris. Just black.

Talia screamed.

She opened her eyes. Dew and Ial each held a shoulder, supporting her weight. Talia tried to push them away, but she didn't have the strength to stand on her own. She looked at her hand. The wound was jagged and raw, but dried of blood.

A light, stronger than the sun beating down in the middle of the day, shot from the center of the stage. The buzzing from the magic drowned out Ial's voice in her ear. The energy from the discharge busted through the arched stone blocks. As the broken stone crashed to the stage, Talia spotted Nomyra still in the center, unflinching. Everyone else moved to the edges. The nadph shuffled backward a few feet, scraping more benches across the stone floor.

The beam of light stopped as suddenly as it had started. It had pierced straight through the roof. The light had blinded their eyes, making the full moon, which peeked through the opening, seem like a dark rock.

The gap destabilized the carefully engineered arches. The surrounding ceiling crumbled at an increasing rate. The falling stones finally forced the stragglers in the hall to rush for the exit.

"I declare Princess Talia Winterlaus the True Heir." Nomyra had lost none of her dramatic air. She walked with purpose to Talia without overtly dodging a single projectile.

The priestess handed the crown to the True Heir. Talia accepted it with her unblemished hand. She wasn't eager to go back to the misty world. She handed the prize to Nyna to put in her bag. A slight scowl crossed Nomyra's face.

"We work as a team, or you can stay here." Talia made a quick count of her companions as she grabbed her sword from the stage. "We're all here. We need to hurry to the rendezvous to meet up with Gregor."

They jumped off the stage in front of the nadph, who protected them from most of the falling stone.

"You must hurry. Fairy magic is not strong enough to stabilize the roof," the ancient one warned the humans.

"Mine can." A shadow blocked the moonlight. Ragaropina hovered over the stage and spoke a few words in her native tongue. The roof stabilized. Some debris that had been on its way to the ground floated in midair.

"Gregor." Talia had never been so happy to see the lordling.

"We saw the light and took it as a signal." Gregor rode the dragon through the hole into the Great Hall. The beast landed with a thud, crushing the already disarrayed benches under her clawed feet.

"Hello, old friend. I'm sorry I did not stay to visit earlier." Ragaropina folded her wings against her back to keep them from scraping the giant tree trunk.

The Great Hall, a place for feasts and ceremonies, now contained two creatures only found in the wildest of imaginations. A tree as tall as the ceiling and as wide as a passenger carriage gesticulated with its long branches. The red-scaled dragon took up half the room with her bulky frame. Her tail flipped back and forth as she sat on her haunches, sharing a conversation with the nadph.

Dew read Talia's mind. "That's a sight I won't easily forget. Which is a good thing because we have to run."

Talia moved toward the dragon, her guardians, the dwarf, and the priestess in tow. Gregor signaled Ragaropina to hunch down, allowing the humans to mount.

"Talia?"

She released Gregor's helping hand at the sound of her mother's voice.

"Mother?" She had a hard time seeing through the debris and darkness. The dragon's flight and the fairy had extinguished most of the torches in the hall.

Queen Shantia and Chary made their way to their beloved girl. Chary visibly shook as she approached the mighty beast by circumventing the talking tree.

"By the Stars, what has happened this night?" the elderly servant muttered.

The queen ignored all sights but the eyes of her daughter.

"I was scared I was going to miss you. I knew you couldn't stay after I overheard your father's plans. Though I didn't imagine such a dramatic exit." Shantia hugged her adult daughter. Talia hoped it wasn't for the last time.

"You can come with us, Mother." Talia walked the queen to the dragon's wing.

"Oh, Darkness, no. I am much too old for an adventure. And my duty is here." Shantia removed her hand from her daughter's. Tears rushed down the older woman's cheeks. "I need to give you this. You need to know the truth of your birth."

The queen tucked a wax-sealed letter into Talia's hand.

Chary hugged Talia. "Your mother has never wanted anything but for you to be happy. As have I."

"We have to go *now*," Priestess Nomyra called from the saddle atop Ragaropina.

"Be wary of that woman." Shantia offered her last bit of motherly advice before her little girl flew away. "Her motives are never easy to see."

"And she is never concerned with anyone's destiny but her own," Chary added.

Talia. and her companions secured themselves in the leather saddle.

"Hold on. There will be some twists and turns to free ourselves of these stone walls," Ragaropina warned as she positioned herself directly below the opening. She bent down in preparation for leaping into the night sky.

"*Stop!*" shouted Tanin from the wings of the stage. Rory tried to hold him back from the dragon's long neck. "You carry fugitives of Tarbin. Turn them in immediately, or face the consequences."

Ragaropina laughed, a rolling, thunderous sound. Talia smelled sulfur coming from the dragon. The same thing had happened before she blew fire on the island.

"Wait. Please don't, Ragaropina." As much as Talia didn't believe her brother had the right or temperament to rule, she couldn't see her twin burned to death.

The dragon twisted her neck around to look at Talia. "As you wish."

Her body aimed to the open sky, Ragaropina pushed with her mighty haunches. The momentum flung the humans backward hard enough to jar loose anything not properly attached. Talia was glad they were securely tied to the saddle. Whoever had designed the massive leather equipment knew the force behind a dragon takeoff.

Guards rushed into the Great Hall bearing torches. They quickly surround the naddle at the orders of the captain.

Nyna shouted above the flapping of the dragon's wings. "We can't leave him behind!"

"Do not worry about me, little one." The nadph moved his face to the top of his trunk, above many of the lower branches so it could be seen from the ceiling. "Philomena and I will take care of ourselves with the help of her sisters. We will meet you at the Tower."

Talia watched the roots of the great tree flex and knock down the soldiers like dominoes. Any torches that flew from their hands to land near the tree were quickly extinguished by fairy magic.

Talia patted Nyna's hand. "I think they can take care of themselves."

The dragon flapped her wings to gain more altitude. She steadied her stroke as she flew larger circles around the city.

Priestess Nomyra insisted. "We need to go the Astro Tower."

Talia had no better solution at the moment. "Astrology central it is."

"Has the central location shifted in the last thousand years?" Ragaropina asked.

"No, ancient one. Astro Tower can be hidden, but not moved." Nomyra sat upon the dragon like she had ridden one her whole life.

Ragaropina turned west. "To the Tower then."

CHAPTER FORTY-NINE

Talia sat by the fire of the camp the companions had chosen for the night. They had made it as far as the farmlands to the west of Tarbinulus. Talia's bones were freezing from the cold wind high above the ground. Most of the companions were asleep among the grove of trees. Ial sat beside her by the fire. Talia had seen her guardians draw straws, and the husbandry guardian had drawn the short one. Talia was glad it was him. He was comfortable sitting for hours without saying a word, and Talia needed time to think.

From inside her tunic, she drew out the letter from her mother. Ial saw her looking at it. He took it from her and broke the wax seal. Without a word, he moved to the opposite side of the fire to give her privacy.

"My sweet baby girl, my Talia, my long-awaited princess,

It is time you learned the truth of your birth. I remember the odd night you were conceived so clearly. Your father had grown distant after so long without an heir. I failed him, and he saw his sovereign kingdom divided among powerful families. Out of desperation, Roland resorted to keeping mistresses, relegating my role to ceremonial with no expectation of childbearing. I have to admit, I felt vindicated when he still failed to produce a child.

Eight months before you and your brother came into this world, I was unexpectedly visited by the king. He came to my chambers and dismissed a flabbergasted Chary. Without a word, Roland loved me with a hunger he had never shown before. He explored my body as if it were new to him, as if it were a privilege to be able to experience my womanhood. When he was spent and I was satisfied in a way I had never known, he quietly covered himself and left.

I go into detail not because it is one of my fondest memories but to contrast it with his second visit that night.

A few hours later, as I lay content in my still-rumpled bed, Roland again visited my chamber. This time, the king burst through the door, loud and drunk. He ripped the sheets off my body and fell upon me like a beast. The stench of his breath and unwashed body made me nauseous. Roland proceeded to take me, despite my protests. He passed out, his dead weight suffocating me. I managed to crawl out of the bed and curl up next to the dimming fire, crying until the morning, when he regained consciousness and left my chamber without glancing in my direction.

I never reconciled the dichotomy of the tenderness with the violence. I had no idea what had changed for Roland between that first and second visit. After everything that has happened this week, with mythical creatures coming to life and magic flying around my castle, I think I know what happened the night you were conceived. I believe two different men visited me. One was your father; and one was your brother's."

Talia paused at the confirmation. Her mother's confession backed up what the nadph had said. *Is that even possible? Can a set of twins have two fathers?* It would explain many things, not least of which was the fact that her blood activated the Holy Gemstones while Tanin's did not. Assuming King Roland had been one of the men who visited his wife's bed, who was the imposter?

Talia folded up the letter into a tight square. She tossed it into the fire. She pulled out the crown from Nyna's bag to watch the flickering of the flames in each facet. Talia was the True Heir. She was to rule her people. But how?

She looked at the snoring dragon, who was wrapped around a dead tree. All she knew was much life on the planet needed the Recharging to be successful. If she had a role in that, she would make it happen. With the help of her companions.

Talia nodded to a spot by the fire. Ial acknowledged her going to bed. He moved around the fire so the light wouldn't blind him from the dangers of the dark.

"Who has the early watch?" Talia asked her guardian.

"Dew."

"Please have her wake me when she gets up. I want to check those rabbit snares to see if we can have fresh meat for breakfast."

"Done." Ial sat with his back to the fire as Talia curled up in a blanket next to Nyna.

ON THE OTHER side of the camp, Nomyra crawled to the edge of the burning embers. She rubbed Krag. It was weakened, but would get a charge in a few weeks. She didn't need to conserve.

She whispered a few words into the coals. The heat singed the ends of her hair. The ashes shook. Something slithered underneath the thin layer, trying to escape. The pieces coalesced into firmly folded parchment paper. Nomyra reached into the heated pit and pulled out the reassembled letter before it could burn again. She shoved it into a hidden pocket of her robe to read at a more convenient time.

She rolled to the other side of the log and pretended to snore gently. Ial stood to pace the clearing without giving the priestess a second glance.

Nomyra's plans had not been fulfilled the way she had envisioned, but everything was proceeding toward the completion of her familial mission. In a little over a year, her destiny would be fulfilled and her ancestor's mistakes corrected. She closed her eyes and fell into a prophetic dream.

ACKNOWLEDGMENTS

None of this would be possible without the belief and constant support of Fern Brady, CEO of Inklings Publishing. She taught me so much. I will always be grateful for her dedication to writers and the publishing industry.

My family remains understanding of my precious writing time. Without their sacrifice, this writing career of mine would be little more than a thought in a dream.

The incredible professionals I've had the pleasure of working with are unparalleled. Tod Tinker for keeping it all straight and making the magic happen in a way that the reader will understand and believe. Stefanie Saw who somehow interpreted my convoluted desires for the cover into something greater than I could have imagined.

Lastly, thank you to the fans who bring the world to life in their imaginations and their hearts. An author couldn't ask for a better group of readers than you. I hope you enjoyed this new edition of *Tarbin's True Heir*. I can't wait to complete this journey with you.

ABOUT THE AUTHOR

Kelly Lynn Colby is a writer of all things fantasy. Whenever she tries to create a mundane story, a dragon pops in to take over. She eventually stopped fighting and caved to the magic. The dragons must have known something she didn't, because her debut novel, *Tarbin's True Heir*, won a bronze medal in the IPPYs for fantasy. You can find her work in the Recharging series as well as numerous short stories in anthology collections. Look for her new paranormal thriller series Emergence, with first book *The Collector*.

If you want to be the first to learn of new releases and giveaways from Kelly, download this free story and join her newsletter here: https://dl.bookfunnel.com/frwef6kmjf.

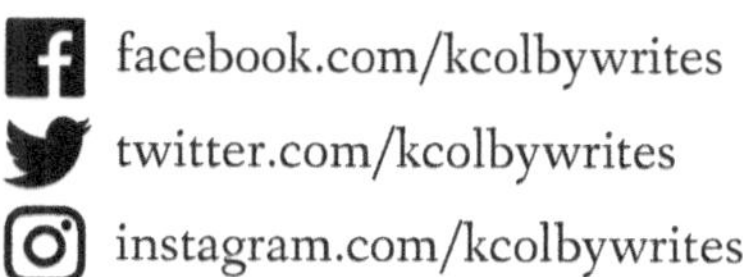

9 781951 445065